About the Author

Phil was first inspired to write when he read *The Lord of the Rings* as a child. Back then the ambition was to create a whole fantasy world with dragons and sword fights but, as George R. R. Martin seems to have cornered that market, he now writes comedy thrillers set in the (almost) real world instead.

He is somewhat obsessed with the public and media's fixation with celebrity, which forms the backdrop to his books. These also tend to feature spies, gangsters, hit men, failed pop stars and daytime-TV presenters.

Phil lives in London with his wife and two children. His main rule in life is to never let tomato ketchup touch any green food. He hasn't yet worked out any deep meaning behind this and suspects it is not the soundest of principles to live by – although it's better than quite a few he's come across down the years. Best not to get him started on that.

D1147574

THE MEAL OF FORTUNE

THE MEAL OF FORTUNE

PHILIP BRADY

This edition first published in 2017

Unbound

6th Floor Mutual House, 70 Conduit Street, London W1S 2GF

www.unbound.com

ISBN (eBook): 978-1911586418
ISBN (Paperback): 978-1911586401

Design by Mecob

Cover images:
©Textures.com
© Shutterstock.com

Printed in Great Britain by Clays Ltd, St Ives plc

MIX
Paper from
responsible sources
FSC® C018072

For Megan, Dylan and Annabel who are everything. And in memory of Christopher Bland and Kevin Kirkwood.

Dear Reader,

The book you are holding came about in a rather different way to most others. It was funded directly by readers through a new website: Unbound.

Unbound is the creation of three writers. We started the company because we believed there had to be a better deal for both writers and readers. On the Unbound website, authors share the ideas for the books they want to write directly with readers. If enough of you support the book by pledging for it in advance, we produce a beautifully bound special subscribers' edition and distribute a regular edition and e-book wherever books are sold, in shops and online.

This new way of publishing is actually a very old idea (Samuel Johnson funded his dictionary this way). We're just using the internet to build each writer a network of patrons. Here, at the back of this book, you'll find the names of all the people who made it happen.

Publishing in this way means readers are no longer just passive consumers of the books they buy, and authors are free to write the books they really want. They get a much fairer return too – half the profits their books generate, rather than a tiny percentage of the cover price.

If you're not yet a subscriber, we hope that you'll want to join our publishing revolution and have your name listed in one of our books in the future. To get you started, here is a £5 discount on your first pledge. Just visit unbound.com, make your pledge and type EUROCHEF in the promo code box when you check out.

Thank you for your support,

Dan, Justin and John
Founders, Unbound

Super Patrons

Paola Griffith
Prof T. G. Griffith
Sian Griffith
Nick Harding
Jessie Hiney
Mark Huband
Emma Hurrell
Jen Inglis
Michael Joyce
Kirstin Kaszubowska
John Kelly
Neil Kenyon
Dan Kieran
Kevin Kirkwood
Jennifer Knox
Stefanie Kudla
Chris Lamb
Andy Last
Elen Lewis
Matt Link
Mark Lyne
Simon Melville
John Mitchinson
Dave Moore
Richard Moss
Malcolm Munro
Jennifer Nadel
David Nicholl
Gitte O Toole
Reynolds Ofori-Koree
Lynn Oliver
Andrew Oliver
Siôn Owen
Robert Parker
Julian Partridge
Robert Pavlov

Libby Pearson
Chris Petter
Justin Pollard
Ann Potter
James Ramshaw
Phil Rock
Will Sanderson
Christopher Satterthwaite
Alexander Schmidt
Daniel Schraibman
Mark Scupholme
Gavin Shields
Charlotte Sinclair
Gillian Slovo
Catherine Southgate
Richard Squire
Imogen Sutton
Michelle Taylor
Anna Terrell
Katherine Thatcher
Claire Thompson
Sarin Tkhar
Piers Tupman
Kirsty Walker
Simon Walsh
Lucy Williams
Victor Wong
Alexander Woolfall
Graham Yarrow
Ali Young

Prologue

Sergei Symenov knew he had drunk more vodka than he should. But then everyone was so generous these days. First Grigor had bought the drinks, then Konstantin, Vassily and finally Grigor again, if he wasn't much mistaken. Oh yes, everyone wanted to be Sergei's friend now that he was going to be famous again.

He stumbled as he stepped into the stairwell, reaching out to steady himself against the wall. The handrail was long gone and the stench of piss and damp burned his nostrils as he started the long slow climb.

Yes, piss. The whole block stank of it– or was it boiled cabbage? Sergei had always struggled to tell the two apart. The smell, whatever it was, seemed to ooze from the crumbling concrete of the walls of the place that had made him such a sorry home for more than 20 years. But it would soon all be a thing of the past and Sergei would be nicely tucked up in a modern apartment befitting a man of his newly restored status.

Befitting a true hero of Russia.

To think the bastards had thought they could take it all away from him. Everything had gone to hell after the communists lost power. Inflation, bread queues and oligarchs. And then they'd decided that he couldn't keep his bear. Dancing bears were not appropriate for the modern Russia, apparently; animal rights or some such pious Western dog shit. Sergei had always looked after that bear well; only beating it when he had to and never chaining it up except at night. Still, he was better off without it. Shit-for-brains bear had never been able to dance anyway.

They'd taken it off to some animal sanctuary, told him he'd be welcome to visit it any time he liked.

Huh! Sergei hadn't liked.

That bear had made its choice and was dead to him now – though as far as he knew it was still alive, all these years later.

He paused for breath halfway up the first flight of stairs.

Normally the steps wouldn't have been a problem, despite his 72 years. All that dancing had kept him in good shape. But tonight, with the vodka inside him, the climb was proving a little harder than usual.

The Singing Cossack, that's what they called him now.

Cossacks, pah. Fucking Ukrainian scum. Stalin had the right idea there. But they'd always had the best dancing east of the Don River and back in the day the suddenly bearless Sergei had been forced to improvise. He'd worked hard on his Cossack moves, learning to fit their ridiculous jig to his own singing. Didn't mean he had to like the filthy horse-molesting bastards.

Sergei pushed off from the wall and started to climb again. He'd have a proper rest on the first-floor landing before tackling the last set of stairs to his apartment. Stumbling as he started to climb again, he put a hand on the cold, bare concrete of the wall to steady himself. That was when he heard the noise behind him. It would be those kids again. All kinds of filth from Chechnya, Armenia and those other stinking yak-infested shitholes ending in 'stan'. Stalin had known what to do with them as well. Not this current president though. Strong man, he was supposed to be. Ha... All piss and wind, if you asked Sergei. Posing with his shirt off like some painted boy-whore when he should have been sorting out the scum polluting Russia's once-great cities.

He headed on up the stairs, more quickly than before. Not that he was scared of the kids. Always hanging round trying to look tough. Didn't understand the meaning of the word. Putin should bring back the Gulags; then they'd know.

But at least Sergei wouldn't have to put up with any of it for much longer. Twenty long years he'd flogged his guts out, singing and dancing while the lazy son-of-a-bitch bear lounged around in its five-star animal hotel. They probably didn't even whip it. How was it supposed to learn discipline?

Twenty years he'd put up with all the laughs and jeers, quarter-full halls and back rooms.

Not anymore.

Soon Sergei would show all Russia what he could do. All Russia, Europe and beyond as well. Show that idle, good-for-nothing bear too. When the money came rolling in he'd buy it back and teach it who was boss again. Things weren't as they'd been in the years after the communists. Everything was for sale in Russia these days.

He reached the landing and carried on up the stairs, deciding against his planned rest. About six steps up the noise came again, much closer this time. Then he felt the hand on his shoulder.

'Let go of me you, Chechen faggot.' He spat the words as he turned.

The man on the step below was a little too old and well-dressed to be one of the deadbeat kids. But he was happy enough to let go, just as soon as he'd yanked Sergei off his feet. And then the Singing Cossack found himself heading back down the stairs he'd just put in such effort to climb. Going much faster this time and without the need of his feet either. His shoulders, elbows, hips did just as well, hitting each step on the way back down to the landing. He tried to stand as the man descended slowly towards him. A second man was approaching up the flight of stairs below. Sergei slumped to the floor again. He hadn't fallen far and, although every part of his body seemed to hurt, he didn't think anything was broken. There was no way he could fight them though. Best to let them take his wallet and be done with it. He groped in his pocket and held it up. The two men stood over Sergei, looking at wallet, then the one who'd pushed him stepped forward and stamped down on his ankle.

Hard.

Sergei screamed in a key he'd never reached during his long singing career as he felt the bones splinter.

The second man bent down and took hold of Sergei's shattered leg, holding it almost gently at first.

'Please, just take it.' Sergei held up the wallet once more.

Then the second man twisted the leg and Sergei screamed again as bone grated on bone. He lay back and closed his eyes, trying not to think about the pain, listening to the two men heading off down the stairs and speaking in a language he did not understand but recognised all the same.

Since when had those Chechen bastards learned to speak English?

Fucking scum. They hadn't even taken his wallet.

And that fucking bear. Wait till Sergei got hold of it. But as he started to drag himself up the stairs he realised the chances of that, and of getting out of this piss-stinking hole, had just been smashed along with the bones of his ankle. He wouldn't be doing any dancing for a long time.

Part One

Rewind about three weeks…

Chapter 1

Every Thursday the music would start in Dermot's head the moment the bell sounded. And even before he got to the front door he'd be dancing inside. The little girl would already be out of the car, running up the path, one hand tucking a lock of long dark hair behind her ear, the other clutching the bag filled with a whole week's worth of things she'd bought to show him.

She'd always be laughing.

The music inside could be anything: that year's big feel-good summer hit or some long-forgotten guilty pleasure with a heavy synth bass and cheesy samples. It didn't matter; it always got him dancing inside.

And every Thursday the little girl would sit up at the kitchen counter to do the homework her mother had so thoughtfully saved up for her one night with Daddy. Still, a little help here and there and they soon had it out of the way. Then it would be time for the bag to reveal its contents. Sometimes one by one, more often all at the same time. Pictures she'd drawn as well as other random (and often unidentifiable) works of art. Stickers (what was it with kids and stickers?) and various little bits and bobs she'd collected along the way. Dermot would laugh and smile while he made her beans on toast. It wasn't that he couldn't cook (OK!). But Thursday was Molly's night and it was her favourite.

At bedtime '*Just one more story*' ended up being three or four as they eked out every last minute of their time together. Their current record stood at eight.

And all the time the dance went on inside his head as the music carried on playing. Shaking, twisting and jiving. Sometimes a little breakdance or maybe even the disco strut.

As a younger man he'd got away with real dancing; at home, in the street, in the lobby of many an overpriced hotel.

Just about anywhere.

A few steps here, a spin or two there, maybe the odd little whoop.

Amazing the allowances people made when you were young and all they wanted was their little own piece of you.

But Dermot had learned long ago to keep it inside. The music, the dancing and a few other things besides.

'The train will soon be arriving in London King's Cross…'

He slipped out of his daydream to find the green of the countryside had given way to the dirty greys and dull browns of the city he'd always called home. So why did it feel like home was 400-odd miles behind him with an eight-year-old girl who still called him Daddy?

Just.

Little wonder the music inside didn't play anymore.

Dermot stayed seated as the train slid to a halt, letting all the other passengers jostle their way off first. Only when the carriage was empty did he reach up and grab his small case from the overhead rail and head for the door.

Scotland, for God's sake.

Actually no: he was going to get it right. *Scotland, for fuck's sake.*

Not that he had any particular beef with the country. He'd just rather his ex-wife hadn't taken his daughter to live there.

With a man called Wayne.

Wanker.

Come on… A Silicon Glen entrepreneur who'd made his first million at about the age of 12, then cashed it all in before the crash to become an organic cheese-maker.

Dermot gave the train a last look of lingering resentment as he stepped down to the platform and headed for the ticket barrier. He shouldn't even have been on the sodding thing in the first place. Sarah's phone call the previous Tuesday had changed that. '*Erm, you see, the thing is…*'

That was the thing about his ex-wife. There was always some sort of 'thing'. This time it was the work deadline that would make it '*just impossible*' for her to bring Molly down to London for half term.

As bloody discussed, agreed and promised.

Sarah was happy enough for him to come up to Scotland to

see Molly. Not to stay with them but there was no reason why he couldn't take his daughter to Edinburgh for a couple of days.

It was a safe enough offer for Sarah to make, knowing he wouldn't be able to drop everything at work or afford the hotel.

Well this time she'd be wrong. On both counts.

'Great, I'll book the train tomorrow.'

'I mean... If you're sure.' A delicious note of doubt had crept into her voice.

'It's fine.'

After weeks of delays Marcus Diesel's new contract was finally edging its way past the collection of pedants and timewasters that the TV-production company insisted on referring to as its legal department. But any further questions the lawyers concocted could be answered easily enough by phone or email.

With no way to un-invite him Sarah had dialled the breeziness back up. 'In that case, Molly's got a surprise. You'll never guess...'

'Daddy, Daddy!' Molly had come charging through the door of the mock Scottish castle she now called home and down the path towards him.

Sarah had stayed in the doorway, the scowl she saved exclusively for Dermot doing little to hide how good she looked. Her blonde hair had been expensively cut into a shiny new bob and she'd lost weight too – something she'd never bothered with when she was with Dermot. But then he could hardly...

Maybe best not to go over all that again.

Wayne at least had shown enough tact to stay well out of sight, no doubt lurking in one of the large feasting halls of what, on closer inspection, appeared to be a genuine Scottish castle. Not such a wanker after all then? Although Dermot didn't plan to let that count in the man's favour.

Molly had wrapped her arms around him in one of those special eight-year-old-hugs that promised to go on forever. Then she let go and looked up at him with her best smile.

'Wayne bought me a pony.'

Of course he had. That would be the surprise Sarah had mentioned. And yes, she'd been right: he'd never have guessed.

Not long ago Dermot had bought his daughter ice creams when there'd been something to celebrate. Now another man was buying her horses.

Wayne's 'tact' in making himself scarce was nothing more than good old-fashioned fear of a punch in the head. Dermot knew he'd been right to avoid a hasty reappraisal of the man's wanker status.

'He's called Nugget. I get to ride him every day.' The words tumbled out as if they were never going to stop. 'And he's got his own special bit of the stable too. It's bigger than your *whole* flat, Daddy.'

Yeah cheers for that, Mol. Was it so wrong to wish the beast a nasty hoof infection or a fatal cheese-churning accident on Wayne?

Two days in Edinburgh had done much to close up the gap driven between Dermot and his daughter by the three months' long separation and the arrival of the bloody horse. Molly had chatted away about old times as they'd done the zoo, the castle, the shops, plenty of cafés and then the zoo again (zoos were a big thing for her). It was all his Thursday nights rolled into one. The horse barely got a look in after the first day.

But all too soon he'd found himself back at Chateau Fromage.

'Bye, darling. I'll see you soon.'

'Bye-bye, Daddy.' She'd said it with a sad little smile. But it had only been little and not really that sad. Then she'd turned away, asking Sarah whether it was too late to have a ride on Nugget.

Dermot had been left to head back to the waiting taxi, wondering if the driver might know where to buy voodoo horse dolls in Edinburgh.

And extra-long pins.

But then he'd had a far better idea.

The station concourse was busy and Dermot dodged through the crowds, weighing up the choice of taxi or underground for the trip across London and home to Chiswick. The station clock read 4.29pm.

So, with an hour of the working day left, he plumped for a taxi. Plenty of time to get on the phone to the production-company lawyers and ask why the bloody hell they were still stalling on Marcus Diesel's contract.

The taxi queue moved with a swiftness that was as unexpected as it was welcome and five minutes later he was in a cab heading along Euston Road, his sleek black phone nestling snugly in his hand. The little device was no ordinary phone though. It was the lightsabre to his Luke Skywalker. In his hands it could be a weapon of almost unimaginable might. All his power (well, all his contacts) dwelled inside the neat glass-and-metal shell. With it he could unleash the force and battle the evil legion of Sith (talentless, wannabe celebs and over-paid fuckwit lawyers).

He was looking at the home screen when the Jedi weapon sprang to life, the name of the dark lord of TV cookery himself written large across the screen. The thought of speaking to Marcus made Dermot's whole face hurt on the best of days. It wasn't for nothing that the man had been voted TV's most annoying man three years on the spin. And that was by a viewing public who only had to watch his show rather than speak to him at least six times a day.

'Marcus, hi.' He took the call reluctantly, trying his hardest to keep the sigh from his voice.

'Dermot what the—'

The rest of what Marcus had to say was drowned out by the siren of a passing fire engine. Not that it mattered; most of it would have been one or other derivative of the word 'fuck'.

'Come again?'

But all Dermot caught were a couple more 'fuck's and maybe a 'bastard' before another fire engine roared by.

'Marcus, I can't hear—'

But the chef had already hung up, presumably happy he'd got his message across.

A combination of poor mobile reception, more emergency vehicles and an overly stubborn receptionist at the production company meant he was well past Shepherd's Bush before he finally got through to the lawyer he needed to speak to. Then the signal went and he lost the call. Dermot looked at the lightsabre lying useless in his hand and decided to give it up for the day.

Fifteen minutes later he was closing the front door of his flat behind him and dumping his case in the narrow hallway as he headed for the sitting room. For five long years the flat had been his sanctuary, coming alive with the sound of Molly's laughter every Thursday night and second weekend.

Now it just felt cold and desolate; the scratched dining table and scruffy green sofas with their mismatched cushions were too big for the undersized sitting room. He tried not to think about that bastard horse lounging about in the comfort of its vast executive stable.

Without Molly's regular visits to the flat he'd decided to forgo the cost of a cleaner and it was starting to show. Then there was the smell drifting from the kitchen, carrying more than a suggestion that he'd forgotten to put the dishwasher on before heading to Scotland.

Dermot took in the mess of papers and used coffee cups on his desk as he thought about fighting his way through the stale stench to tackle the dishwasher. But the prospect of a pint and a pie in his local was always going to win that debate. His stomach was already grumbling as he headed back down the hall and pulled the front door open, only to find someone standing in his way.

'Ah, Mr Jack, hello. My name is Yegor Koslov.'

The man wore an expensive suit and a cheap haircut. The hair was thinning and blond (possibly dyed) and quite a bit too long on top; what the uncharitable might have described as a comb-over. At six foot four he could have pulled it off but at five foot five and a bit he didn't stand a chance.

'You are a very hard man to track down.'

Jesus, that accent; like the first baddie to die in a low-rent spy movie. But when he looked down into the little man's eyes he saw something hard and cold there, something that suggested it would be foolish to underestimate him.

Dermot took a step backwards, ready to close the door. Because, well… It wasn't every day a real-life Russian gangster came calling. The Russian bit he wasn't quite so sure of, although the name and the accent were pretty big clues.

But gangster?

When you'd spend half your life scratching the fleshy underbelly of the entertainment business you knew a crook when you saw one.

'I have a message for you from my employer.' The man smiled, the chill never quite leaving his eyes.

Shit… Mulrooney.

'Look, I can…' Repaying the money he owed the big loan shark wasn't going to be a problem. It just wouldn't be happening today. Or that week even. The 'better idea' that had trumped the voodoo horse doll had also proved a lot more costly. The deposit and three months' rent he'd forked out for a flat in Edinburgh meant he'd be able to go to Scotland and see Molly whenever he liked. But it also meant that he was skint again.

'Tell him—' Dermot took another step backwards. It didn't look like he'd be getting that pie and pint after all. But the little fella wouldn't look quite so tough with a face full of front door. He shoved as hard as he could with his shoulder.

'That's not very friendly, Mr Jack.' Somehow Yegor Koslov had stepped backward and still managed to force his foot between the closing door and frame, moving surprisingly quickly for such a little man. 'Not very friendly at all.'

Then the Russian started to push the door back open. Turned out that he was surprisingly strong for a little man as well.

Chapter 2

The purse hit the floor of the Tube train with a slap. Anna was already on the move as the man reached for it. She grabbed his arm, twisting it up behind his back and forcing his grubby face into the slightly dirtier glass of the carriage door. It all took a second, maybe less. The sort of move she'd practised hundreds of times over on the judo mat, although admittedly there'd not been any train windows there.

'Gerroff me.'

He tried to throw an elbow round to catch her face. Hardly the most chivalrous move Anna had seen.

Or the most effective.

She dodged easily and shoved his head against the door again, perhaps a touch harder than was strictly necessary.

'Think it's big, do you? Stealing from old ladies?'

Up close she could smell him: cheap cider, sweat and three-day-old piss.

'Yer what?' The feigned outrage was laughable. He squirmed again but he was built for stealth and snatching. No match for Anna.

The old lady in question stared at the purse on the floor, only just beginning to cotton on.

A man was at Anna's side now. Youngish and Australian from the accent; little more than a teenager. 'Are you OK?'

Clearly new to London and the world's most antisocial public-transport system, he seemed blissfully unaware of that golden rule – don't get involved. Nobody else ever did.

Except Anna, of course.

'I can handle it.' She cringed at the D-list action-hero dialogue. 'Could you please just give the purse back to the woman over there?'

The Australian obliged and sat back down again, trying not to look too put out.

It was mid-afternoon and the Tube was still pre-rush-hour quiet. Anna had noticed the snatcher the moment she'd stepped into the carriage. There was just something that made her look twice. A certain slyness; little ratty eyes darting around, nose on the sniff for any kind of opportunity.

He'd made his move at the next stop as the old woman got on, dipping a quick hand into her bag and coming up with the purse. A jolt as the train started up had shaken it from his grasp at the crucial moment.

'It fell out. I was just picking it up for her.'

Yeah right. She spun him round and grabbed at the greasy lapels of his jacket; a short sharp knee to the balls was practically her civic duty. But of course she had to show restraint.

'Let me go, please.' The earlier indignation was gone and he was just desperate now, sweat starting to run down his skinny, dirty face.

Anna felt her anger swiftly morph into something closer to pity. Just another hopeless junkie trying to fund his next score. But what should she do now? Involving the police would only make things... Her mind stretched for the type of euphemism her bosses might use.

Complicated.

Yes, that was it.

She kept a tight hold of him as the train slowed for the next station. Then, as the doors opened, she pushed the man out onto the platform, far more gently than he deserved. But he stumbled and fell all the same, shouting the odds as his scrawny arse hit the floor. The small cluster of passengers waiting impatiently to get on let out a collective gasp before stepping around him and boarding as if nothing had happened.

Back in the carriage all eyes were down as the train pulled away. Books, phones, tablets, newspapers and even fingernails had suddenly become ever so much more interesting. Anything to avoid eye contact with the mad woman who'd just...

PUSHED A MAN OUT OF THE FUCKING TRAIN!!!

The OMGs would be clogging up Twitter the minute they got their phone signals back. And the old woman whose purse she'd saved was far too busy thanking the nice Australian boy to give her a second glance. Anna was wondering quite why she'd bothered when she spotted Kate Barnes at the other end of the carriage.

Really? Oh, for fuck's sake.

Staff of Kate's grade rarely slummed it on public transport. Anna cursed the dumb luck that had put her on the same train as the junkie, the old woman's purse and now her sodding boss.

Kate looked at her down the carriage and gave a slow shake of her head. Anna could well imagine how the incident must have looked from her boss's point of view. 'Headstrong', 'impulsive', 'emotional' – those were the words that people had used to describe her when she'd had her last little issue. Right before they'd shoved her into her current dead-end desk job.

They'd be saying the same again when this got round.

Anna started to move down the carriage: better to talk to Kate immediately; make sure her boss understood what had just happened. But then she stopped herself and turned away.

What was the point? Kate would see it exactly as she wanted to.

Their stop was up next so Anna turned and moved towards the doors instead for a quick getaway. Eyes down, she was first off the train, hurrying for the exit, resisting the temptation to run. One old woman had got her purse back. Great, maybe the ungrateful old hag could learn to keep her bag shut in future. Why couldn't she have stayed out of it?

Just three short weeks ago Anna had got back from her holiday with Scott, happy and relaxed (and looking pretty tanned and gorgeous, she thought). She'd headed into work that first morning, adamant she'd give the job one more go, to try to put everything into it.

Now it had all gone to shit.

She reached the escalator, taking the steps two at a time, determined not to give Kate the satisfaction of seeing her cry.

Chapter 3

Dermot didn't know who'd coined that phrase about fear giving you strength but, whoever it was, they were a bloody liar. The door edged slowly inwards as the little Russian continued to push. Yegor Koslov's eyes were even harder and colder than before, his voice level as if he were making no effort at all to open the door. 'Please, Mr Jack, I am just here to talk to you.'

Yeah right. Loan sharks like Mulrooney didn't hire freelance Russian muscle simply to talk. He tried to push the door shut but it was no good. Back when he'd had more money, and hadn't anticipated Russian gangsters trying to force their way into his flat, a wooden floor had seemed just the thing to smarten up his dingy hallway. Right now his feet were struggling to get any sort of purchase on the surface even though it hadn't been polished for months.

'My employer just wants to see you. That is all.'

'I think I'll pass, all the same.'

'Look,' The Russian gave a grunt, the first sign he was making any real effort. 'I will stop pushing if you will and then maybe we can talk.'

Nope, not falling for that one.

'Ow.' The next thing Dermot knew he was pitching forward and smacking his face against the door as the Russian stepped back.

'My fucking nose.'

'I did tell you I was going to stop pushing. My employer, Mr Oleg Bukin, wants to talk to you; that's all.'

Dermot jerked his head back as an arm snaked round the door. Then he noticed the business card the Russian was holding.

'Please take it.'

Oleg Bukin, Chairman Bukin Enterprises. Underneath was an address in Chelsea and then some more words in what he presumed was Russian.

'He is a very rich man and thinks you will want to hear what he has to say. Now, can I come in?'

Not Charlie Mulrooney then. Dermot waited a beat, breathing in deeply as he had one last think about it. Then he stepped backwards, pulling the door open.

'Thank you.' The Russian's smile wasn't the most convincing but it was a least a smile.

'This Mr...' Dermot looked down at the card again. 'Bukin. What does he want?'

'He has heard you work with some of the UK's biggest TV stars.'

'*Daytime*-TV stars,' Dermot corrected, not too proud to admit it. There was big money to be made outside primetime these days.

'Mr Bukin is particularly impressed by your work with Marcus Diesel. He is a big admirer of the man's work.'

Well that was lucky. Dermot's recent sacking by TV gardener Stuart Goodall (a patio-furniture endorsement deal gone sour) meant that the TV chef was his last client standing.

'He has a business proposition for you but wants to talk to you face to face. I am just here to bring the message.' The little man's eye scanned the hallway, moving on to the mess in the living room. Then he wrinkled his nose at the stale smell. 'He flies back to Moscow tomorrow afternoon. He'd appreciate it if you could visit him at the address on the card tomorrow morning at 11 o' clock.'

OK... Dermot held the little man's gaze for a second or so as he pretended to think it over. The negotiation was already on and he needed to play it cool.

The little Russian maintained his cold, hard stare. But there was something else in his eyes, a superior sort of amusement.

'I'll come and see what he has to say.' Dermot broke first. Of course he would, because, well... You didn't go tracking people down, waiting outside their flats and inviting them to meetings in Chelsea unless you were prepared to make it worth their while.

'Look, er, I am sorry about the thing with the door.' Maybe he'd got this Koslov guy all wrong. The man had only been trying to deliver his boss's message.

'It's nothing.' The Russian nodded but there was no hint of

warmth in his smile. 'Until tomorrow then, Mr Jack.' Koslov reached out a hand to shake Dermot's then turned and left, shutting the front door behind him.

Manners, too – Dermot really had misjudged him. The music inside his head was already playing and he broke into a little dance. How fitting it was 'Boogie Baby'; the disco strut from the video was just perfect for an occasion like this.

This Oleg Bukin character clearly meant business and business tended to mean money. Lots of it, too, if Koslov was to be believed.

Oh, yes.

Paying off Charlie Mulrooney would just be the start of it. Dermot was dancing for real now, not caring about the mess all over his desk, the tatty worn-out furniture or the smell from the dishwasher.

Sod the Edinburgh flat. Dermot would be buying himself a castle bigger than Wanker Wayne's. He'd make better organic cheese too (and more of it) and buy Molly her own pet elephant to ride.

They'd see how Nugget the bloody horse liked that.

He carried on the dance into the kitchen and all the way to the fridge, where he reached for a cold beer. People had said a lot of unkind things about Dermot down the years. It was water off a duck's back mainly, but for some reason the one that cut the most was the suggestion that he was a bit of a fool. If only they could see him now, can of premium lager in hand, about to secure a major deal with a real-life Russian billionaire, well... They wouldn't be calling him a fool then, would they?

Chapter 4

The man was a fool; there was no other word for it. Just one quick flick through the thin dossier Oleg Bukin had given him had bought Yegor Koslov to this simplest of conclusions. His first meeting with Dermot Jack had done nothing to change his opinion.

'Go.' He slumped into the front seat of the Mercedes and barked at the driver. The man didn't like it but knew not to answer back to Yegor.

Celebrity agent? It was the job of a fool. The job of just the kind of man that Yegor had always despised.

And yet it had come to this.

He flicked open the dossier and stared at the photo again as the car headed off. Dermot Jack was 34 years old, but he could have passed for younger. He was 5'10", maybe 5'11" but probably told people he was six foot. Thick, dark hair of which he was clearly proud, neatly trimmed around the sides but left longer on the top – presumably to show people just how much of it he had left. Yegor resisted the temptation to touch his own balding head. Dermot looked fit and lean enough, too, but he was probably just built that way. It was hard to imagine a man like him having the discipline to work out regularly.

But, fool or not, Dermot Jack possessed what Yegor could only describe as a certain low cunning. He'd seen it in the man's eyes as he'd weighed up the prospect dangled in front of him. Ha! Had Dermot known the first thing about Oleg Bukin it wouldn't have been cunning in the man's eyes. It would have been sheer, naked terror.

That said, Yegor had built a career on not underestimating even the weakest of opponents. So he'd be watching Dermot very carefully during their time together. The very thought made him feel sick. When Bukin had first spoken of the idea back in Moscow it had seemed such a remote possibility. Now it was less than a day from becoming harsh reality. Then Yegor would be stuck here in London. Not that he had anything against the city itself. The food was acceptable, the people tolerable enough and it didn't rain anyway near as much as he'd been led to believe. The low sunlight of the late-March afternoon made the place look almost appealing. His four previous trips to London had all ended successfully, in that each of the people he'd come to kill had ended up dead. But being here would mean not being in Moscow, not being close to Bukin. Three hard years he'd spent climbing up the ranks of the man's organisation, just to be side-lined at the very moment he needed to be at the heart of things. And by something as trivial as this.

The driver negotiated his way across two lanes of traffic and headed down towards Earl's Court. Soon they'd be back at Bukin's Chelsea home and Yegor could share the 'good news' that the Englishman had agreed to the meeting.

'Do this thing for me, Yegor; you are the only one I can trust.' His boss had put a meaty hand on each of Yegor's shoulders as he'd made the request. 'It will not be for long.'

Not necessarily true.

Yegor knew he could be stuck here for weeks, months even. But if things ran on for too long he'd just have to take matters in hand. Part of him pitied Dermot Jack. But the Englishman had made his choice. He'd have nobody to blame but himself.

The fool.

Chapter 5

Just shy of 10 o'clock the next morning and Anna had already endured the expected dressing-down in Kate Barnes's glass box of an office. The air conditioning was cranked up to the max, adding to the chill of the atmosphere, while the world-class soundproofing would be doing little to disguise the bollocking she was getting from anyone in the main office who cared to glance in.

But then wasn't that partly the point?

Conduct unbecoming... Bringing the department into disrepute... Blah-de-blah-de-fucking-blah. As expected her explanations had been casually swept aside.

It wasn't that Kate was angry, just (pause for a big dramatic sigh) disappointed. Jesus, what was this, kindergarten?

Anna suspected that 'delighted' summed up Kate's feelings a lot more accurately. For some wholly unfathomable reason, her boss had had it in for Anna ever since she'd joined the team. The Tube incident gave Kate a golden opportunity to put a proper fat, black mark against her name.

Another one.

But then Anna could have lived with that. She could have sucked it up. She could have said sorry, buried her head in her endless reports and waited for an opportunity to apply for a transfer. There was bound to be ample time along the way for fantasies of dark revenge on her boss too. But no, Kate had only gone and taken it upstairs. By 10.30 the two of them were sitting in Richard Lawson's office, waiting for round two to begin.

Three floors up, the departmental head's room was a world away from Kate's sterile little box. At one end a leather-topped desk vied for supremacy with an overly fussy marble fireplace. Three large windows looking out across the River Thames and Lambeth Bridge dominated one wall, while high bookshelves covered most of the rest. Pictures of a younger wife who never seemed to change and a boy and a girl at all ages from birth to young adulthood took up what little space remained in between.

Lawson and Kate sat with their backs to the windows, facing Anna across the table he clearly used for bawling-out junior staff who'd beaten people up on the Tube.

For now though Lawson was ignoring Anna as he leafed through a thin folder on the desk in front of him. He was a 'college tie and Mayfair Club' sort of a man; old school to the core, affable and charming until he needed not to be. Maybe he'd been attractive as a younger man but now, neck deep in his fifties, a nasty set of jowls and a heart-attack-red complexion had long since done their worst. Lawson was known for being decent enough; not one to suffer fools gladly although fair with it. But with those rumours of the current chief's early retirement refusing to quite go away he was also hotly tipped for the top job. Anna doubted he was about to let a matter of staff conduct dent his prospects. There was some nipping in the bud to be done here and fair play was unlikely to get much of a look in.

Next to Lawson Kate glowered, her arms crossed over an expensive cream blouse that didn't quite work for her stick-insect-on-a-diet figure. Cold, hard and impenetrable, she brimmed as ever with self-importance and a simmering sense of indignation against the world and pretty much everyone in it.

Anna had heard it said that her boss's hardness meant she was brittle too. That one day, when someone finally found her fault-line and gave it a gentle tap, she'd shatter into thousands of tiny pieces.

Nice theory. More likely she was just a cow.

Lawson finally closed the folder, looking up as he pushed it to one side. 'Miss Preston, I've heard what happened yesterday.' He paused for a big sigh and a shake of the jowls. 'We simply cannot have members of staff behaving like this. Do you realise how stupid this could make us look?' He shook his head sadly as he stood up and turned his back to her, looking out through the window at the murky waters of the river below.

'It isn't the sort of behaviour we expect,' Kate weighed in, laying it on perhaps a little too thick.

But Anna knew her game here: provoke a reaction so Lawson

would see first-hand how there was little or nothing Kate could do to control her junior's behaviour.

Er, sorry. Not falling for that one. 'With respect, I saw a vulnerable old woman being robbed...' She wasn't going to let Kate get away with it either.

'And, with respect, Kate saw it rather differently.' Lawson turned back round to face her again.

'You got the wrong end of the stick and went in off the deep end.' Kate leaned forward, twisting away at the knife.

Long. Slow. Breaths.

'OK, I'm sorry.' More deep breaths. 'Maybe I did get it wrong. It was a mistake to react in the way I did.' The apology was the only way out now that Lawson had come down so firmly on Kate's side.

He nodded, setting his jowls off on another little wobble.

'I thought martial arts were supposed to be about self-control,' Kate probed again.

'She's apologised,' Lawson cut in. 'I think we can probably leave it there this time.' He looked at the two of them in turn, nodding slowly as he sat back down.

Anna couldn't believe she was going to get away that lightly.

The two of them carried on staring at her.

OK, maybe she wasn't.

'Now, we haven't had the chance to catch up for a while, Anna...' Lawson broke the silence a second or so after it had become uncomfortable.

And it was Anna now, not Miss Preston. That had to be a good thing.

'How are things with you otherwise?' He leaned back in his chair, playing the benevolent uncle, perhaps in anticipation of the promotion to come.

'Everything all right at home?'

No, it bloody wasn't. It had only been a week since Scott had walked out. Her long and unpredictable work hours being the excuse he'd used. Nothing at all to do with the little slapper he'd been seen with in a Fulham wine bar.

'All fine, yes.'

Scott was a shit. Anna had thought they'd had such a great holiday together and here he was cheating on her almost the moment they were back. If he hadn't left she'd have kicked him out. But Lawson and Kate Barnes didn't need to know about her domestic troubles.

'And work-wise, everything OK?'

'Yes, good.' She tried for an enthusiastic nod as she thought about the pile of reports on her desk and the long list of shitty tasks Kate would dream up for her.

'Excellent.' Another little nod set the jowls off once more.

'Actually, there was one thing, sir.' Well, he had asked.

Kate shot daggers across the table.

'Go on.' Lawson gave her what he must have believed was an encouraging smile.

'It's just, well…' She thought about the pile of reports again. 'I think I could do more.'

Lawson threw in another noncommittal nod.

'You're doing important work.' Kate seemed to have her heart set on the world record for unbroken scowling in a workplace environment.

'Kate's right, Anna. What you're doing is vital.'

Yes, she knew all that. But then… Well, it wasn't quite what Anna had envisaged when she'd ditched a promising legal career to follow her dead father into MI5.

Chapter 6

Dermot heard a clunk as the automatic gates swung shut behind him. He stopped and stood for a second on the gravel driveway, mentally preparing himself as he looked up at Oleg Bukin's house. The place was on the small side compared with some of its Chelsea neighbours but it reeked of money all the same.

He pulled the card from his pocket to double-check the address. Yep, there was no mistake. And when he looked up again he saw Yegor Koslov frowning down at him from the top of a short flight of steps leading up to the front door.

'Come, Mr Jack.' Yegor gave him a cold smile. 'Oleg Bukin is not always a patient man. It is best not to keep him waiting.'

And suddenly all the doubts from Dermot's largely sleepless night were back. He could be walking straight into a golden opportunity or a… He didn't like to think what might happen if things went sour. And what exactly did he know about these Russians anyway, except that Yegor Koslov was a little crook and his boss was likely to be a far bigger one? The likes of Google and Wikipedia had been curiously reticent on the topic of Oleg Bukin.

But here Dermot was, rushing straight on in without really thinking things through. Just like when he'd borrowed the sodding money from Mulrooney in the first place. Or shelled out the cash he owed the loan shark on the Edinburgh flat. Then there was that unfortunate misunderstanding with that lap dancer in Norwich. But actually none of this was really helping and it was a little too late for second thoughts now. He slipped the card back into his pocket, pleased with how little his hand was shaking, and headed for the door. Because really, what was the worst that could happen?

OK, bad question. He pushed it to the back of his mind along with everything he'd ever heard about the Russian mafia. The man had invited him here to discuss a business proposition. That was all.

And it was 11am on a sunny Monday morning in Chelsea. Yards away expensive foreign nannies would be minding children with names like Jasper and Jemima. Old ladies would be gathered over tea to talk about hats. And preparations for this year's Flower Show would be well under way.

So he'd go inside and listen to what Bukin had to say. Then, if he liked the sound of it, he'd bargain the price up a little then bite the man's arm off somewhere just south of the shoulder. And if he didn't like it he'd make his excuses and walk away. Standard operating procedure for every deal he'd ever done. This was no different.

'Come on, Mr Jack, my employer is a busy man.' Yegor gave an impatient little sigh.

Dermot realised that he'd stopped at the bottom of the steps.

OK... Breathe.

Then he was moving again. One, two, three, four up the steps and in through the door.

That hadn't been so hard, had it? Rhymed as well. Why was he being such a big Jessie?

'Good morning, sir.' A large man who seemed to be dressed as a waiter or a magician emerged from behind the door to push it closed.

Dermot reached out for the wall to steady himself, the man's sudden appearance bringing on something akin to a seizure.

Jesus, get a grip.

There was little time for recovery though, with Koslov already marching off down the hallway on his little legs. Dermot breathed deeply again and followed, his footsteps muffled by the thick gold carpet as he passed a series of expensive-looking paintings in elaborate frames. Each was probably more valuable than the average London flat. This Oleg Bukin character was clearly no stranger to splashing the cash. And from the state of some of the paintings he had a few issues when it came to judgement. All in all the sort of character Dermot liked doing business with.

Ahead of him, Yegor stopped at a set of double doors, throwing another impatient look over his shoulder. Then he knocked once.

A voice rolled through the door like the thunder of an approaching storm. And Dermot was certain some of the paintings shook on the walls. All the doubts came hurtling back again. Surely it wasn't too late to walk calmly back to the front door and ask the nice man to let him out? In fact that was exactly what he was going to do. But then Yegor pushed the door open and he heard the music.

WTF?

That same jaunty tune he must have heard a thousand times down the years. Heard and come to hate.

But he wasn't hating it now. And he wasn't scared any more either as a few things started to fall into place.

The music played on as Dermot stepped into a room that was vast and largely empty. He blinked for a second as his eyes adjusted to the morning sun streaming in through the big bay window. In the far corner three oversized white leather sofas were arranged to face an industrial-sized wall-mounted TV. Pictures much like those from the hall lined the walls. Away off to the right, across the vast swathes of white carpet, an open-plan kitchen of stainless steel and high-gloss white gleamed in the sunlight. The granite-topped island could easily have petitioned for full continental status or thrown its hat in the ring to host the next Olympics.

Everything about the room was white, bright and positively airy. Everything, that was, apart from the big man, dressed in black and hunched forward on the middle sofa. He was apparently far too busy watching telly to even say hello.

Oleg Bukin, Dermot could only presume.

The big man sat perfectly still, eyes fused to the screen as the music chuntered on. Dermot paused, unsure whether to start the journey across the huge room as Bukin continued to watch TV.

'Welcome to my home, Mr Jack.' The voice that had rumbled its way through the door was a lot softer as the man on the sofa finally tore his eyes away from the screen and pushed himself upright with a grunt. 'My name is Oleg Bukin.' He reached for the remote to pause the programme and headed over towards Dermot.

The man looked to be in his early fifties and, like the room, everything about him was huge. But while the room was mostly white, Oleg Bukin's preferred colour was clearly black, from his short hair to his severely cropped beard and deep, dark eyes and the expensive-looking suit sitting snugly across his broad shoulders.

Almost everything.

The long scar that tugged at the corner of his smile before stretching up across his right cheek to the corner of his eye was a deep and angry red.

'Thank you.' Dermot returned the smile, trying not to stare. Probably best not to ask how Bukin had got the scar, or what had happened to whoever had given it to him.

The Russian reached out a massive paw, engulfing Dermot's hand in a firm yet comfortable handshake.

Then he let go and turned to Koslov. 'You may leave us now.'

Yegor looked far from happy but gave a curt little bow, throwing Dermot an evil glance before turning and heading across the wide expanse of carpet and out through the door.

When Dermot looked back at Bukin the big Russian was eyeing him intently once more.

'Come, Mr Jack, we have much to talk about. But first we will watch a little television.' He waved a big hand at the screen. 'It is why you are here after all.' He headed back to the sofa and sat, beckoning Dermot to join him. Then his eyes were back on the big screen as he pressed the remote and the studio audience burst into a round of applause.

Dermot perched next to him as a familiar figure in chef's whites grinned out from the TV. *'Hello and welcome to* The Meal of Fortune. *My name's Marcus Diesel.'*

It wasn't, of course. His real name was Richie Murray but Marcus had taken the stage name early in his career, presumably so people wouldn't actually have to meet him to realise he was a total cock.

'And we're going to spin up some great dishes for you this evening.' It was the same line the chef had trotted out most weekday afternoons for the past decade. That didn't stop the audience letting rip with another blast of applause. Bukin joined in with the clapping as the chef bounded off to meet the day's two oh-so-lucky contestants.

Dermot grabbed another sly look at his host as Marcus introduced himself to Gail from Dorset and Ruth from Nantwich. But the big man ignored him, staring at the TV with almost childlike glee. How could Dermot ever have imagined there was anything to be scared of here? Bukin had probably got that scar opening a tin of biscuits.

'Well, you all know the game…' Marcus launched into a quick summary of the rules. 'We spin the wheel and see which ingredient it lands on. Then it's fastest on the buzzer to answer the question and win the ingredient.'

On screen Ruth and Gail were nodding eagerly at Marcus with near knicker-wetting awe.

On the sofa Oleg Bukin wasn't far behind.

'Then after the break our two chefs will help the contestants prepare the tastiest dishes possible with the ingredients they've won in part one. And someone will walk away with our Meal of Fortune trophy.' He paused to give the camera another big smile and a wink. 'So let's begin, it's time to spin!' Another phrase Marcus reeled out on every show. The studio audience showed its appreciation with a fresh blast of wild applause. Again Bukin joined in.

The chef set the big wheel in motion. It spun madly for about ten seconds before coming to rest on a cartoon onion. Marcus launched into a question about pastry and Gail from Dorset buzzed in to get her first vegetable on the board as Bukin roared his approval from the sofa, slapping Dermot firmly on the back with a meaty fist. This really was a man who knew quality cookery-based light entertainment when he saw it. Dermot had been brought here for one reason and one reason only. To thrash out the details of a proper Russian remake of *The Meal of Fortune*. Real Russian contestants with real Russian vegetables. And Oleg Bukin had clearly decided that Marcus Diesel was the man to show his countrymen how to rustle up a tasty feast with just half a beetroot and a tin of pickled herrings.

'Idiot fucking bitch whore.' Bukin wasn't shy about showing his disapproval as Gail fluffed a simple question about salad dressing. But his smile was quickly back as her opponent answered correctly to claim a pair of salmon fillets – a versatile and highly prized ingredient on *The Meal of Fortune*.

Next up the wheel landed on basmati rice, another valuable ingredient for all true *MOF* aficionados, setting off a ripple of excited chatter among the studio audience as Marcus fired off a question about bacon-curing techniques. Bukin shouted something in Russian and punched the air as Ruth buzzed to claim the prize. And Dermot found himself slipping a zero on the end of the number he'd just started to toy with. The TV show itself would just be the start of it. There'd be exclusive sets of Marcus Diesel-endorsed cookware, launched to coincide with the beginning of series two. Toasted-sandwich maker and kettle gift sets would follow along with a range of stir-in sauces (presumably including various takes on the classic stroganoff) and of course cookbooks – every Christmas for five years on the bounce.

Dermot didn't normally do his mental dance routine when he was sitting down but you had to make exceptions on occasions like this.

A loud buzzer jolted him back into the here and now. Next to him Bukin was leaning forward eagerly. It was time for the day's bonus vegetable.

Many a close-run show had been decided by the bonus-vegetable round and fans rated it as one of the show's true high points. Marcus smiled as he pulled today's prize from his apron pocket with something of a flourish. You had to hand it to the chef: complete arse he may have been but he was a man who knew how to play the big points. It was a skill that would go down as well in Murmansk as it did in Middlesbrough.

'How do you say in English?' Bukin turned to Dermot pointing to the vegetable on screen.

'Turnip.'

'Tuurneep. Very popular in Russia.'

Dermot thought about adding another zero.

Bukin's applause reached new heights as Ruth buzzed in with the right answer. Dermot relaxed back into the sofa, watching happily as the future star of Russian daytime TV ran through a few more questions before wrapping things up for the first half.

'Join us after the break when we'll be cooking up The Meal of Fortune.'

They certainly would. Dermot sat forward in his seat as the image of Marcus's manically grinning face faded, giving way to a series of adverts offering poor people a series of ever-more convenient ways to get into debt.

Marcus Diesel was a 24-carat, copper-bottomed idiot for sure. But he was Dermot's idiot and one who still commanded among the highest fees in daytime TV.

A point Dermot would be making to Oleg Bukin some time very soon.

Chapter 7

'You think you could do more?' Lawson held the encouraging smile.

'Well, I just feel...' In for a penny.

Kate shot Anna another dark look.

'I just feel a bit wasted where I am. I'm a trained intelligence officer. I could make more of a contribution out in the field.'

Kate and Lawson shared a look.

'Take on more responsibility.'

'You think your behaviour today was that of a responsible person? And what about Simon Wells?' Kate said the name with a grim little smile.

Why did it always have come back to Simon bloody Wells? The only mistake she'd ever made – and that had been to trust someone else to do their job properly.

'I think that's all water under the bridge.' Lawson threw Kate another look then turned back to Anna. 'As you know, your father and I were close.' He stood and turned towards the window once again. 'Learned pretty much everything I know from him.'

And why did it always have to come back to her father too?

'The thing I admired most about David was...' Lawson paused and stared out the window.

His patience. Yeah, yeah, yeah...

Always one for playing the long game...

Forty years of service... Practically an institution around here...

Not such an institution around his own house.

'He was a great man for seeing things through.'

Less of a man for seeing his wife and daughter though. But Anna couldn't have loved him more. It was why she'd waited until after his death before following him into the service. She knew he would have been proud but it wasn't the future he'd wanted for her.

'A great man.' Lawson continued to gaze out the window at the Thames, as he shared a private moment with the ghost of his old, dead friend. And when he was done he'd firmly put Anna back in her box.

'Anyway, enough of that.' He finally shook himself out of it and turned to face her once more. 'So you're after something a bit more challenging? What about our Russian friend, Kate? Should be right up Anna's street.'

Come again?

'You *were* saying just yesterday how you needed more arms and legs.'

Hardly a ringing endorsement, but…

'And all the time you've got Anna on your team, raring to go?'

'Well, sir, there are other priorities.'

'I'm sure what she's doing can keep for a few days.'

'Of course.' Kate nodded. She hadn't climbed so far so quickly without knowing how to live to fight another day.

'This is hot off the press.' Lawson flipped the file in front of him open and handed a photograph to Anna.

Anna looked straight into a pair of cold blue eyes, still not quite believing what was happening. The man in the photo was blond and balding, his face set into a scowl. Not the kind of man to mess with lightly, judging by the look of him, although he did appear to be slightly on the short side.

'Russian, goes by the name of Yegor Koslov,' Lawson pressed on. 'Contract killer turned mafia enforcer, although there's nothing we can pin on him. We've been interested in Koslov and the organisation he represents for some time. He was flagged up arriving at Heathrow a few days ago. We've had a team watching him ever since. Everything we have on him is in the file. It isn't much.'

OK. So far, so routine. All they'd want was some extra intel on Koslov. Anna couldn't see this taking her too far from her desk. If anything it was a lowlier task then her usual daily grind.

'We need to know why he's in the UK.' Kate took up the briefing. 'Yesterday he met a man and they rendezvoused again this morning at a house in Chelsea about an hour ago. The surveillance team is outside there now. The address is in the file too. Koslov has been in London for four days and hasn't met anyone. Now he's met this man twice; it must be important.'

Lawson leaned forward, playing tag team with Kate. 'I want you to oversee the operation on this second man. Get down to the house and speak to the surveillance team. We'll give you a couple of juniors to dig up all the info you can. Remember though, your brief is the second man.' He shuffled around in the folder. 'We've got a separate surveillance team for Koslov. Keep your team on the target at all times. Anything you find out could be crucial, however insignificant it seems. Now, any questions?'

'No.' Anna shook her head, still trying to take it all in. Ten minutes ago she'd been up for a disciplinary or worse. Now she was heading up a real operation once again.

'Ah, here it is.' Lawson finished sifting through the file and came up with a second photo and handed it to Anna. 'Name of Dermot...'

The whole room spun, even though she was sitting down.

'... Jack.'

The grin was as cheeky as ever.

The room spun some more.

His hair was just as thick and wavy, the eyes dark and smiley.

Things finally started to stand still again as Anna put the photo down next to the picture of the Russian and looked across the desk with what she hoped was a confident smile.

'I'll get on with it straight away, sir.' She held Lawson's gaze, then Kate's, searching for any hint that she might have given herself away. They'd never let her carry on with it if they suspected she knew the man. That she and Dermot had once been... That would have breached all sorts of protocols.

But there was no sign that either of them was any the wiser.

'If that's all?' She reached across and took the folder, slipping the two photos inside. Then she stood slowly, resisting the urge to turn and rush from the room.

'Yes, thank you. Keep us informed.'

She turned and started to walk, counting out the steps to door slowly in her head.

'Oh, Anna.'

Lawson's words hit like a sniper's bullet between her shoulder blades.

Stay calm.

Deny everything.

They didn't know anything, OK.

Anna reached for one of the breathing-control techniques her martial-arts instructor had taught her. Then she turned back slowly and looked Lawson straight in the eye.

Just one flinch, one flicker and it could all be over.

'This is a matter of national security. I know you won't let us down.' His encouraging smile was back in place.

Only when the door was closed behind her did she let her own smile come.

A real assignment. And all she'd had to do was to stand up for an old lady on the Tube. Maybe there was some justice in the world after all.

Anna pulled the photo out of the folder for a proper look. On closer inspection she could see there were a quite a few more lines round the eyes. And of course the boy she'd known was now a man. But 17 years had done little else to change him. The bastard hadn't even lost any of his precious hair.

She smiled again as she slipped the picture back into the file and thought about Lawson's words.

'A matter of national security.'

Well, well, well. Dermot Jack. What have you gone and got yourself mixed up in now? Anna suspected she might just enjoy finding out.

Chapter 8

Oleg Bukin beamed at him across the rolling granite expanse of the kitchen island as *The Meal of Fortune* theme tune blasted out to signal the start of part two. The adverts had been about halfway through when the Russian had invited Dermot to join him in the kitchen area.

And what more fitting place to start the negotiations. Dermot smiled back then arranged his features into his best bargaining face. 'Mr Bukin—'

But just then a door next to the kitchen area opened and the large man who'd let Dermot into the house appeared carrying two bags. He emptied the contents, laying them in two neat piles on the worktop, before helping Bukin into a bright-white apron. On the TV the theme tune gave way to yet more applause as Marcus crossed the studio to patronise the two low-level celeb chefs who'd be trying to make a meal with the ingredients the contestants had claimed in part one.

'I don't expect you to join me but I do like to cook along.'

Dermot looked at the Russian then down at the two piles of ingredients on the worktop. They were identical to the ones on the TV.

Play along? The guy truly was a *Meal of Fortune* nut. There'd be more than one extra zero on the end of Marcus's fee.

'I get him to watch it first and prepare both sets of ingredients.' Bukin nodded at the other big man's back as he disappeared through the door. His smile might have looked shy were it not for the scar. 'Then I watch on play-back and cook along. Now, you are my guest, Mr Jack – which ingredients should I choose?'

'That one.' Dermot pointed to the pile on the Russian's left.

'Good choice.' Bukin nodded appreciatively. With the salmon, rice and stir-fry veg, Ruth from Nantwich was holding all the aces.

Incorporating the turnip in any meaningful way might pose a challenge but he was going to have to trust in Bukin's culinary skills.

On screen a buzzer sounded and a big clock in the top corner started to count down from 15 minutes.

'I have to thank you, Mr Jack, for bringing us Marcus Diesel. *The Meal of Fortune* has no bigger fan than me in all of Russia.'

Bukin's admiration clearly didn't extend to the guest chefs who did the actual cooking. While on the TV the salmon were already gently frying in a pan with some oil and garlic, in his own kitchen the Russian was soon well off-piste, attacking his fillets with much gusto and what looked like a small cutlass.

'The man who put Marcus Diesel at the very top of TV cooking is a man who can help me, I think.'

Dermot smiled and nodded as he took a step back to avoid the flying bits of fish. He wondered whether to tell Bukin he should probably be getting his rice on.

'So you're interested in working with Marcus?' Dermot weighed in with the opener, leaving Bukin to worry about his own rice.

The Russian just frowned, waving a dismissive hand at the sizzling fillets on the TV before firing up a gas ring to maximum and throwing his own shredded pieces of salmon into a dry wok. Then he got busy with the turnip. Knife in hand again, he made short work of the peeling and chopping before lobbing it in with the salmon. His stir-fry veg went in next, followed by a disturbing amount of soy sauce.

'There'd be a lot of money in a Russian remake,' Dermot pushed on, determined not to lose the initiative.

Bukin stared down at the contents of his wok with a faraway look in his eyes. 'Sadly most Russians do not share my passion for cookery-based TV quizzes.'

Which was exactly why they needed a man like Marcus Diesel beamed into their living rooms five nights a week.

The Russian stirred the contents of his wok before dipping a spoon in for a taste. He screwed up his face then upended the bottle of soy sauce over the wok before finally getting round to the rice. It was going to be chewy at best.

'A Russian remake of *The Meal of Fortune*.' For a second Bukin stared across the kitchen, all misty eyed again. Then he shook his head. 'No. It would never be as good as your original. It is your contacts in the music industry that interest me. You must still know a lot of important people.'

Dermot tried to keep the smile on his face as the all-too-familiar stench of defeat invaded his nostrils – though this could equally have been the salmon starting to catch in the wok.

Yes, he had *known* a lot of important people in the music biz. But the music biz had chewed him up and spat him right across the room a long time ago. Dermot had promised himself he'd never go back. It was a promise he'd never come close to breaking.

Bukin was stirring the wok again now, ignoring the black smoke starting to billow up from the rapidly blackening mess within. He dipped a spoon in for another taste, nodding happily this time. 'I want you to use your contacts to help my daughter. She wants to be a pop star.'

Dermot looked at Bukin and tried to picture his daughter. A stocky peasant girl with a flat voice, flatter feet and an arse like a bison no doubt; her complexion raddled by too much underage vodka and all that wind howling across the Russian steppe. It really was time to make his excuses and get the hell out of there before his lungs endured lasting smoke damage.

'Just listen to her sing.' Bukin flashed another contemptuous look at the TV, where the griddled salmon fillets seemed to be coming along nicely, then muted the sound and reached across to an iPad docked into a speaker on the worktop.

'Let It Go' from *Frozen*. It had been one of Molly's favourites from the previous summer and Dermot recognised the song on about the third beat.

Then the voice cut in; Bukin's daughter presumably. The Russian started to nod his head with the slow beat.

'You must admit she is good, yes?' Bukin killed the music after a couple of verses and a chorus, clearly deeming this sufficient to demonstrate his daughter's musical prowess. He turned the TV volume up again, just as Marcus Diesel, the audience and a big clock on the screen started to count down from ten.

Yes, the girl had a good voice, he'd give her that – but it was still going to be a no. The Russian wouldn't be happy but a limited-edition Marcus Diesel apron would help soften the blow. Maybe he'd even throw in a signed wok to replace the one Bukin was currently ruining.

'It's kind of you to consider me...'

A soft knock on the door cut him off.

'Ah that will be my daughter now.' Bukin beamed at him, the scar once again tugging away at his cheek as he turned off the heat under his charred salmon and started to spoon it out into three dishes, just as the countdown hit zero. 'Her name is Svetlana and she's looking forward to meeting her new agent.'

Hang on...

Suddenly Dermot was angry. Who did this man think he was? Sending that little thug to barge into his flat, then dragging him all the way over to Chelsea when a simple phone call could have saved them both a lot of time and trouble.

'Please forgive her; she does not speak much English.'

The door swung open.

Dermot started to speak but then stopped and decided just to stare for a bit instead. Forget about the lack of English; people would forgive the girl in front of him most things short of culling seal cubs to make a fur bikini that she'd wear only once. Bukin's daughter was quite simply one of the most stunning girls he'd ever met. Much later, he learned the meaning of her name, Svetlana – bringer of light. She smiled shyly as she walked into the room and it was as if the sun had just come out from behind a dark cloud, even though it was already shining brightly through the big windows. And actually, on reflection, she'd probably have got away with the seal cubs and the bikini too.

'I am please to meet you, Meeser Jack.' Her voice was soft and melodic.

Dermot would have put her at about 21 or 22 but she could equally have been a little younger. It was hard to tell which was the darkest: the hair that flowed around her shoulders, or her eyes. The eyes maybe just had it but he would have understood if the hair had demanded a recount. That was where the likeness to Bukin ended. The skin across her high cheekbones was almost pure white and flawless. And then there was the rest of her, all six-odd feet of sheer and unadulterated wow. She was dressed simply in jeans and a plain white T-shirt, but then nothing more was needed.

Dermot zipped through a quick dance routine in his head, finishing up with an ambitious mental backflip and landing it perfectly as he returned her smile.

'We have a deal then, I think, Mr Jack.' Bukin gave him a knowing little nod, a broad grin across his face as he reached over the wok and grasped Dermot's hand.

Oh yes they had a deal. That inconvenient little promise about not working in the music industry wouldn't be troubling him any longer. Dermot felt his own smile spread as the pound signs spun up in his eyes. All those extra zeroes he'd imagined for Marcus Diesel would be nothing compared to what he could make with Svetlana.

'I must go back to Moscow soon but Svetlana will stay in London. Yegor will remain here too as her translator. I think the two of you will get on well.'

Hmmm, it wasn't as if they'd got off to the best of starts. But Dermot for one was prepared to let bygones be bygones. He put both hands on the granite worktop and took a deep breath. Ideally he could have done with a little sit down at this point.

A drink maybe too.

But Bukin was already making his way round the huge island, the smile growing wider with every step. He reached out for Dermot, wrapping him in a big bear hug and lifting him off the floor. When he finally put him down again there were fat tears in the Russian's eyes and big bits of raw salmon from the apron all over Dermot's trousers.

'Thank you, thank you, thank you. This is her dream.' Bukin smiled as the tears rolled down his cheeks.

'No, thank *you*...' Dermot felt the beginnings of tears in his own eyes and not just from the smouldering wok.

Then Svetlana was thanking him in her soft voice and cranking up the sunlight with another smile.

Boom... She really wouldn't have to do too much else. A little pouting and posing for a few photos. Obviously there'd be some singing every now and then. But not too much and from what he'd heard of her demo it wouldn't be a problem. Nothing though, would be as important as that smile.

Bukin had finally noticed the mess he'd made of Dermot's trousers and was apologising and trying to brush it off. Dermot told him not to bother. So Bukin stopped with the job only half done and invited him to stay for lunch instead. And of course Dermot accepted, even though he guessed it would mean sharing the charred contents of the wok.

'I be on the *Topska da Popska, da*?' Svetlana smiled and the room lit up all over again.

Dermot frowned as he worked through the girl's words in his head.

'Yes – you know, where your famous paedophiles say which song is Number 1.' Bukin was nodding enthusiastically now.

'Oh, *Top of the Pops*.' The show hadn't been on for years but never mind. Svetlana was guaranteed to get plenty of airtime elsewhere.

'They show reruns from the eighties all the time in Russia. When Svetlana was a little girl we did not miss an episode. She liked Duran Duran but I was always more of a Kajagoogoo man.'

'*Well that's it, ladies and gentlemen! Join us next time to spin* The Meal of Fortune…' On the TV Marcus said his goodbyes and the theme tune started up again. Next to him Ruth from Nantwich smiled happily, clutching her frying-pan-shaped trophy.

Bukin smiled at the TV and gave a little clap then he grabbed Dermot and Svetlana, leading them round the kitchen island in a wild jig, laughing as he went.

And then Dermot was laughing again too. Wiping the smile off Wanker Wayne's face (and the horse's) would be just the start of it. And what about all those squealing little nobodies who'd stopped returning his calls? The fuckers who'd stopped inviting him to parties. And those back-stabbing bastards who'd, well… Stabbed him in the back. And the front.

Robbie BASTARD Gray too.

Talk about unfinished business.

Oh yes.

Round and round they danced, until Dermot had forgotten his earlier qualms about the Russian-mafia side of things – or quite how badly things had ended last time he was involved with the music biz.

Chapter 9

Whatever Dermot was doing in the Chelsea house he was taking his bloody time about it. Anna stretched out her legs, shifting in the surveillance van's uncomfortable seat as she looked up at the monitor.

The only sign of life from the house across the road had come about half an hour back when someone had opened a downstairs window to let out a worrying cloud of black smoke. But there'd been no alarm or other fuss so they'd just had to carry on watching and waiting.

The house would have been at the top end of the market in most parts of London. For Chelsea it was no more than average, although still likely to carry a price tag somewhere in the low double-digit millions. Way back when, with life treating Dermot more kindly than he'd ever deserved, it was just the sort of place he might have hung out in; drinking overpriced champagne and making inappropriate suggestions to pretty girls.

Girls who'd have been more than happy to say yes.

But the owner of this house had to be well out of a bottom feeder like Dermot's league. Certainly it was too expensive for one of his low-grade TV chefs, however many packet-sauce endorsement deals he might have racked up for them. Still, there were a thousand innocent reasons for Dermot to be visiting. But none of them explained why he'd been met at the door by the same Russian mafia enforcer who'd visited his flat the day before.

Back at base the two juniors she'd been given had already started to build up a picture of Dermot Jack's life. She reached for the folder Lawson had given her and pulled out the picture, just to make sure she wasn't going completely mad. But there he was, grinning back at her.

Thirty-four now (she'd known that) and single (hardly surprising) with a young daughter from a short-lived marriage. Whoever the poor woman was, Anna could only sympathise. She hadn't known about the ex-wife or the daughter, but then she'd stopped following Dermot's life in the tabloids long before the press had themselves lost interest in him.

Still no sign of any movement across the street and the little van was starting to get hot and stuffy now with the midday sun on its roof. Anna shifted again in her seat and turned towards the man in the chair next to her. He ignored her, peering instead at the monitor and fiddling with a couple of knobs. She thought again about striking up a conversation but then decided against it. He'd introduced himself as Stuart, his only words since she'd arrived. He was mid-forties and a surveillance lifer. The kind of man who felt a youngster like Anna should be back at base waiting for his team to tell her what was going on. Not down here, in his face and quite frankly in his way.

'*Don't worry, we've got it covered.*' Those had been his exact words when she'd phoned to say she was on the way down. And almost exactly what she'd been told last time, too, on the Simon Wells operation. That time she'd listened – a mistake she would not be making again.

Nobody had ever been able to say quite how the surveillance team had messed up so spectacularly on the Wells assignment.

'*It wasn't my fault!*' She'd wanted to scream the words back then and still did now. But it had been her operation – the biggest one she'd handled; more responsibility after a string of smaller successes.

Wells hadn't been anything particularly special: late forties and a mid-ranking salesman for an arms company. Big house in North London, beautiful younger wife and two adorable kids at private school. Two golden retrievers, second home in Devon, holidays four times a year.

Gambling debts.

Ah…

Serious ones, too.

Anna had made contact herself, offering to pay off his debts in return for few details about his company's dealings with a certain Kuwaiti 'businessman'. The Kuwaiti oozed respectability, sitting on the board of several children's charities when he wasn't acting as a middleman in the sale of arms to a selection of unsavoury regimes across the Middle East and Africa.

Wells hadn't needed much persuasion. Queen and country and all that.

And those debts of course.

Anna's plan was simple enough. Wells would go into the office at the weekend and download the files they needed. They'd be watching to make sure the coast stayed clear. There was nothing they could have done to stop Wells' boss coming into the office for an unscheduled and highly uncharacteristic Sunday visit. But they could at least have spotted him and warned their man.

Unable to adequately explain the confidential files on the memory stick dangling from his office PC, Wells had been shown the door.

Six months of careful intelligence-gathering down the tube.

The surveillance team had held their hands up. But there'd been suggestions that Anna had been too eager to go for a quick result, her plan ill thought out and too risky. Funny that nobody had raised any such objections when the operation had been signed off. She'd been consigned to desk research ever since.

So this time she was staying put. And no, just for the record, it had nothing to do with the prospect of seeing Dermot Jack again.

Christ no.

Anna reached for her phone as it started to vibrate, hoping for an update from the team. The caller ID read *Scott*.

Great, from one prick to another. He'd been calling about three times a day since he'd dumped her. Wasn't it supposed to work the other way round? So far she'd avoided speaking to him and hadn't listened to any of his messages. She'd have to talk to him at some point though, if just to tell him to fuck off. But now was not that time. Yesterday maybe, stuck behind her desk, she might have taken the call and maybe even listened to what he had to say. But not today, with her own operation…

'Subject One on the move.' The words brought her back to the screen in front of her.

Subject One was Koslov. He scowled as he closed the front door behind him, his eyes scanning round before he trotted down the steps and jumped into the black Mercedes on the gravel driveway. The front gate swung open and the car roared out of the drive and took a left.

'OK. Green One and Two get ready to follow.' Next to her Stuart was speaking into his mic.

A dark-blue Ford slowly detached itself from the curb and followed Koslov's Merc, a man on a scooter dressed as a courier close behind.

'So who's the other car for then?' She turned to Stuart, pointing at the screen at a second black Mercedes which had just edged into sight around the side of the house.

'Beats me. Nobody's been in or out but Koslov and Derm... Hang on.'

The front door opened and Dermot stepped out. Anna clicked the mouse to zoom in on his face; that same grin stretching from ear to bloody ear.

'Car must be for Dermot. Green Three stand by.'

Anna watched as another figure emerged from the doorway. A girl, long dark hair, early twenties and stunning with it. She gave Dermot a long hug then turned back towards the house. No wonder he was smiling.

'Look.' Next to her Stuart was leaning forward as he peered at the screen. 'There's someone else coming out too.'

A big man in a heavy black raincoat appeared, his collar up and a wide-brimmed hat covering his head. He gave the girl a hug, then did the same for Dermot before he hurried down the steps and climbed into the back seat of the Mercedes. The car pulled away as the gates swung open once more. Dermot gave the girl a final wave and headed for the gate on foot.

Shit, this was all happening too fast.

'Can you cover Dermot and the car?' The question was out before she'd had time to think it through.

'No, it's just us and one other unit. If we split the team we'll be too easy to spot. Either that or we'll lose them.'

'Take the man in the car then.' Anna knew it was the right thing to do. 'That's who Dermot was here to meet and he clearly didn't want to be spotted. It's far too warm for that coat and hat.'

'Orders are to follow Subject Two.' Stuart shook his head as he turned to glare at her.

Dermot stopped by the gate, brushing something from his trousers.

'Orders have just changed. Take the car. I can follow Derm... I mean Subject Two on foot.'

'You're not a pro; he'll spot you in ten seconds.'

'He's not a pro either. Follow the second car. That's an order.' The words had come out calm and assured; inside she was feeling anything but.

The surveillance man stared at her, the silence stretching from one second to two and then three before he finally gave in with a sigh. 'OK Green Three, follow the Mercedes; I'll be behind you.'

'Thank you.' She took a breath then stood and pushed the back door of the van open, scanning the pavement opposite for Dermot.

He was about 20 yards away; strolling like he didn't have a care in the world, whistling or humming an annoying little tune no doubt. Well he wouldn't be so cocky if he knew who he'd got himself mixed up with.

Anna waited for a few seconds then crossed the road, staying 30 or so paces behind as Dermot made his way up to the King's Road. Once there he seemed content to amble through the lunchtime crowds, glancing in almost every shop window as he went. It was a known classic counter-surveillance technique; catch the image of whoever was following you in the glass. But Anna was pretty sure he was just window shopping or – more likely, knowing him – checking how his hair looked.

And if he did spot her? So what?

Just a chance coincidence bumping into an old friend, even after all these years. Wasn't a girl allowed to spend her lunch break doing her own bit of shopping on the King's Road?

He walked on further then stopped to pull out his phone, pacing around in a circle on the pavement as he made a call.

Anna ducked across the street, doing a spot of window shopping of her own to keep an eye his reflection as he continued pacing round and round.

'*Your brief is the second man… Keep your team on the target at all times.*' Lawson's words echoed through her head. She'd just gone and done the exact opposite.

But they needed to know more about the man in the coat and hat. Anna had taken the initiative and knew it had been the right call. Besides, she was more than capable of tailing an amateur like Dermot…

She spun round, suddenly realising she couldn't see his reflection. It had disappeared from the window. She scanned quickly up and down the street, trying to spot him through the crowds. But, just like that night all those years before, Dermot Jack was nowhere to be seen.

Chapter 10

Anna took a last deep breath and knocked gently on the door. Then she pushed her way into Lawson's office for her second visit of the day. He was sitting in the same place at the table, another slim folder in front of him and Kate Barnes at his side once more.

The summons had come minutes after she'd got back to the office following two wasted hours, beating herself up as she searched for Dermot around the streets of Chelsea.

'Please sit down, Anna.' Lawson's face was a dangerous shade of crimson, while Kate's had gone the opposite way.

Neither was a good sign.

Just this morning she'd been in here bigging herself up and asking for a more responsible role. But by now they'd know she'd taken the surveillance team off Dermot and then managed to lose him.

What was that about more responsibility?

'That was a big call, to switch the surveillance from Dermot.' Lawson's jowls trembled as his face darkened further.

'Sir I—'

'You went against operational guidelines. Not to mention the advice of an experienced surveillance team member.'

'I'm—'

'There's a reason we have protocols.'

Here it came. The bastard was even smiling now. 'I thought. I'm sorry—'

'You're sorry?' He shook his head and sat back. 'The last thing you need to do is apologise. Protocols are there to be broken if need be. Without your quick thinking we wouldn't have this.' He pulled a photograph from the file. 'The man Dermot Jack met at the house. Your surveillance team only managed to get a clear snap of him at the airport, when he took off his hat for passport control.'

Anna looked down at the livid red scar on the man's cheek.

'His name is Oleg Bukin. He's on the watch list, for God's sake. But we just let him swan in and out of the country as if he owns it.

We could have had him today.' He slammed his hand down on the table.

Beside him Kate had faded to an even paler shade of white. Presumably as the operational lead she'd taken the brunt of the flack before Anna arrived.

'Bukin's an arms dealer. Ex-Red Army weapons to Africa and South America. Nothing that bad in the scheme of things. He's trying to go legit now, like they all do. Oil, media and mining, that sort of thing.'

'So what's so special about him?' Russia and the former Soviet republics were full of men like Bukin peddling ageing weapons to the highest bidder.

'There's been chatter for a while that he's trying to sell something a little more specialised.'

In the world of illegal arms dealing that meant chemical, biological or...

'Old Soviet nuclear materials. It was like the Wild West out there, post-Communism,' Kate chipped in, finally regaining some colour. 'A lot of things went missing. Nobody knows who got hold of what.'

Lawson rubbed at his face, his complexion back close to its normal deep red. 'We missed him this time but he was here for a reason. We need to work out what that is. And how Dermot Jack's involved.'

'What do the FSB think?'

'As you know, we're hardly on the best terms with our Russian friends at present.' Kate shook her head as she threw Anna a withering glance. 'Plus we think Bukin may have high-up connections in the Russian intelligence community. All in all, best not to ask.'

Lawson closed the folder and pushed it across the table. 'Some bedtime reading for you, Anna. You did well today. I want you to run with this now. If Dermot Jack moves, I want to know about it. Find out whatever you can about him. Then we can try to work out what's going on.'

'Yes, sir.'

'What do you need?'

'Second surveillance team: one for Jack, one for the house.' It would mean she didn't have to make any more decisions like the one today.

'No problem.'

'Email and phone surveillance on Dermot too.' That was something else entirely. Anna knew she'd pushed it too far. The surveillance on a private citizen would need a signed order from the Home Secretary. This couldn't be that important.

'Done.' Lawson nodded.

She felt a little thrill run through her; this was *that* important and still he'd put her in charge.

'And keep me informed.' His curt nod indicated that the meeting was over.

She and Kate both stood to leave.

'Not you,' Lawson nodded to Kate. 'I think we need another word. Close the door behind you, Anna.'

She walked slowly to the door, enjoying the feeling of Kate's eyes burning into her back every step of the way. She'd known she'd made the right call with the surveillance and her quick thinking had put her right at the very heart of a vital operation.

She fought to keep the smile from her face as she headed for the lift. A proper operation with electronic surveillance. And yes, of course, this was business. But she wasn't going to kid herself that it wasn't just a little bit personal too, after what Dermot had done.

That though, was something she'd be keeping firmly to herself.

Chapter 11

Lawson waited until the sounded of Anna's footsteps had faded down the corridor. 'Do you think she suspects anything?'

Kate shook her head. 'She's so pleased to be back in the field she can't see any further than that.'

'Good.' Lawson felt relieved. Kate was a good judge of people; this was one of the reasons he'd come to rely on her as his eyes and ears around the place.

Those eyes were looking down at her hands now. There was more to come. He wasn't such a bad judge of people himself. Lawson sat back and waited.

'It's just… Does she have to be quite so involved? It feels risky and…'

'Go on.' They'd been through this on more than one occasion but it was best to keep her onside by letting her think she was having a say.

'She's compromised because of her relationship with Jack.'

'But that's exactly why we need her involved. It might just be helpful if we need to recruit him as an asset. And it was all a long time ago.'

'She doesn't have the experience. That decision today could easily have backfired.'

'Didn't though, did it? Far from it in fact.' Anna had acted swiftly and her father would have been proud. He stifled a pang of guilt as he thought about how he was using his dead friend's daughter. 'Sometimes I think you're too hard on her. She's got the makings of a good operative.'

Kate nodded, still not looking convinced.

'Anna's a proud young woman. We can't reveal that we know about her and Jack. She won't react well if she thinks that's the only reason we got her involved. And we're so close to Bukin now; I can feel it.'

'And you think Dermot Jack is the key?'

He nodded. 'He's definitely important. Bukin wouldn't have risked coming to London to meet him otherwise.'

Kate looked down at her hands again. 'What if Anna decides her loyalties lie with Dermot rather than us?'

Lawson didn't think that was likely, not with all their history. But it was always good to have every base covered.

'If it comes to it we'll just have to deal with that in the appropriate manner.' He hoped for the sake of his dead friend that he'd never be faced with that choice. But then he wasn't about to let the situation with Bukin blow up on his watch. There was only one director general's job and you only ever got one shot at it.

Part Two

Part Two

Chapter 12

Three weeks it had been now, three long frustrating weeks and what? Bugger all. Things had seemed so simple that day in Bukin's house with the beautiful girl smiling at him over the burned salmon stir-fry. Get her a recording deal, make her a star. Who exactly was going to say no?

Just about everyone, as it turned out. And if anyone in the music business did remember the name Dermot Jack after all this time they weren't letting on.

He put the phone down on another not-so-polite refusal and clicked to open his latest email. The steam-powered computer chuntered and whirred, this simplest of tasks almost beyond it now. He sat back, looking at the two photos of Molly that flanked the ancient machine as he waited for the email to open. On the right aged five wearing a pink anorak. On the left aged seven and dressed in the black Puffa jacket that still remained a firm favourite a year later.

This was the extent of his business empire now: the second-hand desk in the corner of his already cosy sitting room, the old computer and the photos of Molly to keep watch over him.

Once upon a time he'd had the smart offices up in Soho; well, as smart as it got over a newsagent's. Meeting rooms, assistants, receptionist, the full works. Opinion though had been sharply divided on his acumen as an agent. While Dermot had rated himself somewhere in the region of professional and proficient his clients had tended to think he was just a little bit shit. Eventually the newsagent had got sick of having to ask for the rent.

One day he'd get it all back, once Svetlana was a star.

The email finally opened up.

'Thank you for your enquiry. Sadly we are not looking to sign any new artists at present...'

They might as well have just told him to fuck right off. He hit the reply button and started to type. 'Dear Beardy Hipster. Thank you for your polite reply. It's clear you know nothing about music and couldn't find your arse with both hands and map. I'd like to...'

Oh what was the point? He stopped and hit the delete key on the flame mail. It was just the standard rejection and he needed to move on. He looked at the next name on the list and opened a new email. 'Dear Zak...' After tapping out the usual pleasantries, he attached the audio track and a set of photos of Svetlana before hitting send. Then he moved on to the next name; there weren't many left on the list. Even an optimist like Dermot had to admit that things weren't looking good.

But at least Charlie Mulrooney hadn't come bothering him for the overdue cash. It was too much to hope the loan shark had succumbed to a heart attack or a vicious gangland slaying. Dermot knew the man would come calling eventually, most likely with some heavy-duty muscle in tow. So, with Marcus Diesel's production company continuing to dick him around over the *Meal of Fortune* contract, getting Svetlana a record deal still seemed the easiest way to get his hands on the money fast.

He'd tried to raise the possibility of an advance with Yegor. The little Russian had just shaken his head, helpfully opining that someone with Dermot's years of showbiz experience should really have grasped the concept of a commission by now.

Little smart-arse tosspot... It was just another example of how these Russians were starting to get on his tits. Dermot fired off another email then sat back in his chair. Bloody Koslov with his ridiculous hair, stupid Bond-villain accent and pumped-up self-importance. The man was a translator, an errand boy, for fuck's sake. The thought that Dermot had once found him scary was, well... Scary.

And Svetlana wasn't much better. Yes, she was beautiful and a bit of pouting was good if you wanted to be a pop diva.

But all the time?

Her smiles from that first day had failed to make any significant sort of reappearance in the weeks since. And, for a girl who was supposed to chasing her dreams, she spent a lot of time on Bukin's big white sofas, watching telly or playing on her phone. Oh and nurturing what looked from Dermot's point of view like a colossal sense of entitlement. Daddy was paying him to make her a star, so she'd just lounge about until it happened.

Great.

At least his weekly phone calls with Bukin had been going OK, despite Yegor's constant warnings about the man's impatience and hints at other things darker and more dangerous. The big Russian had simply listened to Dermot's reports without question before moving on to a few swift anecdotes about the latest *The Meal of Fortune* reruns he'd watched. He was probably just pleased to have his sulky daughter out from under this feet for a few weeks.

Dermot hunched forward over the keyboard again and fired off a few more emails. Then he left a couple of phone messages and sat back once more.

Sod it.

He looked down at the tatty piece of yellowed paper on the desk. It had sat there all day; the faded photo showed a man and a woman hand in hand as they left a nightclub.

More boy and a girl actually.

A 17-year-old Dermot and… Gail, Gail, Gail? What was her name again? Lead singer of some long-forgotten girl band. Gail Storm, that was it. Just the kind of ladette the tabloids had all gone mad over for about five minutes in the nineties. Probably married with two kids and living near Chichester now, grumbling about school fees and the plans to build a supermarket on the outskirts of the village.

He'd found the newspaper article in an old box when he'd been hunting out music-industry contracts. It had given him an idea that he'd been toying with all day. Desperation or borderline genius, he wasn't sure. But then it had worked well enough back then.

Had to be worth a go?

Dermot pulled his face into an expression somewhere between a smile and a grimace as he picked up his phone and selected his least favourite number from his favourites.

'Any fucking news on the contract?' The chef had let it ring for a long time before finally picking up with his typical charm.

'Nice to speak to you too, Marcus. What are you doing tonight?'

Chapter 13

Three weeks it had been now; three long, frustrating weeks. And what? Bugger all.

Anna checked her watch – nearly eight o'clock – and thought about a glass of wine.

It hadn't taken them long to work out what Bukin wanted with Dermot. The doting father shelling out for a top manager to help his daughter to chase her dreams of pop superstardom. Well, what father wouldn't? The other oligarchs all had their football teams; Bukin was just taking a different path.

Anna covered the short distance from sofa to fridge in three paces, then thought better of the wine and reached for a yoghurt instead. She'd found herself drinking a glass or two of white each night as the operation ran out of steam.

Missed quite a few judo classes and gym sessions too.

One thing they *hadn't* worked out was why a man who'd been clever enough to build up a highly illegal import/export business hadn't done a bit more basic research. If he had he'd have soon realised that Dermot wasn't anyone's idea of top talent management. Plenty of minor celebs had tried him out: actors, presenters, weathermen and newsreaders, retired sportsmen.

None of them had seemed to think he was much cop.

And Dermot's involvement with the music business had started and ended way back in the nineties with his mercifully brief brush with boyband fame.

Oh yes, The NewBoyz.

They were, well… five new boys. Handpicked to form the latest manufactured boy band. Despite a level of talent barely threatening the moderate Dermot had somehow managed to bag a spot. A bit of turd-polishing later and their first single went straight into the Top 10. The second made Number 1, with their third perfectly timed to grab the prized top slot at Christmas and hang on well into January. Their debut album went double platinum and their European tour sold out in about 15 seconds. With packed stadium after packed stadium nobody seemed to care that it was derivative shite. A mixture of reworked sixties classics and soppy ballads, all propped up by computer drum beats and overproduced backing tracks with lots of strings.

Cue even bigger second album and longer second world tour.

Then there were those glossy videos: the boys taking it in turns to have their hearts broken by doe-eyed beauties who had trouble keeping their kit on at the sight of an exotic location.

Dermot had actually sung lead on three of their five Number 1 singles, including 'Samba La Bamba Baby', the band's biggest hit.

The inevitable break up came shortly after the Greatest Hits album.

Funny that.

But there was no reasons for fans of the band to lament, not with things looking nicely set for the big race to Number 1 between Dermot and erstwhile bandmate Robbie Gray. Many in the press had tipped Dermot to hit the top spot and go on to be the bigger star.

But then many in the press knew shit all.

Dermot stormed to Number 2 with a cheeky Elton John cover. Fair enough.

But Robbie Gray went straight in at Number 1 and held off Kylie for three further weeks while Dermot slunk back down the charts.

Robbie Gray's next two singles hit Number 1 and his solo album went platinum both sides of the Atlantic. He'd been going platinum ever since. Dermot's next two singles bombed and he went to the pub, where he'd been going ever since.

And that was the last that the music industry had heard of Dermot Jack. But now here he was again, banging on the door with his pretty little Russian songbird in tow, not realising his invitation to the party had been ripped up years ago. It was almost enough to make you feel sorry for him.

Unless you knew that other piece of ancient history that had never made it anywhere near the papers.

Anna and Dermot had been together for nearly a year before he'd joined the band. And he'd promised he'd make it back for her birthday party.

Her sixteenth too. He'd bloody promised.

She'd waiting for him outside the hall where all her friends were celebrating as the long minutes slipped by. Then half an hour.

Then an hour.

Anna hadn't seen Dermot again for another 17 years. Not until three weeks ago.

The fact that she'd been over it years ago (and she really did mean years ago) didn't make him any less of a dick.

A yoghurt. Really?

She headed back to the fridge, previous decision on the wine overturned.

Back on the sofa again she sipped at her drink. All that ancient history was just that: ancient history – and of absolutely no use now. If Bukin's daughter wanted to be a pop star that was hardly MI5's business. And if Daddy was daft enough go with a loser like Dermot that wasn't their concern either. The operation was being officially wound down tomorrow. Other people were crying out for surveillance teams and that growing pile of reports on her desk wasn't going to read itself. Kate had made it clear they were exploring other avenues to get to Bukin. Ones that didn't involve Anna. A debriefing meeting with Lawson had already been arranged for tomorrow morning.

Then that would be that.

She reached for her wine, nearly knocking it over as her phone sprang to life next to the glass. Maybe the surveillance team finally had something?

She looked at the caller ID then let it ring out rather than send the call to voicemail. If her mother thought Anna was screening she'd just ring straight back. There'd be plenty of time to share the news of the breakup with Scott once she was back on the research desk. Her sister's marriage and subsequent regular production of grandchildren (three and counting) had lessened the maternal pressure on Anna in recent years. But her mother had expressed particularly high hopes for Scott, chiefly because she'd failed to see what an utter knob he was.

Not that Anna could really talk about character judgement; her mum hadn't been the one shagging him.

The phone sprang to life once more. Again Anna wondered about ignoring it before snatching it up. She was going to have to tell her mum sometime.

'Dermot and the Russians, they've all headed out together.' Not her mum, then. Stuart from surveillance, his voice muffled inside the cramped van. 'Thought you'd want to know.'

'I'll be right with you.'

'Reckoned you might. Kensington Church Street.' But there was warmth in his voice as he gave the address.

She'd first detected it the day he admitted she'd been right to send the surveillance team after Bukin. It hadn't stopped him giving her a ticking off about losing Dermot and a few refresher tips.

Since then though they'd spent a long time together in the back of the surveillance van and had become something approaching friends. Stuart had done 20 years in the service and remembered her father well. He'd shared a lot of old stories along with photos of his kids.

'I'll be half an hour.' Ten seconds later she had her coat on and was heading for the door, an image of Kate's thin face popping into her head for an unwelcome visit. Anna could just imagine her boss's smile as she dropped by the research team to see how she was settling back in.

It had to be worth a last look, didn't it?

Chapter 14

The car pulled up to the curb and Dermot opened the door and hopped out. Seconds later he pushed through the door to the restaurant, turning to hold it open for Svetlana and Yegor. He was still finding it hard to believe how easily the whole plan had come together.

Svetlana stepped inside, big fur coat held tightly around her. Many small animals from the cold Arctic tundra must have given their lives for that coat but Dermot was more interested in what lay beneath. Or more precisely what didn't.

'Tell her to make it revealing.' His instructions to Yegor had been clear.

Svetlana stopped and let the coat slip slowly from her shoulders as an obliging waiter stepped in behind her to catch it.

She hadn't let him down.

Where most girls would surely have considered a backless dress somewhat daring, Svetlana had gone for virtually frontless and sideless as well. And that was before you got to worrying yourself about the length. The few hints of insubstantial material were somehow held together by what looked like a couple of very thin shoelaces. If the dress had ever heard of Isaac Newton, it was having no truck with his views on gravity. But somehow Svetlana managed to carry it off without looking at all cheap.

'Thanks, mate.'

Dermot turned at the sound of the voice behind him, realising he'd forgotten to let go of the door. Everything that could go wrong with the plan was summed up in the form of the man who'd just walked in behind him.

Marcus Diesel.

The chef had a big grin right across his slobbery chops as he stepped inside. Dermot had run him through the plan that afternoon at a hastily arranged meeting in a Soho café. The emphasis had been on how it would help push things forward with Marcus's contract talks. But the chef had roundly failed to grasp it. In the end Dermot had boiled it down to four easy-to-remember points:

Henri's Restaurant, Kensington.

7.45 sharp.

Hot Russian totty.

Your contract.

GEDDIT?

Oh, and a fifth:

Keep your hands to yourself.

Marcus had looked a little hurt at the last one, or at least pretended to. But the chef had form in this area. Dermot wondered again if this was really such a good idea and whether he should have warned Svetlana what a sex pest the man was. Marcus's whole life had seemed like one long application for a place on the sex offenders' register.

And right now he was looking Svetlana up and down, his jaw bouncing off the spotless tiles of the restaurant floor.

This could go badly.

'Enchanted to meet you.'

Enchanted? Make that really badly.

Marcus bowed (yes, actually bowed) and took Svetlana's hand to kiss it. The grin was still plastered across his ruddy features.

Jesus, all Dermot needed was for Marcus to earn a slap round the face for a lewd suggestion and everything would be ruined. The language barrier might help but it would be no protection against the chef's famously wondering hands.

Bit bloody late to worry about that now though; a waiter was already leading the pair off across the restaurant. Svetlana went first, her eyes on the floor ahead, with Marcus bringing up the rear, his eyes firmly on her rear.

The restaurant was a cacophonous barn of a place, sounds

echoing and amplified off the expanses of wood, metal and fashionably exposed air-conditioning pipes. But it was popular enough, presumably with people who didn't want to actually hear any conversation across the dinner table. The hubbub of chit chat, laughter and cutlery on plates died away as the couple made their way to a strategically chosen table in the very centre of the room.

Men and women alike were trying their best not to gawp too openly at the girl in the dress.

Trying and largely failing.

And of course everyone knew the name of the man accompanying her. Marcus wasn't just famous for his TV show. He was famous for being famous. And while his chef's whites offered him a degree of sartorial safety on screen, off it he was a fashion-free zone. He'd been voted Britain's worst-dressed celebrity almost as often as he'd won the crown of the nation's most annoying. While other celebs attracted eye-watering offers from fashion houses to wear their clothes, Dermot regularly received letters from labels saying they'd prefer it if his client didn't.

Tonight's get-up was a variation on an old Diesel classic – what Dermot liked to refer to as the colour-blind golfer who'd got himself dressed in the dark while wearing a blindfold. The maroon tank top had a nasty zigzag pattern and was matched (but only in the loosest sense) with a green shirt and a tight-ish pair of orange trousers that did few favours for a man pushing 45. But the couple's outfits were certainly getting them noticed. As planned. The phones were already out and soon the images would be trending their way up the social-media charts. The photographer Dermot had tipped off to pap the couple on their way out would do the rest and the pictures would be all over the next morning's tabloids. Come lunchtime the race to find the identity of Marcus's latest squeeze would be well and truly on. And there was no way you could keep weapon-grade gossip like that from the boys and girls of Her Majesty's press. Some ingenious newshound was bound to sniff the story out, or failing that they could just open the email Dermot would be circulating to all the news desks. And wouldn't the media just lap up the Russian beauty and the tale of her childhood dreams of pop stardom turning to dust at the fickle hands of the music biz?

Dermot figured he might find some of his calls or emails got returned at that point. And the publicity wouldn't do Marcus's contract negotiations any harm either.

Two birds, one very large and well-aimed stone.

And all because he'd found that old picture of Gail Storm.

Way back then the first NewBoyz single had been a week from release and the record-company PRs were on the hunt for a way to get the band into the news. Gail, lead singer in a band signed to the same label, had already been seen about town with a couple of actors and a promising young footballer. The pictures had made the papers each time. And it had been Dermot they'd picked. Not Robbie BASTARD Gray. He and Gail had left that club hand in hand and climbed into a taxi. He'd climbed out again just round the corner and caught the bus home, the record label's PR budget not stretching to his cab fare.

Dermot looked across the restaurant to where Marcus and Svetlana had reached their table. The chef pulled back her chair and waited for her to sit down.

So far so gentlemanly. And so un-Marcus. Could it be that he was finally coming down with a dose of manners?

All he had to do was to keep those hands to himself until the snaps were in the bag. The last thing he needed was Svetlana giving him a slap round the face or chucking a glass of red wine over his tank top (not that anyone would have noticed).

Dermot and Yegor followed another waiter to their own table, tucked away in the corner but with a good view of Marcus and Svetlana. The chef was leaning in close now and talking loudly and pointing in true Brit-abroad fashion. Opposite him Svetlana was doing her best to look like she was enjoying herself. Dermot caught her eye and threw in a smile and a reassuring wink. She smiled back and straight away it was like someone had turned the lights up. Not quite the smile she'd dazzled him with that first day but just about the first real one he'd witnessed since.

'Your plan. You think it will work?' Opposite him Yegor smiled too and raised an eyebrow.

Christ, he must be making progress. A smile from each of the Russians within 30 seconds and both seemingly genuine too.

'Let's hope so.' But Dermot was sure that they were nearly home and hosed now.

'The wine list, sir.' A waiter hovered at Dermot's shoulder.

What an excellent idea. It was a bit too early for champagne but he'd certainly be having a glass of something. Yegor may have said no to the advance but he was generous enough with Bukin's money when it came to day-to-day expenses. Dermot ordered a glass of Sauvignon Blanc for himself and a predictable water for the little spoilsport opposite.

The waiter soon returned with the drinks and Dermot took a long sip as he relaxed back into his chair. The music inside started again and soon his foot was tapping once more as another dance routine rolled on in his head.

Chapter 15

'Give the man time, Yegor. This is my daughter, remember; her dream.'

If you asked Yegor, Bukin had chosen a bad time to show such an uncharacteristic bout of patience. Not to mention stupidity.

And all the while things would be moving on back in Russia. Others vying to step into Yegor's shoes; doing and saying things they wouldn't have dared had he been there to slap them down.

But after three weeks, with the fool of an Englishman showing little sign of any progress, Yegor had been hopeful that Bukin's anger would finally force its way to the surface and he'd call Svetlana home.

But not a bit of it.

And now this.

He had to admit that Dermot's plan sounded plausible enough. What had he said to himself about the man's low cunning?

They'd been at the table for close to an hour now and Dermot was still humming away tunelessly and tapping out what could only be a beat as he sipped his second glass of wine. Yegor was the first to accept he knew little about music, but how the man had ever been a pop star was beyond him. He offered up a weary smile and turned his attention back to Svetlana and the idiot chef. If she was at all fazed by tonight's hurriedly arranged little charade it didn't show. But then she was a cold one.

Back when he was starting out with her father Yegor had tried to befriend the girl, figuring she could prove a useful ally.

The looks of distaste that had greeted his every word had quickly shown the futility of that idea and he'd had little to do with her in the intervening years.

Even now, thrown together in London, they'd barely spoken aside from his translations of Dermot's increasingly weak excuses for his lack of success. Svetlana caught him looking, that same old distaste appearing in her eyes. Yegor held her gaze until she looked away as a waiter arrived with their desserts. The chef took another long pull on his wine and stuck his spoon into the dark chocolate mass on his plate, offering it to Svetlana. She allowed him to feed her, even smiling as his other hand crept across the table to rest on hers, playing the part Dermot had given her to perfection. Was there nothing the girl wouldn't stoop to in the pursuit of her cheap dreams of fame? Who was she to look at Yegor with such disgust?

Thank God the evening was nearly over. Across the table Dermot had finished off the last of his own dessert and had finally stopped his infernal humming and tapping. He sat forward now and raised an eager hand for the bill.

'So far so good.' He gave Yegor another of his halfwit grins, eyes shining with the effects of the wine and excitement at the seeming success of his plan.

It was a success that could detain them all in London for a whole lot longer. But Yegor had already decided that this would not be happening.

Dermot kept up the smile as he paid the bill then drained the last of the wine from his glass.

Without an agent (or more accurately with a dead one) there'd be no reason for Svetlana to remain in London.

The man simply had no idea what he'd got himself into. Or what was coming.

No idea at all.

Chapter 16

Dermot swayed, putting a hand on the door to steady himself as he followed Svetlana and Marcus outside. No it wasn't the wine; he'd limited it to just two glasses. But when tomorrow's tabloids headlines swam in front of your eyes they tended to have an unsteadying effect, especially with all that camera-flashing going on.

They'd be getting half a page minimum.

Towards the front, too – big pictures, big headlines, the works.

The camera flashed some more as Marcus turned Svetlana this way and that, like a ballroom dancer, offering up a whole host of new angles for the greedy snapper. You had to give the chef his due: put him in front of the lens and he knew how to perform.

Then he turned Svetlana back towards him and pulled her in for a kiss.

Noooooo…

Dermot watched in horror as the chef's meaty hand, already hovering in the uncertain no-man's land of her lower back, started to creep lower. Any second she was going to slap the stupid fucker round the face and it would all be ruined.

Pleeease…

He held his breath as Marcus's fat, red face homed in on Svetlana's impossibly white skin.

The hand moved lower.

Svetlana stiffened as their lips met. The chef's hand definitely wasn't on her back anymore. Then the kiss was over and Marcus was helping himself to a last little grope before breaking away. The photographer lowered his camera and Dermot breathed again.

The kiss would mean a full page for sure. But Marcus had come pretty fucking close to ruining the whole thing with his wandering hands. Svetlana had Dermot's permission to hit him now. As hard as she liked, too.

But the punch, when it came, wasn't the Russian girl's doing. That particular honour fell to the first of the two masked men who'd just shouldered their way past the photographer.

The man's fist connected with Marcus's nose, redistributing it across several other parts of his face where it wasn't meant to be.

Then the second man got in on the act too.

Svetlana staggered but kept her balance as the photographer raised his camera and started flashing again. Marcus flailed his hands around wildly in what looked more like a deranged dance than an attempt at self-defence. Dermot staggered as someone pushed him out of the way. Then little Yegor was out there in the thick of it. What exactly did the shortarse think he was going to do against the two big fellas?

Nothing, as it turned out.

Yegor ignored the chef and his attackers, grabbing Svetlana instead and pulling her back across the pavement and into the restaurant.

A voice in Dermot's head was screaming at him to help but if his feet were getting the message they were ignoring it. He watched as the latest punch put Marcus on the pavement. A couple of kicks to the ribs for good measure and then the men were off, one pausing just long enough to snap a picture on his phone.

Inside the restaurant waiters would be fussing around Svetlana while the diners who'd flocked to the windows for a better look would be starting to head back to their seats. Yegor would no doubt be dividing his time between speaking into his mobile and throwing the occasional dark look Dermot's way.

But Dermot didn't see any of this as his eyes never left the figure on the floor. He took a long breath and walked slowly across the pavement. 'Are you OK?'

'What the fuck do you think?' Marcus sounded as if his mouth was full of wet tissues. He tried to stand but slumped slowly back to the pavement.

Dermot's phone didn't feel quite so much like a lightsabre as he pulled it out to call for an ambulance. But it did give him a chirpy little beep to tell him he had a message.

A picture of Marcus filled the screen. On the ground, exactly where he was now bleeding all over his orange trousers; the photo taken just seconds before by one of the attackers.

Just two words beneath the picture:

Happy now?

How nice of Charlie Mulrooney to get in touch. And after all this time too.

Chapter 17

Marcus Diesel must seriously have pissed someone off to deserve a kicking like that. But it had all been a huge waste of time. Anna pushed the front door shut then dropped her coat on the table and headed straight for the fridge and the wine.

A sore *Meal of Fortune* loser maybe? Cheated husband? Or someone who just thought the chef was an arsehole? Not that it mattered. Whoever had attacked Marcus Diesel, it had nothing to do with the Russians and was therefore no business of MI5's.

She poured a large glass of wine and headed for the sofa, scanning about for the TV remote. Come the morning Oleg Bukin, Yegor Koslov and Dermot Jack wouldn't be her concern anymore. If Lawson or Kate Barnes had wanted her to be a part of it they'd have found a way to keep her involved already.

But looking on the bright side: as of tomorrow, Dermot would no longer be a person of interest. She could walk up and give him a friendly kick in the balls any time she liked. Or alternatively she could just forget about him like she had done for the past 17 years and get on with her life.

Not back in the research section though. Anna had already decided that was something that wouldn't be happening. She took a long swig of her wine. It would be her last glass of the night. Last glass for a while. Tomorrow was a new start.

She'd hit the gym before work, take it out on the treadmill and punch bag, imagining Kate's face on it for the very last time. Then to work where she'd walk straight in to Lawson's office and resign. Going over Kate's head would rob her boss of a good deal of satisfaction.

Sometimes it was the little things that got you through.

As the spooks didn't tend to bother themselves too much with notice periods – reasons of national security and all that – it wouldn't be long before she would be out. Debriefing, stern reminders of some of the key points of the Official Secrets Act and maybe a warm glass of wine and some crisps. It wouldn't be days but it wouldn't be months either.

Anna took another sip of her wine and searched round again for the remote control. Of course, returning to the law would be the simplest option. Her old firm had always said they'd take her back. And she'd be able to afford a bigger flat; one that wasn't on a main road. Her eyes wandered slowly round the sitting room. What had once seemed cosy, charming and snug now just looked cluttered and frankly small.

But it wouldn't be law; that ship had long since sailed. She reached for her wine again. She'd known she was done with the legal profession when she'd walked away from it the last time. And you know what? The flat was just fine. So what about a charity maybe, or even teaching? Something she'd enjoy and that wouldn't bugger up the rest of her life.

Then she'd have the time to find herself someone she really liked and enjoy herself a little in the trying. With the gym sessions and all that judo under her belt, Anna didn't mind admitting she was pretty hot right now. Dermot might have looked as good as he had all those years ago but she knew that she looked far better, especially with the last remnants of what her mother had always helpfully described as 'puppy fat' long gone.

She'd go for someone who didn't work in the City or claim to know a lot about wine. A graphic designer, perhaps? Maybe a life coach or someone who had a job actually making stuff. Someone who knew how to put a shelf up and could repair his own bike. They'd head out into the country for long walks at weekends and maybe even do cookery or photography courses together.

Anna finally spied the TV remote down between the cushions and fished it out.

The screen pinged to life to reveal a former boxer competing in a celebrity sheep-herding challenge. Hadn't the same man been on a cooking show last week? Anna surfed on through the channels, wondering if she'd find a programme where chefs learned how to box. Might have come in handy for Marcus Diesel earlier on.

She carried on flicking through reality show after reality show.

Baking, diving, dancing, skating, hedge-cutting, dry-stone-walling and even marriage guidance. All sorts of people, so-called celebrities or otherwise, just trying to get their faces on the telly. Little wonder that girls like Svetlana wanted to be pop stars.

Anna certainly had.

She did that little internal cringe thing at the memory and sought sanctuary by finishing her wine in one long glug.

Maybe one more glass?

A pop star – pop *stars*, rather; it had been love's young dream in all its misguided glory. Anna and Dermot, plotting their future singing careers as they played the leads in the school musical.

She flinched again. At least he'd made it though, if only for a little while. Anna pulled herself up and headed fridgewards. Another glass definitely wouldn't hurt.

Of course her father had disapproved. 'Dabbling' in all this acting and singing nonsense was only getting in the way of her proper studies. He wasn't exactly keen on the Dermot side of things either.

But that had changed on the opening night of the musical. The KGB must all have been at a leaving do or something that day as her father managed to make it for once. After the show he pretended not to be wiping a tear from his eye as he gave her one of his big hugs.

'I can't believe you actually came.'

'You were brilliant. I wouldn't have missed it for the world.'

Words like 'dabbling' never surfaced again, although his views on Dermot had remained broadly the same.

It had been a silly old school musical, that was all. But her dad being there had meant everything to Anna. Dermot was welcome to his pop career. Fat lot of good it had done him anyway. Her dad had been proud that night and that had been enough for her.

She surfed on, finally finding the news and then a documentary about human-rights abuse in Guatemala before moving on guiltily to the quarter finals of *Cosy Kitties*, where celebs learned how to knit jumpers for their cats.

Maybe it was the same for Svetlana? Did she just want to make her dad proud? Heartless, murdering arms dealer he may be, but he was her father. And, if she ever did get to perform, Anna doubted that

Bukin would be able to stay away either. Not that it was likely with Dermot in charge of things.

On the TV a former topless model became the latest celebrity kicked off *Cosy Kitties* as her Siamese point-blank refused to wear the little Aran sweater she'd lovingly knitted. The girl wept as they cut to the ads.

Oh for God's sake…

Then a trailer for an upcoming show took Anna right back to her teens; she'd watched the programme religiously every year. Next to her the wine glass was empty again.

Perhaps just another little one.

No. Up early, gym, then into the office and… On the screen the camera homed in on the outside of a distinctive building, the show's familiar title and a date superimposed on the picture. It was barely three weeks away. Anna jolted forward as an image of her father floated back across her mind; a head taller than anyone else at the back of the school hall, clapping wildly as she made her final bow on the stage.

'I wouldn't have missed it for the world.'

And hadn't there been something in Bukin's file about a TV station and…?

Three hours later she was still awake, possibilities dancing wildly in her head. Oh, she'd be seeing Lawson tomorrow morning all right. But not to resign.

A teacher… Charity work? Life coach?

Seriously?

Cookery classes? A man who fixed his own bike?

No way. Not now she'd figured out exactly how Dermot was going to help them get to Oleg Bukin.

Chapter 18

'Who the fuck is it?'

'It's me.' Dermot pushed the door open, not bothering to wait for a reply.

'Some fucking cheek you've got turning up here.' Marcus seemed to have forgotten that he was the one who'd asked for the meeting.

And it was an appointment Dermot could well have done without, the situation with the Russians remaining dangerously un-soothed since last night. Far worse things had happened to the chef before and would no doubt happen again before too long.

'You've seen all this, I suppose?' The chef sat on a stool by his dressing table, one eye covered by a huge steak while the other looked down at a pile of morning papers.

Dermot had. But it was the last thing he needed to be worrying about right now.

Chef Boils Over – hardly the most imaginative of headlines but then it didn't need to be. Not above the picture of Marcus grappling with his attacker. The shot had caught him at probably the one point he looked like he was making a decent fist of fighting back. The story had made pages three, four and five too, although the pictures there didn't paint the chef in quite such a heroic light.

The other tabloids had pretty much followed suit.

'Have you fucking seen what the fuckers have written?'

Yes, he fucking had. And Marcus's little fight had been the talk of the breakfast radio shows that morning. Twitter had been thick with its own trademark brand of pious condemnation, too.

The chef read on anyway. '"Daytime TV's Marcus Diesel could find himself in trouble after publicly brawling outside a popular Kens-ington restaurant while dressed in a pair of bizarre orange trousers."'

Marcus pressed the steak to his eye and shook his head, jabbing at Dermot with his free hand. 'They were ochre, OK. Fucking ochre.'

Dermot took a deep breath; he'd just have to take the chef's word for that. One day soon he'd find himself in the happy position of telling Marcus to piss off for good. Most likely he'd follow up by leaking a couple of unsavoury but essentially truthful tales to the more vindictive journalists he knew.

But today was not that day.

And it wouldn't be anytime soon if he didn't get away from here and give Yegor one good reason why he shouldn't take Svetlana straight back to Moscow.

'It gets worse.'

Sadly a quick escape wasn't looking likely.

'"Police confirmed that they will be looking to question Diesel, 44, following the incident, which happened as he was leaving the restaurant with a lady friend."'

That was the only mention Svetlana had warranted. No photos, no dress, no speculation about the identity of Marcus Diesel's hot new squeeze. Britain's most annoying celebrity getting a punch in the nose was a far better story.

'I know what it says.' Dermot checked his watch, trying not to be too obvious. Yes, he felt guilty that he'd earned Marcus a kicking. But not that guilty.

'And this? "It's not the first time that Marcus, famous for his madcap antics on Channel 5's *The Meal of Fortune*, has been in trouble. In 2013, two women accused him of calling them 'Fxxxing slags' in a West London pub."'

'You did call them "fucking slags".'

'They *were* fucking slags.' Marcus gave Dermot a one-eyed stare; it was his catch-all description of women who didn't succumb to his advances.

'It'll all be over by tomorrow.' As would his deal with Bukin if he didn't get out of here soon.

'That other stuff was years ago and they haven't forgotten about it.' Marcus shook his head and pressed the steak more firmly onto his swollen face.

'How's the eye anyway?' Dermot changed tack, hoping a show of concern might calm things down. 'Aren't you supposed to do that straight away?' He pointed at the steak. There'd been no meat the night before, just a lot of shouting and swearing as Marcus had got himself ejected from A&E. It had taken 10 minutes for them to work out he was basically OK but only half that to complete a diagnosis of total arse.

'I've been doing it half the night and all morning. I'm supposed to be filming in an hour. They're talking about getting Terry fucking Lloyd in to replace me for today. Well they can't. It's my show.'

Terry Lloyd? Dermot didn't like the sound of that; the Russians would have to keep for another five minutes. Talentless though he was, Lloyd was the up and coming man of TV chef-ery and Marcus's new contract remained dangerously unsigned.

'They can sort you out with make-up. I'll have a word with the producer.'

'No, you won't. You've done enough already.' Marcus removed the steak and waved it at Dermot.

The whole area around his right eye was a mess of yellow-and-black bruising, the eye itself almost closed over. He wouldn't be going in front of the camera today or any day soon.

'I should never have agreed to go along with your little stunt. You said this would help my career.'

'I'll sort it out. It might even be good for you in the long run.'

Marcus snorted. 'Didn't see you worrying too much about my career last night.'

'Come on, I've always—'

'More concerned about that Russian tart. Frigid little bitch anyway.' The chef pressed the steak back to his eye.

'It was meant to be good for both your careers. How was I supposed to know some random nutter was going to jump you?'

'Random? It was her they were after.'

'Bollocks.' But he could hardly admit that it was his own financial troubles that had earned Marcus a beating from Mulrooney's heavies.

'Bit of a coincidence, them turning up when I was with her.'

'They didn't punch her in the face.'

'Only 'cause I didn't let them. That's what the papers should have written: how I bravely defended an innocent woman from attack.'

'And she's very grateful. Asked me to pass on her best wishes.' It was probably best to let Marcus feel like the hero.

'What do I get to show for it?' The chef removed the steak again and surveyed his damaged face in the mirror. 'They'll never let me go on like this.' He put the steak back and turned his one good eye back on Dermot.

'It's not the end of the world if you miss a couple of shows.'

'How can you say that?'

'Because we can make this work for you. I'll get a story out about how you're the victim here – a vicious attack by some deranged fans. We could even say you're worried you've got a stalker. You've never had one of those before.'

'A stalker?' Marcus's steak-free eye lit up at the prospect of the latest must-have celeb accessory.

'It'll get the whole story about the risks celebs face going again. You can do a few of the chat shows and win the sympathy vote. A lot of people are disgusted at the abuse hardworking TV stars get.'

Dermot wasn't convinced about that last bit but Marcus was nodding along now. Well either that or trying to work the steak around his battered eye socket.

'Take the whole week off? They'll be begging you to come back when the ratings take a bath.' Dermot took another sly look at his watch. When he looked back at the chef he was shaking his head.

'It's a bit too late for all that now.'

'What? They can't have... You said they were only thinking about...' The bastards.

'No they haven't.' Marcus shook his head again. 'They've been very supportive actually; especially once I'd told them what a dickhead my agent was. You're the one who's sacked, Dermot. Now get the fuck out of my sight.'

'You can't sack me, I've always been your—'

'Not any more. Now piss the fuck off.' Marcus took the steak from his eye and hurled it at his former agent's head.

'No. *You* piss off.' Dermot caught the steak one-handed and threw it straight back.

Chapter 19

Lawson's office, 11.30am. Same table, same places, same drill as all the other times.

'So you don't believe the attack on the chef was connected to Bukin?' If Kate Barnes was at all gleeful at Anna's impending move back to the research desk it wasn't showing.

'No.' Anna shook her head. 'Maybe a stalker or someone with a grudge against Diesel. Nothing to do with the Russians.' It hadn't taken long to finish the debrief on the bizarre events of the previous night. She closed the file in front of her and sat back.

Say it now.

There was a pause as Lawson leaned forward to reach for one of the mini Danish pastries he'd laid on specially for the meeting, even though it was nearly lunchtime.

Come on.

The words were on her lips, all rehearsed and ready to go. But suddenly the whole plan seemed, well... just a bit silly.

It must have been 3am by the time she'd drifted off to sleep, the idea spinning round and round in her head until it was polished and perfect. But never had the cold light of day shone so cold or harshly as it had that morning. Even under the darkly brooding April sky the plan had been exposed as tawdry-looking, imperfect and a bit daft.

More importantly the chance of it working seemed close to zero.

She'd skipped the gym (the second and third glasses of wine had already put paid to that anyway), fretting away the hours before the meeting at her desk in the company of three super-strength lattes and an industrial-sized choc-chip muffin. She looked across at Lawson and Kate now, trying to imagine the words actually coming out of her mouth.

Then trying to imagine her bosses not laughing.

Lawson finished his pastry and looked at her – almost apologetically, it seemed. 'We've given it three weeks and come up with nothing. Resources are tight and there are plenty of other priorities.'

He sounded like a vet telling her that nothing more could be done for a beloved family pet.

'Yes, probably time to call it day.' Kate was somehow managing to sound objective about the whole business. 'When Bukin hears about the attack he'll probably insist Svetlana goes home anyway.'

Lawson sat back and closed his eyes as he rubbed his forehead. 'But maybe... We're getting increasingly strong intelligence that Bukin has got a nuclear weapon and he's close to selling it. This is the only real lead we've had on him in a long time. And it could help us get to others further up the chain.'

It was the first time that any 'others' had been mentioned but Anna had assumed that someone like Bukin wouldn't be at the very top of the food chain. Which was exactly why they needed to...

'What do you think, Anna?' Lawson looked at her encouragingly.

He was actually asking for her opinion?

So say it!

But her idea didn't just seem silly now. It seemed ridiculous.

'There's certainly no point in continuing the current operation.' Anna took a breath, playing for time. 'Dermot's just trying to help the girl to be a pop star.'

This was it: the perfect moment to set out her plan; but somehow she still couldn't quite bring herself to say the words.

Lawson nodded and let out a long sigh. Kate shuffled her own papers and made to stand.

Last chance.

Did it matter if she looked stupid? She had her resignation speech all lined up anyway. (And that would show them.)

So bloody well say it.

'Wait. I think...' Then she stopped, running through the whole stupid, crazy idea in her head again as colour flooded her cheeks.

And she wanted them to take her seriously? Give her more responsibility?

'I think I've got a way we can get to Bukin.'

She imagined their laughter again.

'Go on, then.' Lawson gave her another smile and a shake of his jowls. Probably just humouring her now.

The little scowl that crept across Kate's was the first sign of her boss's displeasure. There'd be plenty more of that to come.

But actually, you know what? Anna held Kate's gaze. She wasn't just some silly little girl from the research team.

'We keep up the surveillance on Svetlana and the house.'

Kate shook her head. 'What, just on the off-chance that Bukin comes back for Father's Day?'

She thought about her father again, standing at the back clapping and smiling.

I wouldn't have missed it for the world.

'No, we lure him here. I've done a little digging and...' She had all the info; all the background, all the justification ready to lay out. Build the case slowly, draw them in and then sell the idea. But sod it. If it was going to sound stupid it was going to sound stupid.

So she just got on and told them straight.

Lawson and Kate looked at each other.

Nobody said anything for quite a long time.

Chapter 20

The video in Dermot's head was stuck on a playback loop as the taxi made the short but slow journey from the TV studio to the restaurant. The steak spinning slowly end over end on its flight through the air before catching Marcus square in his good eye. He would have bet that nine times out of 10 – no, make that 99 times out of 100 – the lump of meat would have sailed harmlessly over the chef's head before hitting the wall. Instead, Marcus had slumped back in the chair holding both eyes as the steak slid down his face cartoon style and landed at his feet with a wet slap.

There'd been no other option for Dermot but to flee. He'd deal with the chef later, once the Russians had calmed down. A grovelling apology and a promise to try to resurrect the idea of Marcus's own chat show should do the trick. He'd nearly managed to land the show a couple of years back; a cookery-based format in the highly prized slot just before *Channel 4 News*. The chef's well-publicised affair with a former model and married mother of two had put paid to his chances and they'd gone with that oily twat from *Bake It!* instead. But, with the show's viewing figures sinking faster than an ill-prepared Victoria sponge, word was the production company was on the hunt for a new host.

He had to sort things with Svetlana first though. She wouldn't be making it as a pop star if Yegor took her back to Russia. Dermot pulled his phone out and thought about sending Marcus a text as the cab crawled up the King's Road. But no, better to let him cool down all on his own. He sent Yegor a quick message instead, promising he wouldn't be more than five minutes. He'd have been there already if they'd been meeting at Bukin's house as usual, but for some reason Svetlana had insisted on a restaurant.

The cab finally pulled up and Dermot climbed out, just as the rain started to fall.

He hurried across the pavement and pushed through the restaurant door, then headed for the corner table where he'd spotted the two Russians.

'You are late.' Yegor stood with a cold glare.

Dermot put on his best smile, even though he was so over the little fella's moodiness and tough guy act by now.

Svetlana stayed sitting. She was dressed all in black with no make-up and looked like she'd been crying. She at least threw him a quick smile.

'Look, er, last night. It was just bad luck.' The words spilled out before Dermot had even sat down.

'I am taking her home.' Yegor's expression didn't change. 'She is in danger—'

'Nyet, nyet.' The tears started to roll down Svetlana's pale face, Yegor's words clearly needed no translation.

'She's right, you can't.' Dermot wasn't having it either.

Yegor ignored him, turning instead to Svetlana and speaking in slow, soft Russian. When he turned back to Dermot, the hard edge was back. 'My mind is made up.'

'Nyet! Nyet! Nyet!' Svetlana slammed her fist on the table as she stood.

'Yegor let's think about this.'

He was just the hired help. Surely it was up to Svetlana? All she had to do was put her foot down and tell him to get back in his box.

She did exactly that, stamping it on the floor as she directed a stream of Russian at her translator.

The waitress who'd been approaching veered away tactically, pretending to be headed for another table.

Yegor shook his head slowly as he replied, his voice still calm. Then he turned to Dermot. 'She is coming home.'

'Isn't that up to her?'

'No. When it is a matter of security, it is up to me.'

They'd see about that. Dermot turned to Svetlana but she was already getting up. She launched another brief volley of Russian at Yegor and stormed off towards the toilets, the tears flowing freely as she went.

Dermot stood and started after her.

'Let her go.' Yegor shook his head. 'We need to talk.'

No, they didn't. Dermot just needed the spoiled little rich girl to quit blubbing in the ladies' and put the jumped-up little translator in his place. What was the point of being a billionaire's daughter if you didn't know how to get your own way?

'I don't want to argue with you, Mr Jack.' Yegor's face softened a little. 'It is not safe for her here. Surely you understand that?'

'They attacked Marcus, not her.' Like the chef, Yegor didn't need to know about Dermot's little difficulties with Charlie Mulrooney.

'They attacked the chef but it was a warning to you, from your fat friend Mulrooney.'

Ah.

This time there was a hint of amusement in Yegor's cold smile. 'You thought we didn't know about him? We did look into your background very carefully.'

'I'll sort Mulrooney out.'

'I'm sure you will. But that's your business. I am taking her home. That is final.'

It was kind of hard to argue with that. Dermot pictured himself getting up and walking out with a sad smile but little in the way of regret. It wasn't as if he'd been getting anywhere with Svetlana's pop career and last night's fiasco would do nothing to help. He could shake Yegor by the hand, maybe even wish him well; send his regards to Oleg Bukin with a signed copy of *The Meal of Fortune Bloopers (Series 3)* DVD.

But then he had just been sacked by his last remaining client and thrown a big steak in the man's face for good measure.

How was he supposed to get even with Wanker Wayne and that bloody horse now?

Then there was all the money he owed Charlie Mulrooney. The loan shark wasn't the kind of man to give such a warning then let things lie.

So no, he wasn't giving up on Svetlana that easily.

'You're just the translator. It's not up to you.' Yegor was about to learn that Dermot was not a man to be dicked about. 'I haven't got her a contract yet but I will and until I do she's staying.'

That had told him. Now all he needed was Svetlana to come back from the toilets (like, sometime today) and back him up with the 'spoiled little rich girl' routine.

But she didn't and the little man opposite him just laughed. 'You really don't know what you are mixed up with, do you, Mr Jack?'

Oh here we go, the poorly veiled threat. It was about the commonest trick in the book.

'Do you have any idea who Oleg Bukin is?'

'No, but I know he doesn't frighten me.' That nasty scar aside, it was kind of hard to be too scared of a big buffoon with a soft spot for cookery-themed light entertainment.

'And I think you'll find I am a little more than a translator.'

I think you'll find I'm a little more than a translator. It was all Dermot could do not to make a mouth out of his hand and repeat the Russian's words in a silly little sing-song voice.

'I am here to protect her.'

Yeah right. But arguing wasn't going to get him anywhere. He had to get Yegor back onside if he was going to convince him to let Svetlana stay. 'Look, her father asked me to make her a star. And that's what I'm going to do. I just need a little more time. She'll be perfectly safe with someone like you here to protect her.'

Touché, Dermot felt.

'You've had more than enough time.' Yegor pulled out his phone. 'But I am a fair man so I will offer you a bargain. We will call Mr Bukin now. You will say that you have done your best but Svetlana is not going to make it as a pop star.'

'And why would I want to do that?'

'Because if you don't, I will tell Mr Bukin that you put his daughter in danger.' Yegor stopped to let the words sink in and leaned in close. 'Then he will tell me to cut your throat.'

Oh please. 'Will he give you a stool so you can reach?'

'You would do well not to mock me.' The little Russian's tone was pure ice now.

Dermot still wasn't buying it. 'You might just be able to manage even on your tiptoes.'

But Yegor wasn't listening anymore, his eyes darting frantically around the restaurant. 'Svetlana, she has been gone a long time no?'

Dermot shrugged; she'd been five minutes at the most. Not so long for a good cry in the toilets after your dreams had been all but shattered.

Yegor sprang to his feet and headed in direction Svetlana had taken.

'Give me a shout if you can't reach the handle.' Dermot whipped his phone out, thinking about calling Marcus to apologise and talk about the chat-show idea.

But Yegor was back before he'd had the chance. 'She's not there.'

'What? You went in?'

'Yes, I went in.'

Jesus, the little pervert. He could get himself arrested for less. 'She's probably just gone for a walk.'

'In this?' Yegor pointed towards the window and the rain that was sheeting down outside. 'We are both dead men if anything happens to her. Dead men, you understand?' The little Russian turned and hurried for the door.

Oh come on.

But there'd been a shrillness in Yegor's voice that Dermot hadn't heard before and something in his eyes that looked disturbingly like fear.

'Hang on.' He jumped up and followed the Russian out into the rain as the cold certainty hit home.

Charlie Mulrooney really wasn't the kind of man to let things lie. Marcus Diesel and his bloody chat show no longer felt quite so important.

Chapter 21

The dark thunderclouds had rolled right in and the rain was coming down heavily by the time the taxi took a right at Albert Bridge and headed up towards the King's Road.

Not ten minutes earlier Anna's words had hung heavily in the air of Lawson's office as the silence stretched on. Lawson had shared another look with Kate before turning slowly back to Anna, an unreadable sort of look on his face. He was going to tell her about her father again. How he'd been a man for seeing things through, not coming up with half-baked ideas that quite frankly could make them all look fucking ridiculous.

'Bring him in.' He'd finally broken the silence as a smile inched across his face.

Bring who…? A second or so more had passed before Anna even started to understand.

'Sir, you don't really think—' Kate shifted uncomfortably as she turned to her boss.

'I'm not seeing any other ideas here. The man's got a nuclear weapon.'

Anna had just carried on staring, not bothered that her mouth was hanging open.

'Well, what are you waiting for? Get Dermot in here now before I change my mind.' The smile faded as he delivered the sting in the tail. 'Then we'll see if this plan of yours has any chance of working.'

The taxi ploughed on, sending big sheets of spray onto the pavement as it hit a puddle. The surveillance team had followed Dermot from home to *The Meal of Fortune* studios and were now waiting outside a restaurant on the King's Road, just before the corner of Old Church St. It seemed he was having lunch with the two Russians, a tense affair she assumed after last night's little goings on.

Despite the heavy rain the traffic was moving easily enough and with any luck she'd get there before Dermot came out. Then it would just be a case of following at a distance and picking him up once he'd parted company with the Russians.

The taxi driver slowed and took a left, honking angrily at some soggy shoppers who'd been daft enough to believe he might take pity and let them cross.

'Green One status, please.' Anna spoke quietly into her lapel mic.

'Subjects are still in the restaurant.'

'Roger that. ETA three minutes.' She cut the communication and peered out through the rain at the spot where she'd lost Dermot back on the first day of the operation. It had been the closest she'd been to him in 17 years. But now...

Shit.

Now she was actually going to come face-to-face with him. The prospect hit her properly for the first time.

What would she say?

What if he didn't recognise her?

God, what would she say then?

Oh, get a grip. She gave herself an internal hard stare. Dermot was going to help catch a man they suspected of having a nuclear weapon. Nothing else mattered here.

'This is Green One. One of the subjects is on the move. Repeat, subject on the move. It's the girl. She's alone. No, wait, she's with a man.'

'Koslov or Jack?' Most likely the Russian. A short lunch, it seemed. Things couldn't have gone well.

'Negative. Not either of them. They're getting into a car.'

Koslov hadn't let the girl out of his sight in all the time the pair had been in London. Something was wrong.

'Other two subjects coming out now: Koslov and Jack. They're running.'

'Just here please.' Anna could see the restaurant sign up ahead now. She pulled out a 20 and pushed it through to the driver as he came to stop.

'The car's on the move. Looks like Koslov and Jack are trying to cut it off.'

'Shit...' Dermot wasn't going to be much use to them if he got himself run over. She climbed out the cab and swung the door shut, trying to see what was happening through the thickening rain.

A running figure appeared, perhaps 50 yards away, splashing through the puddles as he dodged the few pedestrians braving the rain. Another followed close behind.

'Car's turning left. Now it's stopped.'

Anna checked the traffic then jogged across the road towards them.

'Christ, he's going to—'

The roar of an engine cut through the air. Then a dull thud.

'Subject down. Repeat, subject down.'

'Which subject? Repeat, which subject?'

Anna was already sprinting through the puddles by the time she heard the reply.

Chapter 22

'There she is!' Yegor shouted and pointed as he ran.

A short distance up the road Svetlana was being bundled into the back of what looked like a blue Volvo by a man in a beanie. The door closed behind her and the man jumped into the front and started the car.

'They're going to turn left; we can stop them.' Yegor upped his speed as the car moved off. Dermot wiped the rain from his eyes and pounded after him.

Svetlana had been in the ladies' for less than five minutes, but it had been enough for Mulrooney's goons to sneak in and spirit her out of the restaurant. Or maybe they'd just dragged her kicking and screaming past Dermot and Yegor as they'd argued.

Dermot heard a horn blare angrily somewhere ahead and watched the Volvo edge its way slowly past a queue of cars coming in the other direction. Whoever Mulrooney had behind the wheel wasn't much cop as a getaway driver.

Yegor was at the junction now, his little legs carrying him through the puddles surprisingly quickly. He stopped and turned as Dermot caught up.

'Go further down. If they get past me you must stop them.'

And how exactly was he supposed to do that? But then the Russian was already ducking between two parked cars and stepping into the road as the Volvo finally got clear of the traffic and turned into a side street. Dermot sprinted on past a parked lorry and three more cars as another horn sounded, stepping out into the road 20 yards or so behind Yegor.

The Volvo driver leaned on his horn and waved madly at Yegor to get out of the way.

Yegor just started walking forwards instead.

'Stop the car!' The Russian's words were clear even over the noise of the downpour. He was pointing what looked like a gun at the windscreen.

Dermot stared through the rain as the object that looked like a gun revealed itself to be just that.

'Out, now.'

All trace of fear had gone from Koslov's voice. He sounded like a man in control. A man who routinely faced down kidnappers in cars. A man who was a little more than a translator and certainly not one to be mocked about his height.

Shit. Dermot re-ran the gag about the stool in his head. But for perhaps the first time since they'd met he also felt glad Yegor was on his side.

The driver flashed his lights and revved the engine. Yegor took another step forward, gun still raised.

The engine revved some more.

'Get out.'

The engine screeched and the car shot forward and suddenly Yegor wasn't standing in the way anymore. He turned end over end as he flew through the air, much as the steak had done as it hurtled straight at Marcus's eye. The little Russian landed on the bonnet of a red car and an alarm sprang into life, almost drowning out the roar of the car speeding straight down the road.

Towards Dermot.

But wouldn't it have been pretty stupid of Mulrooney to run him down? Surely the whole point of the kidnap was to get his money back – and dead men didn't tend to pay their debts.

Stupid or not the car kept coming.

'Stop!' Dermot raised his own, gunless hand but the car wasn't even slowing. Who exactly was the stupid one now?

The headlights flashed again; the horn was now one continuous note, competing with the blaring of the car alarm, the sound of the rain and the voice that had started shouting at him.

'DERMOT.'

'If they get past me you must stop them.'

'DERMOT!'

Ten yards now but there was still time for the car to stop, even in the wet.

'We are both dead men if anything happens to her.'

'DERRRRMMMOOOOOT!'

An image of his daughter popped into his head, dragging him back from the edge. He leaped across to the other side of the road just in time as the car sped by. If Yegor wanted to get himself run down, that was his lookout. Dermot would find a way to get Svetlana back from Mulrooney that didn't involve ending up as roadkill.

'DERMOT!'

OK, the panic was over now. Thanks and all that, but whoever was shouting his name could stop. He turned to look and found himself face-to-face with a little old lady. Harmless enough, he supposed, even though she was driving her little yellow car straight at him. She wasn't the one doing the shouting though; she was far too busy chatting away on her mobile and looking round for a parking space to even see him.

'DERRRR-MOTTT!'

The old lady finished her call and looked up just as the car reached the place Dermot was standing. For a moment he was flying, which felt reasonably OK. Probably quite similar to what it had been like for Yegor.

And for Marcus's steak.

But flying soon turned into landing.

Which wasn't so good. Lots of bits of him started to hurt and there seemed to be something strange going on with his head.

Everything was a bit wet too.

'Dermot.' The voice was a whisper now as a pair of impossibly big eyes stared down at him.

God they were beautiful.

'You'll be OK.'

He wasn't sure about that. But with eyes like that she could tell him anything.

Eyes like…? Hadn't he seen them somewhere before?

He reached for a name as his lids started to droop. Always been pretty good with names. Except Molly's damned horse; been trying to remember what it was called for days.

Things began to get a little fuzzier, as he felt himself slipping away into the dark.

But that name was on the tip of his tongue.
'Anna?' His eyes snapped open once more, the word on his lips.
No, no, no. The horse wasn't called Anna. It was called Nugget.
But, those eyes…
Darkness finally came.

Part Three

Part Three

Chapter 23

A pair of eyes was looking down at him. Perfectly acceptable eyes, too; they just weren't the beautiful pair he'd seen...

Where exactly had that been again?

That part was proving tricky, although he did remember something about being wet.

The perfectly acceptable eyes blinked once and then a second time. Then they were gone.

There'd also been a name, hadn't there? And something about a car, although it could easily have been a horse. So much easier to stop worrying and go back to sleep.

The memory of the beautiful eyes was with him when he woke again. There was something about a restaurant now. And Russia? Rain as well. (So that's why he'd been wet.)

He didn't feel wet anymore. The bed was comfortable and he was warm.

Something flying through the air?

No, make that someone... Yegor? Little fella, translator. That was the Russian bit covered then. But the name that went with the beautiful eyes still wasn't playing ball. And something else was nagging away.

Sleep stepped in once more.

'We've done all the checks.' A woman spoke first.

Hushed voices pulled him slowly from sleep again. Probably the third time he'd woken but then who was counting?

'Nasty bang on the head, that's all. He should be OK.' The second voice was male, older and sounded sympathetic enough.

Next came footsteps and the sound of a door closing. The silence was interrupted only by a regular beeping noise and something whirring.

When Dermot opened his eyes everything was blurry and a little too bright.

A hospital.

He seemed to be alone in some kind of private room. The whirring and beeping noises were coming from machines on both sides of his head. At the foot of the bed and just off to the left was a door, presumably the one that had just closed. Next to the door a wide window gave him a good view of the main ward where nurses and doctors were going about their business with what looked like reassuring efficiency.

He rested his head on the pillow as sleep came for him once more.

Then he remembered the eyes.

And wasn't there something rather urgent he needed to be doing? But the bed was so soft, the sheets so crisp and comfortable and that whirring sound would have made anyone feel drowsy. All he could think about was those beautiful eyes. Those eyes and a name…

Marcus Diesel.

An image of the chef barged rudely into his head, making itself right at home; nothing new there, then. In Dermot's mind's eye, Marcus was holding a steak. That couldn't be right. The man didn't know one end of a frying pan from the other; wasn't really a chef at all. But then 'cookery presenter' didn't sound half as good.

'Does a chef have to create his own recipes, Dermot? You didn't write your songs.'

No, but he had sung them. Dermot had never found the energy to pursue the argument further.

Then a new image had found its way into his head. The steak again but flying this time.

Oh shit… Sacked by TV's worst-dressed and most annoying man.

Other pieces started to come back.

'I think you'll find I'm a little more than a translator.'

A blue Volvo, the little Russian doing his flying thing, the yellow car and the old woman ON. THE. FUCKING. PHONE!

Svetlana gone.

'*We are both dead men if we don't find her.*'

Given the speed with which the Volvo had hit him, Yegor had to be dead already.

That just left Dermot. He had to get up now. Get out of here, find Mulrooney and bring Svetlana back before Bukin found out. Yegor had had a gun. He'd been desperate enough to face down a speeding car. Desperate or scared enough. He really was a little bit more than a translator. Which meant Bukin was…

A quick look around revealed that he wasn't attached to any of the beeping machines, which seemed like a good start. Even better, his clothes were just a few feet away on a chair. And there, nestling in his jacket pocket or maybe in his trousers, would be his phone. Armed once more with his all-powerful Jedi weapon he'd be in a far better place to take on the dark forces of…

Oh, shut up and get on with it.

His whole body protested as he pulled himself upright.

'*Nasty bang on the head, that's all…*' Yeah, right. Dermot doubted the doctor had ever been mowed down by a mad old woman in a yellow car.

But after a few seconds he found that things didn't seem to hurt quite as much, so maybe the doc knew his stuff after all. Dermot slid himself towards the edge of the bed and placed a foot on the floor. He was about halfway to his clothes when the door opened.

A grey-haired man in a while coat walked in followed by…

'Hello, Dermot.' A wide smile was spread right across her face.

'Anna…?' Dermot's head spun and he wondered whether he should be getting back into bed on account of him seeing things. But no… It just couldn't. It must have been, what…?

'Long time no see.' The smile was still in place.

'Anna? But how? What…?' And those eyes. He felt another wave of fuzziness and reached out for the edge of the bed.

'Well, you always did know how to make a first impression.'

On reflection, her smile was more of a smirk. He followed her gaze downwards.

Right then, somebody round here clearly thought they had a sense of humour. Well they didn't, OK? The hospital gown he was wearing was bright pink and reached only to the very top of his thighs. He wasn't even sure it covered everything it needed to.

Or that he was wearing anything underneath.

'You shouldn't be out of bed.' The doctor stepped towards him with a frown.

Yes, a dignified retreat back under the safety of the covers was exactly what he needed but his brain was far too confused to start issuing orders.

'Anna, it's you… I mean… What are you doing here?'

Back at school his friends had always wondered (sometimes quite cruelly) what he saw in the class 'fat girl'. They wouldn't be calling her fat now. Everything seemed to have pulled itself back into proportion and then some. The jeans, T-shirt and jacket showed off her figure without flaunting it. Her brown hair was shorter and that suited her too. But it was those eyes that kept drawing him back, deep brown and just impossibly large.

'You're looking g-grr-great.' He still hadn't managed to move. 'And have you lost…?' He tried to swallow the words but it was too late.

'Are you saying I was fat?'

'No, well, yes. What I meant was…' He pulled his arms around himself as the temperature in the room plummeted by around a thousand degrees.

'Er… I might just leave you to it.' The doctor coughed and turned away. 'As you seem to have made such a speedy recovery.'

Slow seconds ticked by as the man walked to the door and closed it softly behind him.

'I'm sorry, I… I just don't know what to say.' Dermot cracked first as the silence became unbearable.

'How about not telling me how fat I was.'

'I didn't. You weren't… It's just.'

'Or you could thank me for saving your life.' Her smile was back. 'You did?'

'How else do you think you got out the way of that car?'

'But it hit me.' He held a hand to his head, which had just started to throb.

'No, I pushed you out of the way.'

'Seriously?'

'I think you'd be feeling a lot worse if you'd actually been run over.'

'Thank you.' And thank God she had shed a few pounds. No way would she have been quick enough to push him out the way with all the extra timber she'd been carrying back then.

'You're welcome. Your head did kind of hit the pavement. Sorry about that.' She didn't sound it.

'And you're OK?' Shit. He couldn't believe it had taken him so long to ask. 'It must have been, what…?'

'I'm fine.' Anna pointed to her ripped sleeve with a shrug, the smile lighting up her eyes again. 'Ruined this jacket though.'

'I'm sorry.'

'Didn't like it that much anyway.'

'No, I mean about everything, you know… Back then…'

'That's ancient history.' Her voice was cold again.

'Things were complicated—'

'Seriously, it's fine.'

'But it wasn't my fault.' That just sounded pathetic. But then that's what he had been back then: pathetic and weak.

'It doesn't matter now.' Something lit up her eyes again but it certainly wasn't a smile.

It sounded like it mattered quite a lot. But yes, probably best not to go there right now.

'I can't believe you were there. You know – when I was about to get run over.'

'Listen, it wasn't exactly a coincidence. I think you'd better sit down.'

'I'm all right.' He was going to stand up like a man, gown or no gown (although the pants/no pants question was frankly still a worry).

'I came to find you. I've been watching you for a while.'

OK then, stay calm. He put a hand on the bed to steady himself again and looked into those impossibly large and beautiful eyes.

The impossibly large and beautiful eyes of a dangerous stalker –

one nursing 17 hard years of resentment despite what she'd said about ancient history.

He stole a glance at his clothes on the chair. 'Thanks again for saving me and all.'

Saving him so she could take him back to some creepy old house she'd inherited from a dead aunt. It would be deep in the countryside and a long way from other farms. She'd tie him to a chair and make him sing all his songs while she etched little love hearts and flowers into his chest with a fruit knife. Then she'd start on his back.

'I've really got to get going.' That part was true. If he didn't get Svetlana back soon the chair, the hearts and the fruit knife would be the least of his worries.

'I need to talk to you first.' Her voice had sharper edge to it now. A bit like that fruit knife.

If he could make it to the chair he could get his phone, call the police and tell them about the psycho in his hospital room.

'I work for MI5.'

Psychopath and fantasist.

'You remember we all always thought my dad did something hush-hush for the government?'

All the best fantasies were built on a solid foundation of truth. He took a cautious step towards his clothes.

'Dermot, what are you doing?'

Getting the fuck out of here... But when he looked her in the eye he saw none of the madness of a dangerous psycho. And she was holding an identity card out towards him.

'You really are a spy.'

That would explain the watching bit.

'Counter-intelligence, actually. But most people don't understand the difference.'

'I'd never have guessed.'

'That is kind of the point.'

'But you were going to be a vet.'

'You were going to be a singer?'

Ha, funny. Although he'd forgive her anything now he was sure she wasn't a fantasist stalker. But why would MI5 be interested in him? Maybe she had used her secret-agent skills to track him down for her own stalker purposes. The chair, the hearts and the sharp, little knife edged their way back into the picture.

'We've been watching you and the Russians. I don't think you know how much trouble you're in. Oleg Bukin's not the kind of man you should be involved with.'

Yes, he was beginning to realise that.

'And Koslov's a hired killer. Don't be fooled by his appearance.'

That too but... 'Koslov's dead.' The Russian had flown a long way after the car had hit him.

'No, he's next door.'

'NEXT DOOR! You put me next door to a hired killer?'

'A, he's under armed guard; and B, he's in a coma. It's not life-threatening, more's the pity.' She sighed and shook her head. 'We need to have a serious talk about you and your Russian friends.'

'But I'm just trying to get his daughter—'

'A record deal. We know.'

'It's hardly a crime.'

'Have you listened to any of your old songs recently?'

Yeah, funny again. Lithe athleticism or not he decided he'd preferred the younger, tubbier Anna. Less of a gob on her for one thing.

'What do you think he'll do when he finds out you've lost his daughter?'

'I wasn't responsible for her safety.'

'And he'll see it like that, will he? Perfectly reasonable man is our Oleg.'

Which was why he needed to get out of here right now and get Svetlana back. Or maybe...

'I'm a British citizen. I've got a daughter too. It's your job to protect us.'

'We can't bail out every feckless idiot who gets in over his head. But we *can* help you if you'll help us get to Bukin.'

'Hang on. You just said he was dangerous.'

'He is.'

Dermot thought again of the shrill fear in Koslov's voice. And he was a vicious murdering thug. 'Why would I want to help you?'

'Oh, I don't know. Patriotism, Queen and country?'

'You said I shouldn't be involved with him.' And he was pretty sure he wouldn't have been the Queen's first pick.

'It's a little too late for that. You are involved. And now you've lost his daughter.' She sighed again. 'Do you want me to tell you a little about Oleg Bukin?'

Long before she finished Dermot had decided it might be best to get back into bed after all.

Chapter 24

Well, that had shut him up. Cocky, arrogant, all-in-all a bit of a prick. But then wasn't that exactly what she'd been expecting? Even after all these years.

At least now he was a prick who knew how much trouble he was in. Didn't seem quite so keen to go on dragging up the past either.

Or telling her how fat she'd been.

Much too busy crawling back into bed and feeling sorry for himself. At least he'd covered up the ridiculous pink gown.

She fought back a laugh. The gown must have been about six sizes too small, but Dermot's thighs came close to carrying it off. Not that she'd been looking.

And could he have been more of an arsehole? Assuming that she was some silly little girl who gave any kind of a toss about what had happened in the past? And that feeble attempt at an apology… OK, she'd cut him dead. But he could have tried a bit bloody harder, couldn't he?

None of that mattered right now.

'Are you OK?' Anna looked down at Dermot, trying to find a place in her voice for a small note of sympathy.

'What do you think?'

'Sorry, silly question. But we do need you to tell us everything you can about Oleg Bukin.'

'I didn't know he was an arms dealer. I'm just working for his daughter.'

'And that's all you're doing for him?'

'Oh sorry, did I forget to mention? Koslov thinks he could make it on the stand-up circuit. And Bukin's got an aunt who fancies a crack at presenting *Celebrity Bake Off*. What is this, some sort of interrogation?'

'Er, yes…'

'Christ, Anna, you can't think…? You know me well enough.'

'No, I don't. I don't know you at all.' *You dumped me, remember.*

On my sixteenth birthday… She managed not to say it. 'But I need to know everything about you and Bukin.'

'There is no "me and Bukin". It's business, that's all.' He slumped back on the pillow and looked at the ceiling.

'Look, I believe you.' And she did. Whatever else Dermot was, he was a shit liar. A weakness that probably lay at the heart of his limited success as a showbiz agent. 'But some of my colleagues are a bit more sceptical.'

More than sceptical, if truth be told. After the events of that lunchtime outside the restaurant Kate had been all for calling the operation off again. But Lawson had agreed to let Anna run with it a while longer. If they could persuade Dermot to help get Svetlana back, they could still lure Bukin in.

'Look, I've only met him once.' He pulled himself back up into a sitting position. 'We watched *The Meal of Fortune*. He's a huge Marcus Diesel fan.'

She stifled a laugh as it all fell into place. 'That's why he came to you.'

'And all my past experience of the music industry.'

Past was about right; the poor girl didn't stand a chance of getting a record deal. But there was still one thing Anna didn't quite understand. 'Why did you agree to do it?'

'Oh, I don't know; she's beautiful, she can sing. I thought it would be easy.'

Anna waited, knowing there was more.

'And her dad's loaded. It's complicated. I er… owe someone a bit of money. Charlie Mulrooney, he's a loan shark. This is all a warning. He attacked Marcus last night. Now he's taken Svetlana.'

'Hang on…' Everything up until that point had made sense. She reached into her pocket and pulled out the photo she'd been given by the surveillance team. 'This is the man who took Svetlana. His name's Dmitri Petrov.' She pushed the photo closer to his face. 'Do you know him?'

'Never seen him before. Sounds Russian though.'

'Ten out of ten. Maybe it should have been you who joined MI5?'

'But it was definitely Mulrooney's men who attacked Marcus.'

Anna shrugged. 'Coincidence. What do you think Oleg Bukin will do when he finds out his daughter's been kidnapped?'

'He'll come here of course.' Dermot sat further up in the bed, a big grin on his face. 'That's it. This Petrov guy's working for you. When Bukin comes over here to find Svetlana you can just grab him. Brilliant.'

'I wish it was that easy.' Anna shook her head. They'd considered that one and discounted it. 'Bukin would suspect it was a trap. He'll send someone but he won't come himself. Paternal love doesn't stretch far for a man like him when his own neck's on the line.'

He slumped back down the bed. 'So it could still be Mulrooney?'

'Unlikely. We haven't heard of any domestic crooks importing Russian muscle. But we just need to find her and get her back.'

'"We" as in MI5?'

'No, "we" as in you, me and MI5. We can only help you if you help us. Svetlana's part of the plan.' She was all of the plan, in fact.

'But she could be anywhere by now.'

'Or she could be at Petrov's flat.'

'What... You know where he lives?'

'Camden. It is quite handy being a spy sometimes.'

'You said you weren't a—'

'Just easier for you civilians to understand.'

'What was it a homing device on his car, a satellite tracker?' His eyes shone with excitement at the prospect of all that hi-tech James Bond gadgetry.

'No. We just got his registration number and rang the DVLA. That's how we got his name, too.'

'Oh.' He sounded a bit disappointed.

'We've got a team on the way now but I need to know you're going to help us first. There's no point in us helping you get Svetlana back if you won't help us get to Bukin.'

Anna watched as he laid his head back on the pillow and looked up at the ceiling.

Kate Barnes had scoffed at the whole idea of course. A mercenary like Dermot would never help; never risk his own precious skin. But

Anna knew what he had been like back then, before... Well before he'd decided to reinvent himself as a monumental penis.

The silence dragged on as he carried on staring at the ceiling. If this didn't work she'd be back in the research section by tomorrow. Her whole career was hanging by the thread of his next words.

Bastard.

A thread that came closer to snapping every extra second the silence stretched on.

Finally he managed to drag his eyes away from the ceiling and look at her. 'What if you just gave me the address and I can go and rescue her.'

'Not going to happen.'

'Worth a try.'

'Not really.'

He puffed out his cheeks as he closed his eyes again. When he opened them he was nodding. 'I don't have a choice, do I?'

Seemed like he was catching on fast.

Then he smiled and gave her a little nod.

Ha! Kate Barnes could just about go and... Anna put a hand on the bed to steady herself, then pulled it away as she realised it was virtually on Dermot's thigh.

'What do you need me to do?'

'It's simple...' But it wasn't and it still sounded ridiculous when she thought about it again. Just because Kate and Lawson had gone for it didn't mean that Dermot would agree. He might have been an idiot but he knew more about the entertainment business than all of them put together.

'We need to get to Svetlana as quickly as we can. I'll tell you on the way. It might be useful to have a familiar face on hand when we go into the flat – help calm her down.' It wouldn't actually. They'd send a crash team in through the front door and stick some big guns in Petrov's face. But Anna wasn't about to let Dermot out of her sight in case he did a runner.

'So what are we waiting for?' He grabbed the covers and started to pull them back.

She raised a hand to stop him. 'I think I've seen enough for one day. I'll be outside. You've got two minutes.'

'Anna...'

She paused, already halfway to the door.

'What?'

'We always did make a good team.'

They had, right up until he'd walked out on her.

'Just fuck off and put your trousers on.'

Chapter 25

Fully clothed and free of the ridiculous pink gown, Dermot had started to feel as if he'd regained some semblance of control. But now, given the choice, he'd probably have opted to be back in hospital with his arse hanging out. He put a steadying hand on the car door as Anna threw her little red Fiat round yet another corner.

Next up she accelerated past a white van before cutting smartly in front of it. Well not so smartly in the opinion of the van driver, if his horn-work was anything to go by. She responded with a cheery wave of apology as they sped on round another blind bend on the wrong side of the road. Dermot closed his eyes and grabbed the handle tighter.

He opened them again as he finally felt the car slowing a little and stole a sideways glance at Anna, wondering whether he needed to pinch himself.

God, she was beautiful. Patronising, superior, annoying and probably about to get them both killed.

But, yes, beautiful with it.

He shut his eyes again and gripped even tighter as she accelerated past a taxi. Several turns (most of them illegal) and a couple of red lights later they reached the relative safety of Tottenham Court Road. In theory, they could head straight up towards Euston Road and then Camden beyond without many more of the moves Anna had used to speed her way down the tight side streets of Soho.

'What happens when we get there?' Dermot had previously decided against asking questions in the interests of safety, but it seemed OK now to take a little of her attention away from the road.

'The surveillance guys are watching the flat. There's a police armed-response unit there too. We'll assess the situation when we get there and decide what to do.'

'What if Yegor wakes up?' They'd hurried past the Russian's room on the way out of the hospital. The little hitman was still in a coma but the doctors seemed relatively confident he'd be awake soon.

Awake and looking for answers.

'We've got someone watching him and he's sedated.' She turned to him, taking her eyes off the road for a worryingly long time. 'We think Petrov's working alone so this shouldn't take long.'

'And you've still got no idea why he's taken her. Aren't you secret agents supposed to know that kind of stuff?'

'I'm not an agent; I'm an intelligence officer. The sources and contacts we use to get our information are the agents.'

'So that means I'm a secret—'

'Please. Don't even go there.' She took her eyes off the road once more to give him a disdainful little glance. Then she was braking sharply and flashing her lights as the car in front had the audacity to stop for a red light.

'Wouldn't it be easier if you had a siren?'

'Might attract a bit too much attention.'

'Unlike your driving?'

'I'd forgotten how funny you weren't.'

But at least she had her eyes back on the road now. They drove on in silence, cutting neatly from lane to lane, before filtering off to the left.

'You were going to tell me what you need me to do?' He couldn't help feeling it had been a mistake, agreeing to help without knowing what they wanted. 'I'm happy to stop working for Svetlana, of course.'

'We don't want you to do that.'

'But you said Bukin was a criminal. Why would you want me to help his daughter?'

She turned and smiled at him. 'Because she's the bait.'

'Bait?' He was starting to have an uneasy feeling about this.

'She's his only child and it's her dream to be a pop star. He'll do anything he can to help her career.'

'I think he was hoping I'd do all that.'

'Needs to be a bit more careful who he trusts, then.' She gave him another little smile.

'You're enjoying this, aren't you?' Suddenly he was angry. And how had he ever thought she was attractive?

'Define "this".'

'All of it. Me being in the shit.'

'Wouldn't you in my position?'

'I said I'm sorry about all that.' Or he'd tried to at least.

'Forget it. I'm here to help you now.'

'But only if I help you.'

'We've got a plan, a way to help you kick-start her singing career. Bukin will be so proud he won't be able to stay away when she performs. That's when we get him. But it's got to be something big enough to guarantee he'll come. All we need you to do is persuade Svetlana and Bukin to go for it.'

That didn't sound *so* hard.

'And to ask Bukin to help make it happen. That's the absolute clincher; he'll never think it's a trap if he's helped set it up himself.'

Not quite so simple then. 'Please... just tell me.'

'OK, er...'

And there it was: the hesitation in her voice he'd first caught back in the hospital. He wondered which part of this wasn't going to be good.

Probably all of it.

He closed his eyes as she floored the accelerator and ran another red light.

And then she told him.

Chapter 26

'Thanks, Kate, I'll get back to you.' Richard Lawson put the phone down. The acid stab of heartburn struck before the handset was even back in its cradle.

What a God-awful mess.

The quacks had told him the heartburn was all down to diet. So he'd changed his diet but it had only got worse. Showed how much doctors knew. It was stress, pure and simple. The stress that had put his old friend David Preston in the ground and would get him in the end too.

But not yet. There was so much more he needed to achieve. He reached into his desk drawer for his little pink pills, thought about taking two then threw four down with a swig of water. Shock and awe; that should sort the bastard out.

He pushed his heavy frame from the chair and walked to the window, avoiding a glance in the mirror. In his mind he was still a young man, a fit man even. But a fleeting glimpse of the jowly, ageing heart-attack-in-waiting would shatter that illusion every time.

The view of the river always calmed him, helping him to think too. And thinking was what he needed to do right now. He stared out at the water for a minute or so then strode back to his desk and called his secretary.

'Hold all calls please, Janet.'

'The news' had come just as he was leaving the office the previous evening. An external candidate had thrown her hat in the ring for the DG's job.

Just when he was starting to feel like a shoo-in, too.

He walked back to the window, unsure whether it was merely some chancer or something more politically motivated from White-hall. The service had been under the radar for years now. Doing its job and doing it well without causing their lords and masters down the river any sort of embarrassment. Why would they feel the need to parachute an outsider in at this stage? But then Lawson had learned years ago not to second-guess the politicos.

Outside, the Thames flowed along under a brooding sky while the traffic next to it stood still. Just another normal day.

Not for Richard Lawson it bloody wasn't.

If they could take Oleg Bukin out of circulation then Whitehall's soft little puppet woman would be toast. But then if it all blew up in his face?

He winced as another stab of heartburn struck.

It was a risk he had to take. Bukin was just too dangerous to leave out there. Lawson wouldn't be doing his job if he let this opportunity go to waste. And doing the job had to come first, despite the risks it might pose to his career advancement. Even with the Russian girl's kidnap and the news Kate Barnes had just delivered, Anna's unorthodox plan remained their best option.

He turned away from the window, avoiding the mirror again as he returned to his desk, running over the plan for about the hundredth time as the heartburn mounted another attack. Perhaps not the most audacious operation MI5 had ever run but it had to be pretty damned close. And how on earth had she come up with it? There was definitely more of David Preston in the girl than he'd first thought.

Any fallout could jeopardise his chances of the DG's job. And it wasn't just about him. There was the good of the service to consider too. He was a far better candidate than any little Whitehall pen-pusher. But then there'd been plenty of rogue officers in the past, hadn't there? Probably best to let Anna get on with it but keep things low-key, as off-the-books as possible.

The heartburn fired its most devastating salvo yet as he thought about the question at hand. Was he seriously considering throwing his old friend's daughter to the wolves?

The hot pain burned his chest again. It was a question he hoped he'd never have to answer.

Mainly because he was worried that the answer would be yes.

Chapter 27

The noise of the engine and the other traffic seemed to fade away to nothing as the whole world folded in on itself. Then there was just her and Dermot and the words she'd spoken hanging in the air between them.

Why didn't he just say something? If it was going to be a no, well, that was fine. Just get it out and then at least they'd know where they stood. Then he could fuck off and try to get his precious little Russian girl back on his own; see how that worked for him.

Speech seemed to be beyond him though. He just stared at the road ahead. Then finally he started to shake. Not just a little, but to really, really shake.

She slowed the car. What was the point now anyway? What exactly was the fucking point?

Kate Barnes had been right all along. The realisation came like a slap. And why exactly had Lawson let her carry on with the whole stupid plan? Was it all just to humiliate her, put her back in her place once and for all?

Next to her Dermot's head was in his hands now. She'd known what he was like; of course she had. Known it ever since he'd walked out on her without so much as a goodbye.

He was bent forward now as far as he could go. A quick stab on the brakes and his seatbelt would probably throttle him. It was the least he deserved.

When he finally lifted his head the tears were rolling down his cheeks.

He tried to say something but the words wouldn't come.

Then he threw his head back and laughed and laughed and laughed.

The bloody, bloody bastard.

She'd risked her neck when that car had been about to mow him down. OK, strictly speaking the old bat wasn't going fast enough to kill anything larger than small rabbit. But that wasn't the point…

And this was how he repaid her: by laughing at her plan.

Anna loved her jacket, too, no matter what she'd told him. She looked down at the shredded material of the sleeve.

He sucked in another breath, wiped his eyes and laughed again. 'Anna's that's the most...' His words were lost in another bout of laughter.

Time to stop the car and give him that punch in face he'd had coming for 17 years.

'It's the most...'

Bastard.

'... brilliant thing I've ever heard.'

It was? She studied his face for any hint of sarcasm. 'You mean it?'

But Dermot didn't reply. He was far too busy lunging towards her and grabbing the steering wheel, pulling it round just in time to stop them mounting the kerb and hitting a lamp post.

'Fuck.' She slammed on the brakes and brought them to a stop.

'Jesus, you nearly drove us off the road.' But he didn't stop laughing. 'It's genius. If you knew Bukin, you'd see that straight away. He's so obsessed with his daughter becoming a star.'

Then they were both laughing, big fat tears rolling down their cheeks until the beeping from the growing line of cars behind reminded Anna they still had to rescue Svetlana before any of them could even think about getting her to represent Russia in the Eurovision Song Contest.

Chapter 28

The Eurovision Song Contest.

It really was genius.

He looked across at Anna as she changed down gears to accelerate through another light just as it turned to red.

And, yes, it would work too.

He remembered the pride on Bukin's face as he'd played Svetlana's demo tape. If his daughter represented Russia, Bukin really wouldn't be able to stay away. Getting Bukin to Eurovision wouldn't be a problem but... 'Isn't it kind of illegal? Extraordinary rendition or whatever it's called?' Maybe MI5 didn't bother themselves with such niceties anymore.

She turned to him with a little frown. 'We'll just get the police to arrest him when he gets to London.'

'What? Eurovision's here?'

'That's the whole point.'

'But don't you have to win it to be the host the next year. We never—'

'Don't you remember? "Dum de dum de, Rock the Party"?' She started to sing. 'Dum de dum de, let's get started...'

Of course. DJ Danny Dance – how could he have forgotten? After years of 'nil points' and attempts to sway the voters with big names like Bonny Tyler it was a former roofer from Barnsley who'd finally brought the Euro bacon back for Britain. 'Rock the Party' had gone on to be last summer's biggest hit.

'God, it was crap.' Predictably Molly had loved it.

'Not like your songs then?'

'At least ours... I mean the lyrics. He rhymed "party" with "started".'

'Worked though.'

'True.' But there was another thing niggling away at him. 'Eurovision's in – what? – three weeks? Don't the Russian's already have a contestant?'

'Yep. Sergei Symenov, traditional folk singer.' She gave him another wide smile as she actually slowed and stopped for a traffic light. 'Used to do an act with a bear. It did some Cossack dancing while he sang.'

Those long Russian winter nights must have been a blast.

'They took the bear away after the fall of the Soviet Union.' She smiled and shook her head. 'Political correctness gone mad if you ask me. What's the world come to when a man can't beat up a bear to make it dance?'

Indeed, but bearless or not Symenov was the man in possession of the coveted Eurovision slot.

'Has to do the dancing himself now. Apparently he's a lot better than the bear ever was. But not with a broken ankle.'

'You wouldn't?'

'Us?' Anna shook her head. 'He had a little accident on the stairs of his apartment block.' She looked at her watch. 'About now, in fact. Quite likes a drink, does old Sergei, and the stairs in those old Soviet blocks are a devil to maintain apparently. Lots of unemployed youths hanging around too.'

'Jesus, you did.'

'They'll need to find a replacement pretty damned sharpish.'

'But nobody's ever heard of Svetlana; they'll never pick her.'

'Helps if Daddy's the major shareholder in the TV station that owns the Russian broadcasting rights. Bukin's been trying to go legit for a while now. That's what gave us the idea.'

'You're kidding?'

'Nope.' She turned to him with that smile again. 'All you need to do is persuade him to use his influence to get Svetlana the place.'

That was all was it? But he doubted it would be too hard. The Russian would do almost anything to help his daughter shimmy up the slippery pole of fame.

'And what about the song?' Cover versions wouldn't cut it.

'Sorted. Just in case Bukin needed a little extra persuasion we've got a songwriter with a proven Eurovision track record.'

'Who?'

'DJ Danny Dance, of course, seems like his record company

screwed him over and what money he did make he's pissed up the wall already.'

Dermot knew the feeling all too well.

'He was about to go back to roofing but your assistant called him this afternoon while you were in the hospital. He reckons he's got the perfect song written but the record company won't release it. He's already sent the track over.'

'But I don't have…' He stopped himself and smiled. She really did have all the bases covered. All except the obvious one.

'So we just need to find Svetlana and tell her the good news.' It was as if she could read his mind. But then they'd always been on the same wavelength. It was just like that time when… Probably best not to think about any of that right now.

'We're here.' Ann pulled the car into the kerb. 'Just keep quiet and do as I say. It's the third on the right, ground-floor flat.' She pointed up the road to a house with a red door. 'We've got it under surveillance and—'

She stopped as the front door opened and a thin woman in an unflattering beige blouse stepped out, followed by two armed policemen in black body armour.

'Shit.' Anna jumped out the car and hurried off up the street.

Dermot scrambled out after her. The two women were already arguing by the time he caught up.

'You were supposed to wait.' Anna didn't look happy.

'I'm in charge of this operation.' The thin woman's superior expression more than trumped Anna's black look.

'Hi, I'm Dermot.' He offered a hand.

They both ignored him.

'Good job we went in when we did.' The other woman handed Anna a piece of paper. 'It's a booking confirmation. Two tickets for New York. Flight's at six thirty.'

'That's only a couple of hours.' Dermot did the maths.

'Well you'd better get a move on, then.' The woman's new expression was probably meant to be a smile but it was hard to tell.

'Can't you just hold the plane?' Dermot felt this was a reasonable enough question.

She looked at him like he was an idiot.

'Yes, why not?' It was Anna who asked this time. Not such a stupid question then. 'A girl's been kidnapped.'

'Lawson wants to keep this low profile. We don't want police crawling all over Heathrow and flights being cancelled. If Bukin gets a sniff of our involvement, it's over.'

Who was Lawson? And Dermot wasn't sure that was quite what they'd been asking for; more like a slight delay to one flight.

'And we don't think she has been kidnapped. The surveillance team didn't spot any signs of coercion and we've got eyewitness accounts from the neighbours here saying she got into the taxi with Petrov happily enough.

Dermot looked at Anna. That just didn't make any sense.

'Follow them to the airport and find out what's going on. You've got just enough time.' The thin woman turned and stared at Dermot. 'Anna's told us that she thinks you can convince the girl and her father to go for the bait. Now we'll see if she's right.'

'Let's go.' There was an edge in Anna's voice as she turned away.

'Oh, there's something else you need to know first. It's why we went in without waiting for you.' She leaned forward and spoke softly to Anna.

'Hospital' was the only word that Dermot caught, but from the look on Anna's face he felt certain he knew exactly what had happened.

Chapter 29

'Are you all right, dear?'

Yegor stumbled and almost fell, putting one hand against the rough brickwork of a wall.

Everything spun again.

When his world swam back into focus he was looking down at the face of an old lady, her hand on his arm.

'Thank you; I am fine. Just a headache.'

'There's a hospital just up the road. I could take you.'

NO! The stale smell of her was in his nostrils now. He saw the dirty ragged clothes.

'I said I'm fine.' It took all his strength but he managed to push himself away from the wall and shrug her off.

'Suit yourself, love,' she cackled and walked off.

And then he was walking too, walking and trying to make sense of it all. But all he could think of now was the needle.

He'd been floating just beneath the surface, half in and half out of a dream he could no longer remember. When he opened his eyes the man had been there with his white coat and the needle.

All the years had slid away.

Good, bad. Us, them. East, West. Long, long ago.

A simpler time. And maybe even a better time too?

Until they'd taken him and used needles. Afterwards Yegor had sworn it would never happen to him again. So he'd pushed up at the heavy, heavy weight on his chest, breaking through the surface just as the needle came down towards his arm. Then the man had been falling, white coat flapping, head cracking on the floor.

The second man had come through the door then, running. So Yegor had taken the needle and pushed it right into his leg. The man hadn't seemed so keen on running after that.

Long minutes had crawled by as he dressed. But nobody had come. His phone, his wallet, keys were all there, although wasn't there something missing? And nobody had tried to stop him as he'd walked out either.

The sunlight was hurting his eyes now. His head pounded and his muscles ached with every step. Ahead he saw a bench. Maybe he could sit and rest for a while? But if he sat he'd never get up again. He had to keep on walking. Or…?

So, so stupid.

He stopped and leaned on the wall again. One little bang on the head and he was behaving like a novice. The famous tower with the clock just across the river told him exactly where he was. Bukin's house was less than two miles away. The driver could be here with the car in under ten minutes. He reached for his phone.

Jacket pockets, trousers… Nothing. His wallet was gone too. They'd been there at the hospital with his clothes. He'd seen them. He remembered taking them.

The beggar woman.

The shame of it almost brought him to his knees. Robbed blind by a stinking old babushka. Yegor Koslov's hitman days would be over if word of it ever got round in Moscow.

No choice then. He took a deep breath and pushed away from the wall. If it was two miles then so be it: he'd walk.

One foot in front of the other.

The longer Svetlana was gone the more chance of Bukin finding out. And that would mean death. But at the house there was the car and there was another…

Another gun! A wall of nausea struck as he realised what had been missing from his pile of clothes in the hospital. He remembered pointing it as the car bore down on him. Then nothing. If it had been found the police would be involved.

But what could he do about that now? He just had to put one foot in front of the other. He'd come so far; too far to fail.

One foot in front of the other.

The loan shark Mulrooney had taken the girl. That much was clear. Yegor would kill him first. Any of his men who stood in his way too.

And then it would be time to deal with Dermot Jack. The

Englishman's money troubles had come so close to jeopardising everything.

Explanations would be needed back in Moscow but they'd be far easier with Svetlana safely back under Bukin's roof and the problem dealt with.

Just one foot...

... in front of the other.

The fear drove him on.

Chapter 30

'Last call for flight number BA 352 to New York. Would any remaining passengers please go to gate 73.'

'Does this thing go any faster?' Anna tapped the driver on the shoulder.

He turned to her with a sad shake of his head and pointed to the sign on the yellow plastic dashboard – *Max Speed 5 MPH*.

Every other time she'd been at an airport these mobility vehicles had fair zipped along, their orange flashing lights and sirens beeping as their boy-racer drivers two-wheeled it round corners.

Not today it seemed.

They'd made the airport from Camden in less than 40 minutes; Dermot had held on tight and kept his eyes shut but it hadn't stopped him urging her to run every light. Now it seemed like it would take them as long again to crawl across the terminal.

A call ahead from the car, some serious scrutiny of Anna's ID and a tense phone conversation with the airport's director of operations on his day off had been enough to get them past the security checks. Official MI5 business had been the explanation offered and grudgingly accepted. There'd been one condition though: the security shift manager and his two men were to accompany them. Given the man's girth and inability to walk more than about 10 steps without irreversible pulmonary damage, the mobility vehicle had been the only option.

'There's plenty of time, don't worry.' The shift manager didn't even bother to turn round or to keep the irritation from his voice. He was up front beside the driver, with Anna and Dermot in the middle seat and two more security guards behind.

'They'll take a while boarding. We can always get on the plane if they've already boarded.'

At this rate, the plane would have boarded, taken off and come back for the return flight before they got anywhere near the gate.

Next to her Dermot sighed as the driver slowed first for a shuffling group of pensioners and then for a long snake of French-looking schoolchildren.

'We'll get there.' She turned to him with what she hoped was a reassuring smile. 'You hold back. Let me assess the situation first. This Petrov could be dangerous. And we still don't know exactly what's going on.' They'd gone over that in the car but neither could see why Svetlana might have come of her own free will.

'I still don't understand how they could let Yegor get out of the hospital?'

No, neither did Anna. 'Someone messed up big time; that's all I know.' The man assigned to watch over Koslov had paid for his mistake with a leg full of tranquilliser. His punishment was unlikely to end there when he eventually woke up. 'But we're watching the Chelsea house. Chances are that's where he'll go. We just need to get Svetlana back and take it from there.'

'And if we don't that's it, right? All bets are off.'

'Yes.' Anna didn't like it any more than he did but Kate had been clear. Svetlana's disappearance and now Yegor's escape had made Lawson nervous. They needed to keep everything low-key. Without the Russian girl Dermot would be getting no further assistance from MI5.

'We'll get her back, don't worry. But you need to convince Yegor it was all some misunderstanding.' She held his gaze, hoping she wouldn't see too many signs of weakness.

'He knows about Mulrooney. I'll just say it was him. He saw what his goons did to Marcus.'

'Yes that'll work.' Like all good lies it had more than a grain of plausibility. She gave him another reassuring smile. For a civilian he was coping remarkably with it all.

'*Last call for flight number BA 352 to New York.*'

'Come on, come on.' Dermot was waving his arms around in frustration now.

The driver seemed to be on the point of stopping again for a slow-moving family with a triple buggy but thought better of it.

'*Would all remaining passengers for flight BA 352…*'

Jesus, they got the message OK…

'Actually, Andrew, it might be a good idea to put your foot down a bit.' There was just a hint of nervousness in the security man's voice now: the sound of a someone realising he might be about to let down one of his country's more shadowy security organisations.

Thankfully though they seemed to be on the home straight. Trouble was it looked to be a very long one.

The driver pushed the speed up to seven miles per hour as they trundled past gates 50 and 51 and edged onwards to 52. Next to them, on the travelator, stumbling toddlers and octogenarians with sticks and Zimmer frames smiled across sympathetically as they easily outpaced the mobility vehicle.

'Look out!'

There was a gentle bump and a clatter of wood and metal and they came to a halt.

'Watch where you're fucking going...' The disgruntled cleaner looked down at the overturned cart he'd just pushed into their path.

'Would all remaining passengers for flight...'

The driver checked diligently over his shoulder before reversing slowly away from the overturned cart.

'We're nearly there now.' She reached out a reassuring hand towards Dermot's knee but found only thin air.

'Bugger this.' He was already out of the cart and running.

'Wait, we need to—'

But he was on the travelator now, bounding along like an astronaut on his first moon walk.

Sod it. She hopped off the vehicle and followed him; the shouts of protest from the fat security man and the beeping of his ridiculous little vehicle fading rapidly as she tried to close the gap.

Chapter 31

'Last call for flight number BA 352 to New York…'

Dermot ran past Gate 68 on the left, then 69 as he dodged round another group of dawdling passengers and put in a last lung-burner of a sprint. Behind him he could hear Anna shouting but there was no way he was slowing down.

If they didn't get Svetlana back then MI5 were simply going to abandon Anna's plan and move in on Koslov. That's what Anna had told him. As Plan Bs went it didn't sound like a bad one, at least as far as the spooks were concerned. With Bukin most likely to place the blame for his daughter's disappearance on the man he'd sent to protect her, Yegor might just be willing to drop his boss in it. New name? New face? New identity? The little hitman could certainly do with a new haircut.

But that would leave Dermot hanging in the wind.

And if Yegor didn't break then Bukin would remain a free man with a missing daughter and some serious questions for her agent.

Gates 70 and 71 came and went, then Gate 72. He stumbled and nearly went down but finally he was there.

Gate 73. In front of him a small queue of 20 or so stragglers were waiting to board. He wasn't too late.

'Svetlana!' He shouted her name as his eyes scanned the line of passengers.

He called her name again as he slowed to a stop, even though he could clearly see she wasn't there.

Some of the passengers were looking round at him. A red-faced man shook his head at all the fuss, while his wife contented herself with a bit of tutting. A small child pointed at Dermot and laughed, receiving a sharp yank on the arm from a disapproving parent.

They must be on the plane already. He'd have to wait for the fat man and his buggy to get here.

'Svetlana!' He tried it one more time but it was no good.

The blonde girl near the back of the queue gave him the briefest of glances and turned away again.

A little too quickly.

'Svetlana!' He ran the last few yards.

But she kept her back turned. The man next to her put an arm around her shoulders as they shuffled forward. He'd been wrong; she was just another passenger wondering what all the fuss was about, rather than a fugitive in a wig and sunglasses.

Sunglasses! The sky outside was dull and promised rain. The man was wearing them too.

'Svetlana.'

'Get away from us.' It was the man who gave the game away. His English was heavily accented and he looked to be in his early twenties. He took his glasses off as he turned.

Dmitri Petrov, the man from the photo, stared at Dermot. But there'd been no mention of him being a 6'5" wall of solid muscle.

'Just let her go, OK.' Maybe he should have stayed with the security men and their buggy after all.

The Russian stepped between Dermot and Svetlana and pushed her towards the gate.

A couple more passengers had their boarding passes checked and moved off through the gate.

'Last call for flight…'

'I don't know why you're taking her but—'

Petrov stepped forward and shoved Dermot hard in the chest, sending him sprawling onto the floor.

That set the laughing child off again, earning another rebuke from a flustered mother who seemed to be having trouble locating their boarding passes.

Dermot pushed himself up as footsteps rang out on the floor behind him.

'I thought I told you to wait.' Anna reached down and pulled him back to his feet.

In the distance he heard the shouts of an irate security man and some high-pitched beeping as the cavalry finally trundled their way in.

'You can't her force her to go.' Dermot moved towards the two Russians again.

'He's not forcing me.' Svetlana poked her head around the man mountain in front of her and removed her sunglasses.

'He's not...?' And then... 'Hang on. I thought you didn't speak English.'

'Yegor thought he is my translator, but he was just my keeper.'

'I've got a plan. You can still be a pop star.'

The girl sighed and looked at him pityingly. 'I never wanted to be a pop star. Don't you see?'

Er... No.

'It was all – how would you say it? – a plot. So I could to come to the West and be with Dmitri. My father...' Svetlana spat the word out. 'He hates Dmitri. He does not think he is good enough for me. So he got Koslov to threaten him, to make him go away. Otherwise he would have killed him.'

A bit extreme maybe, but then Dermot wondered how he'd react when some grungy deadbeat started hanging around Molly.

Up ahead the queue shortened again.

'That was two years ago. We've been planning it ever since. I learned English in secret so my father would not suspect.'

'But the whole pop-star thing?'

'He is a very proud man. His rich friends all own their businesses, their hotels and their football clubs but none has a pop star for a daughter. And he really did love your stupid *Top of the Pops*. It was the only way to get him to let me come to London. And now we can disappear together. He must not find out about Dmitri. Please, you cannot tell him.'

'We go now.' Dmitri took her arm and led her gently towards the boarding gate.

The queue in front of them was down to four or five people as the Tannoy put out another last call.

'So that's it: you're just running away.'

'Yes.' Dmitri nudged Svetlana closer to the gate.

'Running away?' Svetlana turned back. Her face was full of anger now. '*Just* running? Let me tell you about my father.'

'No, come on.' Dmitri tugged at Svetlana's arm; he clearly knew there'd be no stopping her if she got into full flow.

'No. I want him to understand.' She shook herself free of her boyfriend's hand. 'My real father is dead. Oleg Bukin murdered him. They said it was an accident at the factory but I know it was not. Bukin was a local party boss under the communists. My mother was the most beautiful girl in the whole town. The only way he could have her was to get rid of my father. I was two years old when my father died. What was my mother to do? She had no money and a child to look after. So eventually she married Oleg Bukin. And when she found out what he'd done it killed her. Not straight away but it killed her in the end. She didn't even fight the sickness when it came. She just gave up. Gave up on herself and gave up on me.'

'Please, we must go now.' Dmitri tugged at her sleeve.

'But I can help you.' The thought hit Dermot harder than Dmitri's shove to the chest. Svetlana wanted to see Bukin behind bars as much as he did.

'How? You are just one man, some show-business person who works with your stupid chefs.'

Harsh but essentially true.

'But it isn't just me, it's—'

'We are going.' Dmitri roared and lunged at him.

But Anna moved faster. One minute the tall Russian was in mid-charge, the next he was flying over her shoulder and landing on the floor with a satisfying slap.

'Dimi.' Svetlana rushed over to her fallen boyfriend and helped him to his feet.

'I'm calling security.' The woman behind the desk was already reaching for a walkie-talkie.

'Don't worry, we're here.' The shift supervisor had managed to prise himself out of the buggy and was waddling over, flanked by his two guards.

'We've got it under control.' Anna flashed him a smile.

'You were supposed to stay with us—'

'Do we need to interrupt your boss's day off again?' She cut him off.

'She's MI5, remember.' Dermot felt it was high time to re-emphasise the point.

'Do you have to tell the whole world?' Anna shook her head and gave him a stern look.

'Sorry.'

She turned to Svetlana and Dmitri, beckoning them away from the remaining passengers. 'It's true, I am with MI5.' Her voice was barely above a whisper. 'We've been trying to get to your father for a long time. We can help you. But only if you help us.'

'British Intelligence?' Dmitri was rubbing his back as head as he looked warily at Anna. 'You don't look like a spy.' But he seemed impressed all the same.

'That's kind of the point.' Dermot stepped in once more.

'It was until you told half the airport.' Anna gave him another of her looks.

'I was only—'

'Can I ask you to board the flight, please?' The woman from the boarding gate had walked over and was right beside them now. She had a job to do and not even a judo-throwing spy was going to stop her.

'Sorry, this is a private conversation.' Anna turned her back on the airline woman and put a hand on the Svetlana's arm.

'You know what Oleg Bukin is, what he does? We can stop him if you help us. Then you'll be safe. I promise.'

'No.' Dmitri grabbed Svetlana's other arm and started pulling her towards the gate. 'This changes nothing. We need to get on the plane.'

'You'll never be rid of him.' Anna wasn't quite finished. 'He'll send Koslov to find you.'

'Ha! Yegor is dead.' Svetlana spat the name. 'We killed him.'

Dmitri handed the two boarding passes to the airline woman who suddenly seemed less keen to have a pair of self-confessed killers on her flight.

'He's not dead and now he's out there somewhere looking for you.'

'Impossible, the car, we hit him…' Suddenly there was doubt in Svetlana's eyes. Fear too.

'Believe me.' Anna nodded grimly at the Russians. 'He's alive and I doubt he's in a very good mood.'

The woman tore the boarding passes and handed the stubs back to Dmitri and Svetlana, happier now that they weren't murderers after all.

'Listen to her.' Dermot tried to sound as calm as Anna. 'Your father will send Yegor after you.'

'He's NOT my father. I hate him.' There were tears in Svetlana's eyes now.

'Please, could you just get on board?' The airline woman wasn't bothering to hide her irritation.

'Just give us a minute, please.' Dermot turned to her, playing the diplomat with his best smile.

'No, they need to come now.'

'Could you please just shut the fuck up.' Anna's approach was just a little more direct.

More effective, too.

'OK, one more minute, that's all.' The woman raised a hand and stepped back. 'I can see it's important.'

'I promise you, we'll get him.' Anna made one last appeal to Svetlana. 'You'll be safe if you help us.'

'We will be safe in America; they'll never find us.' Dmitri made another grab for his girlfriend's arm.

'Until Bukin finds out about Dmitri.' Anna nodded towards Dermot. 'How long do you think he'll hold out once Koslov gets hold of him?'

'Yeah, how long… Hey!' Dermot pulled up short as he realised what she'd just said. But she was probably right.

Tears were running down Svetlana's face as she spoke quietly to Dmitri in Russian.

He had tears in his eyes too, shaking his head as Svetlana reached up and stroked his cheek. Then she turned and faced Dermot and Anna.

'You are right: my stepfather will find me. He will never give up. I asked Dmitri to go but if I stay he says he will stay too.'

She was staying.

'Oh, for God's sake.' The airline woman turned and headed to the desk then spoke into the Tannoy. 'BA flight 352 to New York is now closed.'

Dermot felt himself wobble as the whole airport did a little spin.

'I promise you've made the right decision.' Anna didn't look as if she could believe it either. 'But we need to get you back to the house before Koslov gets suspicious. We'll explain everything on the way.' She grabbed Svetlana by the hand.

'Wait.' Dmitri Petrov pulled himself up to his full height and stared down at Anna and Dermot. 'If anything happens to her I will kill you both myself.'

'And I will kill you if anything happens to Dmitri.' Svetlana's dark eyes bore into Dermot's.

He stared back at the two Russians, not doubting their sincerity for a minute. But with Mulrooney, Yegor Koslov and Oleg Bukin already in the queue, a couple more at the back really didn't make a whole lot of difference.

Chapter 32

And Anna had thought the last bit was hard. She gripped the steering wheel and watched through the windscreen as Dermot and Svetlana approached Bukin's Chelsea house.

Back at the airport she'd been in control; first with the security man and then with the two Russians. She'd played it well enough, even if she said so herself. But now all she could do was sit, watch and wait.

And rely on Dermot.

Fifty yards away he and Svetlana were already across the street and at the front gate. Less than an hour ago the Russian girl had been ready to get on a plane. But here she was now, reaching out towards the security keypad next to the gate instead of enjoying mediocre economy cabin service somewhere over the North Atlantic.

But the girl knew full well what Oleg Bukin was capable of and what he would have done to Dmitri when he finally tracked them down.

Anna felt her grip on the steering wheel tighten again as the pair stepped through the gate. Everything depended on them now – and the little Russian hitman waiting inside.

Kate had got the surveillance team to stakeout the house and wait for Koslov's return. As predicted, he'd come back – about the same time as Anna and Dermot had been persuading Svetlana not to get on the plane. But there'd been no sign of life from the house since apparently.

'You think this will definitely work?' Petrov leaned forward between the seats. It was the fifth or sixth time he'd asked the question in one way or another.

'Yes, I do.'

Did she? It all came down to Koslov's reaction. Whether Dermot was able to convince him to believe that Mulrooney had been behind it all. And that Svetlana was safe now and as desperate as ever to be a pop star.

Anna had explained the plan to Svetlana and Dmitri on the drive

147

back from Heathrow. They'd sat quietly in the back seat as they heard her out. Then, just as Petrov's disbelief had been about into erupt in anger, Svetlana had smiled and put a hand on his arm.

'My stepfather has the money and he knows the people who can do this. If I am in the contest he will come to London. He is a proud man. It is a good plan.'

None of them knew Bukin better than his Svetlana. If she was confident it would work, their chances had to be good.

The girl had leaned forward and smiled again, catching Anna's eye in the mirror. 'You know my father's character well. You must be a good spy.'

Anna had smiled, wondering whether to tell her it was all down to her own father and a silly school play all those years ago. No, that was unlikely to help.

Dermot and Svetlana were at the front door now, the girl reaching into her bag for her keys.

There was really no knowing how Koslov would react and Anna wondered again whether they could have done this some other way? Maybe they should have just thrown the hitman into a cell and gone straight to his boss. But then how to explain to Bukin that his little enforcer had disappeared? That would have spooked him and he might have ordered his daughter home.

This was the only way.

Dermot had nodded slowly when she'd explained he'd have to go in alone with Svetlana. Either he'd been in total shock or was confident in his ability to pull it off.

Or maybe he was just plain stupid? In which case what did that make her?

'It's going to be OK.' She caught Petrov's eye in the mirror and tried to pull a convincing smile.

And it would be, wouldn't it? They'd covered all the other bases; surveillance was in place, armed-response team ready to go in at the first hint of trouble. Dermot's story was well-prepared. Apart from telling the whole damned world she was a spook he'd done well at the airport. Anna was starting to feel a sneaking sense of admiration at the way he'd handled himself today. Not that it made him any less of a prick.

She watched as the front door swung open.

Everything was down to him now.

Oh God.

She elbowed the thought aside as the door swung shut behind Dermot and Svetlana. Then she closed her eyes and gripped the steering wheel tighter still.

Chapter 33

Dermot and Svetlana both stood staring at the hallway through the open door.

Ladies first?

He stepped back, his manners taking charge; or maybe it was just his survival instincts kicking in?

It was a moot point though; Svetlana shook her head and waved him on. She might have signed up to the Eurovision plan, but it didn't mean she'd be leading the way into a confrontation with a dangerously disoriented hitman.

He took a deep breath, conjuring up a picture of Mulrooney's fat red face, Bukin's livid scar then Molly and finally the sodding horse. Was this really the only way?

Bloody MI5.

And bloody Anna.

But he knew she was right. He felt the weight of the hard cold thing tugging at his pocket but it really didn't help.

Fuck's sake, get on with it. He stepped inside.

And nothing happened. The hallway was empty and there didn't seem to be a sound coming from the rest of the house.

OK, so that hadn't been so hard.

'Come on.' Svetlana gave him a little shove in the back.

Easy for her with him up front. She wasn't the one that Koslov would shoot.

'Hello?' his voice sound thin and scared as it echoed down the long white hallway with all the pictures.

No reply.

'Yegor?' He called again then started to walk. Maybe the hitman had passed out again or was having a little nap. So why not just phone Bukin and Svetlana could get 'Daddy' to agree to the plan before Yegor even woke up. Then there wouldn't be a thing the little man could do.

'Hello?'

Still nothing.

He stopped outside the entrance to the big white room where he'd first encountered Bukin and his filthy excuse for cookery. It seemed as good a place as any to start. He paused again then pushed gently on the double doors.

The white walls, the TV, the huge sofa, the kitchen spotless and gleaming... The room was just as it had been the day he had first seen it...

'Stop right there.'

Except for the man standing beside the door pointing a gun at his head. Yegor was so close the bullet would go more or less straight up Dermot's nose if he fired.

'OK, OK.' He raised his hands. Yegor hadn't specifically requested it but it felt like the right thing to do.

'Where's the girl, where's Svet—' The words died on Yegor's lips as Svetlana stepped into the room behind Dermot. He lowered the gun a little, relief etching its way across his pale face.

Then he raised the gun again. 'What is going on?' He stumbled, putting a hand on the wall to steady himself. Sweat had plastered his bad hair down against his forehead and his shirt was untucked. He was shaking and seemed a lot smaller than usual too.

'It's all OK, she's fine.' Dermot lowered his hands a little.

'I just need to sit.' Yegor's voice trembled as he stumbled across to the sofa, the gun still vaguely pointing at Dermot as he beckoned them to follow.

Dermot walked slowly across the deep carpet, Svetlana a step or so behind him.

'Tell me what happened.' The Russian slumped onto the sofa, indicating for Dermot and Svetlana to sit opposite. 'And this had better be very good, Mr Jack.' The tremor was gone from his voice and the gun hand seemed steadier now he was sitting down.

Svetlana got in first, offering up a stream of angry-sounding Russian. But Yegor just waved a dismissive hand, clearly wanting to hear it from Dermot.

'Why don't you just put the gun down and we can talk about this.' He was surprised how level and calm his voice was managing to sound now.

'Just tell me.'

'It was Mulrooney. He took Svetlana. He ran you down.'

'Mulrooney?' Yegor seemed to be struggling to place the name.

'The loan shark. He was a threat, like you said.'

'Of course.' Yegor nodded at the acknowledgement that he'd been right.

'I went to see him, got her back.'

'You? You got her back.' A sound that could have been a laugh came from Yegor's throat. 'How did *you* get her back?'

'Mulrooney's my problem so I sorted it out. I'm sorry you and Svetlana had to be involved.'

'HOW...' Yegor leaned forward, the gun squarely aimed Dermot's forehead. 'DID YOU GET HER BACK?' The strain was showing on his face and his gun hand started to shake again.

'I... Er... I just said I'd pay him back double if he let her go. He's only interested in getting his money.'

'Double?' The sound was definitely a laugh this time. 'Not a bad bargain. You're not as much of an idiot as I thought. But Mr Bukin will hear of this. You put his daughter in danger.'

'You said we were both dead men if we didn't find her?' This was where it could all go wrong. 'Do you want him to find out that you failed to protect her?'

Yegor scowled then sat back rubbing his head; the gun drooped, pointing at the floor. If rushing him had been part of the plan this would have been the time to do it.

'No.' Yegor looked up and shook his head. 'She is in too much danger here. I must tell Mr Bukin and take her home.' He raised the gun again.

'You're not well. We need to get you to a hospital.'

'No...' Yegor stopped again, confusion in his eye. 'I had a gun. What happened to it? If they find my gun the police will be involved.'

'They won't. I picked it up when you got run down.'

It was the story Anna had told him to use to explain why the police hadn't been waiting at Yegor's bedside to question him.

'I've got it here, look...'

Shit.

Dermot realised his mistake before his hand was halfway out of his pocket.

'Drop it.' Yegor lurched to his feet, swaying wildly but managing to keep his own gun pointed at Dermot.

'No it's OK.' He held his hand out.

Fuck. He'd meant to hold it by the barrel but somehow he'd got hold of the wrong end and was pointing it straight at Yegor.

'I said drop it.' The little man had both his hands on his own gun to keep it steady.

Dermot dropped the gun down onto the carpet. 'It's not even loaded. I took the bullets out. Yegor please, you need to put that thing down.'

Svetlana threw in something else in Russia but again Yegor ignored her.

'Give it to me.'

Dermot stood slowly and tried to kick the gun gently in Yegor's direction but it just snagged in the heavy carpet.

'Now.' Yegor was sweating more than ever.

Dermot swung his leg harder, somehow managing to chip the gun out of the heavy pile. It popped up in the air and landed at the Russian's feet.

'Thank you.' Yegor grabbed it before collapsing back onto the sofa. But at least he'd lowered his own gun once more.

'Please, Yegor. You've got to listen to me. We need to call Bukin.' Dermot took some deep breaths, deciding it was time to take control. 'I've got something I need to tell him. A plan to help Svetlana's career. But it's quite urgent.'

'Alright.' Yegor stretched his free hand out towards the phone on the table next to his sofa. 'You can tell him about your plan after I've explained how you nearly got his daughter killed.' His speech was more even now and the shaking had stopped.

'She was never in any danger.'

Next to him Svetlana fired off another stream of Russian but Yegor just turned back to Dermot, shaking his head. 'I told him he was wasting his time with you. What does a man who works with chefs know about the music business? But he loves your ridiculous

Marcus Diesel. I'm glad I didn't stop Mulrooney's men from...' The Russian tailed off as he realised his mistake.

'I'll tell him about that too. That you just stood by and let his hero take a beating. What's he going to say then?'

Yegor stared at him coldly, the gun quivering in his hand as he put the phone to his ear. Then he started speaking in slow deliberate Russian.

Svetlana gasped.

'What did he say?'

But she was too busy listening to reply. And then gasping again.

Yegor stopped and listened. Then he spoke some more.

'What, what did he say?'

Another gasp.

Jesus Christ.

Yegor finally put down the phone and smiled at Dermot.

'You told him.' But he was sure he hadn't heard Mulrooney's name among all the Russian.

'You are right, it is probably best for all of us if Mr Bukin doesn't hear about this unfortunate incident. So I just told him that you have a plan you wanted to share. That is what you wanted, isn't it?'

'Yes, thank you.' So why had he ended the call? Why wasn't Dermot explaining things to Bukin right now? There was definitely something about the little smile on Yegor's face he didn't like.

'Mr Bukin would very much like to hear it.' The smile got nastier. 'So I suggested that it might be better if you told him in person.'

Yessss. Yegor wouldn't be smiling for much longer. Dermot prepared to launch himself into the most ambitious of mental dance routines. They wouldn't even need to bother with the Eurovision plan; they could just grab Bukin when he got off the plane. Yegor had just done Dermot's job for him and lured his boss right into the trap.

That's what all Svetlana's gasping had been about.

Less than a day of helping MI5 and Dermot had already helped bag an evil international arms dealer. This spying lark was a piece of cake.

'He is looking forward to welcoming seeing you tomorrow.'

Just one more day and it would all be over.

'He will send his private jet to take all three of us there.'

Hang on. 'Take us where?'

'Russia, of course.' There was a little glint of something in Koslov's eye.

'You want me to go to Russia?' That was never part of the deal.

But Yegor just sat back and smiled. It was a smile that said the little Russian didn't believe a single one of the lies Dermot had just spun. A smile that said they'd soon be back on the hitman's home turf. And then...? Well, then they'd see, wouldn't they?

Part Four

Chapter 34

Dermot blinked and followed Svetlana out of the plane door and into the late-afternoon Russian sunshine. He was doing his very best not to have a very bad feeling about this.

The first thing he noticed was the snow, or rather the lack of it. He'd kind of been expecting lots of it, rolling miles of cold arctic tundra eventually giving way to dense forest. Yes, he'd definitely assumed there'd be forests. Dour men in army greatcoats and fur hats too, stamping their feet against the cold and looking forward to a warming tot of vodka. Maybe even the distant howl of wolves. But Domodedovo looked reassuring similar to any other European airport he'd ever touched down in. As well as lacking snow, Moscow had to be a good 10 degrees warmer than the chilly London morning he'd left five hours before.

Svetlana was already halfway down the small set of steps hurriedly placed alongside Bukin's little jet by a pair of nervous-looking airport workers. The reputation of its owner clearly went before him. Behind him Dermot heard Yegor cough.

Much too close behind.

He started down the steps. He'd been jollying himself along throughout most of the flight by humming 'Back in the USSR.' Yes, he knew the country wasn't called that anymore. It hadn't even been called that back in 1995 on his only other visit. That had been at the arse end of the NewBoyz's first European tour, with everyone tired and desperate for home. It hadn't stopped him trying to persuade his fellow band members to deviate from their on-stage routine with a cheeky cover version of the Beatles classic. Nobody else had been at all keen and dark mutterings from their stage manager about the trickiness of the harmonies had been enough to put the idea down humanely.

Back then the band had been cheered by a small crowd of teenage girls who'd gathered at the airport to shriek and throw underwear. As ever, Robbie BASTARD Gray had proved the most popular target. Even in far-flung Moscow they had him pegged early on as the big star. But then what had the Russians ever known about music? Quite a lot if his former band mate's success was anything to go by, but then their original Eurovision entry had been a man who used to dance with a bear.

Years later Dermot had found out that the crowd of girls at the airport had been a put-up job by the NewBoyz's Russian record label in a last attempt to bolster lower than anticipated ticket sales. It had been just one of the surprisingly tame revelations in *NewBoyz Confidential*, a snippy little book written by Jerry, their former manager. Promising to lift the lid on one of the biggest boy bands of the nineties, it had focused almost entirely on Robbie Gray: a transparent and only moderately successful attempt to milk the fame of the international megastar. Dermot had come across as little more than a bit-part player. There'd certainly been no mention of him singing lead vocals on three Number 1s. Just the odd name-check or photo caption and the hurtful conclusion on page 96 (oh yes, Jerry; Dermot remembered) that he'd sometimes been 'a bit of a tool'.

He reached the bottom of the stairs and stepped onto Russian soil. No girls and no flying underwear this time. Just a large woman with a clipboard approaching across the tarmac. She wore an overly tight blue uniform, a disapproving scowl and looked like she might have had minor success on the European shot-put circuit sometime around the mid-eighties.

'Welcome to Russia, Mr Jack.' The words didn't come from the sour-faced woman but from Yegor behind.

It sounded more of a threat than a welcome and again Dermot thought back to those little jibes he'd made about the man's height before he'd known quite how dangerous he was. Surely Yegor must know he hadn't really meant anything by them.

Ahead the shot putter was already talking to Svetlana in Russian, breaking into something that may even have been a smile. Then she turned and headed back across the tarmac, beckoning them to follow her.

Dermot kept a few paces behind Svetlana, fighting the gnawing sense of unease and the temptation to look back at Yegor. Remembering the drill, he pulled his phone out, tapping in the innocuous little message that would tell Anna that he'd arrived and everything was OK.

For now.

And it was, wasn't it? He hadn't been drugged and handcuffed to a radiator in a basement. And it didn't look like Yegor was planning to hit him over the head with an old Red Army pistol and bury him in the dense, dark forest that he knew would be out there somewhere.

Less than five minutes later they were outside the terminal building, without having been troubled by customs or passport control. Bukin's cash and connections were clearly enough to smooth their way into the country.

Dermot told the bad feelings where to go as the biggest, blackest limo he'd ever seen purred its way to a stop in front of them and sat gleaming in the sunshine. He thought instead about one of his little dance routines. Maybe the Latino number from the video of 'Gotcha Girl'? Or even the full-on disco moves of 'All Night Party'? Instead he settled for a friendly wave at the airport woman as he relaxed into the soft leather of the back seat beside Svetlana.

Yegor hopped into the front and the car purred silently away, the driver calmly negotiating his way past the taxi rank, the passenger-drop-off point and car-hire offices with their familiar brands and colours. Only the unfamiliar letters of the words on the signs confirmed that they were actually in Russia.

'The journey should take about an hour, Mr Jack.' Yegor turned from the front seat with an insincere smile. 'Make yourself comfortable.'

That was kind of him; an offer of a drink would have been kinder though. A car like this had to have some sort of minibar. But then Yegor hardly looked the type for a couple of afternoon looseners.

They headed down a slip road onto a busy three-lane motorway but turned off again after a few minutes onto a far quieter single-track road. And soon enough Dermot got his forests. Miles and miles of them on either side of the long straight road, the trees seeming to edge in closer the further they went; denser and a lot darker than he'd ever imagined.

And suddenly the whole fragile façade of confidence he'd worked so hard to build was slipping away as he thought about everything Anna had told him about Oleg Bukin. However tightly packed the trees were there'd be plenty of room for shallow graves. The hard, semi-frozen soil would make it impossible to dig too deep and eventually the wolves would get at the bones. But the forest was so vast and so dark that it was unlikely anyone would ever find them.

But all in all it was a bit late for those kinds of worries now. So he closed his eyes and did his best to think of the few positives he could find.

It had all seemed so simple the evening before outside the cosy pub beside the river in Putney. The early-evening sunshine had warmed the terrace, cooking smells had drifted from the kitchen and a group of children around Molly's age had played noisily on the lawn.

With appearances to be maintained he'd left Svetlana at the Chelsea house with Yegor, along with a promise to meet them there at six thirty the next morning to go to the airport; a promise he'd been far from sure of keeping at that point. Once Dmitri had been deposited at a safe house and Anna had phoned in with an update for her thin boss she'd surprised him by suggesting they go to the pub.

'Much safer than HQ. Never know who might be listening. It's full of spies.'

Hardly reassuring.

'Joking.' She must have seen the expression on his face. 'You just looked like you could do with a drink.'

Difficult to argue with that.

'It's a big ask but I know you can do this.' She'd looked him straight in the eye and then sat back with an encouraging smile as she'd raised her glass of wine. It was the same smile she'd used all those years ago to pack him off to the first NewBoyz audition, right at the point when he'd been about to chicken out.

And now she was using the same multipurpose smile to send him to Russia to trap a dangerous international criminal. But he'd been over all that in his own head again and... 'It's fine. I'll do it.' There weren't really any other options.

She'd smiled again. 'I knew you would.'

'Had she?' He'd only decided for sure just then.

But then going to Russia to persuade Bukin seemed a lot less dangerous than fronting up to a gun-toting hitman with a sore head and a serious attitude problem. And Dermot felt he'd managed that one well enough. All he had to do was lay the plan out then leave Svetlana to wrap her stepfather round her little finger.

Later, on the pavement outside the pub, Anna and he had stood awkwardly for a second or two, neither knowing quite how to say goodbye.

'Well, it's been quite a day?' She'd finally broken the silence.

Yep. She could certainly say that. Sacked by Marcus, rescued from (near) death by a long-lost teenage squeeze before talking a girl into entering the Eurovision Song Contest to trap her wicked stepfather.

Oh and then agreeing to go to Russia.

'So I'll see you when I'm back.' He'd done his best to keep it light and breezy.

She'd nodded then stretched up to give him a little kiss on the cheek. 'Be careful, OK.' Then she'd turned and walked off with a glance back, soon lost in the crowds enjoying the evening sunshine.

'So what do you think of our country, Mr Jack?' Yegor Koslov smiled from the front seat as the long miles of dark trees sped by outside.

'There's a lot of forest.'

Yegor nodded like a man who knew how to put a shovel and a patch of woodland to good use. He'd said nothing so far to suggest he didn't believe Dermot's account of events. But then he didn't have to. The look on his face had made clear he wasn't buying any of it. What did that matter though, as long as Bukin went along with the plan?

'If I ask him he will say yes.' Svetlana had been very clear on that.

Dermot stole a look across at her but she was staring out of the window. Back in London the night before she'd quickly got over all that gasping as Yegor revealed the plan. Then she'd turned to Dermot with the smallest of nods, determination and something else that might have been hate shining in her cold dark eyes. Perhaps there was more of Oleg Bukin in her than she'd like to admit.

He turned to stare out of his own window as more miles of forest rolled on by, trying not to think about shallow graves, wolves or that knowing little smile that kept finding its way onto Yegor Koslov's face.

Chapter 35

Yegor rubbed the bruise on the back of his head and tried to relax. Swearing was one of the many things he had always viewed as a weakness in others. It showed a certain lack of emotional control. But quite frankly there were a few things that were fucking bothering him right now.

The feeling had been growing ever since they'd boarded Bukin's jet back in London. How many times had he used it to return to his master's side after the completion of a job? Usually the plane was a haven of peace and calm where he could reflect on the success of another tricky assignment.

Not today.

The Englishman had spent the flight pretending that he was all calm and confident. First humming and tapping some inane tune that sounded a bit like 'Back in the USSR', then pretending to sleep.

Pathetic.

Svetlana had occupied herself by listening to music through a pair of headphones. She'd mouthed the words silently, practicing the lyrics to the song Dermot had given her for Eurovision, no doubt. He'd proudly played it for the two of them, right after he'd laid out the full details of his ridiculous little plan.

A devotee of Russian death metal in his youth, Yegor knew he was hardly in a position to judge, but even so he was pretty sure the song was shit. That said, he'd caught himself humming it on the way to the airport that morning.

He was in no mood for humming now. The nagging feeling had persisted throughout the flight and kept on at him all through the drive to Bukin's home.

Surely he should have been more than happy at the turn of events? This was the return to Russia and the place back at his master's side that he'd craved throughout his long weeks of exile.

He faked a smile as he turned and caught Dermot's eye. If Bukin said yes to the Englishman's plan Yegor would almost certainly have to turn straight round and head back to London to keep watch over

Svetlana again. But the damned singing contest was in less than three weeks and he could manage the situation if he was only away for a short time. No, that wasn't what was worrying him. A sharp stab of pain hit him behind the eyes and he turned to look forwards once again, hand on the back of his head as he waited for it to pass. The pain had been coming on and off since yesterday's incident with the car, making it hard to think straight.

Clarity finally arrived as the agony subsided. His head spun and he was glad to be sitting down. On balance he'd have preferred the pain. It wasn't Bukin saying yes to Dermot's plan that bothered him; it was what might happen if he said no. And all the things that might then be revealed.

The next time the pain came he was ready for it, controlling it, channelling it until he knew exactly what he had to do.

The car sped on through the forest. Bukin's home was close now.

And when they got there Yegor would be ready. He'd seen Dermot looking nervously at the deep, dark forests. Perhaps the Englishman had already realised that there were plenty of places out there where a body would never be found.

Chapter 36

They finally turned off the long straight road onto a smaller one and drove on for a couple more miles. Dermot tried again to fight off those bad feelings as the driver slowed to a stop in front of a gate.

For most self-respecting countries it would have served as a more than adequate border checkpoint with a small but quarrelsome neighbour.

For Oleg Bukin it was a front gate.

A squat concrete building that looked capable of surviving several nuclear strikes lurked next to the gate, while a fence, at least 10 feet high and topped with evil rolls of razor wire, stretched away into the trees on either side.

Eight uniformed men hurried to surround the car. Six of them carried the kind of guns that would have made the SAS feel they'd come to a gunfight with a small spoon. The other two guards struggled to control the huge black dogs that snarled and pulled on their leashes. Someone had clearly decided to see what would happen if you crossed a wolf with a bear. The results of the experiment were currently spraying industrial quantities of spittle over the car windows.

Yegor reached for the door handle.

Was he mad?

The Russian pushed the door open and hopped out. Dermot certainly wouldn't be following unless someone dragged him out by the eye sockets.

The one consolation was that one of the dogs might try to eat Yegor. He was certainly small enough for either of them to get down in a couple of bites. Instead the two beasts just lay on the ground and rolled onto their backs, letting Yegor rub their bellies and ruffle their ears. He stroked and patted them for a couple of minutes before straightening up and exchanging a few words with the men. Handshakes and a good deal of back-slapping followed. But even from inside the car the tension of the atmosphere was clear. Yegor was a lot less popular with the human guards than he was with the dogs. Each of the men topped Yegor by a head and most of a neck too, yet all seemed watchful and wary in the little man's company.

'Great animals once you get to know them.' Yegor's smile seemed almost genuine as he climbed back into the car. 'There are eight of them in all. Mr Bukin bred them himself. We let them loose after dark to patrol the grounds. They don't get fed much in the daytime, so it's best not to go out of the house at night.'

The gate swung smoothly open and the car slid through before picking up speed. Seconds later the fence and the guards and the dogs were behind a bend and then they were out of the trees and Bukin's house was in front of them. Quite a long way in front of them. The forest had been cut back for about a mile in each direction, replaced by wide flat lawns. In the middle sat the 'house,' although 'palace' might have suited it better.

'Built for Count Constantin Romanov, a cousin of Aleksandr III, the second-last tsar.' For some reason Yegor had decided to turn tour guide.

The palace ahead of them was a yellow and white monstrosity of a thing, all columns and ornate statues, topped off with a big gold dome.

The car skirted a round pond with an overly ornate fountain covered in cherubs at its centre, then stopped at the bottom of a wide flight of stairs that swept up to the front door.

'Mr Bukin is very proud of his home and is looking forward to offering you his hospitality.' Yegor's voice couldn't have sounded less welcoming. He jumped out and ran round to open Svetlana's door. But she was already out of the car before he got there. Dermot gave a last check round for dogs before climbing out and following the two Russians up the steps.

Inside was just a rerun of Bukin's Chelsea home, except on a far grander scale. Same sort of pictures in their elaborate frames and the same deep carpet. Maybe he'd just used the offcuts for London. A butler type fussed over Svetlana before turning to take Dermot's coat. And then Yegor was leading them across the entrance hall and pushing on a huge set of double doors.

The room beyond was so vast that Dermot thought at first they'd stepped back outside. But no, it was just simply the largest room he'd ever seen. A row of giant windows ran down one wall while more pictures lined the others. The high arched ceiling was dominated by a huge painting, but given its altitude it was hard to make out the details.

'The ballroom. It is one of the largest in all Russia.'

Yegor wasn't kidding; you could have held a medium-sized rock concert here and still had room for a couple of football matches on the side. Right now, the room was completely empty apart from the man dressed in black on the white sofa watching the huge screen on the wall, which looked about half a mile away.

The little Russian was already moving off that way. Dermot caught Svetlana's eye, thinking about a reassuring wink. She was the one who needed to do the persuading after all. But she just stared back with those cold, hard eyes and gave him a slow nod, then headed after Yegor. Dermot followed, his mouth dry as he tried to remember all the words he planned to say. Maybe it was him, rather than Svetlana, who needed the reassurance.

'*You can do this. I know you can.*' Anna's smile came back to him and he quickened the pace. She worked for MI5. If she thought he could do it then yes, actually, he could.

He wondered what she was doing now. Wouldn't it be harder for her, waiting in London, checking her phone for the news?

No, probably not.

They were about halfway across the room now, the faint strains of *The Meal of Fortune* theme tune sounding thin and tinny in the vast space.

Then Bukin was standing and turning, something small and black in his hand.

Shit... How did he know? There was nowhere to hide in the empty room.

Bukin pointed the remote control at the TV. The image on the screen froze.

Dermot breathed again.

'Mr Jack, welcome to my home.' His voice was more like thunder than ever, as it rumbled round the walls of the huge room.

He put on his best smile and pushed all those doubts as far to the back of his mind as he could.

Chapter 37

Oleg Bukin sat back on the sofa and let rip, his fat belly laugh bouncing off the distant walls. Dermot shifted on the edge of the sofa beside him and breathed again.

Bukin paused to take a breath of his own before launching another barrage of deep guffaws.

Laughter. That had to be good, didn't it?

Dermot had run over the plan, keeping it simple and succinct. If anything it hadn't sounded quite so ridiculous this time.

Svetlana sat nodding eagerly, leaning forward in her chair and catching his eye to let him know it was her turn now. Yegor was in the chair opposite, his expression hard to read. But Marcus Diesel seemed delighted about the whole thing. The chef couldn't stop smiling; the pause button on the TV remote had stopped him midway through his trademark manic grin as he juggled three wooden spoons.

A tosser in far more ways than one.

'So Sergei Symenov was chosen to represent Russia in your Eurovision Singing Contest?' Bukin spoke through his laughter. 'That bear… When he had that bear he was funny. It was the worst dancing bear ever. But afterwards…' He shook his head, a faraway look in his eyes. 'Not everything is better in Russia since we got rid of the communists.' His face almost wistful now. 'They should never have taken the bear away from him.'

Dermot shook his head at this example of political correctness winning out over tradition, wondering when the Russian might get round to the business in hand.

Bukin obliged. Leaning forward, he grabbed the remote and banished the frozen Marcus Diesel from the screen. 'And now that Sergei has lost the chance, you want me to use my influence to help Svetlana take his place.'

'It will be great for her career.'

Now was the time for Svetlana to make big with the eyes and the daddy's-girl smile. Right on cue she rose from her chair and made her way over, signalling to Dermot to budge up so she could squeeze in next to Bukin.

Dermot budged.

'Papa—' Svetlana sat.

Bukin cut across her with a torrent of Russian, his tone hard and cruel. Svetlana reared backwards as if she'd been slapped and tried to speak. But again he cut her off. Then she stood, staring down at him, big fat tears rolling down her cheeks.

What the…

Then she turned and ran away, her sobbing echoing all around the room.

Two pairs of Russian eyes turned to rest on Dermot as the sound of Svetlana's crying faded away across the vast room.

How much did they know? Anna? MI5? The lot?

Svetlana had been sent away to spare her the horrors to come. Dermot looked back across the room as she finally reached the door and closed it behind her. Yegor leaned forward with another of his little smiles. There was no way he could escape and even if he did manage to get out there were those men with the guns and the dogs to think about.

Bukin stared at him, blinked once and began. 'Many men find it hard to say no to my daughter. As her father I find it particularly hard. This is why I let her go to your country to pursue her dream even though I was reluctant.'

OK… The words seemed calm and measured enough, not like those of a man who'd just caught someone he thought he trusted in cahoots with a foreign security service. Dermot breathed deeply and tried to relax.

'Of course she is not my real daughter; you may or may not know that. But I have brought her up as my own and that makes the bond between us even stronger than blood.'

Evidently he hadn't heard Svetlana's views on the subject recently.

'That makes it even harder for me to say no to her. But I can say no to you, Mr Jack. I admire you of course for what you've done with Marcus Diesel, but you are hardly a man to be trusted, given the world you operate in.'

Pot? Kettle? Not that Dermot was about to point that out. And then he was selling the man out to MI5.

'So I want you to tell me why I should do this. Without the help of my daughter's powers of persuasion – which I think you were hoping to use, yes?'

Got it in one. But this sort of thing was home territory to Dermot and he was well prepared. 'The music industry is more competitive than it has ever been—'

'You mean you have struggled to get the record deal you promised?'

'No, I, er.' He couldn't actually remember any specific promise. 'It's just that this would be the perfect way to—'

'You Westerners.' Bukin cut him off again, shaking his head as he climbed to his feet. 'You think we are just greedy oligarchs. That we bribe our way to everything we want?'

Pretty much, yeah.

'So you come here and ask me to use my money to bribe my countrymen because that's the way you think we do things.' Bukin's voice was still calm and level enough. 'Look around you. Look how the world is changing. We are not some oppressed nation, backward and rife with corruption. Moscow has more millionaires than New York or London. More billionaires than both together. We own your hotels, your businesses and your football clubs. Your beautiful women throw themselves at the feet of our sons and we can cut off your gas with just one turn of the tap.'

A lecture on current affairs was about the last thing Dermot had been expecting from a Russian gangster.

'And you think that this is the way I should teach my daughter to behave in life?'

Or on parenting.

'I wanted you to help Svetlana use her own talent, just as I have done myself and just as your Marcus Diesel has too.'

Was arms dealing strictly a talent? And as for Marcus...

'But you just want me to buy success for her.' His voice was less even now as the scar on his cheek turned a deep shade of purple. 'You want to take advantage of some poor man who has had an accident. I could have done that without your help, Mr Jack. I'd even have organised the accident.'

If only he knew.

'And, yes, we have made great strides but corruption is everywhere in our country, even today. I have no doubt that I could arrange this with just one phone call.' Bukin shook his head and turned away. 'But I expected a little more of you, Mr Jack. You have insulted Russia and you have insulted me.'

'No, you don't understand. I have a daughter too. I'd do anything to help her.'

'I understand, and I am a man of the world.' Bukin's tone softened, but only a little and his scar was still a dangerous colour. 'Like you, I know how hard it can be for young people to succeed today, especially in show business. I know that you have to use every advantage – every trick in the book, as you would say. That's why I want to consider what you have said more carefully. You will have my answer in an hour. Yegor will show you to your room.' He turned away and reached for the remote control. On screen Marcus Diesel reappeared. The wooden spoons he'd been juggling went flying across the studio and he leaped back, launching into a quick-fire gag about radishes that had the audience and Oleg Bukin in stitches.

Dermot stood up slowly. At least it wasn't a no, not yet. Bukin had said he'd give it more thought. Although to be honest it looked more like he was just sitting on his fat arse watching telly.

The big man wiped the tears of laughter from his eyes and looked round, surprised that Dermot was still there. 'You will have my answer soon. Now please try to make yourself comfortable.'

No invitation to join him for some telly this time.

The anger began to rise inside as he felt a hand on his shoulder. Yegor moved in behind and gently eased back across the massive ballroom towards the door.

Those MI5 bastards had known it might have come to this. They'd damned well known and they'd sent him anyway.

Anna had sent him.

He took one long last look behind him. On screen Marcus Diesel gave another lunatic grin as they cut to the adverts. *'I'll be back soon.'*

Dermot wasn't sure he could say the same about himself.

Chapter 38

Landed safely.

The simple text had arrived soon after Dermot was scheduled to touch down in Russia. That alone should have meant there was nothing for Anna to worry about. But it had been four hours now since the message and they'd heard nothing more.

'Any news?'

Anna jumped as Kate Barnes perched herself on the edge of the desk; just another friendly colleague stopping for a natter.

As if...

'Shouldn't we have heard something by now?'

It felt more like a playground taunt than a question.

'It's only been a few hours.' Anna heard the edge in her own voice. 'It will have taken a while to get to Bukin's place.'

'Yes...' Kate left it hanging.

Anna forced herself not to rise to it. But her boss did have a point. The drive to Bukin's house shouldn't have taken more than an hour. And if Svetlana was right about her powers of persuasion the answer would have come pretty swiftly. Perhaps they were just celebrating with a few shots of Bukin's best vodka. Anna tried to ignore the sick feeling rising in her stomach as she looked back at her computer screen, wishing the bloody woman would just go away. Once again Kate had been against continuing with the operation after the news that Dermot was expected to travel to Moscow. But Lawson had figured that if Dermot Jack wanted to get on a plane to Russia there was precious little they could do to stop him. And precious little to lose as well, if things did go wrong. Because who was ever going to believe... Well, the Eurovision Song Contest? That wasn't the sort of thing MI5 would ever get involved with, was it?

'You know, I had my doubts about you before this.' Kate brought out a poorly timed smile.

It was all Anna could do to fight back an obvious sigh. Did her boss think she was helping things now?

'I didn't think you were ruthless enough.' She shifted her bony arse on the desk and stared down over her chunky glasses.

Anna tried to look her in the eye but could only focus on the glasses. Kate had taken to wearing them recently, probably in the mistaken belief that they lent her the right combination of gravitas and style. In truth, they just made her ferrety face look even thinner.

'But I was wrong, wasn't I?'

Was that a compliment? Anna felt a twinge of guilt over her bitchy take on her boss's taste in eyewear.

'You *have* got what it takes. Sending a man off to almost certain death. Now that takes guts. And they say that I'm the bitch.'

She was right about the last part. Anna fought back the impulse to grab the stupid glasses and grind them into the floor with her foot.

Kate slipped off the desk with another little smile. 'It's all about making the tough decisions. I'm sure your father would have been proud of you. But I do think we should have heard something by now, don't you?' Kate turned and walked slowly across the office.

Chapter 39

'Make yourself comfortable.' Bukin's very words. Well, the huge guest bedroom certainly provided plenty of opportunities. The four-poster bed looked just the place to kick off his shoes and take a nap, while there were plenty of cupboards in which an industrial-sized drinks cabinet could be lurking.

But if Bukin thought Dermot was just going to waste the hour snoozing or getting pissed he had another think coming. Because without Svetlana's powers of persuasion the Russian would say no to the plan. And then Yegor would be despatched to kill him. Dermot was sure of that now. How could he have been so stupid? Cocky too. Thinking he could just bowl up here and talk the Russian into falling for MI5's little scheme.

Fuck, fuck, fuck.

He stalked around the room, wondering about sending another text.

'Weather here not so good.'

It was the coded message that would tell Anna that Bukin had said no to the plan but that he didn't know about MI5's involvement. But then how was that going to help? Anna had made it clear that he'd be on his own out here. You didn't go telling the Russian intelligence service that you were running an op like this on their soil, so a backup team was out of the question in a country that was still listed as 'friendly'.

There'd be no men in black boiler suits and gas masks abseiling down from swiftly despatched assault helicopters. No windows kicked in or smoke grenades lobbed as a reassuringly authoritative voice told Dermot to hit the deck so they could strafe the building with automatic-weapons fire.

If he was going to get out of this he was going to have to do it himself.

Surely all he needed to do was get out of the house, scoot across the lawn and find a way through the forest and over the fence. Then back to the long straight and flag down a passing car.

Well that would be easy then.

But it had to be better than sitting round here waiting for Yegor to come and kill him. At least the dogs weren't let out until after dark and there had to be a good couple of hours of daylight left.

It would have to be now though. But somehow Dermot had found himself perching on the edge of the bed. He pushed himself to his feet and made for the bedroom door, trying not to think how much his legs were shaking. All he had to do was open it, walk straight through the house and out the front door. Bukin would be too busy watching TV and as long as he managed to avoid Koslov he'd be in the clear. There hadn't been much evidence of other security within the house.

He took a last deep breath and reached for the handle. Then he stopped and listened. What if they'd put a guard outside? And what if it was Yegor himself? The element of surprise was his only advantage and it would be lost.

Dermot turned and ran back past the bed to the four big windows that looked out on the wide lawn. But there seemed no apparent way of getting them to open. Sensible for those long Russian winters no doubt but not quite so handy for a stroll on the lawn or a quick escape. A bang on the glass with first his fist and then a very expensive-looking antique chair made it clear that smashing his way out wasn't an option.

The bathroom then?

He headed through the door and pulled himself up to the little window, not bothering about the tell-tale black marks his shoes were making around the top of the bath. The open window would be enough of a giveaway. And at least this one looked like it was supposed to open.

'Come on.' He undid the latch open and shoved outwards.

Nothing.

Why the fuck wouldn't it move? He banged with his fist, once, twice, three times. Then he noticed the small line of nail heads covered over with white paint.

Jesus.

It would have to be the bedroom door after all. He'd have a decent enough head start as long as they didn't realise he was gone until the hour was up. Dermot forced himself to move; down from the edge of the bath, back into the bedroom and across the thick carpet towards the bedroom door.

The hardest thing, the very hardest thing would be opening the door and stepping out into the corridor.

Breathe, breathe, breathe.

He tried not to think about Bukin, or that look of fear on Yegor's face back in London. *'We're both dead men.'*

If MI5 were to be believed Yegor was a hitman: ruthless, unprincipled and fearless. And he was scared shitless of his boss. How was Dermot supposed to feel?

He reached for the door handle, watching his hand shake as it moved. Hand on the cold metal. All he had to do was...

Then he stopped.

Someone was already turning the handle from the other side. Inching it round bit by bit in exactly the way you'd turn a handle if you didn't want the person in the room to know you were there.

He backed away slowly, thinking about the relative safety that locking himself in the bathroom might bring.

Next he heard a soft click and door started to nudge open. He ran the last few steps to the bathroom, shutting the door behind him and reached for the...

Oh, for fuck's sake. What was it with these Russians? Happy enough to nail the windows shuts but when it came to putting a lock on the bathroom door... Hot bile rose in his stomach at the thought of the faint smile that would be playing on Yegor's lips as he made his way quietly across the room. Bukin must have made his decision early, probably during the first ad break of *The Meal of Fortune*. The little hitman had been despatched to carry out his orders.

Dermot put his ear to the door but there was no sound from the bedroom. There was someone there though; he knew it. And he was certain now that it would be Yegor. Most likely he'd be armed, too. A gun, drawn and sitting snugly in his hand. Or perhaps a knife? But then there were those thick carpets to think about. Bugger to get the blood out of. Blunt instrument then, maybe, or a small syringe loaded with the lethal toxin of some South American tree frog? Then again Yegor may not need a weapon. A man like him would know at least half a dozen ways of killing with his bare hands.

Dermot held his breath and strained to listen for the tell-tale sound of footsteps advancing stealthily across the room. But the sound, when it finally came, was just the other side of the door; someone letting out a long slow breath after doing their own bit of listening.

Then the handle started to turn.

Slowly, steadily and sneakily.

And suddenly Dermot wasn't having it anymore. If anyone was going to be opening the bathroom door and going on the attack it was going to be him.

He grabbed the closest weapon to hand and yanked hard on the door handle.

With only a bath towel as a weapon the element of surprise was going to have to be a bloody big leveller.

But so it proved.

Over Yegor's head the towel went, causing just the right amount of blindness and disorientation. Dermot followed up by spinning the hitman round. The more tangled up he was the better and a spot of dizziness would hardly go amiss. Then Dermot could give him a kick in the bollocks and make a run for it. He carried on wrapping his new weapon round and round. Inside the towel Yegor gave a high-pitched squeal. He sounded a bit like a girl.

Dermot twisted him round again. Come to think of it, the hitman even had legs like a girl too and…

He let go and took a step back, watching as Svetlana battled her way free of the towel.

'I'm sorry; I thought you were Yegor. We've got to get out of here.' Maybe she'd know a better way out than the front door. 'Come on…' He stopped.

The gun in Svetlana's hand had a long tube on the end that he could only assume was a silencer. It was pointing straight at his head.

'It's OK. It's me.' He raised his hands to show he had no more towels or other deadly bathroom accessories. 'Your father's not going to agree to the plan. We need to get out of here.'

For some reason Svetlana was still pointing the gun at him.

'I'm sorry, Dermot.' When she finally spoke her voice was hard. 'You know about Dmitri: you'll tell my stepfather.'

'Of course I won't.' He felt something churn in his guts as he tried to back away.

'You say that now but when he comes to kill you, you'll tell him anything to save your own sorry life.' The tears were rolling down Svetlana's cheeks now. 'Please, you must understand. I am doing this for Dmitri.'

That really wasn't much of a consolation.

Her hand was shaking but the gun was still aimed at his head.

'He might still agree to the plan.'

'You just said yourself he would not.' She took a step backwards but kept the gun pointing at his head. 'Let me tell you a story about Oleg Bukin. It was my tenth birthday. As usual he had bought me lots of presents. I never wanted anything from him but I had seen this beautiful watch. I was just a child and I wanted it so badly.'

Dermot nodded encouragingly, keeping his eyes on the gun. The longer he kept her talking the longer he'd stay alive.

'I opened all my presents but saved the one I hoped was the watch until the very end. Inside I found this.' She waved the neat little gun in her hand. 'He gave a 10-year-old girl a gun. That's what kind of man my stepfather is. He said to me, "We must all learn to protect ourselves. When you can use the gun I will give you the watch." I learned to use the gun. Hours and hours of practice; he made me. I never wore the watch when he finally bought it for me. But now at least I can use the gun to protect myself. And Dmitri.'

'By shooting me?' Dermot prepared to move, wishing he hadn't been so quick to drop the towel as he tried to work out the distance between him and the gun.

'I have to. I'm sorry.'

'No please—' He was already moving when he heard the sharp crack of the gunshot. Dermot closed his eyes and waited for the pain.

When he opened them again Svetlana was still standing there but the gun was pointing at the ground now.

And he wasn't dead either. Or even injured.

The sharp crack came again; it was a knock on the door, not a shot.

'Dermot, can I come in?'

This time it was Yegor Koslov. At least he'd been polite enough to knock. Maybe it was good news.

'Please, you must help me,' Svetlana was pale and shaking now.

Hadn't she been just about to shoot him?

'My stepfather will think there is something going on if he finds me in your bedroom. He'll kill us both.'

'You were going to kill me anyway. I'll still be just as dead.'

'Please.'

'Dermot?' Yegor rapped again. 'Why is the door locked?'

'Hang on.'

'I, er, locked it.' Svetlana looked down at the gun in her hand.

'So you could kill me undisturbed?'

'I was going to make it look like suicide.'

'With a silencer?' Even Dermot thought this sounded unlikely.

'Well, I... Just help me. Please.'

'Dermot. I do have a key.'

'Just a minute, Yegor.' He scanned round the room. It wouldn't look good for him either if Svetlana was found in his room. 'Quickly: in here.' He lowered his voice to a whisper and pointed at the bathroom.

But Svetlana was already dropping to the floor and rolling under the bed. Probably a better hiding place all in all.

'Coming.'

But the key was already turning in the lock. The door swung open and Yegor Koslov strode into the room. The gun in his hand was bigger and uglier than Svetlana's neat little weapon, its silencer far longer.

But that's where the differences ended. It too was pointed directly at Dermot's head.

Chapter 40

Yegor let the door shut behind him. All the time keeping his gun on Dermot. 'I'm sorry, I truly am.'

Wasn't that what Svetlana had just said? He had a lot more trouble believing it from the hitman. 'Bukin's made his decision then?' He looked over his shoulder, knowing the bathroom was out of reach. Not that the door would provide much protection against the heavy artillery in Yegor's hand.

Just for a second the Russian looked confused. But then he smiled. 'He'd made his decision before you left the room. You failed him and you insulted him. People who do that tend to die.'

Dermot tried to ignore the pounding in his head and the slippery feeling in his bowels as once again he tried to judge the distance between himself and the barrel of a gun.

'Of course, he likes to have his fun first.' Yegor took another step into the room.

Dermot fought the temptation to back away. Maybe, just maybe, the hitman would come a little closer then he'd have a chance. He looked over at the bed, thinking that now would have been a good time for Svetlana to come out with her gun blazing.

But then why should she? Yegor was going to kill him. She was about to get exactly what she wanted without getting blood on her hands.

'Right now, he's keeping you waiting. He likes to do that. Then it will be time for the big speech. "I'm a reasonable man etc., etc., etc."' The hitman gave his shoulders a theatrical shrug. '"But you have let me down. You have left me with no choice."' His imitation of Bukin was uncannily good. 'He likes his speeches, but not as much as his torture. You'll say anything at the end to save your life or end it without more pain. And I can't allow that. If you tell him what happened in London, I'm a dead man. It is nothing personal but I have to kill you first.' Yegor took another step forward then stopped, his eyes darting around the room as a faint rustle came from under the bed.

Maybe it was time to fess up about Svetlana, cause enough of a distraction so he could escape. But having one of the two people who wanted him dead safely tucked under the bed improved his odds, however marginally.

Yegor shook his head, clearly deciding he'd imagined the noise. Then he stepped forward again. The gap was down to about three feet now; close enough for Dermot to make a lunge for the gun. He tensed, ready to spring, and then stopped himself. Yegor wasn't going to fall for that. But he knew he had to do something, say something. And fast.

'Please, I've got a daughter.' It was all he could think of. 'She's eight and—'

'A lot of men have daughters. It makes no difference.'

But just for a second he thought he saw something in Yegor's eyes that suggested that it did.

'I have worked hard to get where I am. I cannot allow anything to get in my way.' He moved quickly to cross the gap before Dermot could react and jabbed the gun hard into his ribs as he pushed him towards the bed.

Dermot tried to stand his ground but Yegor pushed him back until he could feel the edge of the bed against the back of his legs.

'Lie down. Mr Bukin will be upset if he knows I have killed you before he's had his sport. It must look like the suicide of a man who knows his plan has failed.'

Yegor had clearly thought out the whole suicide bit better than Svetlana but there was still one flaw.

'Make me.'

'You're forgetting I'm the one with the gun. I could just shoot you now.'

'Then it wouldn't look like suicide.'

'You're going to end up dead whatever happens.' Yegor sighed. 'It'll be so much easier this way.'

'Easier for you maybe.' The longer he stayed off the bed the longer he stayed alive. 'And you wouldn't want it to look like there's been a struggle.' The vase on the bedside table was a nasty shade of green but probably cost more than Dermot had earned in the past decade. He reached out and knocked it over.

The vase teetered for a second before gravity took over and it fell to the floor, bouncing a couple of times before nestling undamaged into the soft carpet.

'So much for the struggle.' Yegor shook his head. Then he shot out a hand and shoved Dermot onto the bed, jabbing the gun into his chest. 'It will look like suicide.'

'Not if you shoot me in the chest.'

'True.' Yegor leaped on top of Dermot, getting a knee on his chest and pressing the gun against his temple. 'That's why you are going to shoot yourself in the head.'

Dermot thrashed and twisted on the bed, grabbing at the Russian's arm, somehow managing to twist it so the gun was pointing past his ear.

'Where will you say I got the gun?'

'Fuck, I don't know.' Yegor let out a grunt as he slowly started to force the barrel back towards Dermot's head.

'You'll need to think of something.' The longer he could keep Yegor talking...

'Just shut up and let me shoot you.'

'There's something I need to tell you.' He kept on pushing but could feel the gun slowly turning. 'It's about Svetlana.' Maybe if she believed he was about to give away her secret, she'd come out from under the bed and she and Yegor would shoot each other.

'I'm not interested...' Yegor pushed harder, forcing his weapon back towards Dermot's temple.

'But she's...' He made one last attempt to push the gun away but Yegor was too strong. 'Please...' He didn't know whether he was talking to the hitman, Svetlana or both of them. 'She's...'

'I don't care.' The hitman grunted as he turned the barrel back against Dermot's temple.

'Please...'

'Mr Jack.'

Yegor leaped up from the bed like a frightened child as the sound of Bukin's voice rumbled through the door. It was followed up by a thumping knock.

'He cannot find me in here. He'll kill me for disobeying him.'

'Mr Jack.' The door shook as Bukin banged again. 'Who are you talking to?'

'I'm, er, just on the phone.' He turned back to Yegor. 'But you said he'll torture me.' Maybe he should just let the hitman kill him and be done with it.

'I'll stop him if you promise to keep quiet. Deal?'

'Deal.' What did he have to lose? Dermot climbed to his feet.

'MISTER JACK.' This time the knock nearly took the door off its hinges.

'Hang on.'

Yegor slipped the gun into his jacket and crouched down ready to roll under the bed.

'No, in here.' Dermot stepped across to block the little Russian, guiding him towards the wardrobe instead.

'Coming.' He pushed Yegor inside and shut the door before hurrying over to let Bukin in.

The big arms dealer strode into the room.

'I have made my decision.'

The look in his eyes had already told Dermot all he needed to know. Just minutes ago there'd been one person in the room who wanted to kill him. Now there were three.

And he really didn't like to think what Bukin might be holding in the hand behind his back.

Chapter 41

Anna sat back in her chair, resisting the temptation to look at her phone again.

'*I think we should have heard something by now.*' The feeling had been building inside her ever since Kate had delivered her parting shot just over an hour ago. A gut-curdling churn that reminded you that your stomach did have a pit and it was not a particularly happy place.

It was that same feeling she'd felt all those years ago. Suddenly she was back there in the school gym that doubled as a dressing room. Five minutes to go till curtain on the school musical. Her dad at the back of the audience. Tension, excitement and last repetitions of lines filling the air all around her. But nothing in the world was going to make Anna go out on that stage.

No way. The thought was frankly inconceivable. Getting to her feet, taking even one step towards the stage?

Wasn't going to happen.

But then he was there, pulling her to her feet, hugging her, telling her she was the best and most beautiful. Telling her she could do it. Telling her that no, she didn't look fat in the dress. She'd fought back, of course, tears smudging her make-up. Telling him she wasn't doing it, not in front of all those people. All of them waiting for her to mess it up so they could laugh at her.

FOR THE REST OF HER LIFE.

So Dermot had started all over again, his voice soft but insistent.

Saying she was brilliant.

That she was beautiful.

And no, the dress DID NOT make her look fat.

That's she'd be fine. In fact, no: she'd be great.

It was only a silly school musical anyway. And hadn't they practised the lines and songs over and over again together? She wouldn't be able to get it wrong if she tried.

Then he'd straightened her wig and given her one of his smiles and told her that maybe it was time to sort out her make-up and get out there and show them.

And that's what they'd done.

When it was over everyone in the audience was on their feet, the clapping perhaps the loudest noise Anna had ever heard. The crowd (because it was a crowd now, not just an audience) parted for the tall figure striding up towards the stage. He hugged her and told her over and over again how proud he was.

She'd caught Dermot's eye then as he smiled and winked at her from the edge of the stage. He was the one who was brilliant. The one who'd always been there for her. That's why it had hurt so much when he'd gone.

The years all slipped back into place and Anna was back at her desk once more.

'*Any news?*' She could just see the look Kate would have on her face the next time she breezed past for an update.

Of course there wouldn't be any fucking news. He'd gone again and wouldn't be coming back.

And it was Anna who'd made him go.

She checked her phone once more for a message she knew now would never be coming.

Chapter 42

'I hope you have managed to make yourself comfortable.'

Dermot took a step back as Bukin bore down on him, trying not to look at the bed, from where there was a faint yet distinct rustling, or the wardrobe, which was emitting a series of strange creaks. He'd let them hide in his room; they could at least have the decency to keep quiet. But then maybe whisking Svetlana out, disarming her and holding the gun to her head was his only chance. With the prospect of bits of his adoptive daughter's brain all over his best guest bedroom Bukin would have to give in to Dermot's demands.

A helicopter, a big bag of cash and the private jet, all fuelled and ready to go at the airport. But if that was the best Plan A he had then he'd better keep thinking.

'I have thought long and hard about what you said to me.'

Yeah... About 40 minutes, to be precise – or an episode and a half of *The Meal of Fortune*. But this was clearly the big speech that Yegor had promised.

'My daughter is very precious to me. I trusted you to help her.'

Or maybe he should just run for it. With Yegor safely in the wardrobe all he needed to do was get past Bukin and he'd have a fighting chance of getting out of the house. He'd worry about the men with the dogs and the guns if he ever got that far.

Plan B was shaping up nicely.

'And now you come back to me with this scheme of yours.'

But Bukin was blocking enough of the doorway for that to be a non-starter.

'So I have considered it and—'

'Yegor's in the closet.' With any luck the little hitman would have no choice but to kick the door open and shoot his boss. Plan C was already shaping up nicely.

'Yes.' Bukin nodded thoughtfully. 'I have always wondered about him. But he is a useful man to have around. Live and let live, I say.'

'No, he really is—' Jesus, he was even pointing at the wardrobe. When exactly had they lowered the entry grades for criminal-master-mind school?

'Please, Mr Jack. I would have expected more tolerance from someone in show business. Whatever our president says about homo-sexuals there is no room for such prejudice in modern Russia. But I am not here to talk about little queers like Yegor.' Bukin took another step forward as he slowly brought his hand from behind his back.

Oh God.

'My daughter has tried so hard, sacrificed so much.'

It had to be now. For a third time Dermot got ready to spring forward at someone who was about to kill him.

'I am sorry Mr Jack…'

All three of them had been sorry but it hadn't stopped them. He shifted his weight forward and started to move.

'Sorry I ever doubted you.'

Eh? He just managed to stop himself springing at Bukin's throat.

'What father wouldn't do this thing when it is within his power? No wonder they call Marcus Diesel "the king of TV cookery" with a man like you behind him.'

Actually it was only Marcus who called himself that but Dermot was already too far into a quick mental salsa routine to care. 'You mean you'll pay the…' He stopped, remembering Bukin's earlier reaction to the word.

The Russian just laughed. 'If you mean bribe then say it. You're right, that is how things do work in Russia, even now. I was maybe a little oversensitive earlier. In this case, a bribe will not be necessary. My partner in the TV station has a cousin. That cousin stole money from another company belonging to me.' Bukin gave a weary shake of his head at such criminal behaviour. 'But I allowed him to live and now the whole family is in my debt. I have made the call and as joint owners we have agreed that my daughter, who is already in London forging a promising pop career, should step in to help Russia in her hour of need. It would be a stain on our country's honour if we were not represented at such a prestigious event as Eurovision.'

Then Bukin stepped forward and wrapped Dermot in one of his

massive bear hugs. When the Russian pulled away there were tears in his eyes. 'I want to give you this as a token of my thanks.'

The object he'd been holding behind his back turned out to be a paper bag. Bukin reached inside and pulled out an extremely old and ornate watch. Dermot didn't know what the sign for roubles was but he was fairly sure there was a pair of them in his eyes.

'It has only sentimental value of course. It belonged to my grandfather and does not even work anymore. But as long as you carry the watch you are under my protection.'

'Thank you.' Dermot reached out and took it. Right now he'd take protection over the cash.

'Yegor will be looking after you. I have decided to send him back to London with you and Svetlana until the competition. I am sure by now you have realised he is a little more than a translator.'

Yes you could say that.

'And next time I see you I will pay you too.'

'Next time?'

Bukin laughed, seeing the question in Dermot's eyes. 'Of course, in London. Russia did not even enter Eurovision under the communists and watching it was banned. But I always found a way. Did you know that since 2000 only the Swedes have had as many top-five finishes as we have? This is something we are very proud of in our country. And now my daughter will compete for Russia. I would not miss this for anything.'

Dermot swayed, placing a steadying hand on the corner of Yegor's wardrobe. He'd only gone and bloody done it.

'Now I have another little surprise for you. The Russian reached into the bag again and pulled out a DVD. 'Box set!'

The Meal of Fortune Just for Starters – The Best of Series One, Two and Three. It was very rare, mainly because it was shit and had sold so few copies.

'Come on. We can watch it now to celebrate.' The big man turned and headed for the door.

Even the prospect of three solid hours of early Marcus Diesel wasn't about to dampen Dermot's spirits. He turned and grabbed his phone from the bedside table. Then, as an afterthought, he reached out and locked the wardrobe door. That would teach Yegor to try to kill him. He followed Bukin from the room with a little skip as he tapped out the agreed text message to Anna.

Chapter 43

Anna ran through the office, phone in her hand, not caring who saw her or what they thought. Round the corner and past her old research desk (wouldn't be seeing that any time soon) and then straight into Kate's office without as much as a knock.

'He's done it.' She waved the phone at her boss.

Kate looked up slowly from her computer screen, trying to look all calm and composed, but just for a second Anna saw something in her eyes. Relief, excitement, triumph.

'And Bukin...?' Kate sounded as if she didn't dare to ask.

'He's coming.'

Now that *had* got Kate's attention. She stood and came round to the front of her desk.

All finished here and coming home tomorrow. Anna held up her phone with the simple coded text that told them Bukin was going to walk right into their trap.

'I suppose congratulations are in order.' Kate offered a limp hand. 'And now I'd better tell Lawson.' The handshake lasted less than a second.

Kate was already reaching for the phone. Anna took it as a dismissal and headed for the door. If Kate wanted to pull rank and try to steal some of the credit then she could go right ahead. Lawson was smart enough to see through it.

'On second thoughts I think we need a little chat first.' Kate replaced the receiver and went back to her chair, motioning for Anna to sit too. 'I've always admired you. You may not think so but I have.'

What was this about? There was something lurking in Kate's eyes. Something that most definitely wasn't good.

'Sending Dermot to Russia, that was a brave move. You must have been pretty confident he'd pull it off.'

Anna threw in a noncommittal shrug, still none the wiser about where this was going.

'Unless of course you had another reason?'

'I don't quite follow.' Anna was sure now that there was a great big bear trap just up ahead but she couldn't spot it.

'Revenge maybe. You know, a woman spurned, even after all these years.' Kate smiled.

Anna tried hard to hide everything that was bubbling up to the surface.

They knew?

'You really thought we didn't know about the two of you?' Her boss tried to stifle a little laugh. 'Oh you hid it well enough; that was quite impressive. But yes, we knew all along.'

Anna felt herself flush as Kate paused to let her take it all in.

'Why else do you think Lawson wanted you on board? We thought you might be able to persuade him to help.'

'You used me.' Anna flushed again at how easily she'd fallen for it.

Kate nodded. 'National security, dear. It's a war out there. One we're in serious danger of losing. We do use people quite a lot all the time.' Then she smiled that thin little smile. 'But we never imagined you'd talk him into going to Russia. Well it looks like your little plan failed.'

'No, it hasn't.' What was Kate on about? 'Bukin's agreed to come.'

'Oh, come on. You didn't seriously think he had a chance of pulling it off, did you? What is it now, seventeen years? That's one hell of a grudge.'

'What? You think I wanted this to fail? That it was all a way of getting my own back?' Anna felt the anger start to nudge her embarrassment aside. 'That's not true.'

'Oh I'm sure that's what you tell yourself.' Kate leaned in closer. 'How you've rationalised this. But deep down? You'd have been happy if it had gone either way.'

'No.' Anna shook her head, trying to control the growing fury. How could Kate even think that? 'I'd never put him in danger.'

'But you did.'

'I mean I wouldn't have let him go if I didn't think he could do it.'

'What, because you still love him?'

'Don't be ridiculous. It was a long time ago. He dumped me; I got over it. That's what people do.' Maybe there was something deep in Kate's past she'd never managed put behind her. Something that had twisted her into the person she was today.

'Anyway it doesn't matter now.' Kate sighed, lowering her voice once more. 'Looks like things worked out. But the bottom line is that you should have told us you knew him at the start. You broke the rules.'

'But you knew I knew him. That's *why* you wanted me on the operation.' Christ's sake, couldn't she make up her mind?

'Yes, but you didn't know that. You should have told us. We would have talked about it and probably decided to carry on.' Kate pulled a small tight smile and sat down again. 'That's why you're off the operation as of now.'

'You can't! It was my idea.' Anna fought for control again, thinking how nice it would be to lean over the desk and slap the smugness right off Kate's pointy little face.'

'And we're very grateful, but it's time for you to move on.'

'You've been after Bukin for months. Now he's coming to London. You know where and you know when. And it's all down to me.'

'And Dermot, surely? He's the one who put his neck on the line.'

'You know what I mean.'

'And as I said everyone's very appreciative. But we can take it from here, thank you. Now I want you to read this please.' Kate took a piece of paper from her desk and handed it across the desk.

Anna took the paper and tried to focus on the words but they all just blurred as the tears welled up. Not that it mattered; she already knew what it would say.

Behaviour unbecoming…

Compromising operational security…

Regretfully inform you…

None of the above.

'You bitch.' Anna dropped the letter and looked Kate in the eye, not caring about the tears any longer.

'It is a promotion.' Kate smiled again.

'Into the research section full time.'

'Well, research is your section. This was only ever a temporary assignment.'

'I'm talking to Lawson.' Anna snatched up the letter and turned.

'Good luck with that.'

Something in Kate's tone made her stop and look down at the letter again, scanning right to the bottom until she reached the name and signature at the end.

Richard Lawson.

The bastard.

'We all felt it was more suited to your, er… abilities.' Kate stood, a dismissive little wave indicating that the meeting was over.

How dare they, how fucking dare…?

Anna launched herself over the desk, then: feet first, taking Kate full in the chest and driving her backwards off her chair. Her boss's head hit the wall with a satisfying thud and Kate slumped to the floor, blood slowly trickling out of her ear down over her torn beige blouse.

Anna shook the fantasy away and headed for the door, not trusting herself to turn and look at Kate again in case the whole thing turned into reality.

Chapter 44

Whoooah... vodka, who said you didn't get hangovers from the stuff? People employed by Russia's ruthless vodka marketing machine no doubt. Dermot and Bukin had spent a good three hours the previous evening watching early episodes of *The Meal of Fortune*. One thing he knew for sure now: those early episodes of the show didn't improve with age. Nor with vodka, although that hadn't stopped Dermot giving it a sporting chance.

That morning he'd only narrowly avoided being sick on Oleg Bukin's best jacket as the Russian had loomed in for his now customary bear hug, on the wide steps of his mansion-cum-palace. Bukin had followed up with one of those two-handed handshakes that people use when they're trying to be overly sincere or imitate the Pope. And then he'd reiterated the promise he'd made the night before.

'I will see you in London, Mr Jack. For Eurovision.'

The Russian had kept his hands in place on the double-handed shake, his dark eyes boring into Dermot as if he could see every last little secret inside.

But then Dermot had remembered the commitment he'd made in return: a meeting with Marcus Diesel for his biggest fan. He told Bukin he'd make the arrangements as soon as he could and the Russian had smiled a happy smile and finally ended the handshake.

Of course he doubted he'd be back on speaking terms with the chef any time soon. But that didn't matter. With MI5 planning to grab Bukin the moment his plane touched down it wasn't a promise he'd need to deliver on.

Svetlana had hugged him then too and whispered something that might have been an apology. Then she'd got back to playing her role of an excited wannabe pop star on the verge of her big break rather than the cold-eyed killer who'd been so keen to put a bullet in his face just a few short hours before.

Dermot knew that, given the option, Svetlana would have been coming straight back to London with him. But Bukin had insisted his daughter stay on in Russia for now. She and Yegor would follow on in a couple of days.

The hitman hadn't looked best pleased with the arrangement. Home advantage hadn't quite panned out as the little fella had expected. Dermot had thrown him a smile as he hopped into the car. It was hard to be too scared of someone who'd spent most of the evening locked in a cupboard.

With Bukin's private jet all to himself Dermot had managed to sleep off the lion's share of the hangover by the time they touched down. He walked out of the small terminal at Biggin Hill feeling far better than he had any right to feel. A little bubble of excitement started to build inside him as his passport was checked and he collected his bag.

He really had done it and now he was returning home a bit of hero. He suddenly realised how much he was looking forward to telling Anna all about it.

But there was no sign of Anna waiting to greet him, just a couple of young looking guys in suits insisting he accompany them to the safe house. From their ages Dermot guessed they must have been well down the pecking order but neither looked too happy at what they seemed to consider a task well beneath them. Didn't they know what he'd just done? Dermot figured probably not: need to know basis and all that.

Both suits stayed quiet throughout the drive, ignoring all Dermot's questions. He quickly gave up, going with his initial assumption that they were so far out of the loop they didn't even know it existed. Anna would have all the answers when they got to the safe house. Hopefully it would be a six-bedroom luxury pad deep in the Surrey countryside, high gates, long gravel drive, Jacuzzi and a drinks cabinet stuffed with single malts. Probably loaned to MI5 by a sympathetic businessman and former spy who still liked to keep his hand in with low-level missions to the less-dangerous regions of the Middle East a couple of times a year.

Turned out that the safe house was a little semi on a soulless new development about 20 minutes' drive from the airport. Dermot could only presume its safety derived from its anonymity, as it displayed no overt signs of security. It was an opinion he swiftly revised when the front door was opened by a man of reassuring size who introduced himself as Joe. But then the giant rather ruined the effect by smiling and making Dermot a surprisingly nice cup of tea with chocolate-chip biscuits on the side. All the while he was chatting away about *The Meal of Fortune*; another big Marcus Diesel fan, it seemed.

Dermot was sitting at the kitchen table brushing crumbs from his trousers when the door opened. But again it wasn't Anna, just her thin-faced boss – '*Please, do call me Kate.*' She scowled sourly and sat down opposite him and said several things, none of which were 'thank you' or 'well done'.

Things like how they'd needed to debrief him in detail.

And how he wouldn't be seeing Anna again.

Ever.

And why? Well, her job was done now. And anything else was classified, wasn't it?

Two hours straight the thin woman asked him the same set of questions. About Bukin, about the Russian trip, Yegor, Svetlana and the layout of the house. Going back over it again and again and again, coming in from different angles and pulling him up on any seeming contradictions or inconsistencies. Hadn't he just gone and bagged Oleg Bukin for them? Yet here she was treating him like some sort of criminal.

All just routine, apparently; not that this made him feel any better. An hour or so in, his hangover had called round again; sitting in his favourite chair, putting its feet up and expecting its own cup of tea. Thankfully big Joe had been on hand with more biscuits.

Finally Kate nodded and sat back, fitting a smile to her face like a pair of badly made false teeth. This and the default scowl appeared to be her only facial expressions. 'You did well.'

'That's it?'

'Yes, you'll appreciate we have to do a complete debrief. But that's it for now. You can leave; we'll be in touch.'

Dermot smiled and sat back, still annoyed at the questioning but impressed with the woman's thoroughness too.

'It's important that you just act normally when Svetlana and Koslov turn up. Just do everything you would do in preparation for a big concert. Rehearsals, dress fittings whatever. We'll be watching and you can call me if there are any problems.' She slipped a card across the desk. 'Then when Bukin comes we'll take him and it will all be over.'

'It's that simple?'

'Pretty much.'

'You don't need me to report in or anything?'

'No.'

Oh.

'Best not actually. Security and all that. We got it from here.'

'And what about Anna?'

'Like I said, she's not involved anymore.'

'But I'd like to...' He wasn't sure what he wanted. She'd appeared back in his life after 17 years and it just felt strange for her to disappear again so suddenly.

'OK, cards on the table.' Kate put her hands down in a gesture that was presumably supposed to inspire trust. 'Miss Preston knew you. We used that to persuade you to help. That was all.'

'I can't even say thank you?'

'No. Any meeting between you and a member of the security services could compromise the whole operation. And it's us who should be thanking you.'

Well she hadn't, not really. Unless that was supposed to be it.

'What about afterwards?' There was so much he hadn't had the chance to explain to Anna.

'Look, whatever happened between you is in the past. Anna's a professional and she was just doing her job.'

That would be about right. She'd used him to get to Bukin; that was all. But Dermot had incinerated all his bridges years ago and didn't really have a right to feel bitter.

'Come on, I'll drop you home.' Kate's facial repertoire stretched to a smile that was in danger of becoming sincere.

'See ya.' Joe gave him a cheery wave from the door. 'And say hi to Marcus for me.'

It was almost fully dark by the time Kate turned the car into Dermot's road. She hadn't asked for any directions or offered anything else by way of conversation during the hour-long trip. She looked over at him, as the car slowed to a stop, a hint of that scowl back on her face. 'We'll be in touch. And remember—'

'Act normally. Yeah I know.' He opened the door, thinking about asking to see Anna one more time. But what was the point? She'd used him. That was all there was to it. That's what these people did.

Suddenly he couldn't bear the thought of seeing her again or spending even another second in Kate's company. He climbed out of the car and closed the door, just about managing a wave as he crossed the road.

Behind him he heard the car start up and pull away.

Good riddance. He'd play his part. Now he just had to wait until they nabbed Bukin and then he could get back to his normal life. Away from Russians and arms dealing and all this top-secret espionage shit. What was the point of luring international criminal masterminds into a trap if you couldn't tell anyone about it? That's why he'd have made a rubbish spy.

He caught himself grinning at the thought as he headed for the path towards his flat.

Then the smile faded away. Even from thirty or so yards away he could see that the front door was ajar. He definitely hadn't left it that way.

Yes, it could have been burglars but it was far more likely to be Mulrooney.

Dermot spun back towards the road but Kate's car was already making the left turn at the end of the road and accelerating away. Looking back at the flat he saw that the lights were on inside.

He took a step back, then another. He'd forgotten all about the loan shark. Little things like that tended to slip your mind when you were off in Russia risking your life. Maybe it was best to leave

Mulrooney to it and come back later? Or lie low in a hotel and get MI5 to sort it all out? He was edging back across the pavement when the door flew open and a figure sprinted towards him up the dark path. Dermot started to turn away then stopped. Wasn't the figure a little too small to be a gangster? Even Yegor wasn't…

'Daddy!' Molly closed the few remaining feet and wrapped her arms around him.

'Sweetheart!' He lifted her up and spun her around just like he used to. 'What are you doing here?'

But she just smiled and laughed as they went round and round.

'Hello, Dermot.' His ex-wife stood in the doorway, the key he'd never bothered to get back dangling from her fingers. 'Haven't you been listening to your phone messages? That's not like you.'

'I've been in Russia.'

'Really?' She shook her head.

'Yes, really. It's a long story and—'

'Let's not worry then; I've got to dash.'

'What?'

'For God's sake! You really didn't listen to your messages, did you?'

'That's what I've been trying to tell you.'

'Well you should check your phone more often.' She turned to Molly. 'Now be good for Daddy.' She leaned over and kissed her daughter on the cheek. 'You did say you'd take her in the holidays, remember?' Sarah was already halfway down the path. 'Any time, you said. Well it's the Easter break now.'

'I just can't…' He felt Molly tense beside him, probably remembering all those times he hadn't been there. 'It's not like that, sweetheart. I'm—'

Sarah turned and took a step back towards him. 'A bit busy right now? How often have we heard that? Well, tough. Wayne's booked a holiday for the two of us. Paris, Rome and then Venice. He needs a break.'

'Must be tough making all that Cheddar.'

Sarah just shook her head.

'Or was it a particularly taxing Wensleydale?'

'Oh grow up.' His ex-wife didn't even bother with a filthy look. 'We'll be away for two weeks. It's a good opportunity for you to actually spend some time with your daughter.'

'I'd get plenty of time to spend with her if you hadn't taken her to—'

'Not now please.'

Sarah raised a hand then walked over to give Molly a hug. 'Bye, sweetie.'

'Bye, Mummy.'

Then she turned and walked quickly to her car.

'No wait...' Dermot started up the path but the car door was already closing. 'Sarah—'

The engine started and the car pulled away. He looked down at Molly with what he hoped was a smile as he led her into the house.

'Can we go to the zoo tomorrow? Please.'

'We'll see.' On any other occasion it would have been an unconditional 'yes'. Why did Sarah have to be so... But then she knew nothing about loan sharks, Russian gangsters or MI5. Best it stayed that way too.

'Come on darling, bedtime.' He needed to get straight on to Kate Barnes.

'Just one story, Daddy, pleeeeease.'

'A short one then. I've just got to make one quick call first.' He pulled out the woman's card from his pocket and started to key in the number. Then he cancelled it and dialled Anna instead.

But the call just rang and rang before eventually going to voicemail.

Part Five

Part Five

Chapter 45

Was it truly all that bad?

Anna skim-read the summary of another report (freight manifests for the Iraqi port of Basra, 24 March–23 April).

Nothing suspicious there. She added it to the pile next to her and grabbed the next summary and started to scan. Two weeks it had been now since her promotion back to the research section. Yes, she knew it was important work. Work that provided the raw data that was the lifeblood of any intelligence operation. But Jesus, checking off the summaries was even more brain destroying than writing them up in the first place.

She put the latest piece of paper down (Sevastopol, 14 March–19 April) and looked around. This cramped corner of the office was now her domain. Four desks and an undersized meeting table, all cordoned off from the rest of the team (and the world) by grey office partitions. Around her the three junior researchers she now managed were all hard at work, their heads down as they scanned and summarised the data for her to check.

Anna rubbed her eyes and stared up at the ceiling, thinking about her fifth coffee of the day then deciding against it. The whole operation against Bukin had been hers. She'd devised it, planned it and even delivered it; she'd recruited Dermot, and Svetlana too. And still they'd kicked her off and were keeping her completely out of the loop. By tomorrow, if everything went to plan, Oleg Bukin would be under arrest and a major threat would have been taken out of circulation. She wondered whether anyone would even bother to tell her.

And it was all down to Anna.

And Dermot of course. The guilt that had been a regular companion over the past fortnight gave her another sharp elbow in the ribs.

She'd sent a man off, possibly to his death, and never even said thank you. Maybe Kate Barnes was right about her after all? Not that she'd been given a choice: all contact with Dermot was forbidden for operational reasons. It made perfect sense but she could have fought harder against it, couldn't she? Kicked up more of a fuss. Although why would she, when her reward was all this? She looked around her little corner and tried not to sigh too loudly.

And hadn't Dermot's phone calls become easier and easier to ignore as time went by? And then eventually, after about a week, he'd stopped ringing altogether. So it wasn't as if he'd tried that hard either.

Yes, he might have done his country a great service. And, yes, maybe the prospect of getting to know him again had been just that little bit intriguing. But at the end of the day he was still a prize dick. Kate and Lawson were welcome to dish out any appreciation that was due. For Anna he'd served his purpose, their long-forgotten relationship giving her the chance to prove herself back in the field. Now it really was time to move on.

But teaching? Charity work? Come on, for fuck's sake. This is what she was meant to do. Kate Barnes had been right about another thing, too: her father would have been proud of her. The Bukin op had been all hers and they would have to give her some credit when it was done. All Anna had to do was keep her head down, keep her nose clean and wait for the opportunity to come again. So, yes, she'd keep reading the summaries, keep compiling her reports and delivering them with a smile at the twice weekly meetings.

She picked up the next summary and finished reading before moving on to the next (Doha, 27 February–25 March). Skimming through the words, she ticked the box that said she agreed with the assessment, and moved on.

However long it took, she'd wait it out. And next time the chance came round nobody would take it away from her.

And if Dermot rang her again? She'd delete the message, just like she had all of the others.

Anna fought back another sigh then reached for the next summary report and started to read.

Chapter 46

Dermot was as ready as he could be but the attack came more quickly than he'd expected. He managed a parry with his left arm then a block with his right but he was wide open now and there was nothing he could do to stop the next strike.

'Yessss.' Molly laughed as she came away with the biggest of the three chips left on Dermot's plate. 'Too slow, Dad.'

'You got me there.' He held up his hands in mock defeat. 'Hey!'

His daughter dived in and grabbed his last two chips.

Dermot sat back and smiled as she quickly wolfed them down. One more day, then it would all be over. And yes, a part of him knew he should have been sitting at home chewing his nails as he worried about hitmen and spies and gangsters. Or maybe on the phone to that awful Barnes woman demanding an update on when exactly they were expecting Bukin to put in an appearance. But he wasn't. He was at the zoo.

Again.

Loving every minute of it too.

There'd been the odd time over the past couple of weeks when he wondered whether he'd slightly overreacted the night he'd got back from Russia to find Molly at his flat.

He'd finally given up on calling Anna after about the tenth go and phoned Kate Barnes instead. To her credit she'd responded quickly enough. By the time he'd put Molly to bed and given her a quick story Kate had been back at the flat. She'd sat calmly in the cramped sitting room, trying not to look too impatient as Dermot had demanded 24-hour protection, a move to a safe house nicer than the one they'd debriefed him in, new identities and God knows what else.

She's nodded her way through every demand, every point Dermot made. And when he'd finished she nodded some more. Then she'd said no. To all of it.

Any deviation from the routine would only make Koslov suspicious. Surely he could see that?

Yeah? Surely she could see that his daughter was asleep in the next room. Not safely tucked-up 500 miles away in Scotland. Yegor was a killer and there was Mulrooney to think about too.

But none of that had made a blind bit of difference to Kate Barnes. They simply couldn't compromise the operation. She'd even suggested that having Molly around made for a better story. If you were selling out a ruthless arms dealer to MI5 it was best not to have your eight-year-old daughter around.

Bitch.

'Come on, let's go and see the monkeys.' Molly leaped up from the table, laughing as she headed off up the path.

'Hang on!' Dermot was slower to stand, fighting to untangle his legs from the picnic table.

The spring sunshine had brought the crowds to the zoo and he had to dodge a couple of buggies then break into a jog to keep up. For a second she was out of sight and a sharp pang of worry did its worst. But then the new red dress he'd bought her flashed into view and he upped the pace, catching up just as she reached the monkey enclosure.

It was their third visit to the zoo during her stay but Molly's enthusiasm was undiminished. Dermot wondered whether it was some kind of therapy. He'd tried his hardest to look sympathetic as she'd told him what had become of the horse. Nugget, it turned out, was a nasty brute with an evil temper that had soon seen him sent away after he'd tried to bite Molly. There'd been talk from Wanker Wayne and her mother about a replacement but this had yet to appear. And Molly hadn't pushed it because she was apparently 'sooo' over horses.

They stood and watched the monkeys getting up to their tricks and his thoughts were soon back on the night of his return from Russia. Dermot had eventually calmed down as Kate reminded him that he was under surveillance. Only 'light-touch surveillance', mind, which appeared to mean that they would be watching him some of the time but not all of it. When and what proportion this 'some' amounted to was not altogether clear.

But in the end she'd convinced him that his own cover story

was the best protection for Molly and him. He was working to help Svetlana become a pop star and had Bukin's promise of protection. Yegor Koslov would be watching over them and the little hitman was more than capable of dealing with a small-time thug like Charlie Mulrooney.

And she'd been right too. There hadn't been so much as a peep from the loan shark. Dermot was too much of a realist to suspect that Mulrooney was doing anything other than biding his time. Maybe MI5 had had a word with him after all, although Kate had said they wouldn't; operational reasons again. But if Dermot was beginning to learn one thing about these spooks it was that they couldn't be trusted. So yes, perhaps they had 'put the frighteners on him', as Mulrooney himself would no doubt have said. Or maybe they'd appealed to his love of Queen and country. Men like him regularly styled themselves as patriots when what they actually meant was bigots. It wasn't beyond the realms of possibility that MI5 might even have paid the loan shark off. But Dermot knew that was too much to hope for. Whatever the reason for Mulrooney's continued absence, it was certainly a welcome one.

Dermot's dealings with the two Russians had been fairly limited too. Yegor's odd visits to the flat to 'check in' had been strangely reassuring, although relations obviously remained strained after the wardrobe incident. He doubted the little hitman had forgiven him for all those height jokes either, but then he had caught Yegor smiling at Molly on a couple of occasions with what appeared to be genuine warmth. And as Kate Barnes had suggested, his daughter's presence seemed to have allayed any previous suspicions the Russian may have had.

Aside from Yegor's visits there'd been the cursory preparations for Eurovision, even though Svetlana wouldn't be getting within 10 miles of the competition. MI5 planned to take Bukin the moment he touched down in the UK. Once her stepfather was in custody Svetlana's regrettable late withdrawal would be announced; a throat infection the pre-prepared excuse. But for now they had to keep up the pretence in front of Yegor. So Dermot had left Molly with their old childminder while he attended Svetlana's dress fittings. The

Russian girl had modelled the gold sparkly dress and platinum-blonde wig with a grudging smile, then followed up with another mumbled apology for trying to shoot him.

The only other times he'd seen Svetlana were for a couple of choreography sessions; again it wasn't worth putting too much effort in since Svetlana wouldn't be getting near the stage. They'd even politely declined the opportunity to rehearse at the venue. On each occasion she'd offered up more mumbled apologies and reassurances that she was keeping up the pretence at home, spending hours in her room with the music up loud, 'rehearsing' her song. DJ Danny had done them proud. 'Viva Let's Party' started as a strings-and-piano-driven pop ballad before morphing into a thumping disco anthem.

Perfect Euro fodder. Given the chance to perform Svetlana might even have been in with an outside chance. Top 10 at the very least; more than enough to launch a decent enough career.

But now wasn't really the time for regrets, considering how badly things could have panned out. And with the Russians keeping themselves largely to themselves, Dermot had been free to spend a lot more quality time with his daughter than he'd anticipated.

The zoo, the London Eye, river trips, Madame Tussauds, the zoo again and the Natural History Museum. Even their unsuccessful trip to Wimbledon Common in search of Wombles had proved enjoyable until Dermot had spotted some wildlife of a rather different kind in the bushes and steered Molly away before she noticed.

There'd been lots of parks and playgrounds too, with a fair few ice creams thrown in along the way. Films and popcorn in the middle of the afternoon as well. Oh, and lots of chatting.

About Mummy, who was 'happy', apparently, and Wayne, who worryingly was 'nice'.

About her new school, where she liked a lot of the girls but didn't yet have a best friend.

And about Scotland, which he was pleased to hear was only 'OK'.

But as always when he had Molly all to himself time had this way of accelerating and the fortnight was now hurtling towards its end. He'd given her the choice the night before of how they would spend their last day together.

'The zoo of course.' Not a second's hesitation.

'What again? OK, then maybe a bit of shopping?' He'd been determined to make it the best day of all to make up for the fact that Molly was going to miss out on going to tomorrow's Eurovision.

Of course he'd love to have taken her but 'Mummy' had already said they were going back to Scotland that evening. The lie had come easily enough. With Bukin safely in custody even Dermot wouldn't be going to the contest. For once his ex-wife had got her timing spot on.

'Come on, Daddy, let's go and see the meerkats.'

'OK.'

They were another favourite of Molly's along with the penguins and spider monkeys. He swallowed back another pang of regret at the thought of her fast-approaching departure and followed her up the path. With the Edinburgh flat he'd be able to go and see her whenever he liked, once he'd squared things off with Mulrooney.

She took his hand, dragging him on through the crowds towards the meerkat enclosure. 'Then we can go and see them feeding the penguins. And then shopping.' She had it all planned out.

'Yes, definitely some shopping.' He smiled down at her, deciding things had worked out pretty well, all in all. OK, he wasn't going to make Svetlana a pop star, but then that wasn't what she wanted. He had helped MI5 lure Bukin into a trap though. Once the Russian was in custody both he and the Russian girl would be safe.

And so what if Anna had used him then spat him out? She was a spy, or whatever.

Had he seriously believed they'd have another chance to get to know each other? Or that she'd even want one? And he could hardly complain given how he'd behaved all those years ago. One thing was certain though: he'd never get the chance to explain that now.

By 2pm Molly had seen enough of the meerkats and it was time to think about heading down to the penguin pool one final time before a taxi to the shops.

'We'll come back next time you're here, sweetheart, I promise.'

She gave the meerkats a final wave and reached for his hand but he was already delving in his jacket pocket as his phone vibrated. It wasn't a number he recognised.

'Hello.'

'Long time no speak, Dermot.'

It had been a while but the voice on the other end was unmistakable. Mulrooney launched into a short preamble about respect before spelling out exactly what he expected Dermot to do and what might happen if he didn't.

Dermot looked at the phone in his hand as the loan shark cut the call.

'Daddy?'

The phone beeped as a text message came in confirming the arrangements.

'Daddy!'

All-powerful Jedi weapon? Yeah right. Who was he trying to kid?

'The penguins. Let's go!'

But there'd be no more penguins today, nor shopping for that matter.

'Give me a second, love.' He scrolled down till he found the number he was after, then made the call, fairly sure he was clean out of other options.

Chapter 47

So much for ignoring all his calls and deleting his messages. But at a push Anna could have explained why she'd answered when she'd seen Dermot's name on her phone's screen.

It was all over now, bar any last shouting that might be involved. The trap was set and about to be sprung. Bukin's private jet would be in the air in a matter of hours. The minute he cleared immigration they'd have him.

So what exactly was the harm in taking one call?

Less easy to justify was the fact that just 40 minutes later she was stepping out of a cab opposite the entrance to London Zoo. And so what if she'd changed her mind and nearly turned back at least five times on the ride across town? That would be no defence at all.

Anna paid the driver and headed across the road, looking at the row of taxis idling invitingly outside the entrance. Even now, it wasn't too late to jump into one and retrace her journey. She'd be back at her desk reading more summaries before anyone missed her.

Karachi, 16 February–23 March.

Muscat, 14 March–19 April.

Jakarta...

Oh for fuck's sake.

She headed past the taxis toward the entrance.

'I need to see you now.'

No 'Hello'; no 'How are you?' In other circumstances she might even have been impressed by his directness. Instead she'd told him to stop pissing her about and cut the call.

Well, almost...

'Please...'

There was just something in his voice.

'Kate Barnes is your handler now.'

'No, I need to see you. I need your help. London Zoo. You've got to come now.'

'I'm not coming to the zoo.' What on earth was he doing there?
'I'm with Molly.'

His daughter. 'Jesus why is she...?' Kate really had kept her in the
dark.

'Sarah left her with me. Please just come.'

'You need to speak to Kate.'

'You're the only one I trust. That's why they involved you in the
first place, because they knew you'd be able to persuade me.'

There was no denying that one. 'Just tell me what's happened.'

'The whole thing, with Bukin. It's off if you don't come.'

'Hang on, you can't just—'

'I'll warn him.'

'Don't be ridiculous.'

'I mean it.'

'OK, OK. I need to tell Kate, bring her with me.'

'No, just you. Café next to the playground and the penguins.
Outside table.'

Then the phone had gone dead.

Anna paid her entrance fee, grabbed a map and followed the path
down the hill, cutting through the slow meandering crowds of
holiday families weighed down with rucksacks and shuffling slowly
along behind baby buggies.

Dermot's directions had been clear enough but she'd expected it
would be hard to spot him in the crowds.

It wasn't.

Easy enough to see the one person in the whole place not having
fun. He sat at a picnic table, coffee cooling in front of him. His whole
body frozen while his eyes darted all around. Cornered and all out of
places to run.

Like prey.

But still she'd felt it. That little burst of joy that had always hit
her back then, every time she'd caught sight of him walking towards
her.

Oh no she bloody hadn't. This was business, nothing else. She'd
only come because he'd sounded desperate enough to compromise

the whole operation. But then she was thinking again of the night of the school musical when he'd talked her down from the high, narrow ledge of her stage fright and made her go out there and absolutely smash it.

Didn't she owe it to him to…?

No, she owed him nothing. This was about the operation, nothing more. She pushed the thought away as she carried on through the crowds. He still hadn't seen her, his eyes on the playground checking on his daughter before darting around the crowd.

It wasn't hard for Anna to spot the girl either. She'd have laid out good money that Molly was the one with the dark curly hair tackling the monkey bars with the same gusto Dermot had bought to every last thing he'd ever taken on. She didn't know too much about children but the girl seemed to be tall for her age (eight, was it?). If Molly had inherited Dermot's dark eyes and easy smile, she was going to be a heartbreaker. Anna found herself smiling at the image of Dermot trying to keep her away from the wrong kinds of boys. Boys just like he'd been, according to her father.

She paused one last time. It wasn't too late to turn and walk away, even now. Maybe she could ring him; pretend she'd never been there and insist he talk to Kate instead.

But Anna knew that was never going to happen. She watched for a minute or two more. Next time he looked her way she stepped forward, throwing in a fake smile and an equally unconvincing wave as if she'd just spotted him.

He returned neither, just stared back blankly.

'He threatened her. He threatened Molly.' Dermot stood as she approached, looking briefly towards the girl on the monkey bars.

'Who?'

'Mulrooney.'

'The loan shark?'

'He's been watching us. He threatened her. I told your boss this would happen; asked for protection but she said no. Hasn't she told you anything?'

'I'm off the operation. We're a security service remember; water-cooler gossip tends to be frowned on.'

'Who's that, Daddy?'

Anna turned to see Molly at the playground gate.

'Just the friend I was telling you about. We need to chat for a minute. Do you want to go and play for a bit longer?'

'I did the monkey rings, all the way across. Did you see?'

'That's brilliant, darling. Can you do them again? We'll watch you.'

The girl ran off to tackle the rings once more, happy now that parental attention had been restored.

'Speak to Kate; explain what's happened.' Anna turned back to Dermot. 'I'm sure she can work something out.'

'It's too late for that. He said if I didn't go to see him he'd find me and Molly.'

'Are you out of your fucking mind?'

'He just wants to know when he's going to get his money. He's old school, wants me to grovel a bit, face-to-face. That's how it works with people like him.'

'And you believe that?' Did he seriously think he'd get away with a slap on the wrists? 'If anything happens to you Koslov will get twitchy and tell Bukin not to come. Is that what you want?'

'Of course not. He's bringing the money. Kate said I can keep it once they've taken Bukin in. I'll have the money to pay Mulrooney by tomorrow. If I go and see him, apologise and say I just need one more day. He'll respect that.'

'Daddy, look.'

They both turned to see Molly halfway across the rings. She reached for the next one but fell short. Dermot gave her a wave of encouragement as she ran back to try again.

'Just call him and tell him you'll bring him the money tomorrow night. You can apologise all you like over the phone.'

'No, he's all about the respect. Said I had to come today or he'll come looking.'

'I'll speak to Kate; we can protect you until tomorrow.'

'If I don't go and see him today it won't be about the money anymore. You can't protect me next month, or next year.'

'Look we—'

'I went to Russia. Persuaded Bukin to go for your whole ludicrous plan. I think I can convince Charlie Mulrooney to hold off for one more day.'

'Daddy.'

In the playground Molly was reaching for the eighth and final ring; arm muscles straining, determination on her face as she hung in the air. Just when Anna felt sure the girl was going to drop she reached out to grab it and swung on to the end.

Dermot smiled and waved again, then turned back to Anna. 'I've got to do this.'

'You're jeopardising the whole operation.' How could he be such an idiot?

'And that's all you care about, isn't it?'

'It's matter of national security.'

'I don't have a choice.'

'Then why drag me all the way over here if you're not going to listen to me?'

'I need your help.'

'If you want backup it's Kate you should be asking. But if Koslov's having you watched it could blow everything. She won't agree to it.'

'I know, it's not that...' He trailed off as he looked over at his daughter, who'd nearly made it across the bars again. 'It'll just be for a couple of hours.'

'What?'

'Daddy, Daddy, I did it!' Molly grabbed the last bar then dropped and came running towards them.

'Oh no...' The penny finally dropped. 'I'm an intelligence officer, not a—'

'Please.'

'Babysitter!'

'Her normal childminder's busy. There's nobody else I can trust. If I tell Kate Barnes she'll stop me going to see him.'

Too bloody right she would. And Anna should do exactly the same.

'I've got to sort this out now.'

'No way.'

But Molly had arrived and was smiling up at her. 'Daddy says you're going to look after me.'

Dermot nodded and mouthed a silent 'thank you'.

'Can we go and see the penguins now please?'

Jesus.

Chapter 48

'Are you sure you're not my daddy's girlfriend?' Molly stared across the table with Dermot's dark eyes and a hint of his cheeky smile. She'd slipped the question in between tiny sips of her orange juice and unfeasibly large bites of rocky road. It was the third time she'd asked. First at the zoo, then in the taxi and now here in the café.

'No, we're just old school friends.' Anna sneaked a look at her phone under the table but there was still no word from Dermot.

'Were you his girlfriend at school?'

'No.' The lie was the easiest option. She sipped her latte and smiled. Did all children ask this many questions?

'I think he'd like you to be his girlfriend. You're very nice.'

Not quite nice enough if the evidence of 17 years ago was anything to go on.

'And you're very pretty.'

'That's very kind of you.' Anna felt the beginnings of a blush. 'But I'm sure your dad's already got a girlfriend.'

'I thought you might be.' A small frown crossed the girl's face. 'Mummy's got a new boyfriend. She's happy now.'

Good on her. Anyone who'd been married to Dermot deserved some kind of break.

'He bought me a horse. He's called Wayne.'

'The horse?'

'No, the boyfriend.' Molly stifled a giggle. 'He lives in Scotland and makes cheese.'

Sounded like a right wanker. Maybe the ex-wife hadn't done so well after all.

'Are you going to be Daddy's girlfriend?'

'No.' But then was it totally inconceivable?

Absolutely.

The idea had managed to wheedle itself into her head on a couple of occasions. Each time she'd treated it with the contempt it deserved.

This time Anna put it on the floor with a judo throw and held on until it promised not to come back. Yes, he'd been brave to go to Russia. And yes, he might have changed. But deep down he'd still be the same old Dermot. She took another sip of her coffee as she sneaked another look at her phone. It had been nearly two hours and she hadn't heard anything from the inconsiderate bastard. So no, he probably hadn't changed. She knew she should definitely think about calling it in.

'Why do you keep doing that?'

'What?'

'Looking at your phone all the time?' Molly surveyed her seriously across the table.

'Oh, just work stuff.'

'Daddy does that too.' Molly shook her head. 'I'm always telling him not to.'

'Good for you.' Anna slipped the phone back into her pocket and tried her best smile, hoping the girl hadn't tuned in to her anxiety.

Back at the zoo Dermot had given his daughter a big hug and promised to return as soon as possible. Once he'd gone they'd headed straight for the penguins. Molly had clapped and laughed at their feeding-time antics while Anna wondered again whether she should have let Dermot go to meet Mulrooney and tried to remember whether her father had ever brought her to the zoo.

She was pretty sure the answer to both questions was no.

Next up Molly had announced she'd had enough animals for the day.

Right then, first mini crisis. Stripped of the readymade entertainment that the zoo provided, Anna had realised she was clueless about how to keep a child occupied. Her dealings with them had been limited to the few friends' babies who'd been sick down her or cried until she'd given them back. Her experience of older children was zero. What did eight-year-old girls like to do? What did they eat and how often? And how frequently did they need to go to the toilet? Would they tell you when it was time or did you have to keep asking them to avoid unfortunate accidents?

'Daddy did say we could go shopping.'

Good for Daddy. Outside the zoo Anna had headed for the cab rank and asked for Regent Street and Hamleys.

The world's most famous toy shop had occupied them for the best part of an hour. And with Molly in full-on shopping mode Anna had time to worry her phone, putting in three calls to Dermot, all of which went straight to voicemail. When they'd finally emerged into the warm afternoon sunshine there'd been no word from him and Molly had managed to put one stuffed pony, a necklace-making kit and a set of fairy books on Anna's credit card. Next it had been the Disney store, conveniently sited next door to ensnare any parents who might not have spent quite enough in Hamleys. A couple of over-priced soft toys later Anna had suggested a sit down and a drink. She and her credit card needed a break and the girl must need a wee by now.

'When's Daddy coming back?'

Molly's chatter had dwindled as she'd emptied all the bags out onto the café table to look at her purchases then carefully replaced them one by one. But with the last of her drink and rocky road finished she was starting to get restless.

'Soon.' Anna nursed her coffee, wondering how much longer she could eke out the café visit, or put off calling Kate Barnes. 'He said he'd call when he's finished.'

So why hadn't he? However many bloody times she went over it she couldn't believe he'd been stupid enough to go and see Mulrooney.

Or that she'd let him.

'Is he with Svetlana?' A little wave of excitement rippled through the girl's voice.

'I'm not sure but it's got something to do with the competition tomorrow.' Dermot's excuse to his daughter of some last-minute arrangements had been plausible enough.

'Daddy's helping her to be a real-life pop star.'

Molly clearly still dwelled in a rosy world of innocence where Dermot was a godlike figure incapable of wrongdoing. She'd learn soon enough about daddies and their great big clomping feet of clay.

But hopefully not today.

Anna sneaked another look at her phone.

'He hasn't even let me meet her.'

'Sorry who?' She realised she'd zoned out from Molly's busy chattering.

'Svetlana.'

With characters like Koslov around she wasn't surprised. 'I'm sure she's just been very busy.'

'And Mummy's taking me back to Scotland tonight.' The first whingy note crept into the girl's voice. 'I won't even get to go to Eurovision.'

'Probably finishes after your bedtime.' Anna had no idea what time an eight-year-old would go to bed but was pretty sure she was on safe territory here.

'That's what Daddy said too.'

'Now, do you need another wee?'

'No, can we do some more shopping?'

'Good idea.' Anna finished her coffee and climbed to her feet. She'd give Dermot another half hour before calling it in and taking the consequences.

Molly leaped up and grabbed her bags, the lure of the shops enough to take her mind off her father's prolonged absence.

Anna pulled out her phone to give Dermot another try as they headed out of the café. Then stopped.

Shit.

'What shops are we going to?'

Just for a second she thought she'd seen a familiar face among the crowds on the pavement opposite.

'Anna?'

The face was gone now.

'Let's just walk a bit and see what we find.' She led Molly out onto the street.

He'd already been turning away when she'd seen him. Turning just a little too quickly; the sudden movement was what had first caught her eye.

But it couldn't be, could it?

Anna knew what she'd just seen though. She thought about all the counter-surveillance checks she'd been taught. Then she counted up all times she'd used them as they'd trailed round the shops.

Precisely none.

How could she have been so stupid? She hadn't done any of the checks at the zoo either. That was just sloppy. But then she could hardly have expected...

'Let's go in here.' Anna breathed deeply, her heart going up through the gears in her chest as she led Molly into a clothes shop. Two new questions had just pushed her worries about Dermot down a couple of notches.

Why exactly was Yegor Koslov following her?

And exactly how much did he know?

Chapter 49

'What do you think?'

Charlie Mulrooney waved a fat red hand around his office. It was everything that Bukin's minimalist white home was not. Thick cream carpet, overly ornate desk and chairs, bookshelves weighed down with what looked like golfing trophies. Above the desk a very fake-looking stag's head was mounted on a plastic 'wood-effect' shield.

'Important to show a bit of class.' The voice was pure East End with a smatter of faux BBC laid over for effect. 'Need to send the right messages to your business associates, don't you think?'

The message that Mulrooney's office sent was that it was a glorified Portakabin full of over-priced tat, uncomfortably close to a busy flyover. And from the look of his clothes Mulrooney himself seemed intent on persuading the world that he was a relatively prosperous auctioneer or a minor country landowner. His light-green tweed suit was matched with a yellow shirt and purple pocket handkerchief. None of them went with the angry roast-beef-red of his big wide face. However he dressed it wasn't hard to tell that Mulrooney was an angry man.

Angry and dangerous.

Dermot cleared his throat. 'Thanks for seeing me.' It was important to get the level of respect just right. 'I just wanted to apolo—'

'Cost me a small fortune on their own.' Mulrooney cut across him and waved at one of the chairs.

It didn't feel quite the right time to point out that someone must have seen him coming.

'I do a lot for our local charities too.' His dark little piggy eyes bored into Dermot and he rolled his big shoulders inside the tight green suit. Mulrooney pointed to a line of pictures along one wall. 'Frames cost me a pretty penny. But you have to do your bit, don't you?'

Yes, you did. So maybe he should have forgotten the frames and given the extra cash to charity too.

The pictures showed Mulrooney at a selection of celebrity

events. In each and every one his big red face beamed out at the camera as he handed over cheques to an assortment of soap stars, Page Three girls and the odd boxer or snooker player.

'Plays havoc with the old waistline, all these charity dinners.' He patted the wodge of gut that was making a brave bid for freedom over the waistband of his trousers. 'Nobody could ever accuse me of being cheap, could they?'

Dermot shook his head as if it had been the furthest thought from his mind.

'So I'm sorry if you think I was threatening your daughter.'

Dermot didn't *think*; he *knew*. But again it hardly seemed the time to make the point.

'That would have been cheap, you see.' Those little piggy eyes bored into him again. 'A bit like not paying me what you owe.'

'I'm sorry that—'

'Like you, I'm a busy man, Mr Jack.' Mulrooney cut across him again. 'So I hope you don't mind waiting while I attend to a couple of pressing matters.'

'No, that's fine.'

Was it?

Mulrooney picked up the gold telephone from his desk and dialled. 'David could you come in here for a second please?'

The sound of lumbering came from the corridor outside, then a knock before the door opened and a tall fat man stepped into the room followed by an even taller thin one.

'Mr Jack, my associates David and Robert.'

Dave and Bob. For associates read goons. It was hard to tell which one looked the more dangerous. Fatty was egg-bald and scowled as if that simple fact of his lack of hair made him mad every last second of each and every day. The thin one looked sour despite a full head of dull-brown hair. Maybe he just liked frowning. Both had the obligatory full set of hard-man tattoos.

'Would you show Mr Jack the waiting room please?'

'Of course, guv… I mean *sir*.'

'You can't get the staff anymore, Mr Jack.' Mulrooney shook his fat red head, piggy eyes rolling towards the ceiling. '"Guv"? I mean to say, what am I – some kind of criminal?' He barked out a laugh.

'Come this way please, sir.' The fat one stepped back and pointed towards the door.

'Can I just make a call first?' Dermot pulled his phone out. If they were going to keep him waiting he'd better let Anna know.

'Best not, son.' The thin one stepped forward and whipped the phone out of his hand.

'Hey—'

The look in the big men's eyes suggested that arguing wouldn't be Dermot's best decision of the day. Although maybe coming here in the first place was already shaping up to be the worst.

'I won't keep you waiting long, Mr Jack. Then we can sort out our little misunderstanding. Now if you'll just go with David and Robert.'

Dermot headed out into the corridor unsure why it needed two of them to show him the waiting room.

'In here please.' Fatty opened a door and shoved him hard in the back.

He pitched forward into a dark room, stumbling as he tried to regain his balance as the door swung shut behind him. Then he fell over something that could have been a mop and banged his shin on what felt like a pile of paving slabs.

Dave and Bob both laughed from the other side of the door. 'They always do that.'

He heard the sound of a key turning in a lock.

At first he'd shouted, begged even, but none of it had done any good. And now, what must have been a good couple of hours later, he was still in there. When he did get out he could compare notes with Yegor about the inside of cupboards – although, to be fair to the little Russian, at least he'd gone in voluntarily.

Dermot held his breath and listened, trying not to let the fear creep up on him again. But the noises were just the same as they had been over the past hours: the dull drone of traffic on the North Circular road, Charlie Mulrooney's muffled voice on the phone and the odd belch and grunt from whichever of the two thugs was standing guard outside the door.

But if this was the loan shark's idea of a punishment it was one he was more than capable of taking. And what had Mulrooney said?

'Then we can sort out our little misunderstanding.'

Dermot owed him money; the loan shark wasn't going to do anything that would stop him paying it back. Maybe a minor beating? A black eye like Marcus's?

But whatever was going to happen he hoped it would be soon. Molly and Anna would be starting to worry and he was getting rather desperate for the toilet. He listened again, sensing a change in the background noises. More creaking and a faint burp from just outside. The hum of the cars on the flyover was there too. But Mulrooney's voice on the phone was missing now. A door opened and a set of heavy footsteps made their way down the corridor. Next there was more creaking and then light flooded into the store room. Much of it was blocked out a second or so later as Mulrooney's big face loomed through the door.

'Sorry to keep you waiting, but as I said I'm a busy man. A lot of things to deal with.' The implication was that he would have been less busy were it not for toe rags like Dermot reneging on their commitments.

'That's OK.' Dermot smiled as if he'd spent the whole time in a comfy waiting room with an ample supply of tea and biscuits, browsing a selection of glossy magazines.

Charlie's face disappeared and the fat goon reached in and pulled Dermot through the door, nearly removing both arms from their sockets.

He rubbed one shoulder then the other, blinking back at the late-afternoon sunlight streaming in through the office window.

'Problem with tossers like you is you've got no respect. Ain't that right, David?'

'Yes, boss.'

'I'm sorry. I'll get you the money tomorrow. All of it.'

'Time you learned a little lesson.'

Dermot looked back at the dark little room.

'Don't be a wanker.' The fat goon again. 'That's wasn't a lesson.'

A big smile curled its way across Mulrooney's face. 'Like I told you, I just had a few things to do.'

Why hadn't he listened to Anna?

He looked one way down the corridor then the other. To the left Mulrooney's office and to the right the door to the outside and freedom. He was fairly sure he could outrun Mulrooney and the fat thug. The thin one might be more of a problem; just depended how close by he was lurking.

Surely he could have taken Molly and hidden somewhere until tomorrow. But no, he'd thought he could play the big man just because he'd gone to Russia and faced down Bukin. Thought he could bowl up with his winning smile and sort the whole mess out with a few half-baked excuses. The kind of excuses a man like Mulrooney must hear every day.

'In my line of work I can't have little scrotes like you behaving with a lack of respect.'

'I'm sorry. I said I can pay tomorrow. I'll give you more. Double.' Surely that would be enough.

'It's not about the money anymore, Mr Jack. It's about you not taking the piss. If other people think they can take the piss too where would I be?'

'Please—' Dermot eyed the door again, ready to make a break for it.

But the fat thug stepped forward and put a heavy hand on his shoulder.

Mulrooney's big smile was back. 'You and Robert take him in the van. I've just got a couple more things to see to. I'll follow in the motor.' He turned to Dermot. 'We're all going for a little drive, Mr Jack. Now won't that be nice?'

Chapter 50

'Shall we go in here? You could get a nice card for Daddy to say thanks.'

'OK.' Molly smiled up at her and led the way into the shop before charging off.

It was a good 10 minutes now since Anna had first spotted Koslov. Since then she'd caught his reflection in three different shop windows as she led Molly slowly along Oxford Street.

It was definitely him, she was sure of it.

And she was equally confident that he didn't know he'd been spotted.

He must have been following Dermot and switched to follow her and Molly at the zoo. She'd forced herself to think calmly and come up with the only credible explanation. But then why had he been following Dermot in the first place? Did he suspect something?

But no, he couldn't.

Again Anna had worked it through and reached the most sensible conclusion: the Russian was simply taking his protection duties seriously.

'What about this one?' Molly held up an oversized card with dogs on it.

'I think he'd love it.' She handed Molly a £5 note and the girl ran off to pay.

Anna took another deep breath; feeling calmer now, back in control after the initial shock. This is where she was meant to be. No, not in a card shop, but out in field, making decisions as things unfolded, dealing with situations as they arose. Whatever reasons Koslov had for following them didn't matter right now. Anna's priority was to lose him. She could hardly have him following her back to Thames House.

Thankfully getting rid of a tail was pretty much counter-surveillance 1.0. Actually 1.0 would have been doing the sodding checks to make sure she wasn't being followed in the first place. It was a little late for that now.

Molly came back with the card in a bag and handed Anna the change.

'Come on then.' She smiled down at the girl, fighting the nerves rising up inside again as she headed for the door.

There was no sign of Koslov as they came out of the shop into the bright afternoon sunshine. Then again, she hadn't expected there would be. He'd be there somewhere though; Anna was sure of it. What she didn't know was whether he had other watchers out there. Best just to get on with it. She took Molly's hand and headed for the pedestrian crossing.

The first thing to remember was that she was in control here, not Koslov. Running a surveillance op on foot for any length of time was difficult, even with a whole team. You couldn't let anyone get too close in case they were spotted and if you hung back too far you'd soon lose the target.

So yes, it would be easy enough to get rid of the tail; the trick would be to do it without Koslov realising it had been deliberate. Something like that might set all sorts of alarm bells running in the Russian's head.

The lights turned green and she led Molly across the road and headed along the wide pavement, worrying about ringing Dermot again.

But no, he'd have to wait.

She steered the girl towards the nearest department store. With multiple floors, as well as lots of exits, lifts and stairs – not to mention crowds of shoppers – department stores offered literally hundreds of opportunities to ditch a tail. It was one of the first things they were taught in counter-surveillance training. MI5 folklore even suggested that Harrods' popularity with overseas visitors was due in part to the sheer number of foreign agents using the sprawling Kensington store to lose whoever might be tailing them.

But other department stores were available and the one in front of them would do just as well.

She pushed through the door, gripping Molly's hand a little tighter as they started to negotiate the maze of cosmetics counters, slowing as they approached the bank of lifts. This was going to be so easy. Wait until the lift doors were about to close then dart across and in. She'd just look like someone running to catch a lift and the little Russian wouldn't be able to follow for fear of giving himself away. They'd go up a couple of floors then back down the stairs in case he stayed watching the lifts. Then out a different exit and into a cab. Like she'd said to herself, easy.

A lift door pinged open and a stream of shoppers charged out.

Wait for it, wait for it...

Now.

'Let's get that one.' She pulled Molly behind her as she headed for the lift.

But the girl yanked her hand away. 'I need the toilet.'

The moment was lost as the lift door slid shut.

'You said no when I asked you in the café.' Anna tried to keep the exasperation from her voice.

'It's not a wee.' A look of horror had spread across the child's face as she jiggled up and down. Then she was moving, pulling Anna into the ladies' next to the lift, stopping only to hand over her shopping bags before bolting for a cubicle.

Talk about timing, but there was no need to panic. Once Molly had finished her 'not a wee' they'd simply amble out and do the lift trick all over again. Or maybe they could just...

Anna smiled to herself as the girl emerged from the cubicle and skipped over to wash her hands.

... Leave by the other exit she'd just spotted.

Even if Koslov did have a full surveillance team they'd be unlikely to know there was a second way out of the ladies'. It bought them out in the lighting department at the opposite side of the lifts from the cosmetic counters where Koslov would most likely still be lurking.

'Time to go, I think.' She took Molly's hand and guided the girl out onto the street in time to flag down a passing taxi. It would be another few minutes before Koslov even suspected anything was amiss.

One tail lost. Maybe not quite as planned, but just as effectively.

She pulled her phone out, feeling a sudden urge to tell Dermot all about their escape. But there was still no message from him and when she rang it went straight to voicemail again.

Chapter 51

'Where are you taking me?' Dermot banged on the van wall again.

Up front in the cab Dave and Bob just ignored him, like they had for the whole trip so far. With the early-evening traffic and a minor argument between the two of them about the route, the little drive had already taken the best part of 40 minutes.

At least they hadn't tied him up, although that was only because they didn't need to. Dermot had tried the back door as soon as he'd felt the van coming to a stop at the first traffic light or turning. First he'd worked the handle and then given the whole thing a damned good kicking.

No joy and a lot of nasty laughter from the pair up front. Seemed he wouldn't be getting out until they arrived wherever they were going.

And now it looked like they were nearly there. He put a hand on the bench seat to steady himself as the van slowed and turned to the right, then started to bump across a far less even surface.

Dermot's limited knowledge of the criminal underworld, gleaned mainly from gangster movies, told him that none of this was likely to be good. He felt his stomach shift. Taking him for a little drive meant they didn't want to leave any evidence of his 'little lesson' on their own patch. And the bumpy surface beneath the van's wheels would be a large patch of deserted wasteland. Any minute they'd pull up in front of a tumbledown old warehouse, its windows long gone and half the roof open to the sky. Exactly the kind of place men like Mulrooney brought people when they planned to make them disappear.

Stop it. His imagination and too many bad gangster films.

The van bumped on, a sharp reminder of how much he needed to go to the toilet. Then finally they slowed to a stop.

Next he heard the sound of front doors opening and some whispered conversation he couldn't catch. Then footsteps.

Dermot stood, bracing himself against the van walls. As soon as they opened the doors he'd dart through and make a run for it.

The back door swung open to reveal Dave and Bob, side by side and completely blocking his escape. No room for darting or running. Something told him they might just have done this sort of thing before.

Over their shoulders he could see a tumbledown old warehouse, its windows long gone and half the roof open to the sky. Exactly the kind of place...

'Out.' Dave, the fat one, gestured with his head.

Dermot clambered out of the van without further encouragement, not sure his shoulder could take another yanking or his overfull bladder too many more jolts. He moved slowly, partly the bladder again and partly to give himself time to look around. Just the warehouse ahead and a red Jaguar bumping tentatively towards them over the open ground. Even at this distance it was impossible to mistake the deep-red hue of Mulrooney's face behind the wheel.

With all that open ground, running wasn't an option. His best shot had to be his highly honed negotiating skills; failing that, a bit of simple begging and pleading. Whatever Mulrooney said about respect, it would all come down to money in the end. Dermot had to remember that. All of this was just about frightening him.

'Inside now.' Dave prodded him in the back.

'Nice and quiet round here, don't you think. Nobody to overhear us either.' Mulrooney emerged from his car as the two thugs took it in turns to shove Dermot towards a doorless opening in the warehouse wall. He toppled forward, tripping over a bit of old pipe and going down hard.

'Get up.' Rough hands pulled him to his feet.

Another shove nearly sent him down again but he managed to stay upright and keep moving for the doorway.

The interior of the warehouse was just how Dermot's movie-inspired imagination would have pictured it. Bare concrete floor all broken up in places, bits of woodwork and piping lying around. But at least there was no chair in the middle of the floor and no blue plastic twine to tie him up while they cut bits of his face off.

'Over there.' Bob, the thin one, now seemed to be solely in charge of pushing duties. He gave Dermot another heavy shunt in the back, sending him stumbling into the middle of the room.

Dave retrieved a chair from behind a pile of rubble and pushed Dermot down onto it. Next he produced some blue plastic twine from his trouser pocket and tied him to the chair.

Mulrooney walked slowly through the doorway and picked his way across the floor, his big ruddy face darkening with rage.

'Please! I said I'd pay.' Dermot fought hard to control his bladder.

'You've been a naughty boy.' Mulrooney's punch to the ribs knocked both Dermot and the chair to the floor before it had even taken the breath out of him. Pain exploded across his ribs and up to his right shoulder, which had taken the brunt of the fall.

'Get him up.'

The two goons hauled the chair upright again. This time Mulrooney kicked the legs from under it, throwing Dermot down onto his other shoulder. His head smacked hard on the ground, sending the whole room into a fast spin. He fought hard to stop his bladder releasing itself as the fat one pulled the chair upright once more.

'All I ask for…' Just one punch and a kick and Mulrooney was already blowing hard. 'Is a bit of fucking respect.'

Jesus, this wasn't just some gangster shtick he'd learned from TV or films – Mulrooney believed all this shit. But listening to him was preferable to being punched or kicked, so Dermot would take a lecture if he had to.

'Have you shown me any respect?'

'I'm sorry. Like I said, I can pay you tomorrow. All of it.'

'Tomorrow, tomorrow. Do you know how many times I've heard that?' Mulrooney bent down so his piggy eyes were level with Dermot's. When he spoke again much of the anger seemed to have gone from his voice. 'You could have come to me earlier, explained the situation, asked for more time. I can be a reasonable man.'

The chair, the plastic twine and the warehouse suggested not.

'I said I can pay you more.'

'You're starting to insult me now, Dermot. Don't you see, it's not just about the money.'

But there was a flicker, something in Mulrooney's eyes. You couldn't eat respect. For a loan shark it was always going to come back to the cash in the end.

Mulrooney leaned his fat face in close. What had been a flicker in his eyes was now something more; the same thing Dermot had seen time and time again across the negotiating table.

Pure, naked, unadulterated greed.

Any second now he'd hear those two little words. The ones that told him it was over and that all it came down to now was the money.

How much?

The big gangster straightened up, his eyes never leaving Dermot's, a slow smile playing across his lips as he worked out where to set his price. He nodded once and spoke the two words.

'Kill him.'

'No, listen –.'

'Too late for that.'

'Please.' First he'd tell them he was under the protection of Oleg Bukin, a crook bigger and far scarier than Mulrooney would ever be. And if that didn't work he'd spill the beans about MI5. Mulrooney wouldn't be stupid enough to mix it with the spooks. 'If anything happens to me—'

'Yeah, yeah.' The big man was already turning and walking away with a dismissive wave of a fat hand.

'I'm done with scum like you.'

Dave and Bob were coming in from the left and right.

'Wait…' He closed his eyes, waiting for the punches as his bladder started to loosen.

Nothing happened.

When he eventually opened his eyes again Mulrooney and his two goons were stood like statues, disbelief scrawled roughly across their faces as they stared at the man in the doorway.

'Gentlemen, Mr Jack is under the protection of Oleg Bukin.' Yegor Koslov looked comically small in comparison to Mulrooney and his men. But then none of them had a gun.

'I don't know who you are but I'm warning you, stay out of this,' Mulrooney snarled. 'He owes me.' He looked at the gun warily but didn't seem likely to back down any time soon.

'Nevertheless I must insist.' The Russian's eyes flicked to Dermot and then back to Mulrooney and his men. 'Mr Bukin would not be happy if he got hurt.'

'I don't care what your Mr Bukin thinks. You're making a big mistake.' Mulrooney moved forward, his men turning away from Dermot to back him up.

'Am I?' Yegor sighed and shook his head. 'I get paid extremely well to deal with men far more dangerous than you.'

Mulrooney let out a growl like a chained animal, the gun the only thing stopping him from flying at Yegor. A pair of metallic snicks rang round the walls of the empty warehouse as Dave and Bob released the blades of the flick knives in their hands.

Again Dermot nearly lost control of his bladder as he realised the knives must have been for use on his face.

The two goons stepped up to flank Mulrooney then all three started to close in on Yegor. But if the little man was troubled by the odds it didn't show. He just held his ground and smiled his little smile.

'I could kill you all now but I have no quarrel with you and neither does Mr Bukin. And it might lead to some unfortunate questions from your police. It's in both our interests to solve this more amicably.'

Or he could just shoot the bastards. Since when had hitmen been so bothered about the police?

'Think about it.' Yegor's voice was low and calm. 'You're a smart man.'

That was open to debate if you asked Dermot. But Mulrooney at least had the sense to raise a hand and stop his men closing in further.

'Thank you.' Yegor lowered the gun a fraction but kept it pointed at Mulrooney. 'Now tomorrow night Mr Bukin's daughter will sing for Russia at the Eurovision Song Contest. It is all thanks to that man you've got tied to that chair over there. Mr Bukin is very grateful and would be upset if anything happens to him. He will also be bringing £100,000 cash as a payment for Mr Jack. How much does he owe you?'

'Twenty large. Ten of it overdue.'

Liar: it was fifteen. And the first down payment was only five.

'And he's already said he's happy to pay you double? That's right isn't it, Dermot?'

'Yes.' Dermot nodded. 'Remember back at your office before we came…' He stopped short as he realised Yegor hadn't been there. So how did he know about that? Shit, he realised the little hitman was talking about the lie Dermot had spun him after Svetlana's supposed kidnap. He'd told the Russian he'd offered to pay Mulrooney double what he owed him in return for her release.

Mulrooney was looking dangerously confused now.

If Yegor found out that Mulrooney hadn't kidnapped Svetlana things were only going to get nastier.

'Yes, remember?'

'Oh yes.' Mulrooney nodded, still looking confused.

'So £40,000 then?' Yegor let the gun fall a little further. 'That seems reasonable to me.'

But the cogs were still moving slowly inside Mulrooney's big red head. Any minute now he was going to ask the question that could make the whole story unravel.

'Tell you what, let's make it fifty.' Dermot pitched in with a last desperate offer. Money had to be the best way to distract a loan shark.

Mulrooney looked over at him then turned back to Yegor, a smile creeping slowly across his face. 'Why don't we make it sixty, to compensate me for all the inconvenience?'

Yegor shrugged. 'Now you're just being greedy but that's up to Mr Jack. Dermot?'

'OK.' He nodded. He'd happily have gone for the full 100 to stop the whole kidnap story unravelling on him.

'We're agreed, then.' Yegor pulled an envelope from his pocket and stepped forward to hand it to Mulrooney. 'You are welcome to join Mr Bukin as a guest in his box. Then Dermot can pay you directly after the show.'

Mulrooney's sausage fingers tore into the envelope, emerging with a pair of Eurovision tickets. 'Nah, more of a jazz man myself.' He offered the tickets back to Yegor. 'Thank your boss for me all the same.'

The Russian waved him away. 'Keep them; you might change your mind. Your friends look like they appreciate a bit of pop music.'

Dave and Bob both snarled and stepped forward but Mulrooney raised a hand.

'Until tomorrow, Dermot.' He smiled his big nasty smile. 'Give me a bell right after the show. I'll tell you where to bring my seventy grand.'

Hang on, hadn't they just agreed... Dermot opened his mouth but closed it again. It was a small price to pay.

'A pleasure doing business with you, Mr Koslov. Give this back to him would you.' He reached out and handed Dermot's phone to Yegor. 'He'll be needing it to call me about the money.' Mulrooney turned and led his two goons away.

Yegor waited until they'd gone then tucked the gun back into his jacket.

'Jesus, fuck. He was going to kill me.' Both of Dermot's legs started to tremble and he leaned forward and sprayed vomit all over the floor, his shoes and good portion of his trousers.

'Yes, I think he was.'

'Then you saved my life. Thank you.'

The hitman just shrugged. 'Strange, isn't it?' He strolled slowly across to Dermot's chair and looked down at him, shaking his head. 'In Moscow I was going to kill you.' He reached down and untied the knot in the plastic twine.

'Thanks.' Dermot rubbed his wrists, wiped his mouth with the back of his hand and stood, hoping his shaking legs would keep him up.

A sudden bout of dizziness had him reaching a hand out to steady himself on the chair and Dermot wondered whether he wouldn't be better off having another sit down. His ribs were aching from the punches and both shoulders and his head were throbbing too. But it didn't feel like there'd be any lasting damage. Eventually the dizziness started to pass.

Yegor looked him up and down with a shake of the head. 'As I told your friend Mulrooney, Mr Bukin would be displeased if I let anything happen to you. But if that changes and I have to kill you in the future then I will.'

'Thanks all the same.' Just when Dermot was thinking of adding the hitman to his Christmas list.

'What I do not understand is why you came to see him?'

No, neither did Dermot, not anymore. 'He threatened Molly, said he'd hurt her if I didn't come. He said he just wanted to talk.'

'Then you are a bigger fool than I thought. Brave maybe but still a fool. You should have called me.' He shook his head again. 'Come on.' Yegor turned and headed for the door.

There was no sign of the van or Mulrooney's car when they got outside. Instead a black Mercedes was bumping its way across the rough ground.

'I came by taxi but understandably the driver didn't want to stick around. Vassily will drive us back.'

The car pulled up and the driver walked round to open both rear doors. They were back on the road and heading towards Central London before Yegor spoke again. 'You should ring that pretty girlfriend of yours. Tell her you'll pick up your daughter soon.'

Shit, it was long past the time that Anna would have started to worry. Molly too. And... God, Sarah was due to come round and get her in two hours. But...

'How do you know about—?'

'I saw you with her at the zoo.'

The penny didn't so much drop as plummet. 'You've been following me.'

'No, I've been protecting you. That's my job, remember.'

Christ. Dermot thought desperately back to his conversation with Anna at the zoo. Could Yegor have overheard them?

'Bit out of your league, isn't she?'

Yeah right. Like a short-arse like Yegor would stand a chance. He and Anna had been an item. And when this was all over they might even...

No, that was ridiculous. Dermot caught a grip of himself as he pulled out his phone. Eight missed calls and ten texts all from Anna. Probably best to keep it to a text for now.

'All good coming home now. Meet at my flat six-ish?'

At least Yegor didn't seem to suspect anything. He turned back to the little Russian as the next question hit him. 'So why didn't you do something sooner? Not that I want to sound ungrateful. But they had me locked in a cupboard for about two hours.'

'In a cupboard? Maybe now we are even then, after Moscow.' Yegor smiled. 'I wasn't following you. I was following your daughter and the woman.'

'Molly, why?'

'Men like Mulrooney are dangerous, unpredictable. After what he did to your chef friend I thought he might target your daughter. And I thought you might be able to look after yourself for one afternoon.'

'How did you find me then?'

'*This watch belonged to my grandfather… As long as you carry it you are under my protection.*' Yegor's impression of Bukin was surprisingly good. He'd got the arms' dealers little speech word perfect too, but then he had been listening from inside the cupboard. 'It has a tracking device inside.' The Russian pulled his phone from his jacket and showed it to Dermot. A red dot blinked in the middle of the screen. 'This is you. Mr Bukin does not like to leave things to chance.' He turned away and looked out of the window.

They drove on in silence for 10 minutes as Dermot ran through it all in his head. He'd had no contact with MI5 until Anna today; done nothing to give himself away. Yegor couldn't know anything. He stared out his own window for a bit until finally he couldn't wait any longer.

'Yegor?'

No response.

'Yegor?'

Nothing.

'YEGOR!'

'No more questions please – and you don't need to thank me again, OK? I was just doing my job.'

'No, it's not that. I, er… just really need the toilet.'

'Couldn't you have gone before we left?' Yegor sighed then knocked on the glass partition behind the driver, indicating for him to pull up in front of an uninviting-looking pub.

'Thanks. I'll only be a minute.'

The driver had already leaped out and run round to open the door. Dermot manoeuvred his aching body from the car and turned to see Yegor climbing out too.

'I'm not letting you out of my sight.' The Russian pulled a small packet of wet wipes from his pocket. 'They often come in handy in my line of work. Now get yourself cleaned up too. You don't want your daughter to see you covered in vomit.'

Quite right.

'Or your girlfriend.'

'She not my…' He stopped, far better to let Yegor believe it. And the Russian was right: he didn't want Anna to see him like this. He took the wipes with a smile. 'I didn't know you cared.'

'I don't. Now hurry up.' Yegor walked past him and headed for the pub.

Dermot limped along behind him. By tomorrow the hitman would be in custody alongside his boss. After what Yegor had just done for him Dermot almost felt guilty.

But only almost.

Chapter 52

Yegor yawned and rubbed his eyes as the taxi headed back from Chiswick to Chelsea. Dermot was due to come over to Bukin's house to discuss final preparations with Svetlana once his ex-wife had collected the little girl. So it had seemed sensible to leave him the Mercedes and driver. It might just keep him out of trouble. And in truth Vassily wasn't just a driver. He'd be more than capable of handling himself if Mulrooney did try anything else tonight. Not that Yegor thought the man would. The prospect of £70,000 of Oleg Bukin's money should be more than enough to keep him happy for 24 hours. But after everything that had happened today... Well, you couldn't be too careful.

Of all the stupid things Dermot could have done. Yegor hadn't been lying when he'd told him how brave he thought he'd been. But bravery and stupidity, while often close companions, had never been close to forming a winning combination.

He rubbed his eyes again as the taxi skirted Hammersmith roundabout. It had been nothing but luck that had seen him arrive in time to stop Mulrooney's goons killing Dermot.

Blind luck.

To think, if he hadn't lost the woman and little girl in the department store he probably wouldn't have checked the tracker and wondered what the hell Dermot was doing way out in East London. And to say Bukin would not have been happy was an understatement. For a second his stomach lurched again; that same churning he'd felt when he realised he might not get to Dermot in time.

But he had got there and dealt with the threat from Mulrooney. Despite his bravado and story about not wanting to involve the police, Yegor knew he'd have been hard pressed to deal with all three men – even with the gun. One of them would have got to him before he'd got a third shot off and with the flick knives things might have got difficult.

So negotiation had been the only way.

And now everything was alright again. Svetlana was in her

damned singing contest. Bukin would be there to watch her. And once that was all done Yegor could get back to Moscow, where he needed to be.

Yes, everything was under control, except... There was still something nagging away at the edges of his mind. And just because he couldn't quite put his finger on it that didn't mean it wasn't there.

The taxi turned left and headed down past Earl's Court. He'd have time to take a shower and a have short sleep before Dermot arrived. The nagging little fears were probably just down to fatigue and the stress of having his own plans put on hold while he was stuck in London. Yegor closed his eyes as the steady movement of the cab offered the enticing promise of sleep. But that little worry was picking away at the edges of his brain.

It was that same nagging uncertainly that had made him decide to follow Dermot and his daughter that morning.

Well, that and the boredom.

With Svetlana announcing she'd be spending another day at home, Yegor had been free to head out alone. He'd almost called it off when Dermot's cab had dropped them at the zoo. But without anything else urgent to do he'd decided to stick with it. Single-handed surveillance like this was the real deal, especially when the subject knew you. He'd spent the morning following Dermot and the little girl round the meerkats, penguins and monkeys, enjoying putting his surveillance skills to the test the old-fashioned way.

Of course, if he had been spotted he had the readymade excuse of protective surveillance. But in truth it had never been part of the reason, whatever he'd told Dermot earlier.

By early afternoon he'd been ready to quit again. But then the woman had arrived.

Interesting?

Or not.

Just his girlfriend probably. They'd certainly had a big enough row but the body language had been a bit stand-offish. So maybe theirs was a relationship that had yet to begin or had already ended. Either way she was much too good for Dermot. But then he had been a pop star once; surprising the number of beautiful women who would throw themselves at the feet of a man like that.

Dermot's abrupt departure had caught Yegor on the hop, if he was honest. He would have needed to move fast to catch up with him, drastically increasing the chances of detection. So he'd settled on tailing the woman instead; she also had a very cute ass.

Things had been a lot simpler after that. The woman didn't know him and, although the girl had seen him on the few occasions he'd visited Dermot's flat, she was far too busy with the animals and then the shops to look behind her. So with the risk of detection a lot lower he'd stayed close. Only once did he think the woman might have noticed him; just a fleeting glance through the café window when he'd been a fraction slow to turn away. But then she was an attractive woman and probably accustomed to having men look her up and down.

By the time Yegor lost them in the department store he'd been about to give it up anyway. When they hadn't emerged from the toilets after 10 minutes he'd wandered round to the other side of the lifts and discovered the second exit in the lighting department. They must have headed out that way and would be long gone. He'd done well though. Several hours of single-handed surveillance and he'd only been undone by a factor totally outside his control.

'Whereabouts, guv?'

Yegor's eyes snapped open as the taxi made its final turning. He pointed at the big gates in front of Bukin's house and jumped out, offering payment and a tip that was unlikely to get him noticed either way.

He was already through the gate and heading for the front door when he heard the sound of tyres on gravel behind him. It couldn't be Dermot already. He turned to see Pytor in the other Mercedes. It swung past him and stopped outside the front door. The driver climbed out and opened the back door for Svetlana.

'Where have you been?' Yegor fought to keep the anger from his voice.

'I got bored.' She shook her head, that familiar look of casual loathing on her face. 'Just a little shopping. Pytor was with me all the time.'

'I don't care. You weren't supposed to go out without me.'

'Well I did and now I'm back. You are not my keeper.'

'That's exactly what I am while we are in London.'

The driver was opening the boot, sensibly staying out of it as he retrieved an armful of shopping bags.

'We only went to Knightsbridge.' The English place name sounded alien among the Russian words. The she turned and stomped off towards the door, leaving Pytor to follow with the brightly coloured bags. The purple one, two yellows and the dark-green one with the famous name.

Yegor almost smiled. He'd spent many an hour in Harrods during his London assignments, pretending to browse like any other rich Russian as he'd run his counter-surveillance checks. In one entrance, up the lift, down another lift, up the stairs and out another entrance. Department stores had always been the very best place to lose a…

Jesus… Yegor stopped dead, catching another last flash of that green bag as Svetlana and the driver headed into the house.

The little glance through the café window. She must have spotted him then. But she hadn't panicked, leading him round a few more shops, playing it oh-so cool before finding an opportunity to innocently slip away.

Yegor put a hand against the Mercedes to steady himself. If there was one thing harder than maintaining a single-handed tail it was losing a tail without letting on you knew you'd been spotted. In his experience, you only acquired those sorts of skills in one particular line of work. That's why the woman was well out of Dermot's league. She wasn't his girlfriend; she was his handler.

MI5, MI6, private contractor? What did it matter? She was a pro.

Except she wasn't, was she? The whole thing was pure coincidence. He hurried up the steps to the front door. It wasn't as if a busy department store was a hard place to lose track of someone. Children managed to get themselves lost all the time without the benefit of any counter-surveillance training at all.

He definitely needed a shower and a sleep. Maybe then he'd stop being so fucking paranoid.

But the idea had taken root now, worming its way deeper into Yegor's brain. He jogged upstairs to his room, in desperate need of a sit down and a think.

MI5? MI6? What could their involvement mean? What did they want? And what did they know? Far too late to warn Bukin off. It would raise certain questions around why Yegor had only just discovered the threat. And what evidence did he actually have? A woman and child he'd lost in a crowded department store and a Harrods bag. His boss would just laugh at him.

But there was something wrong here; Yegor could see that now. The whole Eurovision plan and the ever so timely injury to Russia's previous entrant. It all just felt a bit neat. His sixth sense had kept him alive all these years and he wasn't about to go ignoring it now. He pulled out his phone and scrolled through the photos he'd taken while tailing the woman and Dermot's daughter. The best one was in the café, a head shot of the woman over the little girl's shoulder. He attached it to an email, typed out a short message and hit send. It paid to be well connected in his line of work, almost as much as it paid to be paranoid. He'd have the answer back in less than an hour.

And if his suspicious were justified?

There would still be time to salvage things if he moved quickly enough. He might yet find a way to turn the whole situation to his advantage.

Chapter 53

'Daddy, daddy.' Molly broke away from Anna and charged up the path to the open front doorway, straight into Dermot's arms.

Anna paid off the cab driver and followed, trying to keep her expression as neutral as possible. She hadn't known whether to feel relieved or just plain furious with him from the moment she received his text. Right now she was edging towards the furious side of things.

'... And then we saw the penguins again then went to Hamleys and...'

Dermot was still crouching down, Molly's arms round his neck as she went through the day on fast-forward.

Everything apart from being followed by a murderous hitman.

'Thank you.' He looked up at her with the eyes of a puppy that hoped it was adorable enough to get away with whatever it had just done.

Well that wasn't going to work.

He straightened and took Molly's hand, offering Anna a tentative smile. 'Do you want to come in?'

'Best not.'

No, the best thing she could do was to get the hell away from there and pretend she hadn't broken her boss's strict orders about contacting him. But she was still angry and wanted some answers first.

'Molly, sweetheart, why don't you say thank you then go inside and start your packing. Mummy will be here to get you in about an hour. I just need to have a little chat with Anna.'

Quite right they did.

The girl beamed up at her then gave her a hug. 'Thank you.' Then she gathered up her shopping and ran inside.

'What the hell do you think you were doing?' As soon as Molly was out of sight down the hallway Anna moved forward and pushed him hard in the chest.

'Everything's OK.' He winced as he stepped backwards.

'Doesn't look OK.' She reached out to push him again.

'Please.' Dermot held up a hand. 'It's just a few bruises, that's all.'

'What did he do to you?'

'Nothing; it was fine.'

But there was something in his eyes that said that this was nowhere near the truth.

Anna raised a hand again. 'You could have compromised the whole mission. If Koslov finds out that Mulrooney's throwing his weight around he'll think Svetlana's in danger.

'Yegor knows already. He came and helped me.'

'But he was…' She stopped. Most of all they needed Dermot to stay calm until they'd taken Bukin. Revealing that she and Molly had been tailed by the hitman was unlikely to help.

'Yes, he told me about that.' Dermot gave her a crooked little smile. 'Quite taken with you is our Yegor. Thinks you're a bit out of my league.'

She *was* out of his fucking league. 'So how did he find you?'

'Tracking device.' He pulled an old watch from his pocket. 'Bukin gave it to me, told me it was some kind of token and if I carried it I would be guaranteed his protection. I didn't realise he meant it so literally.'

'And you don't think Yegor suspects anything?'

'No. He was just protecting us. He's shit scared of Bukin and what he'll do if anything happens to me.'

OK, that was good. With Yegor still in the dark she had no reason to come clean about today's events to her bosses.

'As far as Kate's concerned today didn't happen.'

'Of course. That's why I called you, not her.' He caught her eye, holding her gaze until she looked away.

'Well I guess this is it then.' Suddenly she didn't know what else to say. 'I'd better be going. I'm off the assignment remember?' There really wasn't any further reason to hang around.

'At least we get to say goodbye this time.' He gave her another smile. 'Third time lucky eh?'

'Something like that.' She took a step back, trying for her own smile as the silence stretched on into a whole new brand of awkwardness. Why hadn't she just turned and walked away?

'Anna, I just wanted to say—'

'Don't, OK… It was all such a long time ago.' And, yes, maybe it would have been nice to meet for a drink or two, get to know each other a bit. But that particular baggage trolley had been full long ago.

'No, I just wanted to say thank you for looking after Molly today. You really were the only one I could trust.'

Oh.

'She's a great kid. Hasn't worked out what an idiot her dad is yet but I suspect that'll come.'

'I'm sure it will.' He reached out and hugged her, wincing a little as she gave a gentle squeeze back.

'Bye then.'

'Bye.' This time she turned quickly and walked away. Something seemed to have found its way into her eyes and they were starting to water. She certainly wouldn't have wanted him to think she was crying.

A brisk 10-minute walk took Anna up onto Chiswick High Road. She was well on her way to the Tube station when her phone started to vibrate.

They'd said their goodbyes. Whatever he wanted she had nothing else to say to him. All things considered they'd manage to part with their dignity and pretty much everything else intact. Couldn't he just leave it at that?

She pulled the phone out ready to bounce him straight to voice-mail.

Kate Barnes's name filled the screen.

Shit.

She thought about bumping the call anyway but that would only make things worse. 'Kate, hello.' She tried to keep it bright and breezy.

'Anna, I, er, we…' Kate's voice had an edge to it. 'We need to talk.'

Of course they did. Anna had disobeyed a direct order and nearly jeopardised the whole mission. Had she seriously believed she was going to get away with it?

'Something happened today. Something, er, unfortunate.'

Interesting choice of words. Kate was just toying with her.

'Something that could compromise our whole operation.'

Anna could hardly disagree with that one. She'd ridden off on her white horse as soon as Dermot had called, risking everything because he needed a spot of babysitting. She should have known they'd have him under surveillance.

'We need to ask a favour…'

That couldn't be right.

'We need you back on the Bukin operation.'

'Sorry?'

'We need you back on.'

They didn't know. About Dermot, Molly and the zoo. About Yegor Koslov or Charlie Mulrooney. About any of it.

Anna listened as Kate talked some more.

What had she said to herself? That things would work out if she just kept her head down and bided her time. Not that she's been doing quite that today. But she was back on the operation with another chance to prove what she could do. Anna felt herself smiling.

She'd probably even get to see Dermot again too. For some reason, her smile didn't fade at the thought.

In fact, she carried on beaming away like an idiot right up to the moment that Kate told her why they needed her back on the operation.

And what they wanted her to do.

Then she wasn't smiling anymore.

Chapter 54

'Do you know where your green top is?' Dermot checked his watch as he sifted through the pile of clean washing again and came up empty-handed. How could it be 6.55 already?

'I'm wearing it.' His daughter came into the bedroom with a smile.

Loan sharks and hitmen would be nothing compared to his ex-wife's wrath if Molly wasn't packed and ready to go when she turned up.

'And check under the bed for socks and things.'

He headed to the kitchen, where the tumble drier with the last of Molly's clothes was finished but insisting on staying locked for a few more crucial minutes.

'Come on, come on...'

It finally beeped and he bent down, his ribs protesting as he pulled the door open. The clothes were the only just on the right side of damp but would have to do.

The doorbell rang a couple of minutes later. Sarah somehow managed to make the usually cheery little bing-bong sound insistent and harsh.

'Hi.' she gave him a suspiciously friendly smile as he threw the door open, then looked down at the packed rucksack in hand. 'She's all packed?'

'Of course.' Hopefully Sarah wouldn't notice the steam rising from the hot damp clothes he'd shoved in at the top.

'Mummy!' Molly came careering down the hall and into her mother's arms.

'Sweetheart, I've missed you so much.'

Not quite enough to stop her fucking off on holiday with Wayne for a fortnight. But Dermot stopped himself. What he needed right now was for his daughter to make a quick departure, not another row with Sarah. The sooner Molly was on her way back to Scotland and away from Mulrooney, Bukin and Yegor the better.

For once though, Sarah seemed keen to linger. 'Go and get the rest of your things, darling. I need a quick word with Daddy.' She turned back to Dermot. 'Aren't you going to ask me in?'

Really?

'I thought you'd be keen to get away.' Their dealings of the past three years had taken place exclusively on doorsteps.

'Things to do, places to be, Dermot? All of them more important than taking care of your daughter.' She pushed past him and headed for the kitchen.

Hadn't he been looking after her for the past two weeks? Suddenly he was angry.

'No cheesemonger?' He followed her to the kitchen and looked out of the window, unable to resist the jibe. Wayne would be lurking somewhere out there behind the wheel of an offensively expensive 4X4. But there was just the little old Honda he recognised as belonging to Sarah's mother.

'He's a fromagier. A cheesemonger just sells cheese.'

Well that told him.

She paused as her face set itself into a Botox-defying scowl. 'Don't say I told you so, OK, but Wayne and I have decided to call it a day.' She stormed over to fill the kettle she'd bought Dermot one birthday before she'd decided he was a prick.

'I don't want to tell Molly yet. OK?'

He nodded, his heart doing little somersaults as he thought about a quick mental dance routine – disco strut twice round the kitchen and maybe a couple of spins. There'd be plenty of time for Molly to hear the happy news later.

'Of course we're not going back to Scotland.'

He forced back a smile. 'But where will you…?' A horrible thought slipped across his mind.

'At Mum's for a few days until we work something out.'

He breathed again. Sarah's mother's place in Watford would do just as well as Scotland until Bukin was behind bars and Mulrooney had his cash.

'Christ, he was such a…' Sarah shook her head.

'Wanker?' This time he couldn't resist.

'Don't start…' But when she turned the scowl was gone and she was laughing. 'Tosser.'

'Who, me?'

'No, Wayne. And you.'

But it felt like a barrier had come down. Just maybe they could start to put all the toxic sniping behind them and act like two civilised human beings for the sake of their daughter.

'Christ, Dermot, why do I always...?'

Whoa! He held a hand up. Giving his ex-wife relationship advice would be a step too far too soon. Thankfully Molly's knock saved him.

'Darling, come here.' Sarah hugged her daughter again. 'We're going to stay at Nana's for a bit.'

Molly stood deep in thought for a second or so, probably working it all out. Then she nodded, a big smile spreading across her face. 'That means I can come to Eurovision tomorrow night.' Her eyes had become impossibly large as they looked up at him.

No, it bloody didn't. But that was OK. However much relations might have started to thaw, Sarah wouldn't be supporting any plan that would earn him serious hero points with their daughter.

'Why not? You know how much she'd love to. She texted me all about it, while I was away. I'd enjoy it too.'

No doubt she would. Sarah always had been a freeloader.

'Please, Daddy, please.'

'It's sold out.' Lame but it was all he could think of.

Sarah snorted her derision. 'You're the manager of one of the contestants and you can't get a ticket for your daughter?'

Molly looked up at him with those big eyes.

'It's not been held in the UK for nearly 20 years; tickets are like gold dust. They've been going for hundreds on the black market, thousands even.' He needed to close down the conversation quickly before either of them spotted the fistful of complementary tickets he'd left out on the kitchen table.

Thankfully Sarah, whose eye for detail was usually so unerring, was far too busy being indignant. And Molly was yet to learn that it paid not to be quite so trusting once in a while.

Mother and daughter left soon after that. Molly with a big hug, despite the Eurovision let down, and Sarah back in something like her usual post-Dermot huff.

Dermot took a shower and tidied the flat, killing the hour and a half he had before it was time to head over to Chelsea. Bukin's driver took little more than 15 minutes to get them there in the late-evening traffic. And all the way Dermot was thinking about Molly and how she wouldn't be going back to Scotland after all.

The car pulled through the gate and rolled up to the front door of Bukin's house. Dermot hopped out, every bit the conscientious manager, calling to calm his client's nerves on the eve of her big performance. Not long now until he could drop the whole pretence. The moment the Russian's plane touched down MI5 would grab him and that would be that.

'Come in, Dermot.' Yegor opened the front door, his smile if anything more self-satisfied than usual. 'I trust you are feeling a little better.'

Dermot followed the hitman as he headed off down the hallway, already planning his getaway. A quick chat with Svetlana for form's sake, then perhaps a casual query as to Bukin's estimated time of arrival. He'd be an hour tops before heading home for an early night. Hopefully he'd wake up tomorrow to find that Bukin was already behind bars.

Then he heard the music.

Just like on that first day, six weeks and 100 years before.

The double doors to the big, white room burst open and suddenly he was in the clutches of 18 stone of hairy arms dealer.

The Meal of Fortune theme tune played on.

'Mr Jack! Come in.'

He was here.

'I thought I'd surprise you.'

He'd certainly done that. MI5 too, by the looks of it. Because for some reason he didn't seem to be in fucking custody.

'I think we have time for a couple of episodes…'

'Mr Bukin. A pleasure as ever.' Dermot's phone started to vibrate in his pocket. 'But I need to talk to Svetlana first – make sure she's ready for tomorrow.'

'She's my daughter. Svetlana was born ready.' Bukin waved a dismissive hand. 'Come on, we watch, yes. Then you can tell me all about Eurovision. You've always got to worry about the Swedes. But the Germans are strong this year and a lot of people are talking about the Danes too.'

Why hadn't they taken him in?

'Have to watch out for the Lithuanians, too.' Bukin pretended to spit on the carpet. 'Sneaky bunch of bastards but they know how to hold a tune.'

He felt his phone vibrate again. Probably Molly wanting to say good night or Sarah ready to berate him about some lost item of clothing.

'Svetlana has a great chance.' It was all he could think of to say.

'Yes of course. And tomorrow I will have your money for you.' The Russian put an arm round Dermot's shoulder and led him into the sitting room.

His phone stopped then started up again straight away.

'But I am disappointed with you.' Bukin was all mock-seriousness now. 'You haven't told me when I am going to meet the man himself.' He pointed to the screen where Marcus Diesel was fawning over a female contestant.

'He's coming tomorrow night.' The lie came easily enough. In truth he had sent Marcus a pair of the complementary tickets as a peace offering but had no idea if the chef was planning to make an appearance.

'Thank you.' Bukin smiled like a child at the prospect of meeting his idol in the flesh.

Not that he ever would. As soon as MI5 knew he was here they'd come for him.

Dermot's phone buzzed again.

'Excuse me, I've just got to…' He pulled the phone out, even though it had stopped vibrating, and backed through the door and up the hallway.

He had to get on to Kate Barnes now and tell her Bukin was here. How the hell had they missed him?

Svetlana was standing at the end of the hall, her eyes silently asking the same question. He tried for an encouraging smile as he watched the big tears form in her eyes. Then she turned and ran away up the stairs.

When he looked back down at this phone he saw there were six missed calls.

All from Anna.

So he dialled her number instead of Kate's.

She picked up before he'd even heard it ring. 'Where the hell have you been…?'

'Bukin's here.' He looked up and down the hallway, dropping his voice to a whisper. 'You need to tell Kate now.'

'Where are you?'

'At his house. Did you hear me? Bukin's here.'

'We know—'

'What do you mean you know? You should have arrested him. You promised.'

'Look, er…'

'Anna?'

'We need to talk, OK?'

'NO! You need to come and arrest him.' He looked up and down the hallway again but it was still empty. 'You said you'd take him as soon as he landed…' His brain finally caught up. 'And why are you…? You're supposed to be off the operation.'

'I'm back on.'

'Come on, Mr Jack; I am about to start the programme.' Bukin poked his head round the sitting-room door. 'It's season seven, my favourite.'

'Just a minute.' He gave Bukin a thumbs-up.

'We need to meet and it needs to be now.' Anna's voice was insistent but there was something else there. Something that sounded worryingly like fear.

'What's happened? Why haven't you taken him?'

'Mr Jack, come on…' Bukin beckoned again.

'Everything's going to be OK. We just need to talk.'

'What's happened?'

'There's been a slight change of plan, that all. But we do need to meet.'

'Mr Jack…'

'Coming,' he called down the hallway to Bukin before lowering his voice. 'Please. Just tell me.'

So she did.

Fuck.

Part Six

Part Six

Chapter 55

The car moved forward 20 or so yards and came to a halt as the traffic slowed once again. Dermot peered forward over the driver's shoulder, focusing on the dome of the O2 Arena through the drops of rain on the Mercedes' windscreen. They couldn't be more than five minutes away now.

Outside the pavements were packed with brightly dressed Euro-vision-goers, chatting and laughing as they made their way through the light rain. A pair of blonde girls in yellow and blue with plastic Viking helmets waved and giggled as they crossed the road in front of them; no prizes for guessing where they were from. There were plenty of flags in evidence too: German ones, and French, Italian and Spanish, plus a dozen more Dermot didn't recognise. A lot of people seemed to be dressed in orange, but then wherever there was a party the Dutch always seemed to be out in force.

'Are you OK?' He turned to Svetlana in the back seat next to him.

She just carried on staring out the window at the crowds as the car crawled its way forward again. But what exactly did he expect after the bombshell Anna had asked him to drop on the girl last night?

'Come on, Mr Jack…' Bukin had called again from the sitting-room door.

Dermot had waved once more, indicating that he'd only be a minute or so more and that Bukin should get on and start the episode without him. No further encouragement needed, the Russian had ducked back into the sitting room and seconds later *The Meal of Fortune* theme tune began blasting out.

Then Anna had told him again.

The tune had come to an end, a round of applause almost drowning out her words.

'Hello and welcome to The Meal of Fortune.'

'Look, it's a delay that's all; 24 hours and then we'll take him. It's no big deal.'

But he'd heard the hesitation in her voice, the nervousness too.

'*My name's Marcus Diesel and...*'

'We've had some more intel – from the FSB; they're Russian intelligence. Something important.' She'd gone on to explain that the intel in question was that Bukin was planning his rendezvous with the buyer from the terrorist cell at Eurovision itself. Somehow the FSB had also got wind that MI5 was interested in Bukin and put in a slightly panicked call telling them about the rendezvous and asking them to let it take place.

No, Anna had explained, they didn't know how the Russians had got wind of Bukin's plans or MI5's involvement for that matter. But then the Russians did have spies too and had been pretty handy at this kind of shit back in the day.

'As soon as the meeting's taken place we can move on Bukin. That's the deal: we get him, and they get the terrorist.' Anna had sounded calmer then, more assured. 'The Russians are happy with that.'

'So they're in charge now, is that it?'

'No. But this is way bigger than Bukin now. We can help them take out a terrorist cell. It's an opportunity to build some bridges too – relations with the FSB haven't been so good recently. It's one more day. We just need you to keep Svetlana calm. That's all.'

All...?

A round of laughter rang out from the TV.

'Mr Jack, you are missing the best bits.'

'Coming, just some er... last-minute arrangements.'

'Just talk to her.' Anna's voice had grown more insistent again. 'Explain that it will be so much worse for Bukin if we catch him red-handed with a terrorist. Tell her there's a bigger picture here.'

He was pretty sure that she'd be happier with the far smaller one where Bukin got arrested ASAP and she rode off into the sunset with Dmitri.

'And I'll still get the money?' Charlie Mulrooney's big red face chose that moment to force its way back into his head.

'Yes, you'll get your money.'

The way she'd said it made him sound grabby and cheap. Rather than someone who'd put his life on the line… But what was the point?

'Mr Jack…' Bukin called out again.

'I've got to go.'

'You'll talk to her, persuade her it's all OK?'

'Yes.' What choice did he have?

'I'll see you tomorrow night. I'm your liaison on the ground.'

OK… Dermot wasn't altogether sure how he felt about that.

But she'd already cut the call. He'd stood for a minute composing himself before heading in to watch TV with a man he'd expected to be under lock and key by now.

The crowds on the pavements were getting thicker the closer the Mercedes got to the venue. Now they were reduced to nudging forward a few feet at a time. But they were nearly at the entrance. And somewhere inside Bukin and Koslov would be waiting.

And Anna.

He'd been certain he'd seen the last of her yesterday evening when she'd walked off up the path. Half of him had wanted to call out and ask her to wait while the other half was all for running after her.

But not now.

He knew it wasn't Anna he should be angry with. That bloody Barnes woman and her shadowy bosses had put her up to it. But then Anna had gone along with it, using him to keep their operation on track just as she'd been using him right from the start.

So yes, tonight would definitely be the last time Dermot would be seeing her.

He peered out of the windscreen again as the car moved forward and the rain started to come down harder. When he turned back towards Svetlana she was staring at him, the same anger he'd seen in those black eyes the night before. She held his gaze for a minute then turned to look back out the window.

Bukin had guffawed his way through the first half of *The Meal of Fortune*, giving Dermot a hearty slap on the back almost every time

Marcus opened his mouth. Never had an illegal arms dealer looked closer to wetting himself all over his best sofa. Dermot had waited for the first ad break then asked for directions to the toilet, the excuse he needed to creep up to Svetlana's room to break the happy news.

He'd found her sitting on her bed, the earlier tears already replaced by that cold, hard look he was coming to know so well. Her expression had remained fixed as he'd explained it all, keeping his voice low as he listened for the tell-tale footsteps of the little hitman on the stairs.

He'd expected the tears to come again but she just sat there quietly, staring at him with those cold, dark eyes. Just when he'd given up on getting any kind of response she'd nodded once.

'I will do whatever it takes. Now please go. Everything must seem normal.'

He'd been back on the sofa next to Bukin before the second half of the show started.

The car moved forward again, jolting him back to the present once more as they turned in through the gates. An echo of all that long-forgotten excitement fizzed up inside him as he looked up at the brightly lit venue. Just like he'd felt back in the day with the NewBoyz; that pre-gig buzz that you knew would just keep on going through the show and for most of the night afterwards.

The car turned, swinging off towards the entrance to the back-stage area. To his right Dermot could see the queues of people waiting to get in. Blues and yellows and oranges and every other colour under the sun lighting up the dull evening, as the line snaked back from the entrance and right out onto the road.

And this wasn't just any gig. Not 400 people in a hall in Leeds or Northampton, or even 5,000 in Barcelona, Munich or Paris.

It was the Eurovision Song Contest.

20,000 in the audience.

Hundreds of millions at home in front of the TV. Right across Europe – and the world.

And MI5's change of plan meant Svetlana would be a part of it after all.

And Dermot would be too.

He was a long, long way from TV chefs and saucepan endorsement deals now.

Except he wasn't, not really. And with Svetlana up second-to-last Bukin's rendezvous was certain to have happened long before she got anywhere near the stage. Once the Russian had been arrested they'd announce her withdrawal. Somehow it felt crueller than not being involved at all.

But what if...? What if the rendezvous didn't happen until after she was due on stage?

Her demo tape showed she could certainly sing. And with her looks she'd have no trouble making it in the music business. She might have no interest in being a pop star right now. But after she'd been up on that stage in front of all those people?

In the audience, watching at home right across the world.

Surely she'd catch the bug, wouldn't she?

With Bukin safely in jail Dermot would be able to sit down with Svetlana and persuade her to re-evaluate a few things. Such a shame to let all that talent go to waste.

He looked out at the queue of people again. Laughing, smiling and joking as they stood patiently in the rain. Then he shook his head, smiling to himself as he chased the silly little daydream away. Bukin was a dangerous criminal, Yegor a killer. So, no, he didn't want the rendezvous to be delayed until after Svetlana had powered her way through DJ Danny Dance's undeniably catchy, if annoying, lyrics. The sooner it was all over the better.

This time when he looked at Svetlana he got a nervous little smile in return. He nodded and smiled back then gazed out at the crowds one last time as the car swung around the back of the arena and slowed to a stop.

They'd arrived.

Chapter 56

'Emperor and Hunter have just entered the building. Repeat, Emperor and Hunter have arrived.'

'Roger that.'

Emperor and Hunter – Bukin and Koslov, of course. Anna listened to the words in her earpiece as she scanned the arena, a mixture of excitement, guilt and no little dread building up inside her. She'd picked her vantage point well, high to the left of the stage at the front of the top tier of seats, which banked steeply up to the roof behind her. Far below, technicians scurried round like high-tech ants on the stage, making final preparations as the seats around the auditorium filled with brightly clothed people, the excited buzz of their conversation easily drowning out the background music.

She let her eyes wander round the arena again, trying and failing to spot the six other MI5 team members she knew were stationed in the crowd. Finally, she looked back at the private box, almost directly opposite her and slightly below on the middle tier.

It was still empty but had been booked two weeks before in the name of one Victor Mandlikov, the same alias Bukin had used to enter the country. It had to be where he and Koslov were planning to watch the show.

And most likely where the rendezvous with the terrorist was going to take place too. Every word and action would be caught on the hidden cameras and microphones they'd installed.

Anna leaned forward on the railings, watching as more people flooded into the arena, jostling happily as they headed for their seats, all those feelings welling up inside her once again. Excitement… certainly. She was back on the assignment. This was her plan and her trap they were about to spring.

And guilt. Yes, that too. However strong the justification, the promises they'd made to Dermot and Svetlana had been broken.

The promises she had made.

Then there was the background feeling of complete and utter terror.

'*Everything's going to be fine.*' How many times had she told Dermot that? But the longer it took to bring Bukin into custody the more things there were that could go wrong.

'*Rock solid.*' That's how she'd described the Russian intelligence to Dermot. But could she really be so sure?

Sometimes these sorts of rendezvous didn't happen for one reason or another. And sometimes the information was just plain wrong. A source being played, getting the wrong end of the stick, even feeding their handler a whole pile of shit. Anna looked around the arena, trying not to think about it. Everything was as it should be. Dermot and Svetlana were safely in the dressing room, the teams were in position and all the exits were covered. Soon enough Bukin would be taking his seat. And then, once the rendezvous had happened, they'd have him.

She touched her jacket pocket, feeling the hard shape of the small handgun through the material. Every member of the surveillance team had been issued with one. Not that they expected it to come to that. Once they had the order to go, it would be the two separate snatch teams that went in to take the terrorist and Bukin. The Met's SCO19 firearms team were stationed outside as backup.

Her eyes scrolled round the auditorium again as she forced herself to stay calm.

The only real concern was the lack of security around Svetlana and Dermot. But with Bukin likely to head down there to wish his daughter good luck at some point, they'd decided against putting anyone too close. It was too much of a risk with a professional like Koslov involved.

But that didn't mean Anna had to feel good about it. Or about the fact that they were relying on two wholly untrained assets to keep their cool. And that was before she got to the lack of any real contingency plan. If Bukin didn't meet his contact here they were simply to keep tailing him and see what happened. Not great as Plan Bs went, but then the last-minute timing of the Russian tip-off meant they were largely busking it.

She turned again to look back at Bukin's box.

Still empty.

'This is Green One. Emperor and Hunter are heading up stairwell seven now.'

Sounded like they were headed to the box. But until she had eyeballs on them, confirmed for herself that Bukin was here in the flesh, she wasn't taking anything for granted.

Anna did one more quick scan around the crowd, checking for anything out of place, but there was nothing. Only 10 minutes or so now until the first act was due on stage. Most of the seats were full. And the music had been cranked right up, filling the auditorium with a pulsating Eurobeat, presumably to get the audience in the mood for lots more of the exact same to come.

Eyes back to Bukin's box. Still empty.

'This is Control. Do you read me, Green Two?' Kate Barnes' voice brayed out of her earpiece. Green Two was Anna; at least they'd kept it simple, avoiding any Eurovision-themed codenames.

When she'd first been told she was back on the assignment Anna had hoped they might give her operational control. No such luck. They'd really only needed her to bring Dermot round and Kate had made it clear that she herself would be taking the lead role on the ground. And didn't everyone just know it. She'd spent the whole time pestering Anna and the team for updates instead of just waiting for them to report in.

But this time at least there was something to tell; the door at the back of Bukin's box had just swung open.

'Emperor and Hunter entering the box.' Anna watched as Yegor Koslov slipped in first. She held up her phone, using the camera on it to magnify her view, knowing she'd look like any another excited punter taking a picture.

Koslov moved swiftly as he checked under the seats but the tech team had hidden the mics so well he'd never find them. His eyes swept the crowd before he turned and beckoned for his boss to follow.

Even at a distance Oleg Bukin looked every inch the man his file made him out to be. Although the supersized fizzy drink and bumper bucket of popcorn slightly spoiled the whole effect somewhat.

'OK, they're in.' Anna watched as Bukin flopped down in his seat, shovelling a huge handful of popcorn straight into his mouth.

'Copy that.' Kate's voice came back on the radio. 'Check on Princess and Joker.'

Svetlana and Dermot. Who on earth had made up these names?

Maybe on reflection a Eurovision theme wouldn't have been a bad idea.

'They probably need a little bit of TLC right now. But don't stay too long in case Bukin decides to visit.'

Yes, yes. They'd agreed all this beforehand, there was no need for Kate to be telling her again.

But Anna knew it wasn't just that. A part of her had been hoping it would all be done and dusted by now. For operational reasons, of course, but also because… well, it would mean she wouldn't have to see Dermot again.

'At least we get to say goodbye this time… third time lucky, eh?'

'Something like that.'

Last night's parting had felt appropriate somehow. Maybe not quite a resolution but good enough. And after all this time there really wasn't anything left to resolve.

Now she'd have to see him again, talk to him and then… then see the assignment through like a good little spook. After that she'd walk away without a backward glance. Wouldn't be getting anything in her eye this time either.

Over in his box Bukin took a long pull from his straw then followed it up with another fistful of popcorn before offering the bucket to Yegor.

The little hitman declined. No popcorn on duty, clearly.

His boss just shrugged, took another handful from the bucket and stuck his nose into the souvenir programme. He looked for all the world like a man hunkering down for an evening of cheesy pop-based entertainment, not a serious criminal about to conclude a highly illegal arms deal with a gang of desperate terrorists.

Maybe the Russian's intel really was off the mark? Anna didn't want to think about that. She turned and headed off down the stairs to see Svetlana and Dermot. Maybe if she went slowly enough the rendezvous would have taken place before she got anywhere near the dressing room? Then she could walk away and leave someone else to tie up the loose ends with Dermot.

Hmmm, funny then that she was taking the stairs two at a time…

Chapter 57

First it was the drums. The drums always came first. Then the bass and the keyboards, then the guitar, pounding through the intro towards the first verse. Dermot closed his eyes and just for a second he was back there with the NewBoyz all over again.

Every night a different stage.

Nationwide tour.

European tour.

Then the world...

OK, they'd never quite made the world. He opened his eyes, ditching the daydream in favour of the three Latvian women in what he assumed was some sort of national dress. They bopped up and down as if they were on springs and smiled manically as they sang.

He turned from the TV and glanced round the dressing room once more. It was surprisingly spacious; certainly the whole of the NewBoyz had got changed in far less space when they'd been setting out. But then this was Eurovision.

'All OK?' He looked across at Svetlana.

She swivelled in her chair and nodded gravely, probably wishing he'd quit asking how she was.

She spun slowly back to the mirror and the finishing touches of her heavy stage make-up. Important to keep up appearances until the very end.

Dermot let his eyes wander around the room again, taking it all in as he remembered what those last-minute preparations had been like.

The mirror and dressing table in front of Svetlana.

The open make-up bag.

The long blonde wig on the back of a chair.

The clothes rail where Svetlana's sparkly gold dress hung next to the door to the little bathroom.

He looked back at the TV as the Latvians swung into what was hopefully the final chorus. Traditional Baltic ballad meets juiced up Eurobeat? Meets, takes an instant dislike to and then beats the shit out of, more like. It may well have been a huge honour to be kicking off the show but it seemed unlikely that act number one would be troubling the scorers. The Latvians would have struggled to carry a tune in a rucksack.

Dermot gave them a few more seconds – definitely a '*nil points*' – then diverted all his attention back to worrying.

'*Just sit tight.*' That's what Anna had told him. '*Stay in the dressing room and we'll tell you when it's all over.*'

Easy for her to say. She wasn't the one stuck in here not knowing what was going on. He directed a smile at Svetlana's reflection, putting on a brave face for about the thousandth time.

On the screen the Latvians had taken their bow to what seemed like overgenerous applause and left the stage. Next up was an attractive Belgian girl dressed in black belting out something half decent, in whichever of their languages the Belgians choose to sing in. She finished and bowed, smiling happily and waving as the crowd clapped a little less enthusiastically than they had for the Latvians. In Eurovision as in life there was precious little justice.

The under-appreciated Belgian girl was followed by a bunch of young Slovenian lads, all white T-shirts and hair gel, looking and sounding suspiciously like a manufactured Irish boy band. They punched their way through a chunky power ballad and ran smiling and waving from the stage to the loudest applause so far. Three acts down and Dermot had the Slovenes pegged as early favourites. Next up was a group of young Irish lads, all white T-shirts and hair gel, looking and sounding suspiciously like a manufactured Slovenian boy band. They bounced on and nailed their own generic power ballad. If it was hard to distinguish from the previous offering, the crowd didn't seem to mind. And so what if it was the same old shite that the NewBoyz had churned out in the nineties? Dermot certainly hadn't heard himself complaining back then.

He looked back at Svetlana again, reminding himself that none of what was happening on the stage really mattered. Because very soon, while some other set of over or underdressed Europeans camped it up to a pounding beat or churned out another dreary ballad, Oleg Bukin would meet a man about a bomb.

And then they'd have him.

The Irish were harmonising their way to a finish when the door opened and Anna walked in.

'In position.' She spoke into her lapel, clearly talking to some hidden microphone. 'Princess and Joker in place.'

No guesses who was who.

'What's happening?' Dermot knew it sounded short but he couldn't help himself.

'Bukin's here. He's in his box.' Anna looked at them both in turn. 'All we have to do now is wait.'

OK… Cold, distant and a little business-like. But wasn't that exactly what you wanted in a spy you were trusting with your life?

'How many acts have been on?'

'Four now.'

'Any good?' She gave him the first hint of a smile.

'What do you think?' He smiled back. She might have broken her previous promise but she was here to see it through. The least he could do was be civil.

Anna turned towards Svetlana. 'There's still plenty of time. It's unlikely you'll have to go on stage.'

'If I have to I will be fine.' The Russian girl shrugged, strangely unconcerned about the prospect of singing in front of 20,000 people.

Maybe he really could persuade her that a career in music was the right choice after all.

Svetlana picked up her hairbrush and started miming the words of her song with a smile. 'See, I have been practising.'

Anna caught his eye and suddenly they were both smiling again.

And properly this time as well.

Then she laughed and he was laughing too.

Seventeen years dropped away in a drumbeat and they were teenagers again, laughing at everything they thought was ludicrous in the crazy, crazy world around them.

Jesus, they'd just gone and set a trap for an arms dealer with a girl lip-synching into a hairbrush. Maybe they should meet for a drink after it was all done.

'It is live though.' Anna's laugh was gone almost as quickly as it had come, her smile fading too.

'Yes, live.' Svetlana smiled and nodded, pointing at the TV. 'I mime so people think I am good. That's what they all do.'

It's certainly what the Latvians should have done.

Anna shook her head. 'If you do go on, you actually have to sing.'

'But you have recorded a track for me to mime to, no?' The Russian girl's smile was gone now.

Dermot looked at her then turned slowly back at Anna, thinking about the demo tape he'd heard and the rather obvious question he hadn't thought to ask.

Chapter 58

'You didn't even ask her.' Fuck's sake, how could he have been so stupid?

'She's on second-last. She won't have to sing anyway.' Dermot looked down, avoiding her eye.

'But you didn't ask, did you?'

'No, I didn't, OK. But I heard the demo. It sounded just like the version from *Frozen.*' Dermot turned to Svetlana. 'Tell her.'

'That *was* the version from *Frozen.* I only needed to fool my stepfather, so he'd let me come to London.' The Russian girl shook her head as the tears started to form in her eyes.

OK, deep breaths, long, deep breaths. Think it through.

Dermot was right: Svetlana wouldn't have to sing. As long as Bukin pulled his finger out and got on with the rendezvous everything was still going to be all right.

'This is Green Two, copy? Any move from Emperor or Hunter?' Anna spoke into the radio on her lapel.

'Negative. He's eating popcorn, watching the show.'

'Of course I can't sing. I never wanted to be a pop star, remember.' Svetlana turned to Dermot. 'I just wanted to be with Dmitri. And they always mimed on your *Top of the Pops.*'

She did have a point.

'And you…' Svetlana turned on Anna now. 'You said you'd arrest my stepfather when he landed. None of this should be happening.'

'OK, OK, let's just keep cool here.' Another fair point but the last thing Anna needed was for Dermot or Svetlana to lose it now. 'You were going to pull out anyway after we'd taken Bukin. A throat infection – that's what we agreed.' The solution was clear enough. 'We'll just stick to that.'

'Yes.' Dermot nodded his agreement.

'No.' Svetlana shook her head, the tears flowing freely now as the panic rose in her voice. 'You do not know him; he is suspicious of everything. He will know something is wrong. Please, you must let me go with

Dmitri now. Give us a chance to get away from him. He will never leave me alone. Not until I am dead.'

'You're right. He'll never leave you alone. You can't just run. That won't work.' Right now, Anna was struggling to think of anything that would. 'We can protect you.'

'You think so?' Svetlana shook her head.

Anna reached into her pocket and slowly pulled out the gun. 'If it comes to it, yes.'

'With that.' The Russian girl looked at the little gun and turned away in disgust, pulling her sparkly gold dress off the clothes rail and throwing it to the floor.

'Do you think you could at least try to sing?' Anna slipped the gun away before it attracted any more ridicule.

'No, I cannot sing. He will know it was all a trick.'

'Not even for Dmitri?'

'You bitch.' Svetlana turned back to her. 'Don't use him to threaten me.'

'I'm just trying to help you, Svetlana.'

But that just seemed to enrage the Russian girl more. She grabbed a blonde wig from the back of the chair and threw it at Anna.

'You were going to wear this?' Anna caught the wig as a crazy, stupid, impossible plan popped into her head.

No way...

'In Russia, all the pop stars are blonde. Just like prostitutes. It is what my stepfather will expect to see.'

'Then that's what we'll give him.' Anna slipped the wig onto her head, picked up the dress and held it up in front of her as she turned to Dermot.

'*It's not you they'll see out there...*' She remembered his words like it was yesterday; how he'd bent down with an encouraging smile to straighten her wig.

'Oh no.' Dermot took a step a forward.

'Got any better ideas?'

'You don't even look like her.'

'We're about the same height and build. With the wig and the make-up and the lights nobody will see the difference.'

'Bukin will. He's her father.'

'He is NOT my father!'

'OK, OK.'

'From up there in his box? Come on.' Anna turned back to the mirror, a weird feeling bubbling up inside her. She could do this.

'But you can't sing either and...'

'Fuck off! I was always better than you at school.' She wasn't letting that one past.

'You were at school together?' Svetlana looked at each of them in turn.

'It's a long story.' One Anna didn't feel they had the time for now.

'She got stage fright.' Dermot clearly felt differently. 'If I hadn't been there she'd never have gone on the stage.'

'I was 15, OK!'

'And what makes you think you can do it now? In front of all those people? There were only about 50 back then.'

'There were a lot more than that.' There'd been 300 at least; Anna could have sworn it.

'You're not doing it.' Dermot lunged in, making a made a grab for the wig. 'You'll ruin everything.'

'Ruin everything?' Anna ducked away, failing to fight the anger rising inside her. 'I'm not the one who forgot to check she could actually sing.'

'This is just because you're jealous, isn't it?'

'Jealous... What the...?' What was he talking about now?

'I got my break and you didn't. You're still desperate for your shot at fame.'

'Oh, don't be such an arsehole.' Anna couldn't believe what she was hearing. 'You think I'd do this if I didn't have to?'

'Have to? You *want* to.' He stepped towards her now, the colour rising in his cheeks.

Just one more step and God forgive her she'd...

'Stop it!' Suddenly Svetlana was between them, holding up her arms. 'Stop it both of you.'

They turned and stared at her.

'Thank you.' Svetlana stepped back again. 'Can you sing?' She wiped her eyes on her sleeve as she looked at them both in turn.

'Yes.' Anna got there first, throwing Dermot a filthy look, daring him to deny it.

'Can she?' The Russian girl looked at him.

'Kind of.' He gave a sour little nod.

Well, thanks for the vote of fucking confidence.

'And you'll do it?' Svetlana looked back at Anna again.

'Yes.' No hesitation. She swallowed as the enormity of what she'd just signed up for hit home. But, yes, she would do it.

'You think it'll be easy going out there?' Dermot still wasn't having any of it.

'No. But it's what I've got to do. Look, it probably won't come to that anyway.' But even as she said it she realised a little part of her was hoping… 'We just need to be prepared.'

He shook his head again but any last resistance seemed to be ebbing away.

'It's our best chance.' Anna turned back to Svetlana. 'Now call your father.'

'I told you, he is not my father!'

'Sorry. Your stepfather. Ask him to come down here to wish you luck. Then put on the wig and dress before he comes. If he sees you like that it's what he'll expect to see on stage.'

The Russian girl nodded, the beginnings of a smile on her face. Anna stole a brief glance at Dermot but he refused to catch her eye. Svetlana pulled out her phone and dialled; a quick blast of Russian was followed by a smile as she cut the connection. 'He's coming down. Now get out, both of you. I need to change.' She touched Anna's hand as she took the wig and dress. 'And thank you.'

Anna made for the door, trying to catch Dermot's eye. She could bloody well do this. Wouldn't have hurt for him to give her a little confidence boost, just like he had back then.

But Dermot kept his eyes on the floor and any encouragement to himself as he pushed through the dressing-room door and headed out into the corridor.

Chapter 59

The Lithuanians, some sort of folk-rock band, hadn't been much kop. Neither had the Portuguese rapper nor the downbeat dirge offered up by an elderly Swiss drum, banjo and ukulele combo. The cheers from the audience were muted at best for all three. But that was nothing compared to the reaction Anna was going to get when she died out there on stage. These were trained singers – well, maybe not the Latvians – whereas she was... Dermot tried not to think about it, turning back to the screen where a duo of Germans girls in plaits and not much else were treating the audience to a surprisingly un-Teutonic piece of frothy synth pop.

Svetlana glanced up at the screen with a snort and got back to nervously adjusting her wig. It had been 20 minutes since she'd called Bukin and there was still no sign of him. With any luck he'd be doing a little arms-dealing on his way down and MI5 would swoop. More likely he didn't want to miss the Danes, a modern-day ABBA-esque foursome who were a lot of people's idea of favourites.

The Germans finished off with broad smiles then waved happily as they ran off stage to huge applause. Again Dermot fought the temptation to run down the corridor and into the ladies' toilet where Anna was hiding to drag her out and talk some sense into her.

What made her think she could just go out there and convince everyone she was a pop star? If Bukin found out he'd been played before the trap was sprung it wouldn't be her taking the rap. How could her MI5 bosses even let her consider it?

Well, he'd just have to come up with another plan to stop her doing it. So he paced the floor as the Germans were followed by a nervous-sounding Bulgarian duet singing something jazzy.

'He will come. Do not worry.' Svetlana turned again, biting her lip, one hand adjusting the wig some more.

That wasn't what he was worried about.

'And he will think it is me. It is a good plan.'

No it wasn't. And Svetlana wasn't going to convince him other-wise if she couldn't even stop fidgeting.

Come on; think, man. He paced the room as the Bulgarians pushed on, finally managing to hit their straps somewhere in the middle of the second verse, a little too late to turn it round if truth be told.

Then finally a knock on the door.

Svetlana started and then turned back to the mirror, catching his eye in the reflection with a small nod.

'OK.'

She fired off a couple of words in Russian and the door opened. Yegor came in first, eyes darting, a small black gun held down by his side. He looked just a little annoyed when his boss strolled straight on in before he'd given the all-clear. The big man was in his habitual black suit but had switched to a pink shirt, presumably in honour of the occasion. He was carrying a small red, white and blue Russian flag in one hand. He crossed the room in a couple of long strides and wrapped Svetlana in a big hug, Russian words tumbling from his mouth and a tear on his scarred cheek.

'My daughter, I am so proud of her.' Eventually he let her go, switching to English as he turned to Dermot. A smile tugged at his scar as he offered him the mini flag. 'I told her she looks like a real pop star.' Then he leaned in and lowered his voice. 'Personally I think she's dressed like a whore but that seems to be the fashion these days. And I told her it does not matter if she does not win. She has already made me proud.'

Well thank fuck for that.

Dermot took the flag, wondering whether to give it a merry little wave; but then he really didn't like the way Yegor was looking at him.

Svetlana threw her arms round Bukin's thick red neck again and launched into another stream of Russian.

'This will be the start of a great career.' Bukin untangled himself from Svetlana and threw a dismissive glance at the TV, where the Bulgarians were trudging off to more mute applause. 'Those Bulgars never could sing in time. If I were a betting man my money would be on the Slovenians. I quite liked the Belgian girl too but I think Yegor's got a soft spot for those Irish boys.' He gave Dermot a big fat wink.

All in a day's work for the put-upon hired thug. The hitman just nodded at his boss then got back to smiling coldly in Dermot's direction.

'No one's been great so far. Svetlana's got as good a chance as any.' Dermot felt he needed to say something and the words were out before he could stop himself.

Great, big up her chances why don't you?

Svetlana threw him an odd little look.

The girl couldn't even sing and Anna was likely to curl up and die with stage fright. But playing the confident agent was all part of the show he had to put on.

'Thank you.' Bukin's face hardly seemed big enough to hold his rapidly spreading smile. 'You have always believed in my daughter.' Then the Russian shook his head and waved his finger in mock admonishment. 'But everyone's talking about those Danes and there's always the Swedes.'

'True.' Dermot nodded gravely at this piece of sage Eurovision wisdom, sneaking another look at Yegor.

But even the hitman seemed to be more interested in proceedings on the TV, where a Finnish Country and Western quintet were sawing their way through their first verse.

The big Russian stepped forward and took Dermot by the shoulders. 'I want to thank you again for everything you've done for my daughter. Tonight you will have your reward, just as I have promised.'

Yes, the money; he'd forgotten about that. He looked from Bukin to Yegor and back again but neither seemed to be carrying a handy briefcase stuffed with cash.

Bukin caught the confusion on his face and smiled. 'After the show. Unfortunately tonight is not just about pleasure for me. I have a little business to conduct. When it is done I will have your money.'

The devious bastard. He was going to pay Dermot with the money he got from the terrorists. Presumably they'd agreed some sort of down payment.

Bukin gave him another grin then turned to Svetlana, switching back for a few last words of Russian.

She hugged him once more, coming away with tears in her eyes.

'Come on, Yegor, I don't want to miss the Austrians. And the Swedes will be on soon.'

The hitman nodded, catching Dermot's eye and holding his gaze for what felt like just a little too long. Then he pushed through the door and led Bukin out of the room.

Svetlana slumped back into her chair with a deep sigh of relief, wiping away her fake tears as the door closed behind them. 'He will believe it is me now.'

'Yes, he will.' Right until the moment Anna opened her mouth to sing. Dermot leaned back against the wall and closed his eyes. He snapped them open again.

The Austrians and the Swedes?

Was it a special code to tell Yegor that it was time for the rendezvous? No, he suspected not. Bukin just didn't want to miss any more of the show. Dermot was certain now that there wouldn't be any arms dealing done until each and every last performer had sung.

He mustered a weak smile for Svetlana and pulled out his phone to tell Anna she'd better come back and get herself ready to go out on stage.

Chapter 60

'There.' Svetlana applied the finishing touches to Anna's make-up and took a step back. 'Nobody will ever be able to tell you're not me.'

Anna smiled at the Russian girl and checked herself out in the mirror. The face staring back was supposed to look young and beautiful and full of hope.

And you know what? It did.

The eyes shiny and dark, the deep red of the lipstick showing off the smile. And when she stood the sheer sparkly dress fitted her perfectly in all the right places.

'You are beautiful.' Svetlana smiled back, a faraway sort of look in her eye.

'Thank you.' Anna smiled again, wondering whether, deep down, the Russian girl yearned to go out on that stage and sing herself.

But Svetlana wasn't going to get the chance because it would be Anna out there. She felt another little shiver. Fear? Excitement? It was almost impossible to tell. But this was what she'd always wanted, wasn't it?

On the TV a troupe of tap-dancing Poles made their way off stage to generous enough applause. Next up were the Moldovans.

She turned from the screen, checking out the dress once more then trying to catch Dermot's eye in the mirror. But he just sat with his head in his hands, staring at the floor. At least he'd given up trying to talk her out of it.

On the TV a trio of men marched grimly out on to the stage wearing what must have been the red and white national dress of Moldova. Anna turned, trying to catch Dermot's eye again but he didn't look up. Why couldn't he just believe in her? She could do this.

Only if she had to, of course. There were 12 acts to go and it was still unlikely she'd get on stage, whatever Dermot had said about Bukin's determination to watch the show through to the end.

OK, make that 11, including the Moldovans.

Anna was sure Bukin would make the rendezvous long before she got near the stage. There was too much at stake for him to delay.

And if he didn't?

She fought back another little wave of excitement.

That wasn't going to happen, OK. She sat back in the chair and picked up the lyric sheet, going over the words one more time, just in case.

Verse, chorus, verse, chorus, chorus, verse, instrumental then repeat chorus three more times, or was it four. Key change before the second-last chorus then up another key for the finale.

Easy.

DJ Danny really had done them proud.

She glanced in the mirror again but Dermot was still staring at the floor, refusing to look at her.

Jesus. Wasn't she doing this to save his sorry little arse? The least he could do was... Oh forget it. Anna read the lyrics once more then turned and plucked the small lapel-mic-cum-receiver from her jacket on the back of her chair and pinned it to the shoulder of her sparkly dress. Of course her comms link would need to be turned off before she went on stage. Anna had already decided that Kate Barnes and the rest of the MI5 team didn't need to know about her little plan. Best not to give the game away by belting out DJ Danny's inane but catchy lyrics down the secure channel. But for now she needed to stay in touch.

The Moldovans rounded off their upbeat little jingle and took their bows.

Ten to go.

'Green Two to Control, copy? Status on Emperor and Hunter?'

'Back in the box watching the show.'

'Roger that.' Part of Anna had hoped that they might make the rendezvous on the way back, while the other part had kept its fingers firmly crossed that they wouldn't.

Next she reached into her jacket pocket and pulled out the gun. But however small and neat it was, there was nowhere to hide it in the tight sparkly dress.

'Guess I won't need it anyway.' She smiled at Svetlana as she slipped the gun back into her jacket.

'Control to all units. Looks like he's waiting until Svetlana's had her moment of fame.' Kate's words were matter of fact. If they had to wait, then they had to wait. No sweat either way.

Easy enough for her to say. Kate wasn't the one who'd have to go out there and sing. The reality of the situation chose that moment to give Anna a slap round the face. She swivelled to look at Dermot again but he only had eyes for the TV now, still refusing to offer up any sort of help.

Tosser.

What had happened to the boy at the school musical?

But she wasn't going to show the same sort of weakness. Not today.

Anna turned back to mirror. Just one glance at that beautiful girl would be enough. But wasn't the make-up that little bit heavy? The sheer dress suddenly looked bulgy in all the wrong places too. And on the lyric sheet DJ Danny's simple words had magically changed themselves into tongue-twisting couplets of near-Shakespearean degree. How was she supposed to remember to do that double chorus after verse two or hit those tricky key changes at the end?

On screen the Moldovans had been replaced by a group of brightly dressed Norwegians, who smiled happily as they stomped and hollered their way about the stage.

Nine more to go after these.

Jesus, if they could do it she could...

Anna reeled as she stood up too quickly; only a steadying hand on the dressing table stopped her from going over as all the blood drained from her head. A clammy coldness swept in like a weather front across her face.

Hot bile rose.

Who the hell was she trying to kid?

She just about managed to reach the bathroom and slam the door before puking her guts up in the sink.

Chapter 61

'Are you OK?'

No reply from behind the bathroom door.

Dermot knocked again. 'Anna?' He'd bloody known this would happen; the whole idea was just stupid. Why had she ever thought...?

'Please. I'm OK. Just give me a minute or two.'

It sounded like she needed a little longer than that. A couple of decades or so longer.

'She'll be fine.' He turned to Svetlana, determined to put a brave face on it for her sake at least. 'Like I said, always used to get a touch of stage fright before our school plays.'

'But she will go on, yes? Anna must be a strong person to be one of your spies.'

'Yes.' Dermot could only hope that MI5 training stretched to handling stage fright. 'There's still plenty of time for your fath... for Bukin to make the rendezvous.' But he knew neither of them believed it would happen.

Svetlana nodded and smiled. ' Maybe it is best if you give her a few minutes' peace.'

With just nine more songs to go there were limits to the amount of peace Anna was going to get. But it seemed a sensible suggestion all the same.

'You go outside. I will stay here in case she needs anything. I think maybe the two of you are, how do you say it? "Winding each other up".'

Yep, that was pretty much how you'd said it, if you were being polite. Svetlana put a hand on Dermot's arm and guided him towards the door. He looked up at the TV screen where the Italians were failing to blend something screechy and operatic with a furious dance beat.

Christ, if that's all Anna was up against, she'd be fine.

More than fine.

It didn't really matter how bad she was; Bukin had said he was already proud of Svetlana. But it was getting Anna out on stage in the first place that was the issue.

The corridor outside the dressing rooms was busy with the after-show buzz. He took a deep breath, craving a cigarette for the first time in years as he leaned back against the wall. Then he pushed off and headed for a quick walk to clear his head. Around him the performers were spilling out of their dressing rooms, rivalry temporarily put aside as they chatted and mingled happily over open bottles and plastic cups. Different languages sounded out from every doorway he passed, the excitement sounding much the same in each tongue. He could almost taste the feeling, even after all these years. Yes he'd have given just about anything to be back there again. A couple of drinks with the boys after the show and maybe a spliff or two courtesy of the tour manager. There'd always been the promise of a club later on too. But it had always been that immediate post-gig moment that he'd trea-sured the most.

No wonder Anna craved her own little bit of it.

Just doing her job. Yeah right; she wasn't fooling him. When she'd first held the gold sparkly dress in front of her, he'd recognised that hunger in her eyes. Shame she'd rather spoiled it all by running off to be sick in the toilet. What he should do was go back in there right now and bring her out here to feel the buzz.

She wouldn't have any doubts then.

In fact that's exactly what he was going to do. He looked around again at the laughing Serbians, exultant Danes (everyone's new favourites after their rousing Euro-anthem) and jubilant Portuguese. Further down the corridor the Slovenian and Irish boy bands were happily mingling and totally indistinguishable now. Then came a roar and the Italians returned, like a Roman legion in its triumph. (And they'd been totally crap.)

But then he noticed the others. One of the Bulgarians was softly punching a wall while the Belgian woman sat on her own crying, despite her more than credible early performance. Then there were the Latvians who'd opened the whole show, two hours and about a million years ago. They stood in a row along the wall, national costumes crumpled and askew, sullenly passed around an almost empty bottle of filthy-looking vodka. This was the night they'd dreamed about, practised and rehearsed for. The biggest night of their lives and now the post-performance adrenalin had worn off they knew they'd hadn't been up to the mark.

Anna was better off staying in the dressing room. Though it was probably best if he got back in there to make sure she'd stopped hiding in the toilet. He was just turning to head back to the dressing room when his phone started to ring.

Sarah. His ex-wife's name glowed menacingly from the screen.

What did she want now? But with his lightsabre he could strike her down – well, send her call to voicemail. But then the nicer he was to Sarah, the easier she'd make it for him to see Molly.

'Hello.' He tried for bright, breezy and happy to be receiving her call.

'Dermot, hi, I—'

The rest was drowned out as someone opened a door and the music from the stage echoed loudly down the corridor.

That would be the Greeks. Hip hop grappling with soft rock.

'Where are you?' The door closed and her voice came through again.

'At Eurovision. You know that.'

'No, I mean where—'

'The dressing room. Look, Svetlana's on soon. I need to go.'

She said something but her voice was lost as the music got louder again.

'I can't hear you. I'll have to call you—' Then he stopped and took the phone away from his ear. The door at the end had swung shut and the music in the corridor wasn't that loud. It was coming from the phone.

Shit. 'Where are you?'

'We're here.'

'Where?' Although he already knew the answer.

'Eurovision, in the audience. I still know a few people who'll get a little girl a ticket even if her dad can't.'

Nooooo. If Wayne had held off on being a wanker for a few more days his daughter would have been safely back in Scotland by now.

Watford with Sarah's mum would have been fine too. Anywhere but here.

'Molly wants to come down and wish Svetlana luck before she goes on.'

Quickly, think... 'We're backstage. I can't get you in.' Feeble but good enough.

'That's OK, we've got passes. As I said, I know a few people.'

'She's about to go on. She needs to focus.' It was a perfectly credible reason.

'She's your daughter.'

'I'm sorry. I—'

'God, you were always such a knob. You're just jealous because you couldn't get her a ticket and I could.'

'I'm not fucking jealous, I'm—' He stopped. Rising to Sarah's bait was the last thing he needed to be doing right now. And far better all round for her to think he was an arse than to find out the real reason he didn't want his daughter anywhere near the dressing room. 'There just isn't time now. Make sure Molly gives her a big cheer. I'll come and find you after the show. She can meet her then.' He cut the call before Sarah could protest and slumped back against the wall, wondering whether the Latvians might be up for sharing their vodka.

But he had to make sure that neither Bukin nor Yegor suspected a thing. Anna had to sing, stage fright or no stage fright.

He headed back down the corridor. He'd persuaded her to go on stage all those years ago. He'd just have to do it again.

Chapter 62

OK, OK...

Anna took a deep breath and rearranged her face into something she hoped came close to an apologetic smile. Just go out there, explain she couldn't do it and say they'd have to go back to Plan A. A throat infection was a perfectly credible explanation after all. She took another deep breath and brushed at a damp spot on the dress where she'd dabbed off a splash of sick. Then she opened the bathroom door, excuses and apologies at the ready.

A new sensation lurched its way around her stomach as she looked around the empty dressing room. Different but no more pleasant than the one she'd been battling with in the bathroom.

Fuck.

She looked around the room again, hoping that both Dermot and Svetlana might be hiding in the ludicrously small space under the dressing table.

They weren't.

They'd done a runner.

On the TV screen an Albanian girl band was heading out onto the stage. Plenty of appreciative applause for the low-cut leather cat-suits. Anna grabbed the programme and scanned down the list.

Just five songs to go.

All of this was her fault. Getting all up herself, saying she could go on stage, and then running off to the toilets to be sick, forgetting that she was actually here to babysit Svetlana and Dermot. And how could she blame them for disappearing? Anyone with any sense would have known it was time to take their chances.

Fuck.

She'd have to call it in, admit she's messed up. Bukin would most likely get away now and the research desk would be the least of Anna's worries.

She spun round as the door opened. Then Dermot barrelled in.

Thank God for that. It was as close as Dermot would ever get to being a knight in shining armour. Svetlana couldn't be far behind him.

'Listen, I've been thinking and—' The sulky face was gone now, replaced by something like his old smile.

'Me too.' She tried to smile back. 'You were right. I can't do it. I was stupid to think—' She stopped as his smile wavered.

'No, that's what I was about to say. I was wrong: you can do it.'

'I can't.' Anna felt the hot tears start to prickle in her eyes. 'I just can't.' She wiped the tears away. 'I should never have suggested it.'

'But you can, don't you see?' There was something different in his eyes now.

And suddenly the two of them were right back there in that school hall again.

'You were always better than me. I just got the lucky break.'

'That's not true. I was just this fat girl, you were—' Hang on, had he really said she'd been better?

'Listen to me.' He smiled again. 'Don't you get it? Remember all those warm-up exercises we used to do? They were to keep *me* calm, not you. I could never have done it without you.'

'But I was one who was terrified.' Anna wasn't sure she was quite ready to believe him.

'I never thought you were nervous; not until that last time. You were always so calm. And so brilliant.'

'Did you always get nervous?'

'Always.'

'Even with the NewBoyz?'

'God yeah, even worse; threw up every time before we went on. Was a bit of a joke with the other guys. But I always went out and did it.' He turned and pointed to the TV. 'Look at that lot.' The Albanian girls were murdering a poppy number that was destined for a washing-powder ad back in their home country if someone ever sang it properly. 'You're far better than they are.'

'I am?'

'Yes.' He looked at her and smiled. 'Definitely.'

Anna breathed in deeply. Well, OK, she bloody well *could* do it. Because she wasn't the scared fat girl in the badly fitting dress anymore. In fact – she checked the mirror again – her costume was looking pretty damned hot again actually: shimmery and tight in all the right places. Even the damp patch where she'd washed off the sick was barely noticeable now.

'Yes.' She couldn't help the smile spreading across her face. 'I can do this.'

'I knew you could.' He smiled back.

'You just stay here and make sure Svetlana…' It was only then that she realised the Russian girl still hadn't come back in. 'Where is she?'

'I thought she must be…' Dermot trailed off, nodded towards the bathroom. 'I thought she was in here with you.'

'No, I just came out of the bathroom. *Neither* of you were here.'

'But I was only outside in the corridor.'

'You left her on her own in here?'

'She told me to go outside, give you a few minutes to calm down.'

'That was her idea?'

'Yes. I didn't go far. She must have just slipped out too.'

'She's done a runner.'

'But where would she…?'

'Anywhere away from Bukin if she thought I wasn't going to sing.' Then she had another thought and reached for her jacket, feeling sick all over again.

The pocket was empty.

'She's taken my gun.' Something unpleasant edged its way to the front of her mind. '"*He'll never leave me alone until I'm dead.*" That's what she said isn't it?'

Anna felt like hitting herself in the face. How could she have been so stupid? 'She's not trying to get away; she's going to kill him.'

Stupid, stupid, stuuuupid.

'She knows how to use it too.' Dermot stared back at her, his mouth gaping wide. 'Bukin made her learn to shoot when she was a kid.'

'But Yegor… She won't stand a chance.' Anna tried to think. 'Best scenario, Bukin will get spooked and run, then the rendezvous won't happen. Worse, we have a full-blown shootout at the Eurovision Song Contest.'

'Call your team. If she's heading for his box they can stop her.'

Yes, it was the only way. And it was Anna who should have thought of that, not him. She turned her head to speak into her mic then stopped. 'No, too obvious. We still can't afford to let Yegor and Bukin know we're involved. They'd just call the rendezvous off and walk away. Then we'll lose the terrorists. You'll have to go and stop her.'

'Me? You're the spy.'

'And you were the singer. But I'm the one about to go out on stage.' Anna tried to think. 'Just get to the box before she does. Stop her outside and tell her I'm going to sing. She won't do it then.'

He just stood there staring at her.

'It's the only way.' He had to see that she was right. 'You went to Russia, talked Bukin into all this. You can do it. I know you can.'

The Albanians had finally put their washing-powder song out of its misery and were waving happily as they left the stage. And still Dermot stood there staring.

'Come on.'

'OK.' Finally, he nodded and turned for the door.

Five more songs. Or was it four now...?

Then he stopped and turned back. 'I know you can go out there, if you have to.' He made to take a step back towards her.

'Thank you.' She raised a hand. 'And it does mean a lot, what you said before.'

He took another step towards her.

'But can you please just get a move on?'

He stopped.

'Like *now*.'

He hesitated for a second or so more then turned and ran for the door.

Chapter 63

Dermot hit the stairwell door and charged through.

Nothing.

Ahead the corridor curved away to the left behind the private boxes. It was empty as far as he could see. If Svetlana had already made it into the box then it was over. Even if she hadn't shot him, Bukin might just have noticed she wasn't all dressed up for her performance.

And that she had a gun.

He ran on, counting down the box numbers, knowing he needed some sort of miracle now.

207, 208, 209...

Svetlana had a head start of about 10 minutes.

... 210, 211, 212...

The corridor ahead was still empty and silent as he sprinted round the bend. No way could he have beaten her here.

... 213, 214, 215...

Had there been more time to think about things he knew he would have been scared witless right now.

... 216, 217...

But if Anna could do what she had to do, then so could he.

... 218, 219...

He hadn't been sure he'd be able to convince her at first. But then he'd remembered the little white lie that had set Marcus Diesel's career on his way.

... 220, 221, 222, 223...

With filming due to roll on the first-ever *Meal of Fortune* a certain wannabe TV chef had been crying himself out of a job in the toilets.

It hadn't even been live, for God's sake. A certain washed-up pop star and wannabe manager had leaned against the hand basin, seeing his commission heading down the pan and decided that it wasn't going to happen.

... 224, 225...

A bit of blatant flattery and that little white lie about his own stage fright with the NewBoyz and the rest was daytime–TV history.

... 226...

And yes, it was a lie but it had worked with Marcus Diesel and had apparently done the trick with Anna too.

... 227, 228, 229...

But now it looked like it was all going to be for nothing. Dermot urged his legs to give him one last burst.

... 230, 231, 232...

He slowed to a halt and looked at the empty corridor.

... 233. Bukin's box, the door ajar.

Svetlana must be inside already. Any second now he'd hear the crack of the gunshot as Yegor fired first, gunning down the girl who Bukin thought of as his daughter. Then, well... Bukin would either kill Yegor or send him after Dermot... Charlie Mulrooney wouldn't get a look in.

He pushed the door an inch or so, heart still pounding from the running. He had to do this. He could still get in there, quietly grab her before anyone noticed and sneak her out. Bukin would be too busy watching the show, although Yegor would probably be a little more attentive.

Another inch.

The first thing he saw was the little hitman, sitting upright and alert as usual, head moving slowly from side to side as he scanned for threats in the audience. Next to him Oleg Bukin was stuffing a huge fistful of popcorn into his mouth. He leaned forward and clapped, then turned to Yegor with a smile. Apart from the two Russians the box was empty. Dermot swivelled round quickly, half-expecting to see Svetlana bearing down on him with the gun. But the corridor was still empty and quiet. He took a step back, pulling the door gently to as he fought to get his breath back. Somehow he'd managed to get there first. All he had to do now was wait until she turned up and convince her that Anna was going to sing; that it would all be OK.

Then maybe she wasn't coming this way? What if she'd found her way into the box above or next door? Or perhaps she was somewhere else in the arena, aiming her gun at Bukin right now?

Perhaps she was waiting to see if Anna went on stage or not? It was only two more songs now. Dermot felt a little surge of hope. But then Svetlana's last view of Anna had been the back of the sparkly dress as she ran to the toilets to throw up.

So there was no way Svetlana would wait and see whether Anna managed to pluck up the courage to sing. He remembered the quiet desperation in her voice.

'He will never leave me alone. Not until I am dead.'

He had to find her. Head back to the stairs, out into the auditorium; surely he'd be able to spot the only person in the whole place aiming a gun?

'Not until I am dead.'

That's what she'd said, wasn't it?

'... I am dead.'

He stopped as the words ran through his head one more time and he finally realised where Svetlana would be.

Then Dermot was running faster than he'd ever run in his life. Even though he knew he was already much too late.

Chapter 64

'OK, received and understood.' Anna had checked in with Kate and the team more in hope than anything else. She reached down and flicked the switch to turn her lapel mic off. She wouldn't be needing that for the next few minutes.

Bukin was still sitting happily in his seat, eating popcorn and watching the show. There would be no last-minute reprieve.

But looking on the bright side, at least the Russian hadn't been shot. Dermot must have got to Svetlana and talked her down. Either that or... *No*, she wasn't even going to think it. She wouldn't have sent Dermot after her if she hadn't believed he could handle it.

Or if she'd had any other options.

She shook her head. He'd be fine. Everything would be fine now as long as she could get out there and sing.

Anna peered through a gap in the curtain in front of her, out to the stage and the bright lights. Then on to the noisy darkness beyond, where the audience were clapping and cheering the act from Malta. The curtain opened wide and the Maltese came past her, the last of them turning and bowing, in no hurry to leave the stage. There were five, all dressed in loose-fitting white trousers and black shirts, open to reveal a lot of finely waxed chest. They whooped and high-fived each other as they came. One of them paused to look her up and down with a wink.

See, what had she told herself? Hot...

'Two minutes.' The girl with the clipboard sidled up to her and smiled in a way that Anna could only assume was meant to be reassuring.

It wasn't.

It was the same smile she'd worn as she barged through the dressing-room door 10 minutes or so before. Anna had tried to smile back then nodded dumbly as she followed the girl out of the dressing room. The walk to the backstage area was little more than a blur now.

'Ninety seconds.'

No way. It seemed like only a second and a half since it had been two minutes. Outside, the applause for the Maltese was finally dying away.

She closed her eyes and breathed in deeply, trying to recall the techniques her judo instructor had taught her to keep calm, then reaching for the voice exercises she and Dermot had done so long ago.

But none came.

Instead she tried to run over the lyrics in her head but each and every one of DJ Danny's words had her tongue tripping and twisting.

'One minute.'

That hadn't been another thirty seconds. Anna wondered whether it would be possible to force the clipboard into the girl's wide, grinning mouth.

'And now, ladies and gentlemen, our penultimate act of the evening—'

'Thirty seconds.'

Anna closed her eyes again and tried to let the gentle vibrations of the floor soothe her. But there was no music and no applause now. The floor was still; any shaking was in her legs. Her head felt hot under the wig, the dress clingy and tight, and her impossibly high heels were taking small but painful bites out of her feet.

'Ten seconds.'

She felt sweat forming at the top of her back.

And then she was turning, ready to run.

'Five.'

Her make-up must have been running a treat now, too.

It didn't matter what was at stake – she simply couldn't do it.

'Go.'

NO!

And then for some reason she found herself stepping forward.

So she stopped.

More sweat, the dress clinging even more tightly.

Clipboard girl snarled in her ear and gave her a little push. And then she was out beyond the curtain.

Shit, it was bright out here.

Thirty feet or so away at the front of the stage stood a single microphone stand. It took Anna a second or so to realise it was for her. She'd never make it all the way over there. And past the microphone, in the abyss beyond the stage's edge, the shifting darkness of the crowd was like a rolling sea on a restless night.

OK, she was definitely going to have to run now.

One little step back, then another. She stopped as a low noise rolled over the edge of the stage and washed all around her.

Clapping, they were clapping.

Clapping her.

There was even the odd whoop and whistle. She took a step forward and the noise increased. Then another and another and another.

More noise.

Somewhere out there Oleg Bukin was watching. Yegor Koslov too, plus all of her MI5 colleagues.

One of them was bound to recognise her. A bit fucking late to worry about that now.

She carried on walking; five steps more now. Then four, then three, then two, then just the one.

She reached out and took the microphone as the applause roared in her ears. Wasn't this great? Anna felt her face almost smile. They loved her and she hadn't even had to...

Ah...

With all her efforts focused on just stepping out onto the stage she'd forgotten all about the singing part.

The applause started to die down as the first few melancholy chords rang out from the keyboard.

She tried to remember the lines again but none of the words were there now.

Then the drumbeat started but the lyrics were still nowhere to be found.

A guitar picked up the volume, strummed chords circling steadily back round towards her cue. People were already clapping along to the beat.

Anna closed her eyes as she counted down in her head. When she opened her mouth to sing, she still wasn't sure what words, if any, would find their way out.

Chapter 65

Dermot pushed through the backstage door just in time to see Anna disappearing out past the curtain.

And he was the one who'd talked her into going out there.

'Wait—' His shout was cut short as he ran into what must have been the largest of the Maltese singers making his way off the stage. The man was far too busy laughing, high-fiving his mates and wearing his ridiculous costume to be looking where he was bloody well going. Dermot bounced off the big singer's shoulder and hit the floor, all the breath knocked out of him. The Maltese bent down, helping him to his feet and generally being overly apologetic and solicitous. Dermot managed a smile as he fought to get his breath back and waved the apologies away. The Maltese grinned back then meted out a hearty and wholly unnecessary slap on the back before following his friends. Dermot bent double, the returning breath all but knocked out of him once more. But he had to get up, had to move. Had to stop...

And that's when he saw her, 20 or so yards away and half-hidden behind one of the big amplifiers. She was looking out at the stage through a gap between the two giant video screens. If the Maltese guy hadn't bumped into him he'd never have noticed her.

The applause died away as the soft chords of the intro started up. The Russian girl slowly raised an arm. Even from that distance Dermot could see the hand at the end of it was holding a gun.

'No!' His shout was lost as the drums and guitar kicked in. He tried to run but stumbled again, pulling himself back up in time to see Svetlana's gun pointing straight out at the stage.

He shouted again, even though he knew it was no use, so he did his best to run instead. Ten yards away, then five, then three. The sound of the music was covering his footsteps and Svetlana hadn't seen him. He launched himself into a dive.

The Russian girl looked round at the very last second and performed a neat little sidestep. Dermot flew right on past her and crashed into the amplifier.

Fuck! That hurt.

But his dive had been enough to put her off her aim. He scrambled back to his feet, fighting to get his breath again and somehow putting himself right between Svetlana's gun and the stage.

'Get out of my way.' It was almost as if she was looking straight through him. 'I'll shoot you if I have to.'

He stood his ground, one ear on the music as the band headed for the last chords of the intro, praying that Anna would hit her cue.

'Move.' Svetlana's gun was aimed straight at his chest.

The piano, guitar and drums played on. And then Anna was singing, her vocals coming in bang on time. A bit shaky first. And if *he'd* noticed, Svetlana would have too. But it didn't matter. She was out there and everyone would think she really was the Russian girl.

'I will shoot you.'

'No, wait. Listen, she's doing great. It's going to be OK.' And she was. Second line in and Anna was nailing it, her voice ringing out in perfect tune.

'It's too late for that.'

'Listen to her. Bukin will think it's you. He'll be so proud of you.'

'I never wanted to make him proud.' Svetlana spat the words. 'I just want to be free.'

OK, wrong thing to say. 'But he won't suspect anything. He'll make the rendezvous and then they'll take him. It will all be over.'

'And if he sees me die it will be over too. He'll leave me alone. It is better this way.'

'He's your stepfather. If he's sees you get shot he'll come straight down. Then he'll know it's not you.'

'Ha! You think so?' Svetlana spat out a short sharp laugh. 'He's a coward. He'll get himself out of here and worry about me later. He'll never know it's not me out there. He'll think I am dead. And your MI5 will never admit it was one of their spies.'

She did have a point there.

Svetlana shifted to the left to get a clear shot. Dermot moved too and the gun was aimed straight at his chest once more.

On stage Anna hit another flattish note then recovered and powered on towards the chorus.

'Get out of the way or I will shoot.'

'No, you won't, because you're not like Bukin.' He could only hope he was right.

Anna hit the chorus, belting out the words, in tune again.

There were tears in Svetlana's eyes now. 'Nobody has ever done anything to help me get away from him. I've got to do this for myself. It's my last chance.'

'I'm helping you now. And she's helping you.' Anna was probably about a third of the way through the song now. If he could just keep Svetlana talking or maybe distract her and make a grab for the gun?

'I will kill you, Dermot.' Svetlana took a step back as if she'd read his thoughts, brushing angrily at the tears with her free hand. 'Think of your daughter.'

And he did. Sitting out there clapping and cheering, his failure to get her a ticket likely to be long forgotten. And then he thought about her growing up in another man's house. Not Wanker Wayne now, but whoever Sarah eventually washed up with. A man who'd never be her father. A man who might come to treat her as Oleg Bukin had treated Svetlana.

'Can you really do this to Molly?' There was pity in Svetlana's voice now, but not too much. The tears seemed to have gone as well.

Dermot looked at her arm. It was rock steady; the gun still pointed straight at his chest.

An image of Molly filled his head again as he closed his eyes and slowly started to step aside.

'Can *you* do it to her?' Then he opened them again and stood his ground instead, trying to forget about the gun as he looked her in the eye; hoping what he saw there justified the biggest chance he'd ever taken. 'You won't take another little girl's father away. Not after what Bukin did to you.'

'Get out of the way.' Svetlana raised the gun so it was pointing at his head.

The chorus started up again. Anna's voice soaring high to hit every note. Was the bloody song never going to end?

'Give me the gun.' Dermot reached out his hand as the music

311

looped back round and Anna launched into yet another chorus, even managing to hit the tricky key change.

'Please, you must understand.' The tears were back in her eyes now but her arm was still steady and the gun still aimed right at his head. 'I have to do this.'

'No.' Dermot stretched his hand out further, trying not to shut his eyes as his fingers closed in on the gun. 'You don't.'

Svetlana took a step back, both hands on the gun as she slowly lowered it to point directly at his heart. Dermot tore his gaze away from the weapon and looked her straight in the eye.

And that's how they stayed as Anna repeated the sodding chorus over and over again until the song finally ended.

Silence for a beat.

Then the cheering, whooping and shouting started up all around the auditorium. Behind him Anna would be smiling and bowing now. Then she'd be walking off to safety.

But the clapping and shouting just carried on and on. He kept his eyes on Svetlana, sure that Anna was still out there bowing, smiling and waving some more, rather than getting the fuck off the stage.

He kept up the eye contact as the applause got louder then finally started to fade.

Only then did Svetlana hand him the gun.

'Thank you.' He reached out and took it gently from her hand, wondering for a moment what to do with it before slipping it into his jacket pocket.

The tears were running down her face now and her shoulders were shaking.

Dermot felt himself sway just a little, queasy at the thought of what he'd just done. She really could have killed him.

'You did the right thing.' His head spun as another wave of nausea washed over him.

But there was no time for any of that right now. He had to get Svetlana back to the dressing room before Bukin came down to congratulate her. Then everything might just be OK.

He grabbed the hand she'd just been using to point the gun at him and started to run.

Chapter 66

Yegor walked quickly down the stairs, Bukin a couple of steps behind him. Sometimes Yegor just had to admire the old bastard.

Times like these.

Crude and violent his boss might be but nothing was ever left to chance. The man was quite simply a genius.

Barely a minute ago Bukin had been standing up in his box with popcorn crumbs all down his suit. He'd clapped and swayed, that idiotic grin all over his fat red face, as his daughter belted out her song. She was – Yegor had to admit – surprisingly good. Even his untrained ear had detected a couple of bum notes but nobody, least of all Bukin, seemed to care.

Then midway through the third chorus Bukin had turned away, tapped Yegor on the shoulder and nodded towards the exit as he brushed the popcorn from his trousers.

Brilliant.

His boss had planned it all along: make the rendezvous with the terrorists when his daughter was actually on the stage.

The man knew nothing about MI5's clumsy attempt at a trap but he was still taking all the right precautions, focused as ever on the little details.

Yes, there was a lot to admire about Oleg Bukin. Yegor opened the door at the bottom of the steps and raised a hand for his boss to wait while he checked all was clear. With the crowd watching the last act the corridor was deserted. He waved for Bukin to follow him and then headed off once more, the dull thud of the music echoing along behind them.

Everything was in place now and they'd soon be out of here and on the plane back to Russia. It had been a close thing though; best not to think about what would have happened if he hadn't followed his gut and decided to tail the woman the day before. The irony of it all was that it was the sheer quality of the woman's tradecraft that had given her away in the end, rather than any mistake. Giving him the slip like that; it had been just a little too perfect.

Once he'd 'made' her for a spook it had taken just that one picture message to verify the fact. A phone call soon after had started off the necessary chain of actions that had meant Oleg Bukin wouldn't be walking into a trap. By the time Yegor had gone to bed the previous evening everything had been back under control.

He pushed through another set of doors and beckoned for his boss to follow again. The music grew fainter as the doors swung closed behind them. He slowed as they approached a corner, raising a hand to indicate that his boss should stay back again until he'd checked the coast was clear.

But Bukin was up alongside him. 'How can I ever thank you, Yegor?' The big man smiled down at him. 'You have kept my daughter safe. I must do something to reward your loyalty.'

His boss would probably have a different view if he knew how close they had come to disaster.

'Once tonight is over you will come back to Russia with me. I have big plans for you.'

'Thank you.' Not quite as big as his own plans, Yegor was prepared to bet. And to think he'd almost allowed it all to be snatched away.

'Where to now?' Happy that it was safe to move on, he turned to his boss for further directions. Bukin hadn't even told him where the rendezvous was going to take place. Irritating though that was, it demonstrated again the big man's attention to detail.

'We're nearly there. It's right at the end and then left.'

Yegor ran the instruction against the detailed plan of the arena he'd committed to memory. But surely that would take them back to the... He nearly laughed out loud. It was perfect.

Me? Rendezvousing with a terrorist? In my daughter's dressing room. I think you've got the wrong arms dealer.

Every last detail covered.

Sheer genius.

Chapter 67

The sound of the crowd was still in Anna's ears, the adrenalin pumping as she hurried down the corridor, fighting the temptation to turn around. Then she'd run back to the stage, elbow aside the mediocre folk rock combo from the Former Yugoslav Republic of Macedonia aside and demand an encore.

All the things that might have been sped through her mind. All the possibilities and different lives that might have opened up for her.

And she knew that somewhere her dad would be smiling down on her.

Shaking his head certainly at the stroke she'd just pulled, but smiling because she'd had the guts to keep the assignment on track. All they had to do now was wait for the rendezvous and move in.

Shit.

She reached down to turn her comms link back on. It had been at least three minutes since she'd left the stage. 'Green Two. Just checking in. Status on subjects?'

'Anna, is that you, where have you been?' Kate sounded taut and unhappy but not the least bit suspicious that one of her team had just been on stage performing for Russia.

'Sorry, problem with the comms. What's the status?'

'Emperor and Hunter are on the move. North stairwell.'

They could have been making their way to the rendezvous or simply coming down to congratulate Svetlana.

'Looks like they're going to the dressing room.'

So she just needed to make sure she stayed out the way of Bukin, Koslov and her MI5 colleagues until she'd got changed. She turned and headed for the ladies' toilet where the bag with her clothes was hidden. There'd be no time to get back to the dressing room and give the dress back to Svetlana. Hopefully Dermot had found her and got her back in time. They'd just have to play it by ear on the dress front, say she'd already got changed.

'Red One in place?' Anna could hear the strain in Kate's voice as she asked for news from the two Red teams, the designated snatch squads.

'Affirmative.'

'Red Two?'

'In position.'

Both the voices that came back were far calmer than Kate's.

'Emperor and Hunter are going into the dressing room now.'

Anna upped the pace, taking a right then a left.

'Control this is Red Two. There's another subject going in. He's got a briefcase with him. I think this is it.' The voice was tense but excited. 'Repeat, second subject going in.'

Oh the clever, clever bastard, holding the rendezvous in Svetlana's dressing room. Anna stopped and took off her high heels then broke into a jog.

'Rendezvous complete, repeat, rendezvous complete. Second subject has just come out. Repeat: second subject has come out.'

'Red One visual?'

'Affirmative.'

'Red Two?'

'Visual confirmed'

'Move in. Take him now.'

Anna slowed to a walk and then stopped and listened for a few seconds until a voice came back over the radio.

'Red One to Control, second subject secure.'

Anna felt the smile spread across her face as she started to jog again. They'd taken the terrorist. Now they were free to move on Bukin.

'Control to all units. Great work, everyone. Status on Emperor and Hunter?' Kate's voice had all its usual authority and confidence back now that things were going her way.

'Still in the dressing room.'

'OK, stand down.'

Anna stopped as the words sunk in. 'Control? What did you say?'

Silence.

'Green Two to Control. Repeat, what did you say? We're supposed to take Bukin now.'

'Sorry, Anna, that was never the plan.' Kate didn't sound very sorry. 'We've picked up the terrorist and Bukin goes free; that's what we agreed with the Russians.'

'And you didn't think I needed to know?' The bastards had tricked her. Not just Kate but Lawson too. They'd got her back in because they needed her to get Dermot on side. But they hadn't trusted her enough to tell her the truth.

'Operation complete; stand down. That means you too, Anna.'

'But we promised Dermot. We promised Svetlana.'

'And the situation changed so we responded accordingly. Stand down.'

'Sorry, not reading you. Trouble with the comms again.' Not that Kate was going to fall for that one.

'Repeat, stand down. Do you copy? It's over, Anna.'

No it bloody wasn't. She'd promised Dermot and Svetlana they'd take Bukin; the very least she could do was warn them, try to get them out of there. She switched off her transmitter, turned and ran...

'Ooofff...!'

Straight into someone who was standing right behind her.

'Just get the fuck out of my—' She tried to push past but something hard smashed into her head.

Then everything spun and faded away.

Chapter 68

'Come on.' Dermot tightened his grip on Svetlana's wrist as he pulled her through the last set of doors. With all the other acts up in the performers' lounge to watch the results, the corridor outside the dressing rooms was quiet and empty again; just a few stray plastic cups and the Latvian's empty vodka bottle remained.

And now they'd made it. Svetlana's dressing room was just a little bit further down on the left. Anna had only finished singing about five minutes before. There was no way Bukin could have got all the way down here yet.

He reached the door, pushed it open and pulled Svetlana inside, then stopped.

Oleg Bukin sat in the chair by the mirror. The ever-faithful Yegor Koslov at his shoulder.

The two Russians looked them up and down, clearly noticing the distinct lack of costume and wig on Svetlana and probably the extreme panic all over Dermot's face.

He opened his mouth to speak but Bukin was already out of the chair and on the move. He tried to get out of the way but the big Russian charged passed him, grabbed Svetlana and lifted her high into the air. He followed up with his customary stream of quick-fire Russian.

He hadn't noticed... anything...

Sadly the same couldn't be said for Yegor Koslov. But then he was paid to notice things like missing dresses and errant wigs. The little hitman looked at Dermot with a cold inquisitive smile. So Dermot upped the stakes with a nod and a raised eyebrow to remind Yegor that he wasn't above mentioning the regrettable lapse in security that had occurred the last time they'd been in London.

Yegor held his gaze, forcing Dermot to raise his eyebrow further. How could he make himself any clearer? Yegor had better keep it shut or else.

Bukin was still twirling Svetlana around and around, oblivious to the silent standoff.

Yegor maintained eye contact for a second or so longer but the smile was gone now. He finally looked away, warning heeded.

'Where are her dress and the wig?'

Or not.

'She, er…' *Think man, think.* 'Got changed.'

Well that sounded convincing.

'There's a small dressing room just behind the stage. Sometimes the performers get a bit hot and want to change quickly…'

'They get a bit hot?'

'You know, the lights and all…'

'The lights?'

'Yes…' Far-fetched it may have been but surely less so than assuming MI5 were using Eurovision to trap Bukin and that one of their officers had just sung in his daughter's place.

'I understand.' Yegor nodded, either finally taking the fucking hint or accepting that Svetlana might actually have got a bit warm in her tight sparkly dress.

'Tonight she will win, yes…' Bukin gave Svetlana a final twirl and put her back down. 'And you, my friend.' He turned to Dermot. 'How can I ever thank you? You've made her dreams come true. And mine.'

It was Dermot's turn to be caught up in the great bear hug and lifted off the ground.

A couple of spins and a big wet, bristly kiss later Bukin put him down. Then the Russian stepped back, a look of mock-horror spreading across his face. 'What am I thinking? Am I such an uncouth peasant I know nothing of gratitude?' He turned and picked up a small black suitcase from beside the chair.

To Dermot's inexpert eye, it looked just the right size to hold £100,000 in cash.

'This is for you.' Bukin held out the case.

'Thank you.' A big stupid grin to match Oleg Bukin's was already spreading across Dermot's face as he reached out to grab it.

Behind him Svetlana was sobbing gently, her tears genuine now. In the corner Yegor was smiling that knowing little smile again. But even he couldn't ruin things now.

'Although money alone can never repay my debt.'

Bukin certainly didn't need to worry about that. He'd be paying with a lot more than money once the rendezvous with the terrorist had...

Dermot looked down at the case again.

Hadn't Bukin said he'd have the money *after* he'd conducted his business? The rendezvous must have happened already. But MI5 had promised to take him immediately.

'*The very second...*' Those had been Anna's exact words.

'But Mr Jack – haven't you been a little forgetful?'

No, it was the bloody spooks who appeared to have done the forgetting, not him.

'Marcus Diesel. You promised.'

'He's, um...' Shit, he'd never expected that he'd have to deliver on the promise. Bukin was supposed to be in custody by now.

The silence stretched on.

But then thankfully the door crashed open and MI5 finally came storming in to keep their own promise.

Anna led the charge, still in her stage costume and wig. It gave the game away slightly but that hardly mattered now. Besides, when you're about to take down a criminal arms dealer you don't always have time to get changed. Her blonde wig was all askew and she seemed to be bleeding from the head. But still she'd been determined to be the one to take Bukin. It was the kind of professionalism that made the British security services the envy of the world. But then wasn't the man following her sort of holding her up?

Holding her up and pushing her too.

And didn't he look a bit like...

Suddenly Svetlana wasn't crying anymore. Yegor's smile had vanished. And even Bukin had stopped laughing. In fact, nobody was doing anything much but stare at the figures in the doorway. Dermot's fingers just managed to brush against the handle of the suitcase before Bukin pulled it away. The absence of Marcus Diesel was the very least of his problems now.

Chapter 69

'Nobody move.'

Anna's head hurt like hell but at least she was fully awake now, her mind clear again. An arm held her tightly around her stomach, another around her neck. Her head felt strangely heavy but she managed to lift it for a second or so and open her eyes. Then she slumped forward again, having seen all she needed to see.

They were in the dressing room. Svetlana and Dermot were nearest to the door, silent and pale. Across from them Yegor Koslov stood calmly next to Oleg Bukin, who was turning an alarming shade of red. But who was behind her? One of the terrorists? FSB? An officer from another foreign intelligence agency on the trail of the nuclear materials?

She was pushed forward, her feet lifting off the ground now, as the person behind her advanced further into the room.

'I've got his daughter.' The voice that came over her shoulder was pure sandpaper, East London, hard and rough.

'I think that you'll find that you haven't.' It was Koslov who replied, sounding suspiciously like he was seeing the funny side of things.

'Yegor, who is this man?' Bukin turned to the hitman.

'The loan shark I told you about. The one who's been causing trouble.' Yegor turned to the new arrival. 'I thought you said you were more of a jazz man, Mr Mulrooney.'

Mulrooney? Jesus, she'd only gone and allowed herself to be taken by some second-rate thug.

'Got bored of waiting. Now give me the money or I'll break her neck.'

'Go ahead.' Bukin gave a shrug before turning and glaring at Dermot.

'But she's your daughter.' Mulrooney was starting to sound a little less sure of himself.

'No.' Yegor Koslov spoke slowly now as if he was dealing with a child. '*That* is his daughter.' He pointed at Svetlana.

Mulrooney swung Anna round as he turned to look at the Russian girl. And Anna knew she had to act fast, get her feet back on the ground and try a judo throw. Not much of a plan but it was all she had right now. But the loan shark was holding her too tightly.

'Tell me what is going on, Mr Jack?' Bukin's voice was low but the words were clear and hard.

'Yes, if that's his daughter why wasn't she on the stage?' There was confusion in the voice behind her.

Bukin looked at the gangster with a sigh. 'That's what I am hoping to find out, if you'd just give me a minute.' The Russian turned back to Dermot. 'I'm waiting, Mr Jack.'

'Who's this then?' Mulrooney wasn't giving up that easily. He gave Anna a rough shake.

'Please, could you just… Yegor, if this man doesn't be quiet then shoot him.'

The hitman's gun was pointed at Mulrooney's head before Bukin had finished the sentence.

Anna felt the big man try to hunker down behind her.

Great, from mere hostage to human shield. But she had to stay calm, stay in control and get her feet on the ground for the throw.

'Please let her go.' Dermot finally found his voice. 'You know she's not his daughter.'

'I think we have established that,' Mulrooney sneered at him. 'But I still want my money.'

'Mr Jack has some explaining to do.' Yegor kept his gun pointed at Anna and Mulrooney. 'And I don't think he'll have any money for you today.'

'I knew I shouldn't have trusted you, you little toe-rag.'

'If you leave now I won't shoot you.' Koslov was by far the calmest man in the room but even he sounded like his patience was wearing thin.

'You promised you'd make my daughter a star.' All Bukin's attention was on Dermot now. 'Then you get this tone-deaf whore to sing in her place. I want an explanation.'

Tone deaf, really?

'Well, it's, er...'

If ever there'd been a bad time for Dermot to lose the gift of the gab, this was it. She needed him to say something, anything; give her enough time to throw Mulrooney over her shoulder and make a dive for Yegor's gun.

'I'll count to three, Mr Jack.' The scar on the Russian's check was throbbing dangerously. 'One.'

'I WANT MY MONEY.' Mulrooney lifted Anna higher in the air to give himself more cover.

'Final warning, Mr Mulrooney.' Yegor's gun now seemed to be pointing right between her eyes.

'Bastards.' The loan shark took a step backwards, dragging her with him.

Then finally Anna manged to get her feet onto the ground. She braced herself, getting ready for the throw.

But then the gangster edged backwards again, dragging her off her feet once more. The wig slipped down further, partly blocking her vision.

'Two.'

Anna tried one last time to get her footing as Mulrooney pulled her towards the door. Then he gave her a hard shove and she was stumbling across the room, arms wind-milling as she fought to keep her balance.

Oleg Bukin stepped forward to catch her before she fell. The big softie. Maybe the age of chivalry was alive and well after all?

Or maybe not.

He spun her round to face Dermot, a fat arm fastening itself tightly round her neck. She heard the door slam as Mulrooney made his getaway.

'Now.' She felt Bukin's spittle on the side of her face. 'Tell me what's going on or I'll break her fucking neck.'

Anna squirmed and wriggled but it was no use, the Russian's hold was far stronger than Mulrooney's had been and she couldn't get her feet back on the ground.

But at least with the loan shark gone Yegor's gun wasn't pointed at her face anymore. The little hitman was aiming at the middle of Dermot's chest instead. Svetlana ran to the corner, sobbing loudly. And Dermot looked like he wanted to cry too. Instead he arranged his features into what he must have hoped resembled his best game face and looked Bukin straight in the eye. 'Well, you see...'

Anna felt Bukin's grip tighten around her neck.

'If you'll just let me explain.' Dermot caught her eye and nodded. Oh shit, he was playing for time. Because...

Well, because he still expected the rest of the MI5 team to come crashing in to save them all.

Because that had been what Anna had promised. If anyone was going to do the saving, it would have to be her. Problem was Anna didn't have the first idea how.

Chapter 70

'I will kill her.' Bukin grunted as he stepped forward, Anna's feet once again dragging across the floor as he pushed her in front of him.

Dermot didn't doubt that for a second. But still he couldn't think of what to say. Where the fuck were MI5 anyway? He wasn't sure how much more stalling he could do.

'Who is she?'

Just a little longer and they'd be here. He felt the weight of Anna's gun in his jacket pocket. It was right there next to his chest, but it might as well have been a million miles away. Yegor would shoot him before he got near it.

'The truth please, Mr Jack.' The scar on Bukin's cheek throbbed darkly as it dragged his mouth up into a snarl.

'She is a singer.' The truth would have been a really bad idea, so he used the next thing that came into his head.

'But my daughter is a singer.' For a moment Bukin looked puzzled then the anger spread back across his face again.

'It's just that Svetlana, well…' This time the truth was all there was. 'She can't actually sing.'

Bukin stared at him for a very long time. When he finally spoke his voice was hard and cold. 'You dare to insult my daughter? She has the voice of an angel. I have heard her on the tape singing that song from *Frozen*. I trusted you. My daughter trusted you. And this is how you repay us? Kill him, Yegor.'

'Papa, no.' In the corner Svetlana had stopped crying. 'I singing no.'

What?

'I cannot sing… tonight.' Svetlana coughed and gave Dermot what he supposed was a meaningful look.

But meaning what?

Bukin replied in Russian then turned to Dermot 'I have heard her. So have you.'

'Tonight, no sing.'

Eh? Then Dermot started to understand. She was trying to tell him something without giving away the fact that her English was better than she'd led Bukin to believe.

There it was, that look again. And another cough.

She was going to have to give him a little more than that. 'TONIGHT.'

He finally got it. 'Svetlana is a wonderful singer but she cannot sing tonight. She has a throat infection.' The same lie they'd planned on using to withdraw Svetlana from the competition. And if it was good enough for the Eurovision organisers...

The anger still blazed in Bukin's eyes but now there was doubt there too. Half a lifetime on the seedier margins of the entertainment business had taught Dermot how to recognise an opening. 'If she hadn't sung tonight, she would have missed her big chance. And all because of a sore throat.' He held Bukin's gaze, warming to his theme now. 'I'd never have forgiven myself if I'd let that happen. You paid me to help her become famous and that's what I've done. Nobody will ever know.'

'I will know!' Bukin was shouting again, the rage back in his eyes. 'I will always know it was a lie.'

'If you don't like my methods, well then I'm sorry.' It was all or nothing now. 'It's what I had to do. And when her voice is better she will make you proud. She will make all of Russia proud.' Dermot held Bukin's eye, hoping he hadn't overegged it with the 'all Russia' bit.

But Svetlana came to the rescue again, speaking in Russian now, her words thick with emotion and her big dark eyes moist with tears. Maybe she couldn't sing for toffee but when it came to acting? Something in Oleg Bukin's big ugly face softened then and Dermot knew they were winning. Then he looked at Anna; he realised that it would all be for nothing. The blonde wig was still askew and her head still lolled to the side. But her eyes were wide open and focused; the brain behind them calculating the odds.

Right now she didn't need to do a thing. But no, she was going to try out some martial-arts move and get them all killed.

His anger started to boil, just as Bukin's was cooling. He'd had things covered before she'd let Mulrooney drag her into the room.

And he had them back under control now. Why did she have to ruin it all with her secret-agent shit?

He tried to catch her eye. But she was far too busy stealing a quick glance at Yegor before lowering her eyes to the floor once more as she got ready to make the move. He had to get her away from Bukin right now. 'Please let her go.' He stepped forward. 'You heard the audience. They thought she was great.'

The Russian looked at him, a smile spreading across his face to replace the last traces of anger. 'All right, Mr Jack. Let's see if you're right. And if not...' He left it hanging and looked over at Svetlana, nodding his head at the TV, which was playing silently in the corner. 'Turn it up.'

What?

Svetlana stepped over and grabbed the remote from the dressing table.

'OK, it's the moment you've all been waiting for...' On screen the presenter was all fake tan, Botox and an insincere smile. 'Let's get the score from our first jury, in Norway.' On screen the presenter faded out to be replaced by a giant scoreboard.

Trial by Eurovision jury. Dermot felt everything wobble a bit as he realised what Bukin meant.

'Serbia eight points,' the voice from Norway boomed out.

But then why not? Anna had done OK, hadn't she?

'Finland ten points.'

He caught her eye and shook his head again, begging her to wait just a few more seconds.

Russia. Russia, please Russia!

'Denmark twelve points.'

No surprise there. The Danes were the favourites. But no need to panic either. There were plenty of points to play for. Bukin's eyes remained glued to the screen as they moved on to the Greek jury. A few points would keep him interested until MI5 finally got round to kicking the door in.

'Denmark eight points.'

Come on!

'Switzerland ten points.'

Pleeeeaaase!

'*Bosnia twelve points.*'

But they'd been really crap.

Bukin frowned, probably thinking the same, but his eyes stayed on the TV.

'*Bit of a surprise there with the Bosnians claiming twelve points. But we've seen it all before with the Eurovision judges.*' The host's voice cut in. '*Let's go over to the Netherlands.*'

'*France eight points.*'

Maybe Anna's way was the best after all. And if she was still planning on a judo move, now would probably be as good a time as any with Bukin staring at the TV.

'*Sweden ten points.*'

It was no disgrace to be beaten by the Swedes; surely Bukin would see that.

'*Slovenia twelve points.*'

The boy band. Again they hadn't been anything better than average.

'*It's already looking like a very open contest this year.*' The host cut in again. '*Now let's cross to Riga for the Latvian jury.*'

'*Finland eight points.*'

Bukin shook his head and swore.

If Anna could just throw Bukin it would be all the distraction Dermot needed to pull out the gun and start shooting.

'*Estonia ten points.*'

He tried to catch her eye but she was too busy staring at the TV. Oh Jesus…

Dermot stole another glance at Yegor. But the hitman stared back with a little smile, the only other person in the room not watching the TV.

'*Lithuania twelve points.*'

Bukin swore again.

Do it… Now, for fuck's sake.

'*The Balkan nations showing their traditional solidarity.*' The smiling face of the presenter filled the screen. '*And now let's go over to Lisbon.*'

But Oleg Bukin wasn't interested in the musical tastes of the

Portuguese. 'I have seen enough.' He turned away from the screen. 'You have dishonoured my daughter and dishonoured my country.'

In the corner Svetlana was crying again, although Dermot doubted that her honour had much to do with it.

'*Spain eight points.*'

Bukin looked briefly back at the TV to confirm this latest humiliation.

'*Hungary ten points.*'

And MI5 weren't coming either. Dermot realised that now.

'*Belarus twelve points.*'

'*And now it's over to Paris.*' The orange host appeared again with another fake smile.

Belafuckingrus. They'd been worse than the Bosnians.

'*Belarus eight points.*'

Not according to the French.

'Even with her throat infection, Svetlana would have sung better.' Bukin waved dismissively at the screen where the scoreboard showed a big fat zero next to Russia.

'*Bosnia ten points.*'

Oh come on.

Dermot finally caught Anna's eye and offered up a silent prayer of thanks. She nodded as she shifted her position, looking round the room again, working the angles and the odds.

This was it.

'*Latvia twelve points.*'

'*Maximum points for the plucky Baltic nation. Time now to hear from Moldova.*'

'See, even those Latvian dogs are beating her.' Bukin shook his head in disgust. 'It is a humiliation.'

Dermot tensed, ready to go for the gun as soon as Anna moved.

'*Norway eight points.*'

'*Some welcome points tonight for the Norwegians. A lot of people's favourites before the start.*'

'Kill him, Yegor.'

Just for a moment the hitman's eyes flicked over to his master to confirm the order. Dermot started to move his hand slowly towards his pocket. Maybe, just maybe he could get to the gun.

'*Greece ten points.*'

'I'm sorry, Dermot, I truly am.' Yegor's gun was pointed right between his eyes.

'I said kill him.'

'No please.' Dermot started to move, knowing it wouldn't do any good at all.

'*Russia twelve points.*'

'Hang on!'

Chapter 71

'Hang on!'

The words stopped Anna just as she was about to make the throw. It took her a second or so to realise she had been the one who'd spoken.

'*Well, there you go.*' The host beamed insincerely from the screen again. '*She was a bit flat in places but Russia's Svetlana finally gets on the board.*'

A bit flat? When exactly had she been flat?

Behind her Anna felt Bukin relax his grip a little. She got ready to make the throw then dive in under the aim of Koslov's gun.

'We can still do it.'

This time it was Dermot's words that stopped her. He and Svetlana were both staring at the TV and even Koslov seemed to be taking more than a passing interest now. Bukin gave her a shove from behind as he hustled forward for a better view, but his grip loosened even more.

Do it!

'*Here are the results from the Maltese jury.*'

Now, while he's off guard.

'*Greece eight points.*'

Just one more result. If Russia didn't get a twelve she'd make the throw.

'*Germany ten points.*'

'Come on.' Dermot clenched his fists.

Bukin loosened his grip a little more and Koslov's gun dropped a fraction.

'*Russia twelve points.*'

'Yessss!' Dermot punched the air.

Now! The voice was screaming inside her head; it was the perfect time. But the voice on the TV was more persuasive. '*Let's cross over to Stockholm for the votes from Sweden.*'

Surely the nation that had given ABBA to the world would know a good performance when they heard one.

'*Croatia eight points.*'

She held her breath and looked round the room. Dermot's fists were still clenched. Bukin's grip was looser now. Koslov's gun was lower again.

'*Russia ten points.*'

Not the full twelve but Sweden had come through for them when they'd needed it most. And a ten from the Swedes had to be worth twelve of anyone else's points. The big scoreboard showed that Svetlana was already up to fourth place.

No, not Svetlana. Anna.

'*Portugal twelve points.*'

'*Now it's over to Baku to hear from the Azerbaijan jury.*'

'*Greece eight points.*'

'Come on…' Dermot edged closer to the screen.

'*Bosnia ten points.*'

It was Anna they were voting for. She'd gone out on stage and sung (and no, she really hadn't been flat). The voters had loved her.

'*Denmark twelve points.*'

Not in Azerbaijan, it seemed.

'*More welcome points there for the pre-competition favourites.*' The host smiled out from the screen again before his face gave way to the scoreboard once more.

Bukin's grip tightened again as the Slovenians took their turn.

'*Finland eight points.*'

It was just a blip; it had to be. She was on a roll now.

'*Denmark ten points.*'

With the dangerous Danes out of the way that left the top spot free for…

'*Bosnia twelve points.*'

Oh for fuck's sake, not again.

'Svetlana will never win.' Oleg Bukin turned from the screen; clearly he'd seen enough.

Anna felt his grip tighten as he lifted her into the air once more and turned to Dermot.

'She has got a few points but you and your cheap Western whore have still insulted my daughter.'

Two lots of twelve points and a ten from the Swedes – it was hardly an insult. But the time for arguing was over. Anna had to get her feet back on the ground to gain some purchase for the throw. And she had to do it now. She screwed her eyes up tight and tried to wriggle free but he was just too strong.

'Kill him, Yegor. Hold still, you bitch...' Bukin's words died on his tongue.

When Anna opened her eyes everyone in the room was motionless. Everyone except Dermot and the gun he now seemed to be pointing at her head. Her gun, the one he must have taken from Svetlana, was shaking around wildly in his hand.

'Let her go or I'll shoot.' Dermot's voice was shaking almost as much as the gun.

Anna couldn't think of a single way in which this helped. She struggled again to get her feet on the ground but it was still no use.

'Let her go.' Dermot's voice was steadier now.

The same could not be said for the gun. One minute it was pointing at Anna's head and the next it was aimed high over her shoulder. Almost everything in the room was in danger apart from Oleg Bukin. She squirmed and wriggled again but still couldn't get a firm footing for the throw.

'Put the gun down, Dermot, or I will have to shoot you.' Koslov spoke softly and slowly, his gun steady, trained on the middle of Dermot's chest.

'Not until he lets her go.'

'That isn't going to happen, Dermot. Drop the gun.'

'*Greece eight points.*' The next jury started on their scores.

'Let her go.'

'*Portugal ten points.*'

'No, you put the gun down.'

'*Russia twelve points.*'

'Look.' Anna nodded towards the TV again but nobody else was interested now.

'Just shoot him, Yegor.' Bukin was starting to sound more than a little irritated with his hitman's tardiness.

'Last chance, Dermot.'

'Shoot him. NOW!'

'NO. LET. HER. GO.'

And that's when Anna knew he wasn't going to back down. Of all the stupid, stubborn and brave... But then he had no choice. And neither did she. Anna screwed her eyes shut and tried again to get in position for the throw. But it was just no use.

'Russia eight points.'

Anna thought about her father. What would he have done right now? But then she doubted he'd ever found himself in a situation quite like this.

'Germany ten points.'

In the corner Svetlana was sobbing loudly, knowing she'd be going back to Russia with Bukin when it was all done.

'Portugal twelve points.'

'Let's go over to the Slovenian jury.'

Fuck the Slovenian jury! She strained again but again Bukin was just too big and too strong.

'Moldova eight points.'

'Put it down now, Dermot.'

'Norway ten points.'

Svetlana stepped forward and shouted something in Russian. Whether by chance or design she'd put herself directly between Dermot and Yegor's gun.

Bukin shouted out in Russian, the fear obvious in his voice, as he realised the danger.

'Aim high, Dermot.' The words were out before Anna could stop them. His gun hand was still shaking wildly but Koslov wouldn't dare fire now.

Why didn't he just pull the trigger, dammit?

But then Dermot wasn't even looking where his gun was pointing anymore; he was staring at the door instead.

Svetlana wasn't shouting anymore either. Just taking a couple of steps back out of Koslov's line of fire.

'*Serbia twelve points.*'

And even the hitman was staring open-mouthed at the figure who'd just stepped into the room.

'Dermot, what's going on?' The man in the doorway looked round, his idiotic grin slowly fading.

Anna could almost feel the slack-jawed look of surprise on Bukin's face. It was all the distraction she needed to finally get her feet into position, shift her weight forward and launch the bastard over her shoulder.

And that's when someone finally got round to firing a gun.

Chapter 72

Bukin roared with pain as he hit the floor. The double-take at the sight of his culinary-TV hero had given Anna the chance she needed.

'What's going on?' Marcus Diesel repeated the question.

'You shot me in the leg.' Yegor sounded more surprised than hurt. Surprised and extremely pissed off. 'In the fucking leg.' The hitman went down on one knee then crumpled slowly to the floor.

Dermot stared down at the gun in his hand, thin trails of smoke drifting up from the barrel.

'Dermot, please tell me what's happening?' Marcus was still standing open-mouthed in the doorway.

He'd heard nothing from the chef since sending him the free tickets, so had assumed he wouldn't be coming.

Bukin was the first person in the room to make a move, pushing himself upwards as he tried to get to his feet. But Anna soon put paid to that, diving on top of him and rolling him onto his front before putting the Russian into a painful-looking headlock.

'Drop it.' Yegor pulled himself up into a sitting position, one hand on the patch of blood spreading on his thigh. Unfortunately the other hand was holding his gun and pointing it at Anna's head. 'Now, Dermot.'

'You just shot him.' Marcus Diesel found his voice again.

'Shut up and get over there,' Yegor snarled at the chef.

'But he shot you.'

'Yes, I'm aware of that. Against the wall now.' Yegor's voice was starting to sound shaky.

'Dermot?' The chef remained frozen where he was.

'Yes, I fucking shot him, OK. Now just shut up and do as he says.'

The chef hurried over to stand next to Svetlana.

'That's better.' Yegor sounded calmer now. 'Now put the gun down or she dies.' He looked like he'd lost a lot of blood but he was still in control.

'Don't do it.' Anna was breathing hard as she fought to keep Bukin under control.

'I won't hurt her if you drop the gun. You have my word.'

'No.' Anna forced Bukin's head down to the floor as he struggled again.

'Last chance, Dermot. I will kill her.'

'Don't.'

'Finland eight points.'

But what else was he supposed do? Shoot Koslov in the other leg? He dropped the gun.

'Now kick it over here.'

'Russia ten points.'

Dermot kicked it.

'Now you, let go of him and put your hands in the air.' Yegor managed to pull himself to his feet without taking the gun off Anna. Blood was flowing through his fingers where he was holding his leg but he looked steady enough.

'Denmark twelve points.'

Anna sighed, shaking her head at Dermot then taking a last look at the gun as she stood up, leaving Bukin on the floor.

'He would have killed you.'

She just shook her head again as she raised her hands.

'Now back away, both of you. Against the wall.'

Dermot moved over next to Marcus but Bukin had other plans for Anna. She'd taken only a couple of steps before he'd hauled himself up and slapped her hard around the face. She staggered back, trying to stay on her feet as Bukin stepped forward and hit her again. This time she went down, her wig sliding off altogether.

'I'll kill you for that, bitch.' Bukin reached down for the gun Dermot had dropped.

'No!'

The voice carried such authority that Bukin stopped and stared at Yegor Koslov.

'What did you say to me?' The Russian's voice rose in anger as he looked at the wounded man.

'I said no.' The strain in Yegor's voice was clear now. 'You have to go now, before it's too late.'

'Not until I've killed them both.' Bukin grabbed Anna's gun and stood over her. 'I am sorry that you've had to witness this, Mr Diesel.'

'If you kill her, you're a dead man.'

Bukin spun round towards Yegor. 'You dare to tell me—'

'She's British intelligence, MI5.'

Hang on, how did...?

'Leave now and you can walk away from this. Kill her and they'll never stop coming after you.'

'But how do you know this?' Bukin asked the question on everyone's lips.

'It's what you pay me for. This was all a trap, just to get you to come here so they could arrest you.' Yegor swayed. His breathing was ragged now, his right trouser leg soaked with blood. 'I found out too late; you were already in the country. But I have a good contact in the FSB. I persuaded him to leak information about your rendezvous to MI5 in return for your freedom. They have taken the terrorist instead of you. That was our agreement.'

Bukin paused to think it through before nodding, perhaps in acknowledgement of his henchman's cleverness. 'Still they must die.' He pointed the gun at Anna's head.

Yegor put a hand on the wall to steady himself. 'Kill her and even I won't be able to protect you.'

Right now it was Anna and Dermot he was protecting. And if he passed out, that protection would be gone.

Bukin looked at Yegor then back at Anna on the floor, his gun still aimed at her. Then he shrugged.

'I suppose you are right.' He gave Dermot a long last glare as he lowered the gun, then beckoned towards Svetlana as he headed for the door. 'Come, my daughter. Let us leave them to their lies and plots.' His voice was still tight with anger. 'I am sorry they have used you in this way. I blame myself for not protecting you.'

'No.' Svetlana stayed where she was next to Marcus. 'I am not coming back with you.' Her voice didn't falter as she finally stood up to the man who'd called himself her father for all those years.

341

Bukin turned, the black rage spreading across his face, but it drained away as he looked from Svetlana to Marcus and back again. 'You're staying with him?'

'You need to go now.' Yegor had slumped down to the floor again. 'I... I will not be able to make it.'

Bukin threw a quick glance of contempt at his fallen henchman then turned back to extend a hand to Marcus. 'Something good has come of this. I never got to tell you what a big fan I am. I will be honoured to welcome a man such as you into my family.'

'Go now.' Yegor's voice was quieter, the gun resting on the ground.

Marcus was looking dangerously confused, a look Dermot had seen a thousand times or more. Usually just before the chef opened his mouth and stuck his foot in it.

'My own daughter marrying one of the greats of TV cookery.' Bukin was beaming now. 'No man could be more proud. Winning Eurovision would have been nothing compared to this.'

Marcus looked at Dermot then back at Bukin, his mouth starting to open.

Please, please. Just don't. Better that Bukin believed that than...

'I am not marrying this fat pig.' In the end it was Svetlana who gave the game away.

'Steady on.' The chef looked genuinely hurt.

'And I am *not* your daughter.'

What exactly had been wrong with pretending she *was* marrying Marcus? Bukin would have given his blessing and fucked off smartish. Then they would all have been safe.

'I am sorry.' She turned to Dermot with tears in her eyes. 'I will never be truly free of him if I carry on pretending.'

Just a little longer would have been nice.

'My daughter—'

'I said, I am *not* your daughter. You killed my father and that killed my mother.' Svetlana stepped forward and shouted the words in Bukin's face.

'I loved your mother.' The big Russian paused, a look of confusion on his face now. 'You're speaking English. How...?'

CHAPTER 72

'Being a popstar, it was just a trick to get away from you. I learned in secret, so I could come here and be with Dmitri.'

'That son of a dockyard whore!' Anger flashed in Bukin's eyes again. 'I should have killed him when I had the chance.'

'If you touch him, I will kill you myself. I HATE YOU.'

Dermot could only watch as the big Russian started to tremble, the scar on his cheek throbbing viciously.

'And I'll kill myself before I come back with you.'

Bukin's scar throbbed more, turning a deadly shade of red. He started to raise the gun, but then his whole face seemed to crumple, as if something inside him had broken.

'I took you into my house. I loved you like you were my own.' The big Russian's hand fell back to his side as fat tears started to roll from his eyes.

'You must go now.' Yegor tried to push himself back up but looked to be fading fast now.

Bukin ignored him. His eyes stayed fixed on Svetlana as the gun slipped from his hand. He stared at her for a few seconds more and then turned and ran from the room.

Anna was the first to move, grabbing the gun and pointing it at Yegor. But that wasn't necessary. The hitman had dropped his own gun. Dermot was sure he saw the vague tracings of a smile as the little Russian closed his eyes for the last time, his head dropping slowly to the floor.

They'd done it. Bukin was gone, Yegor was dead and wasn't that a briefcase full of cash lying on the floor. Given the chance Dermot might have taken a quiet moment to savour it all.

Maybe a little dance inside, even?

But then Svetlana was sobbing and hugging him and Marcus was waving his arms around demanding all sorts of answers. And then he wasn't thinking about them either.

'Daddy, Daddy, Daddy.'

Molly ran across the room and jumped into his arms, so nothing else really mattered now.

Not his ex-wife, who'd followed his daughter in and was berating him for not answering his phone.

Nor Marcus Diesel, who'd stopped his questions and was busy looking Sarah up and down, a sly grin spreading across his lecherous chops.

Nor Yegor Koslov, who was still dead in the corner.

And not even Anna, who caught his eye with a faint smile. They'd have plenty of time later to work things out. Maybe a drink. Maybe…

But right now it was all about Molly.

'Russia twelve points.'

'Look, Daddy.' His daughter pointed at the TV where the final scores were coming in.

A picture of the plucky Bosnians filled the screen, heads in hands as they tried to come to terms with being overhauled on the line by a single point. Then the camera was panning around to catch the smiles and tears of the winner.

Well it could pan all it liked; it wouldn't find her. Because the first – and certainly the last – MI5 officer to win the Eurovision Song Contest for Russia was standing right next to…

But when Dermot turned to her again, Anna had already slipped away.

Epilogue

Meet me. St James's Park, bench by the lake. Midday
Friday. I'll find U… A xxx

Dermot checked the text message for what must have been about
the hundredth time. Why hadn't she just called him like any normal
person? Or maybe answered when he'd rung her. But she was a
spook; nothing about her would ever be normal. And that was something he was going to have to get used to if they were ever going
to… He tried to put the idea out of his mind. It was a big 'if'…

But then why else would she want to meet up? He looked at his
watch again.

12.15.

He'd already promised himself he'd wait until half past and no
longer. But he already knew he'd be waiting well after that if it came
to it. He looked left and then right along the path but the bright May
weather had brought the locals out to supplement the tourists. The
lakeside pathway was crowded in both directions and there was no
way he'd spot her until she was almost with him. He slipped off his
jacket and put it on the bench next to him, staring down the length
of the lake towards Whitehall and the London Eye looming beyond.

Two weeks it had been since Eurovision and the text message
was the first time he'd heard from her. One minute she'd been
standing next to him and then she was gone. There'd been little time
to think about it then as he concentrated on keeping Molly's attention
away from the body of the dead hitman in the corner.

He'd expected a phone call from her or a visit the next day and
again the day after that.

But no, nothing. Just the call from the Kate Barnes woman to
thank him again for all his efforts and remind him of his obligation to
keep quiet about everything that had happened.

The only number he had for Anna kept going straight to voicemail. So he'd finally taken the hint and conceded that he wouldn't be
seeing her again. But then with Molly around he hadn't exactly had

time to brood. Sarah had asked if he could lookafter her for another week while she sorted things out in Scotland and another week while she went on holiday with her, er... new boyfriend. At least she'd had the decency to sound a little embarrassed. Not that he minded. Sarah was welcome to take a permanent holiday if it meant he got to spend more time with Molly.

The last week had revolved around drop-offs and pick-ups as Molly settled into the new school her mother had somehow managed to wangle her into. Sarah had decided to rent a flat in Hammersmith, close enough to Chiswick to make Thursday nights and every second weekend a reality again. He'd already cancelled the lease on the Edinburgh flat.

So with all that going on there'd been no time brood over Anna. Not until she'd sent him the text at least.

He pulled out his phone to check again that he'd got it right just as she came into view behind a group of Spanish-looking teenagers. Anna ambled slowly up the path, sunglasses covering her eyes, long brown hair flowing loose and one hand clutching an ice cream as if she didn't have a single care in the whole world. The teenagers split and he saw the tall guy next to her, arm round her shoulder, bending in for a kiss.

Dermot shook his head and looked away.

Not Anna then.

He checked the text again. But he was right where was supposed to be, when he was supposed to be there.

It was Anna who wasn't.

He was just scanning up and down the path again when someone sat down next to him.

'Hello, Dermot.'

He turned, trying his best not to look too startled. The man looked to be in his mid-fifties, red, jowly and a little out of breath; defying the heat in jacket, shirt and tie.

'Who are you?'

The lined face looked kindly enough but there was something in the clear blue eyes that suggested he was well used to getting his own way.

Something familiar too.

'There's nothing to worry about. I suppose you could say I am Anna's boss.' The voice was deep and calm.

Again he felt that little tug of recognition. Had the man been one of the MI5 officers at Eurovision? Dermot didn't think so but he was sure he'd seen him before.

'Where's Anna?' He looked round but there was no sign of her. 'She texted me.'

'Well it only said "A", actually. Sorry, that was our little ruse.' He stuck out a hand. 'You can call me Richard. There's something we need to talk to you about. Something quite important.'

'We…?' So maybe she was coming. Someone sat down on the other side of him.

He turned with a smile and looked straight into the eyes of a dead Russian hitman. The last time he'd seen Yegor Koslov he'd shot him in the leg. Shot him and killed him. The Russian didn't seem the type to let bygones be bygones. Dermot tried to stand but the man who'd introduced himself as Richard had a hand on his arm. 'Please don't make a scene, Mr Jack. You're perfectly safe. This is very important.'

'Don't worry. I'm not going to hurt you.' Yegor's bad Bond-villain accent had been replaced by near-perfect English.

'But you're dead…'

'Apparently not.'

The little Russian looked quite different too. The poorly cut blond hair was now brown and shorter and he was dressed more casually than before, a T-shirt and jeans replacing his habitual suit. Getting shot had clearly worked wonders for the man.

'I'm afraid I haven't been entirely straight with you, Dermot.' The smile in his eyes was warm, without a hint of its previous mockery. 'When I said I had a good contact in the FSB I was talking about myself. I work for the Russian secret service. I've been under cover for three years, posing as a hitman called Yegor Koslov, to infiltrate Bukin's organisation.'

'So Yegor's not—'

'Not real, no.'

'What do I call you then?'

'No real need to call me anything but probably easiest to stick with Yegor.'

'And you're a spy too?'

'Well, counter-intelligence, like Miss Preston and your friends from MI5. But it's a small difference to most people.'

'I'm sorry, I didn't know.'

'That's kind of the point.'

'But I shot you.'

'You did, yes.' The smile never left the man's face.

'And you don't kill people?'

The Russian paused for a second before answering. 'Only ones who are a threat to my country.'

Ah.

'But in Moscow you were going to…?'

'I could not afford to let Bukin to lose faith in me; it would have threatened my operation. So yes, you were a danger then but not anymore.' He let that one hang for a second or two. 'I'll explain, but first I need you to give me Bukin's watch.'

The watch! It had become something of a good luck charm for Dermot. Pretty much everything had gone right since Bukin had given it to him. Molly was back, he was square with Mulrooney and Svetlana had won Eurovision.

No, Anna had won it.

But most importantly he wasn't dead.

'Please.' Yegor's smile was back but it wasn't a request.

Dermot pulled the watch from his pocket and gave it to him.

The little Russian turned it over in his hand a couple of times. Then he pulled a penknife from his pocket and carefully prised the back off before removing a folded-up piece of paper and what looked like a SIM card. He replaced the cover and handed the watch back to Dermot. 'All yours. It might even work now.'

'I don't understand.'

But Yegor wasn't listening. He unfolded the paper and studied the contents for a few seconds, then took out a wallet and slipped it inside. When he looked up again he was smiling as if a great weight had just been lifted from his shoulders.

Next he held up the SIM card. 'The tracking device.' He dropped it and ground it into the gravel with his foot.

'Remember what Bukin told you – that as long as you had this watch you were under his protection?'

'Yes, you found me at the warehouse.'

'That was fortunate.' But Yegor was shaking his head. 'I certainly wouldn't be too grateful to him.'

Dermot was lost now.

'The piece of paper contains details of the location for the nuclear materials he was trying to sell. When you told him about your Eurovision plan he decided it would make the perfect place for the rendezvous with the terrorists. Bukin didn't want to bring anything incriminating into the country himself, in case he was caught. So he used you as his mule. He gave the terrorist a second tracker for the watch when they met. The agreement was that they would come to collect the watch and the instructions later that night. And then they would have killed you.'

Some lucky charm. 'You mean I've been carrying these around for two weeks? They could have—'

'No. Only the terrorist who was captured at Eurovision knew you had the location. We only found out a few days ago. I wanted to come and retrieve the information sooner but we've had to do a certain amount of negotiating with MI5 and I did have a bullet in my leg.'

'Our Russian friends didn't quite trust us to do the job.' Richard sounded more than a little testy.

'Are you surprised? If you'd told us of your operation earlier things would have been a lot simpler.' Yegor turned to Dermot. 'I also wanted to thank you.'

'But I shot you?'

'Yes, we'd known for a long time that the people Bukin represents had nuclear materials and were looking for a buyer. All that time I spent on the inside, undercover – and then just as the sale was getting close he sent me to London to babysit Svetlana. I had to no choice. To refuse him would have meant losing his confidence.'

'And how did you know MI5 were involved?' The question had been troubling Dermot ever since the night of Eurovision.

'It's the kind of thing I am trained to know. You wouldn't expect me to give all our trade secrets away.' He smiled across at Richard. 'But I didn't realise until the day before the contest. It was too late to warn Bukin off; and if MI5 had moved on him, three years of work would have been ruined and lives put at risk. So we tipped them off about the rendezvous and in return they let Bukin go free.'

'But why tell Bukin that Anna was MI5? He could have killed her.'

'He would have killed her if I hadn't. You as well. Then he would have been arrested. This way he is free and eventually he will lead us to the people he represents and the other nuclear materials they still have.'

'But he thinks Yegor Koslov is dead. You can't carry on pretending to work for him.'

'That is why I wanted to thank you.' Yegor smiled again. 'Although I doubt my superiors are quite so pleased.' He reached into his jeans pocket and pulled out a photograph.

A little blonde girl sitting on a swing smiled back at the camera. She must have been a couple of years younger than Molly.

'I had not seen my daughter in over two years. It was simply too dangerous. If Bukin had discovered my true identity she and my wife could have been in danger. But now that Yegor Koslov is dead I cannot go back under cover. I have a safe job behind a desk and I can live with them again.'

'So you wanted me to shoot you? You planned it.'

Yegor laughed as he shook his head. 'No. I am not that clever, or that brave. But when you shot me I saw the opportunity. I knew if Bukin believed I was dying and left without me that I would be free.'

'But there was so much blood. I thought you were dead.'

'It would have hurt less if you'd shot me in the chest. I was wearing a Kevlar vest. That is where you are supposed to aim.'

'That's where I was aiming.'

Yegor shrugged. 'I suppose the blood made it look more real-istic.'

Richard coughed. 'Time to wrap things up gentlemen.'

'Of course.' The Russian nodded and got to his feet. 'You and your family have nothing to fear now from Oleg Bukin. And the little problem with your fat gangster friend is OK? Now there's someone I would happily have killed.'

'All fine now he's got his money.'

'Thank you again.' The Russian reached out a hand. 'You are a far braver man than I first took you for.'

Dermot shook his hand. 'And thanks again for saving my life.'

Then the man Dermot knew as Yegor Koslov gave him a little nod then turned and limped away without a backward glance.

Dermot watched until the Russian disappeared into the crowd. When he turned, Richard was staring intently at him. Something stirred in his memory again.

'Sorry about that, old boy. The Russians insisted on getting the information themselves. Didn't want us to see it, apparently.' He shook his head as if he didn't know what the world was coming to. 'We'd like to express our thanks too. Things looked tight for a bit but you came through in the end.'

'I want to see Anna.' He wasn't that interested in this man's gratitude.

Richard shook his head. 'You live in very different worlds. She's a highly trained intelligence officer with a great career in front of her and you're a...' He left it hanging but his distaste was clear enough. 'She'd have to choose between you and her job, and MI5 can't afford to lose good people.'

'Let me see her.' He wasn't being fobbed off that easily.

'She's made her decision. It would be best all round if you didn't try to contact her again, old boy.' Richard put a hand on his shoulder.

'Best all round if you didn't try to contact her...'

Those same words came tumbling back down the years.

'Old boy...'

'You!' Finally Dermot knew then where they'd met before.

Richard's features and expression were still the same, although masked now in a face that was older, redder and far, far fatter. But it was the voice that Dermot remembered most strongly, even though their single meeting had been years before.

'I did wonder whether you'd recognised me.'

'I think we need to have a little word...'

Dermot had been heading out of the station, about to break into a jog, when he'd felt the hand on his shoulder.

'Won't take a minute.'

The first thing he'd felt was irritation. He'd been running late for Anna's sixteenth birthday party and knew she'd be worried.

Richard had guided him to a bench then pulled the pictures out from his jacket pocket; Dermot in the back of the tour bus taking cocaine with one of the NewBoyz' backing singers.

'Anna's father thought you should see these.'

Then he'd explained how the pictures would find their way to the papers if he ever tried to see Anna again. And how Dermot was sure to be thrown out of the band and most likely go to prison.

'No photos this time?'

'No, not this time no. It was cheap but it was for the best then and it's for the best now.'

'Her dad got you to threaten me.' Dermot felt himself redden as his anger grew. 'How do you think she'd feel if I told her that?'

'I suspect she'd be quite disappointed in you. All I did was give you a choice. And you chose your singing career over her. Fat lot of good it did you, by the way, although my wife did quite like you. Daughter was always more of a Robbie Gray fan.'

Fear... that's all he'd felt back then. He'd known Anna's dad was something to do with the security services. The guilt at what he'd done to Anna had only come later. By then it was far too late. Much easier to bury it and try not to look back. But, now, well he was older and not so easily scared. After everything he'd just been through, Dermot wasn't going to be warned off quite so easily. 'She'd understand if I told her now.'

'Maybe she would.' Richard didn't sound so sure. 'She might not be so understanding when it comes to her father. How do you think she'd feel if you told her what he did?'

'I think she'd want to know the truth.'

'Would she? She worshipped the man, still does. He had his reasons, good ones too. We took the pictures but you were the one taking the drugs.'

'You can't stop me from seeing her.'

Richard sounded tired now. 'Believe me, we can. But I don't think that will be necessary. She's got a career ahead of her and some good memories of her father. Do you really want to take those away from her?'

Dermot closed his eyes and thought for a second. 'No, no, I don't.' Richard was right.

'So I've got your word that you won't try to contact her?'

'Yes.' He'd been wrong to walk away from her back then. But it would be just as wrong to do the opposite now.

Richard held his gaze for a moment and nodded. 'I meant what I said by the way. You did well. But you know you can't talk about any of this.'

Dermot nodded.

'If you don't mind I think we should catch up from time to time, just to see how things are going.' Richard held his gaze for a few seconds longer, the subtlety of his words taking nothing away from the hidden threat. 'You never know. You might even be able to help us out again.'

Dermot certainly hoped not.

'Goodbye, Mr Jack.' Then, like Yegor Koslov, Richard stood and walked away without a backward glance.

Dermot got to his feet and started after him then stopped himself. Instead he turned, letting out a long, slow sigh as he headed off in the other direction along the lake. There'd be plenty of time to brood over Anna later, to think about what might have been. But right now he should be heading back so he wasn't late to collect Molly from school.

He strolled on through the warm afternoon sun, wondering vaguely what to cook for her supper, knowing it would beans on toast again. He was just dodging round a group of tourists at the end of the lake and heading for the Tube station when his phone started to ring.

He whipped it out, hoping it might be... the caller ID read *Marcus Diesel*.

Into every life a little rain must fall. He went to bounce it to voicemail but the chef would just keep calling.

'It's me.' Marcus sounded as if he was two paces away rather than in the Caribbean with his new girlfriend. A woman also known as Dermot's ex-wife. You had to hand it to the man, he knew how to move quickly.

'Yes?' They hadn't spoken since Eurovision night. Marcus was no longer his client or his problem.

'We need to talk.'

'If it's about Sarah then it's fine. I'm cool with that.'

'Christ, Dermot, how did you put up with her for so long?'

He smiled. Sarah and Marcus certainly deserved each other, although the idea of the chef becoming Molly's stepfather was one he simply wasn't prepared to entertain. Luckily it didn't sound like that was going to happen.

'I've sacked my new manager. I want you to work for me again.'

'What about all those saucepan endorsements he was going to get you?'

'He was just too focused on cookery. I can be bigger than that and you're the man to help me. All this stuff with Svetlana got me thinking. I want to be a pop star.'

'Everyone wants to be a pop star, Marcus, even me.'

'You *were* a pop star.'

'Believe me, it isn't all it's cracked up to be. Look where it got me, working for you. Anyway, you can't sing.'

'Does that matter?'

'Not particularly. But you're a 45-year-old man who wears orange trousers.'

'They were ochre, OK.'

'Whatever.

'Please, Dermot.'

'I'll think about it.' It was the only way he'd get Marcus off the phone.

'That means no, doesn't it?'

'Yes, it does. Say hello to Sarah for me. Bye.'

'Wait.'

'I'm not doing this, Marcus. But I'll give you a bit of advice for free. Maybe it will help.'

'What?' The eagerness in the chef's voice was almost pitiful.

'You're quite big in Russia apparently.'

'I am.,.?'

Dermot cut the call but he knew the victory would be short-lived. The chef would just ring straight back and keep ringing. So he did something he hadn't done in years: turned his phone off completely. The Jedi weapon beeped as the screen went black. No calls, no texts, no emails, no dark side. Because right now he had an appointment with his daughter and the biggest milkshake she was ever likely to see.

A song started in his head as he headed on along the path. And suddenly he was into his favourite dance routine. Not in his head this time but out there for everyone to see.

Step, step, step, step and turn. Step, step, step, step. Turn. And point.

YESSSSS!!!!!

*

Anna finally let herself relax as she watched the Russian turn and walk away, keeping her eyes on the screen as Lawson and Dermot exchanged a few more words. She knew her boss would be explaining how things had to be, just as he'd explained them to her. She had hoped that Lawson would let her act as chaperone for Dermot's meeting with Russian. At least then she'd be able to say goodbye properly. But even that had been denied her and she'd had to settle for a place in the back of the surveillance van. They were parked up several hundred yards away but patched into the CCTV covering the park for a grandstand view.

Cleaning up the Eurovision mess had proved easier than she'd anticipated. The Russians were grateful that their operation hadn't been blown. Somewhat surprisingly Anna seemed to be getting a lot of credit for that. And with the man they had known as Koslov only injured, nobody was asking too many difficult questions about the shooting of a member of Russia's security services on British soil. And the terrorist they'd picked up was apparently giving them all sorts of useful information too.

The old director general's retirement had been announced a few days later with Lawson swiftly confirmed as the new boss. Things had happened quickly after that. Kate Barnes had been rewarded with a promotion to a different section and Lawson had offered Anna Kate's job. She'd accepted straight away. Not that she'd totally forgiven him for keeping her in the dark on the Bukin operation. But if she was serious about a career in MI5 she'd just have to move on from that.

Of course she could have jacked it in for a pop career but then it wasn't like she could ever tell anyone she'd won the Eurovision Song Contest.

But who exactly would believe that?

And yes, she had occasionally caught herself daydreaming about what might have been. But the security service was where she was meant to be.

All the loose ends were tied up, then.

All except Dermot.

Anna watched on the monitor as he and Lawson said their good-byes and headed off in opposite directions. Her eyes followed Dermot up the side of the lake until he stopped and answered his phone. She may well have been dead if he hadn't stood up to Bukin in the dressing room. It had to be one of the bravest things Anna had ever seen. She was still finding it hard to accept that she was never going to get the chance to say thank you.

'OK, let's go.' She spoke to the driver via the intercom and reached for the switch to turn off the monitor.

On screen Dermot was ending his phone call and staring wistfully out across the lake. Was he thinking about her now?

Anna liked to think so.

Things could have worked out so differently if he had turned up for her birthday party.

If he hadn't been such a selfish prick.

Could still do now, if she defied Lawson and threw away her career. She could be out of the van and with Dermot in less than two minutes.

But then that would have been a terrible idea.

So she watched instead as he walked away, laughing now through the tears as his walk turned into a funny little sort of dance. Suddenly the years fell away and she was back in the school hall with Dermot smiling that ridiculous smile as he disco strutted towards her. She reached out and flipped the switch, shaking her head as the screen went blank and Dermot and his dance disappeared.

A really terrible idea.

Acknowledgements

I'd like to thank everyone at Unbound for giving me the chance to make *The Meal of Fortune* a reality. Everyone who chipped in on the crowdfunding too. I hope you find the book funny and enjoyable.

All the members of my writing group that evolved from the Faber course, led, marshalled and cajoled by the brilliant Gillian Slovo, have made such a huge contribution through their comments, advice and support. I hope that I have been as helpful to you all as you have been to me.

And, of course, Megan, Dylan and Annabel for everything and putting up with long hours in the study that have finally got this rather silly book over the line.

A couple of things I should mention

Sometimes reality can be a bit inconvenient. However late Easter falls the school holidays never stretch into May, so are unlikely to coincide with the Eurovision Song Contest. And, since 2004, Eurovision has included two semi-finals for all but the five biggest countries (France, Spain, UK, Italy and Germany). This means it would not be possible now for a Russian entry to go straight through to the final. These are details though and relatively minor ones as far as I am concerned.

Patrons List

Kate Arnot
Ruth Barker
Lauren Bloch
Simon Chase
Michael Daniel
Andrew Davison
Sarah Deo
John Dexter
Rich Gregory
Claire Halford
Patricia Ibarrola
Simon Jones
Terry Leahy
Chris Lukehurst
Sara Lumley
Rosemary Maxfield
Bob McSorley
Tyson Mercan
Sarah Mitchell
Chris Nicolson
Philip Omar
Alan Outten
Penny Reeves
Madeleine Reid
Edd Ross
Viv Sedov
Sarah Stollard
Matthew Sturge
Rupa Tailor
Mike Scott Thomson
Amy Tsao
Debby Turner

Michael Wright
Ruriko Yamada

Tinker Tailor Soldier Chef

Anna Preston and Dermot Jack will return in *Tinker Tailor Soldier Chef*, joining forces once more in a desperate bid to stop one of the world's most secretive intelligence organisations from bringing the British economy to its knees.